On Lone Star Trail

Books by Amanda Cabot

Historical Romance

TEXAS DREAMS SERIES

Paper Roses

Scattered Petals

Tomorrow's Garden

WESTWARD WINDS SERIES

Summer of Promise

Waiting for Spring

With Autumn's Return

Christmas Roses

One Little Word: A Sincerely Yours Novella

Contemporary Romance

TEXAS CROSSROADS SERIES

At Bluebonnet Lake

In Firefly Valley

On Lone Star Trail

TEXAS CROSSROADS #3

On Lone Star Trail

A Novel

Amanda Cabot

Revell
a division of Baker Publishing Group
Grand Rapids, Michigan

Published by Revell
a division of Baker Publishing Group
P.O. Box 6287, Grand Rapids, MI 49516-6287
www.revellbooks.com

Printed in the United States of America

Library of Congress Cataloging-in-Publication Data
Cabot, Amanda, 1948–
On lone star trail : a novel / Amanda Cabot.
pages ; cm — (Texas crossroads ; #3)
ISBN 978-0-8007-3433-6 (pbk.)
1. Title.
PS3603.A35O5 2016
813′.6—dc23 2015022782

This book is a work of fiction. Names, characters, places, and incidents are the product of the author's imagination or are used fictitiously.

16 17 18 19 20 21 22 7 6 5 4 3 2 1

For April Kihlstrom,
award-winning author, kindred spirit,
and the best of speaking and signing partners.
I miss the April and Amanda gigs.

1

Relax. Gillian Hodge forced her fingers to stop gripping the steering wheel as if it were a lifeline. This wasn't her Carnegie Hall debut or the finals of the Brooks competition when so much was riding on the outcome. This was a vacation, for Pete's sake. A week with her best friend and the woman who'd been a surrogate grandmother. She should be filled with anticipation, counting the minutes until she arrived, not wound as tightly as a metronome.

Gillian took a deep breath, exhaling slowly. In, out. In, out. The technique had never failed when she'd used it before performances, and it did not fail now. She could feel her neck and shoulder muscles relaxing as she repeated the slow, even breathing. The tension began to drain, and for the first time since she'd left the freeway, Gillian looked at her surroundings rather than concentrating on the highway.

Kate was right. The Texas Hill Country was particularly beautiful in the spring. It had been lovely when she'd been here for Kate's wedding last September, but the fresh green of spring grasses and leaves and the patches of vividly colored wildflowers turned what had been simply lovely into something spectacular. No wonder Kate kept raving about her new home.

Though it was still difficult to believe that Kate, a dyed-in-the-wool city girl like Gillian, had given up a major promotion and traded a glamorous life as an advertising executive to run a small resort in the middle of Texas, that was exactly what had happened. Of course, one particular man had a lot to do with Kate's decision. She had come to Texas almost kicking and screaming and had discovered true love.

Gillian's smile faded. Despite her father's advice that marriage was what Gillian needed, she wasn't looking for love at Rainbow's End, just a change of scenery and a chance to rest. Months of physical therapy had not accomplished its goal. Her dreams had been crushed—literally—leaving her no choice but to build a new life. At this point, Gillian had no idea of what the future would bring other than that concert stages would not be part of it. After six months of dwelling on what she could no longer do, it was time to discover what other talents she had. But before she did that, she wanted time with the people who'd known her before her name ever graced a marquee.

Breathe in. Breathe out. Focus on the progress you're making, not what you can't do. The scars will fade, and so will the memories. Brushing aside the memories that had so far refused to fade, Gillian scanned the roadway, smiling when she saw what appeared to be an armor-plated animal lumbering along the shoulder. Who wouldn't smile at an armadillo? They looked like something out of prehistoric times. Though she thought they were supposed to be nocturnal, what did she know? Other than her weekend trip for Kate's wedding, the only parts of Texas Gillian had seen were airports, hotels, and concert halls. The only armadillos she'd seen were the stuffed varieties in airport gift shops.

The chuckle that curved her lips upward died as she glanced in the rearview mirror. It couldn't be. Not now. Not here. Gripping the steering wheel so tightly her knuckles whitened, Gillian stared at the approaching vehicle. The bright red motorcycle, the black-clad rider, the black and red helmet were indelibly etched in her memory along with the damage they had wrought.

She bit her lip, trying to tamp down the fear. It couldn't be the same one. *That* motorcycle was almost two thousand miles away. There must be hundreds, perhaps thousands, of men in black leather riding red motorcycles. There was no reason to believe this was the one who had changed her life.

He was going faster now, that horrible red machine eating up the distance between them. Maybe it was the same motorcycle after all. *That* one had been going too fast. Though the police had cited the rider for excessive speed, witnesses had said there was no sign of reckless driving, claiming the crash was an accident. An accident that would haunt Gillian for the rest of her life.

She slowed the car, wanting the bike to pass her. The sooner it was out of her sight, the better. Dimly, she was aware of clouds blocking the sun. In mere seconds, the day—like her mood—had gone from bright and sunny to ominously dark. It wasn't an omen, a portent, or a warning. It was simply a change of weather. And yet Gillian could not tamp back the sense of foreboding. She flinched as a crack of thunder split the sky and the deluge began. Within seconds, the pavement had gone from dry to wet. And still the motorcycle drew closer.

He was in the left lane now, getting ready to pass. Gillian's eyes widened and her heart began to pound. No! Not again! No!

He probably shouldn't have detoured. TJ Benjamin frowned as he headed north. Deb would never have done it. She made plans, developed itineraries, and followed them. Deb never took a detour, and none of her plans involved a motorcycle or sleeping under the stars. As much as she loved traveling, she also loved her creature comforts. That's why she'd insisted on renting a class A motor home equipped with air conditioning and a microwave. There was no roughing it for Deb. But Deb wasn't here, and he had no reason not to detour.

TJ gave the throttle another twist. Speed might not be the cure for everything, but it did help clear away melancholy. So did the countryside. He was deep in the heart of his home state on a beautiful early April day. If only he let himself, he could find reasons to smile.

As if on cue, a hawk soared above him, looking for an afternoon snack and making TJ grin as his stomach rumbled. He could use a snack himself, something warm instead of the energy bars that had become a staple of his diet. He'd stop in the next town and find a greasy spoon. Meanwhile, he was going to enjoy the detour.

He leaned back and started to relax. Though he'd traveled many of the state's highways, TJ had never explored this part of the Hill Country. His plan had been to continue on US 90 heading west. If he'd followed that plan, he would have reached Big Bend today. Instead, when he'd seen the sign pointing toward Dupree, the town that claimed to be the Heart of the Hills, something had urged him to turn, so here he was heading north. The old TJ wouldn't have done that. But, like Deb, the old TJ was gone.

So what if he was a day or two late getting to Big Bend? The park wasn't going anywhere. It wasn't like he had anyone waiting for him or had anything planned after that. Big Bend was the last item on the bucket list. Once he'd seen it, he would . . .

TJ frowned. The problem was that he didn't know how to finish the sentence. His frown turned into a wry smile as he felt a moment of sympathy for his former students with their complaints about open-ended questions. Multiple choice quizzes were definitely easier.

The hawk, more single-minded than TJ, swooped down and landed on the ground, its head diving into a hole. It appeared the hawk had found its prey.

Focusing on the highway in front of him, TJ noticed a light blue sedan in the distance. It had been little more than a speck when he'd seen it from the top of the last hill, but it was much larger now. Judging from the way he was catching it, it must be going under the speed limit. Probably tourists looking at the Hill Country's fabled spring wildflowers. If that's what they wanted, they'd come to the right place. Bluebonnets carpeted the meadows, their color providing a vivid contrast to the green hills.

TJ had seen his share of bluebonnets, but these were extra special. Though his stomach was protesting his decision, he pulled off the road and reached into his saddlebags for the digital SLR that had cost more than a month's pay. As he rotated the polarizing filter to deepen the hue of the flowers, TJ scowled at the realization that a dark cloud was approaching. He probably shouldn't have stopped, but the bluebonnets were as enticing as the road itself had been.

While his head told him to skip the pictures, his heart rejoiced at the sight of the deep blue flowers with the white and yellow tips, and he carefully composed the shots. It might be foolish. It wasn't as if he was going to try to sell the photos. That had been Deb's dream, not his, and yet he couldn't deny the pleasure of composing a picture that lifted his spirits and made him happy, if only for a moment.

With the camera once more safely stowed, he climbed on the bike and headed north, determined to reach Dupree before the rain began. The last sign had said it was only ten miles farther. With a little luck he could get there and find shelter from the storm that seemed to be gaining on him. The thought had no sooner lodged itself in his brain than the clouds opened and the deluge began.

As raindrops dotted his windshield and slid down his helmet, TJ shook his head. He should have known this would happen. It was just another in the string of bad things that had plagued his life for the past eighteen months.

The blue sedan was only a short distance in front of him now, rooster tails rising from its rear tires. TJ hated rooster tails. They weren't a problem in an RV or even in a car, but they did nasty things to a motorcycle, throwing dirty water on the windshield and reducing the already lowered visibility. There was only one solution.

A quick twist of the throttle and he'd accelerated enough to pull into the left lane. It would take no more than a couple seconds to pass the car. Only one person inside, he noticed as he approached the sedan. A woman. And then TJ felt his bike begin to hydroplane.

Braking did no good. The bike had a mind of its own, and right now that mind was making it slide. *Please, God*, he prayed as he attempted to keep the bike upright. *Keep me from hitting the car.* Though God hadn't answered his other prayers, this time was different. The bike slid past the car's front fender, then skidded into the guardrail. The next thing TJ knew, he was flying over the handlebars.

No! No! No! Gillian stared in horror as the motorcycle crashed into the guardrail, catapulting the rider into the air. With memories of another motorcycle on another day flashing before her, she stomped the brakes. She hated motorcycles! They were nothing but trouble. Big trouble.

Switching on her emergency flashers, Gillian backed up slowly until she was next to the bike, then shifted the car into park. The rain had stopped as suddenly as it began, but the damage was done. The bike had crashed, and the rider . . . She grabbed her cell phone, frowning at the absence of bars. Kate had joked about the spotty cell service, but this was no joking matter. The rider could be seriously injured, just as she had been that day.

Forcing the painful thoughts aside, Gillian climbed out of the car and approached the guardrail. Deliberately averting her gaze to avoid looking at the bike, she stared at the rider.

"Are you all right?" Gillian called to the man who was lying motionless on the ground. *Please, Lord, let him be all right.* Though she'd spent more than her share of time in hospitals, she knew nothing about CPR and almost as little about first aid.

She started to climb over the guardrail, but as she did, the motorcyclist stood. *Thank you*, she said silently. The man appeared to be checking various body parts as he shook first one arm, then another before repeating the process with his legs. It was only when he extended his left hand a second time and winced as he clenched the fist that Gillian felt herself grow weak.

"Just bruises," he announced. His voice was brusque, almost as if he was unaccustomed to talking aloud. Or perhaps it was the effort of pretending he wasn't injured. Gillian was certain that, even if his only injuries were bruises, they were painful ones.

As he took the helmet off, she saw that his dark brown hair was pulled into a ponytail and that he sported a beard sorely in need of trimming. If she'd had to describe him in one word, it would be scruffy. And then she saw his eyes. Almost as dark brown as his hair, they were so filled with sorrow that Gillian felt tears well in hers. Something had hurt this man deeply, and her instincts told her it was not having crashed his bike.

"Are you sure?" she asked, surprised that her voice sounded so calm. Inside she was anything but calm. Just the sight of a red motorcycle was enough to send her into a panic, and one with a crumpled front fender brought back memories that still had the power to paralyze her.

"I was going to call 911, but there's no cell service." She held up her phone.

The man shook his head as he bent to inspect his bike. "There's nothing the EMTs can do. They can't fix this." He pointed to the front wheel. The fender had been bent so severely that it had cut the tire. Gillian glanced at the bike. Even if he'd somehow been able to straighten the fender, there was no way to repair the tire.

"It's not going anywhere," he said, confirming her thought.

Though the sun was once again warming the air, Gillian shivered. She'd come to Texas to relax, to try to forget about motorcycles and the damage they could do, and here she was, only feet from another motorcycle crash.

Instinct urged her to flee, and yet while she wanted nothing to do with motorcycles or the men who rode them, she could not. She couldn't let him stand here waiting for a truck to rescue him. What if his injuries were more serious than he believed and he collapsed? He might still be in shock and unaware of how badly he'd been hurt. Gillian knew that was possible, because the full scope of pain hadn't hit her until she'd been in the ambulance, being rushed to the ER.

"Where were you headed? I'd be glad to take you to the next town." Glad was an exaggeration, but Gillian knew she couldn't abandon this man.

As he straightened, she revised her first impression. He was taller than she'd thought, probably six feet, and though it was hard to tell through the leather, he appeared well muscled.

The man nodded in what seemed like a grudging response to her offer. "The next town's where I was headed. Dupree. The place that advertises itself as the Heart of the Hills."

A frisson of something—apprehension, excitement, Gillian wasn't sure which—made its way down her spine. It was probably a coincidence that he had the same destination. "That's where I'm going too. A friend of mine owns the resort there. Is that where you're heading?"

It wasn't Gillian's imagination that he stiffened. "I just wanted an afternoon snack. Now it's looking like I'm going to need some repairs. Expensive repairs," he muttered so softly she almost missed the words.

As another car drove by, Gillian was tempted to flag it down and ask the driver to take care of the man who seemed as prickly as the cactus that lined the highway. Instead, she forced herself to smile as she said, "I don't know about repairs, but Kate can provide that snack and a nice warm, dry cabin."

"I'm afraid not."

The way he was balking made Gillian suspect money was an issue. What he didn't know was that it wouldn't be an issue at Rainbow's End. Kate and her husband had a sliding rate scale, and on numerous occasions that scale slid all the way to zero.

"You're wet, you're hurt, and your bike is in even worse shape. Let's get you to Rainbow's End and sort the rest of it out there."

"Are you always so bossy?" The man took a step toward her, his halting gait proof that he'd done more than bruise himself. Gillian wouldn't be surprised if he'd pulled a ligament or suffered one of those deep tissue bruises that some people claimed were worse than broken bones.

"I'm usually much worse," she said. "Besides, it doesn't look as if you've got a lot of alternatives."

"Good point." He stared at his bike for a moment, indecision etched on his face, then limped toward it. After unlatching one of the saddlebags, he pulled out a backpack and tossed it onto the backseat of Gillian's car, then opened the driver's door for her.

"Thanks, Miss . . ." As he extended his hand for a shake, he let his voice trail off, clearly expecting Gillian to offer her name.

"Hodge," she said. "Gillian Hodge. And you're . . ."

The man's shake was firm, and if he noticed that she winced ever so slightly at the contact, he said nothing. "I'm TJ Benjamin, and as you can see, I'm having a very bad day."

"It could have been worse," she said bluntly. "You could have hurt an innocent bystander."

2

She was unlike any woman he'd ever met. The women he knew—Deb included—would say something more after the zinger she'd hurled at him. Instead, Gillian Hodge simply started the engine and pulled onto the road. She didn't seem troubled by the silence, but she was definitely troubled by something. There was no mistaking the way her lips tensed when she looked in the rearview mirror.

TJ was doing his own share of tensing each time he glanced at the side mirror, but he had a good reason. That was his bike, his sole form of transportation, his home on wheels, he'd left chained to the guardrail.

When the car crested a hill and the bike was no longer visible, TJ forced himself to relax. It was unlikely anyone would try to steal it, but the simple fact was, there was nothing he could do if someone with a pair of bolt cutters, a truck with ramps, and a larcenous frame of mind came along. He needed to think about something else, like the woman in the driver's seat.

As she exhaled, almost as if in relief, he glanced at her. For the first time since she'd pulled back onto the highway, her fingers no longer had a death grip on the steering wheel. It might be coincidence, but TJ couldn't help wondering whether there was a connection between her tension and his motorcycle.

As he thought back, he realized that her reaction to it had been unusual. Though he would have expected dismay or sympathy, there'd been fear in Gillian's eyes when she'd looked at the mangled bike, and when he'd been chaining it to the guardrail, she'd kept her eyes fixed on the horizon.

And then there was her comment about hurting innocent bystanders. TJ had been tempted to ask her what she meant, but the anguish in her expression had stopped him. It was probably cowardly, but the truth was, he didn't want to know. There had been a time when he would have tried to comfort someone in her situation, but he was out of that business now. Firsthand experience had taught TJ how empty words of comfort could be.

"Have you been to Dupree before?" It was odd, being the one to break the silence, but it had begun to feel oppressive, at least to him. There was something wrong with sitting so quietly in a car with Gillian Hodge, especially when the combination of the silence and Gillian herself sent TJ's thoughts in dangerous directions.

He studied the woman who'd rescued him. She wasn't the most beautiful woman he'd ever met, but she was strikingly attractive with that auburn hair and those brilliant green eyes. Her features were classic, a fact that the severe hairdo highlighted. Though long, wavy hair seemed to be the hairstyle many women liked, Gillian's was pulled back into a formal bun that reminded him of the ice-skaters he'd seen on TV.

He judged her to be at least eight inches shorter than his six feet, and though that made her a bit shorter than average, she didn't seem to feel the need to wear those ridiculously high heels. Instead she was clad in jeans, ankle-height boots with sensible heels, and a tailored shirt. The outfit looked ordinary, but something told TJ it had cost more than he imagined. Deb had warned him that sometimes the simplest clothes—a little black dress, for example—were outrageously expensive.

Seemingly unaware of his scrutiny, Gillian nodded. "I was here once before. I came for my best friend's wedding last September."

"The friend who owns the resort?"

Another nod, this time accompanied by a smile that made TJ revise his opinion. When she smiled, Gillian Hodge *was* the most beautiful woman he'd met.

"Kate and her husband are the least likely people to open a resort," Gillian said, visibly relaxing as she spoke of her friend. "Kate used to be an advertising executive, and her husband owned a big software company in Silicon Valley. Now they're innkeepers." Gillian chuckled, as if amused by the idea.

TJ had to admit that those were not the backgrounds he would have expected for innkeepers. Some of his fellow teachers had talked about opening B&Bs when they retired, claiming that years of dealing with unruly students was the perfect preparation for handling demanding guests. TJ wondered how people more accustomed to structured meetings and PowerPoint presentations were dealing with the unpredictable behavior of tourists. He wouldn't ask, because he really didn't care. What he cared about was the woman driving him to Dupree.

"What about you?"

Gillian appeared startled by the question. "What do you mean?"

"What do you do for a living?"

It was the wrong question. Though he'd thought it innocuous enough, the way her fingers once again clutched the steering wheel told TJ he'd hit a sensitive nerve. Her lips flattened, and for a second he wondered if she'd refuse to answer. But then she shrugged. "I'm temporarily unemployed."

And obviously unhappy about it. He wouldn't pry into the circumstances, because if he did, he might find himself feeling he should offer advice, something he had no intention of doing. Instead, TJ said, "Me too."

He suspected that was one of the few things he had in common with Gillian. She had East Coast big city stamped all over her, but even though he'd lived in a suburb of Houston, TJ had never considered himself a city man. Give him wide open spaces any day. Wide open spaces and his bike, not an air-conditioned sedan that allowed you to see but not hear, feel, and even taste the countryside. TJ grinned, wondering how Miss Big City would have dealt with bugs on her teeth. Not well, he suspected.

They lapsed into silence, but this time it felt more comfortable, perhaps because they'd both begun to relax. Before he had to search for another topic of conversation, Gillian made a left turn at the sign that welcomed them to Dupree, the Heart of the Hills. A gas station sat a few yards behind the sign. Perfect.

"You can let me off here," TJ said. "They're bound to have a tow truck." He had no way of knowing whether anyone there could repair motorcycles, but he wanted to believe that chances were good, since the damage was simply metal and rubber. Engine repairs were trickier.

Gillian shook her head and showed no sign of slowing. "The deal was to take you to Rainbow's End. That's where we're going."

Whatever her job had been, one thing was clear: the woman was used to being in charge. TJ settled back in the seat, resigning himself to seeing her friend's resort. There was no way he would stay there, but the place would have a phone. And, if he was lucky, Dupree would have a motorcycle shop.

As he glanced at the street sign, TJ blinked. "Lone Star Trail?"

Gillian laughed, the sound so sweet it made him smile. "It sounds silly, doesn't it? Kate told me it used to be called Main Street, but a hundred years ago, someone decided to go for something more Texan." She turned, giving TJ a conspiratorial smile. "There's more. We have to climb Ranger Hill to get to the resort. Believe it or not, Rainbow's End is located on Bluebonnet Lake, and there's even a place called Firefly Valley."

She probably didn't realize it, but that was the longest speech TJ had heard her give. It seemed Gillian preferred talking about inanimate objects rather than people. He wondered why.

Since he didn't have to concentrate on driving, TJ looked around as they drove through what appeared to be an ordinary small town's downtown area. A few empty stores were nestled among the collection of establishments typical for a town of less than six hundred: a theater, bank, grocery store, two churches, and a few other small businesses. Dupree was what TJ had always called a blink town. "Don't blink, or you'll miss it," he used to tell Deb when they'd approach other similarly sized towns.

He wasn't blinking now, and he wasn't blinking when Gillian told him they'd reached the summit of Ranger Hill. With the sun still high in the western sky, he saw the sparkle of a small lake and the metal roofs of cabins at what must be the resort. As his gaze turned to the left, TJ felt his heart begin to thud. RVs. A field filled with RVs.

He closed his eyes and clenched his teeth, willing his pulse to return to normal. He wouldn't stay here. He couldn't. This was not the place for him.

TJ forced his eyes open but kept his gaze focused on the resort, as if by ignoring them, he could make the RVs disappear. He hadn't been inside an RV campground in almost two years, and he wasn't going to start now. Just being this close was making the sweat break out on his forehead.

Seemingly unaware of his distress, Gillian gestured toward the wrought-iron gate as she turned onto a multicolored gravel driveway. "I like the sign. Don't you?"

TJ stared. Though the gate itself was ordinary, the sign was not. As might be expected, the sign featured a rainbow, but instead of the fabled pot of gold, this rainbow ended in what appeared to be Noah's ark.

Two years ago, TJ would have smiled in delight that instead of animals peering from the windows, the ark bore a heart with a cross in its center and that the sign proclaimed this to be Rainbow's End, the Heart and Soul of the Hill Country. Today he could barely repress his shudder. An obviously Christian resort with RVs parked across the road was the last place he wanted to be.

"It's . . ." He struggled for a word, finally settling on *unique*.

"That it is," Gillian said as she drove a short distance along the road and parked in front of a Tyrolean-style building with a discreet sign identifying it as the office. "C'mon. I'll introduce you to Kate and Greg."

Though he was tempted to walk away, TJ knew that would accomplish nothing. As uncomfortable as he felt, he needed to get his bike repaired and find a place to sleep tonight.

"Ms. Hodge!" The teenager behind the desk of the nicely appointed office jumped up from her seat. "It's so cool that you're here." The grin on her face and the light in her eyes did a good job of conveying more excitement than TJ had ever seen on a desk clerk's face. Gillian's friend must have told the staff to make her feel welcome. Apparently unfazed by the bubbling enthusiasm, Gillian simply smiled.

"Kate's on a conference call now," the girl said as she gestured toward the back of the building. "She said to tell you to make yourself at home in her apartment. You know where that is, don't you?"

Gillian nodded as she settled her bag on her shoulder. "I need to see Greg first." She gave TJ a quick smile before she turned back to the teenager. "This gentleman needs a room for a few days."

As if on cue, a brown-haired man about TJ's height entered the office. So this was the California software mogul. Other than his undeniable air of command, he looked like many of the men TJ had met along his travels, but Gillian was right. TJ wouldn't have pegged him for an innkeeper.

"Did I hear my name?" Greg hugged Gillian, then held her at arm's length to study her. "Welcome back," he said with a warm smile before he glanced at TJ. "Who's your friend?"

Tired of being treated as if he couldn't speak, TJ nodded brusquely. "TJ Benjamin," he said, extending his hand for the obligatory shake. "Gillian was kind enough to give me a ride after my motorcycle had an unfortunate encounter with a guardrail. I'm looking for a place to camp while it's being fixed."

"You're in good hands, TJ," Gillian said, giving him a small wave as she headed toward the back of the building, clearly eager to see her friend.

"Where's your bike?" Greg asked.

When TJ explained, Greg nodded. "I have the best mechanic in Dupree on staff here. If Eric St. George can't fix your bike, no one can. C'mon." Greg headed outside. "When we bought the truck for Rainbow's End, Eric insisted on getting ramps. Now I know why."

Greg led the way to a small parking lot hidden from the office by tall shrubs. Though the white pickup he approached had the Rainbow's End logo on the sides, it was the van next to it that caught TJ's attention. The van had been transformed from an ordinary white vehicle into what appeared to be a motorized ark, with the Rainbow's End logo covering not only the sides but also the front and back, making it a rolling advertisement for the resort.

"This was Eric's idea too," Greg said. "I don't know what Kate and I did before he joined us. As you can see, the man's got great ideas, and he's a wiz at anything mechanical. God knew what he was doing when he sent Eric back here."

God. Of course. A man who owned a Christian resort would believe that God was the giver of all good things. He probably had Jeremiah 29:11 and Romans 8:28 tattooed on his chest. TJ did not.

When they reached the accident site, Greg whistled. "You

were right about close encounters. That was one of the worst." He frowned as he looked at the crumpled front wheel, and TJ winced. The damage was worse than he remembered. Fortunately, sheet metal and rubber could be replaced . . . for a price.

Greg patted the handlebars. "Nice bike."

"It was." And it would be again, if this Eric person was as good as Greg claimed.

With Greg's assistance, it was a simple matter to haul the bike into the truck, and within minutes TJ was headed back to Dupree. This time he knew not to look to the left as they descended into Firefly Valley.

"Eric's already left for the day," Greg said when they reached the resort, "but I'll have him start on your bike first thing in the morning. Meanwhile, let's get you settled. I've got two cabins vacant tonight. Would you prefer lakefront or tree views?"

TJ shook his head as he climbed out of the truck. Unlike the people he knew—ordinary people with ordinary incomes—Greg was wealthy. He'd probably never been in TJ's situation. "There's no easy way to say this, but I can't afford either. I was looking for a place where I could pitch my tent." He hadn't slept in a real bed in a place with walls since he'd left Houston.

Greg stopped and turned to face TJ, his expression saying he realized TJ did not want the conversation overheard. "I'm afraid there are no campgrounds in Dupree, and the local ranchers aren't especially happy about folks camping on their land."

"What about the RVs?" Though the thought made him cringe, there didn't appear to be any alternatives.

Greg's face softened. "That's not a campground, even though it might look like it. A fire last December left two dozen families homeless. They're living there until the new apartment complex is finished." He clapped TJ on the shoulder and turned toward the office. "The only place to stay is here."

Was this how animals felt when they were cornered? TJ didn't know. All he knew was that he didn't like the feeling. "I can't accept charity."

"It won't be charity." There was no hint of pity in Greg's voice, nothing other than the steely determination that had likely propelled him to success. "Trust me, TJ. There are plenty of ways for you to pay for your room and board. Now, c'mon. I won't take no for an answer."

Though his instincts told him to run, there was nowhere to go, and so TJ followed Greg into the office, telling himself this was only temporary. In a day or two, he'd be on the road again.

3

"You look wonderful!" Gillian exclaimed as her best friend entered the apartment. Gillian had let herself into the suite of rooms over the Rainbow's End dining room only a few minutes before and had felt the tension that had plagued her ever since she'd seen the motorcycle in her rearview mirror drain as she curled up in one of Kate's comfortable chairs. Now Kate was here, her face beaming with a welcoming smile.

Gillian rose and took a step toward her friend, her arms opening for a hug. This was why she had come, for the unconditional love and acceptance she knew Kate and her grandmother would provide. Though their lives had changed dramatically over the last year, Gillian knew nothing could change that.

"I look fat," Kate said with a rueful look at her once-trim waistline.

"You're glowing," Gillian insisted. "Pregnancy definitely agrees with you." Kate had always been beautiful. The unexpected combination of brown eyes and blonde hair made most men take a second look, but today she'd gone beyond beautiful to radiant. Gillian enfolded her in her arms, both of them laughing at the awkwardness the baby bump added to their embrace. "Oh, Kate, I'm so happy for you."

"And I'm so happy that you're here," Kate said as she returned the hug before leading Gillian to the long couch where they could sit with their arms around each other as they'd done as children. "Greg and I are going to do our best to convince you to stay for more than a week. That's why we've put you in Isaiah."

Though she wasn't certain where that particular cabin was located, Gillian remembered that Kate and Greg had replaced the numbers on the cabins with biblical names.

"Lakeside?" Gillian asked.

Kate shook her head. "No, but it's even better. Isaiah used to be our cook's cabin. It's more like an apartment than a cabin, because it has two bedrooms and a small kitchen. Although," Kate added with a wry smile, "I doubt you'll use the kitchen. Carmen's cooking is out of this world."

Gillian matched Kate's grin. "I remember. The meals here are guaranteed to fatten up everyone. But where's Carmen living?"

"Back in town. Her husband's here now, and when their old house went on the market, Carmen and Eric bought it. I've been saving Isaiah for you."

"It sounds wonderful." And it did. Although Rainbow's End's cabins weren't luxurious and boasted none of the amenities that had once been part of Gillian's life, they were comfortable. She didn't need a hundred TV channels or a whirlpool bath. What she needed was a place to relax. She was giving herself a week here. At the end, she would return to Chicago and attempt to piece together a new life.

"So, tell me about your trip," Kate encouraged.

Though Gillian would have preferred to talk about the baby, she knew how single-minded Kate could be. Until Gillian satisfied her curiosity, there would be no discussion of anything else.

"The trip was uneventful," she said, trying but failing to keep her voice even, "until a man crashed his motorcycle." Gillian shuddered at the memory.

"That must have been scary."

"It was." Gillian closed her eyes for a second as the memories threatened to erupt. "TJ was lucky. The bike's in bad shape, but he doesn't seem to have any permanent damage. Greg's taking care of him, probably putting him up in a cabin tonight." It was easier—far easier—to talk about TJ than to relive the moment when the motorcycle spun out of control.

"What about you?" Kate tightened her grip on Gillian's waist in what Gillian knew was an attempt to comfort her.

There was no reason to lie. This was Kate, the woman Gillian had called even before she told her father what had happened on that New York street last September. "I had another flashback. It didn't help that TJ's bike is the same color as the other one. For an instant, I thought it was happening again."

"Oh, Gillian." Kate reached for Gillian's right hand. "I'm so sorry." She turned Gillian's hand over and began to inspect the back. If the web of scars that had yet to fade shocked her, she gave no sign. "What did the new doctor say?"

"The same as all the others. I've regained 90 percent of my mobility, and that's all I can expect." Gillian tried to keep the bitterness from her voice as she said, "It's enough to do almost everything except play on a concert stage again. Gillian Hodge, the woman who won the Brooks and was touted as the new Van Cliburn, is no more."

As tears filled her eyes, Gillian brushed them away. "I'm sorry, Kate. I didn't come here to cry on your shoulder. It's just some days the fact that I have no idea what to do next is scary. Music was my whole life for more than twenty years, and now there's nothing."

This was the first time Gillian had voiced those words. Though the psychologist her father had insisted she consult had told her that anger and depression were normal stages in the healing process and had urged her to vent her feelings, she had not. Despite his impressive degrees, he was a stranger, and Gillian did not confide in strangers. She hadn't even shared her deepest feelings with her father once she'd realized that his anger still hadn't subsided. Dad's stock answer was to make the motorcyclist pay, even though Gillian had told him she saw no point in suing the rider, that money wouldn't restore her hand. Dad didn't understand that what she wanted most was to put the accident behind her and build a future. But Kate had always understood.

Kate nodded. "I won't offer platitudes, because I'm sure you've already heard a lifetime's worth. I just wish there were something I could do." That was Kate, the woman who was born to solve problems.

"You already have." Gillian turned to gaze out the window, admiring the way the sun sparkled on Bluebonnet Lake. "You gave me a place to escape. I love my father, but you know what he's like—as opinionated as ever. He's convinced the only thing that makes sense is for me to find a nice man—his words, not mine—who'll take care of me for the rest of my life." Gillian shook her head in exasperation. "I don't need a husband, and I most certainly do not need a caretaker. What I need is a new career."

Kate's eyes took on a distant look, telling Gillian she was searching for the right words. "Your dad loves you," she said slowly. "He's only trying to help."

"I know." Gillian had never doubted that, though as a teenager she'd chafed at what she considered her father's overprotectiveness. It was only when she'd become an adult that she'd realized how difficult it must have been for him, becoming a parent for the second time when he was over forty. Many men would have considered that enough of a challenge, but for Dad the challenge had been multiplied many times by Mom's death. Single parents had a tough life.

"Did I tell you he invited me to go on the cruise with him?"

Kate shook her head. "Obviously, you refused."

"Obviously. It's a singles' cruise. I still don't understand why he picked that one, other than that it's going to places he wanted to see, but it's definitely not the cruise for me. The last thing I need is professional matchmakers helping my father find the perfect man for me. At least I don't have to worry about that here."

Kate's lips twitched as if she were trying to repress a smile. "There's something I need to tell you."

Gillian raised an eyebrow. "And that would be . . ."

"Dupree has a trio of matchmakers that would put those professionals to shame."

Just what Gillian didn't need.

4

God had a strange sense of humor. TJ closed the door and looked around. He could practically hear heavenly laughter as God watched him settle into a cabin named Moses. There was definite irony in a man who used to be called the RV Reverend being stranded at a Christian resort within walking distance of two dozen RVs. The cabin's name was a nice touch too. Moses might have led the Israelites out of Egypt and delivered the Ten Commandments to them, but he'd also been prevented from entering the Promised Land.

Some would say there was a message in all this, and perhaps there was. TJ was no Moses, but he knew beyond the shadow of a doubt that after everything that had happened in the last eighteen months, he had no right to enter the Promised Land.

He shook his head. There was no point in remembering the past. The present was all he had, a present that included a damaged motorcycle and a surprisingly comfortable cabin.

The furnishings were simple but tasteful, with one of the most beautiful quilts TJ had ever seen covering the bed and a smaller one hanging on the wall. No doubt about it; sleeping in a bed would feel good, and the small but spotlessly clean bathroom looked inviting too.

As TJ walked into the bathroom, he caught a glimpse of himself in the mirror and did a double take. He hadn't realized how scruffy he looked. It was a wonder Gillian offered him a ride and that Greg hadn't pretended they had no vacancies. If he'd been the innkeeper, TJ would have had second and third thoughts about renting to someone who looked like him, especially when he'd admitted to being short on cash. The beard had to go.

Five minutes later, TJ stared at his reflection. Better, but now his hair looked wrong. If his bike weren't wrecked, he'd have ridden into Dupree for a haircut. Not styled, just cut. Now there was only one choice. He dug into his pack and pulled out the scissors. It wouldn't be perfect, but he wouldn't look like a homeless vagabond, even if that was exactly what he was.

His spirits restored by a shower that felt even better than he'd expected, TJ slid into clean jeans and a western-style shirt before heading for the dining room. A quick glance at his watch confirmed he would be on time. Greg had explained that there was only one seating for supper, adding that the meal was served family style. If TJ had had any doubt about God's sense of humor, that would have clinched it. He no longer had a family.

Though part of the same building as the office and reachable from the long hallway on the east side, the dining room also had an outside entrance. As TJ entered the room, he barely had time to register the coffered ceiling, the beautifully paneled walls featuring more of the finely made quilts he'd seen in his cabin, and the unusual tables before Greg clapped him on the shoulder.

"Looks like you did more than take a shower. I almost didn't recognize you," Greg said as he directed TJ toward one of the tables. There were five of them, all round and seating eight each. Nothing unusual about that, but what appeared to be lazy Susans laden with pitchers and serving bowls in their center did surprise TJ. He'd never seen tables like these. Of course, he'd never been in a resort like Rainbow's End before.

As he approached the table, Gillian's eyes widened, probably in a reaction to TJ's new appearance. Her self-confessed bossiness seemed to have vanished, and she had been engrossed in an animated discussion with a pretty blonde whose rounded belly left no doubt that she was pregnant.

"This is my wife Kate." Greg gave the blonde's shoulder a gentle squeeze that sent pain ricocheting through TJ. How many times had he touched Deb in the same way? Though the first raw grief had faded, there were still times like this when the memory of all he'd lost ambushed him. He took a deep breath, trying to tamp down the pain.

"Of course you know Gillian." Greg was still speaking. "Let me introduce you to the others at our table." They turned out to be two brothers and their wives, who spent at least one vacation together each year and who'd come to the Hill Country in search of wildflowers.

TJ gave them a perfunctory smile as his pulse returned to normal. Fortunately the attacks, as he referred to the waves of sorrow that turned his legs to rubber and made him feel as if his heart were being squeezed by a vise, now lasted only seconds rather than debilitating him for hours.

When everyone was seated and TJ found himself between Gillian and Kate, Greg rose to give thanks for the food as well as Gillian and TJ's safe arrival.

"You picked the perfect day to arrive," Kate told TJ after the amen. Like Gillian's, her voice bore no trace of a Texas drawl, confirming Gillian's story that Kate was a transplant. In her casual maternity clothes, she did not look like a former Manhattan advertising executive, but what did TJ know about Manhattan advertising executives?

"Tonight's one of my favorite meals," Kate told him.

A soft chuckle was Gillian's response. "Don't let her fool you. I'm sure she says the same thing every day."

"Can I help it if I like Carmen's cooking? Besides, I'm eating for two, and right now everything tastes wonderful." Kate spun the lazy Susan slightly and reached for a biscuit. "Don't be shy, TJ. I know for a fact that there's at least one more tray of biscuits in the oven in case anyone wants second helpings."

It was ordinary conversation, the gentle banter of friends and family, and though he hadn't expected it, TJ found himself relaxing as the meal progressed. The food was delicious and more plentiful than any he'd had in the past year. Chicken fricassee on top of what were probably prize-winning flaky biscuits, accompanied by bowls of peas, glazed carrots, a green salad, coleslaw, and a molded salad. It might not be a gourmet meal, but TJ couldn't recall when he'd enjoyed one more.

He was savoring the delicately flavored fricassee when Kate turned to him. "Tell us a little bit about yourself, TJ. What do you do when you're not riding your motorcycle?"

The last thing TJ wanted was to talk about himself. That was one of the reasons he'd avoided campgrounds for the last year. Folks in campgrounds were friendly, their questions as well-meaning as Kate's. There had been a time when TJ had enjoyed that friendliness, when he'd gone out of his way to encourage it, but not now. Still, he had to give Kate an answer. He doubted she'd believe the truth, that the bike had been his life for a year.

TJ had broken the lease on his apartment, sold his belongings, paid off his bills, bought the bike, and headed out, determined to finish Deb's bucket list. There was no need to share that or that traveling alone had occasionally been lonely and that there were times when he wondered what he'd do next.

He split another biscuit as he said, "I used to teach high school. History." There. If he was lucky, that would be enough to satisfy everyone's curiosity. He wasn't lucky.

"And you're on sabbatical." Gillian's expression reflected surprise and something else. If he'd had to describe it, TJ would have said it was disdain, but that made no sense. Why should she care how he used to earn his living?

"Not exactly, but I am taking some time off to see this country."

If he'd wanted to discourage conversation, TJ had failed. Interest shone from Gillian's green eyes, erasing the fleeting moment of disdain or whatever it had been. "Have you seen a lot?"

He nodded. "Every national park in the lower forty-eight except for Big Bend. I was on my way there when I took a detour and wound up here." TJ slid a forkful of peas into his mouth, hoping that would end the discussion.

While the two couples on the opposite side of the table discussed the lack of nighttime activities in Dupree, Greg leaned forward to address TJ. "I'm glad you took that detour. Your being a teacher is an answer to prayer."

"And how would that be? I can't imagine that history lessons are part of the entertainment here." He also couldn't imagine being the answer to anyone's prayer.

Greg reached for the pitcher of water and refilled Kate's glass. "You're right about that, but the fact that you know more about teenagers than either Kate or me just might solve the problem you and I discussed."

TJ had to admire Greg's tact. Instead of saying that whatever he had in mind would be a way for TJ to pay for his stay here, he simply alluded to a problem.

"How?" TJ took another bite of fricassee, hoping the answer wouldn't destroy his appetite.

"Kate and I are worried about the kids living in Firefly Valley. That's where the RVs are parked," he explained. "There's no TV or cell coverage there, and that's rough for the kids, especially the teenagers who can't drive. They're bored."

"Greg and I've invited them to come here," Kate interjected, "but no one seems interested."

"And you think I can help." His day just kept getting worse. It was bad enough knowing all those RVs were so close. Now he was expected to go over there and face the memory of the summers he and Deb had spent traveling the country in their motor home. If TJ agreed to Greg's suggestion, he'd be surrounded by kids and even more memories. Still, how could he refuse when he was here, eating Greg and Kate's food, planning to sleep in one of their cabins?

Before he could respond, Gillian touched his arm. "I'll go with you."

Why had she said that? Gillian could have kicked herself for volunteering to have anything to do with teenagers. She knew as little about them as Kate and Greg, and yet she couldn't help feeling sorry for TJ. She'd seen the pain in his eyes when he admitted he'd been a teacher, and that had touched a chord deep inside her.

"Those who can, do." Her father's words reverberated through her brain, reminding Gillian of the day she'd announced that she wanted to be a music teacher. Dad had scowled, his expression forbidding as he continued. "Those who can't, teach. Only losers teach, and you are not a loser, Gillian. You're a Hodge. You're meant for better things than teaching."

Had TJ heard similar disparaging remarks? Gillian didn't know. What she did know was that something was wrong, something TJ did not want to discuss, something tied to teaching. There had been a note of finality when he'd said "used to teach," a hint of melancholy that made her imagine herself pronouncing similar words.

"I used to be a concert pianist." Though she'd never actually said that, she knew that one day she would have to, and it would undoubtedly be painful. TJ was already at that point, and the anguish she'd seen before he lowered his eyes made her wish there were some way to ease it.

"I'm not sure how much help I can be," she told him, trying to keep her voice light, "but I've always heard there's safety in numbers."

He shrugged. "Sure, why not?" Though he didn't sound thrilled, what could she expect? The man was having a bad day. Not only had he crashed his bike, but he was now sporting the worst haircut Gillian had ever seen. She had to admit that the clean-shaven look was an improvement over the scruffy beard, but that naturally curly hair of his needed more than a rough hacking.

When her nephew's hair had shown a tendency to wave, her brother George and sister-in-law Lisa had searched for the right stylist to tame it. Of course, George and Lisa were more concerned about appearances than TJ seemed to be. Gillian suspected the man had never worn, much less owned, a tuxedo. His clothing was clean and serviceable but bore none of the designer labels that were so important to her brother.

"The image you project is important," George used to say, parroting their father. If TJ had heard the adage, he either disagreed or had a very different image in mind. Rough rather than refined. To Gillian's surprise, she found rough appealing.

As the conversation switched to Texas politics, she said little, content to watch the way TJ challenged the others. Though never confrontational, he asked probing questions that elicited surprising responses. She doubted even George, a proud graduate of Harvard Law School, could have done a better job of changing the other guests' opinions.

"You win." One of the men raised his hands in surrender.

"It's not a matter of win or lose," TJ said. "It's a matter of thinking. I just wanted you to consider the other side. The truth is, I agree with your position."

After a second of shocked silence, everyone laughed. "Good job, TJ." The man lowered his arms and grinned, obviously pleased by the apparent U-turn.

Good job indeed. Who would have guessed that the rough-around-the-edges man was a skilled orator?

5

The meal ended with the best chocolate pound cake Gillian had ever eaten, leaving her feeling as if she wouldn't need to eat again for a week. She rose and told TJ she'd meet him in front of the office in ten minutes. To her surprise, though TJ had taken seconds of almost everything, he emerged holding a large bag of groceries.

"More food?" She groaned at the thought.

"Take a look." TJ tilted the bag so she could see the contents. "Carmen had everything I needed in her pantry." Gillian smiled. The food wasn't for them. It was for the bored teenagers. Though she would not have thought of providing food, TJ's knowledge of kids was evident.

"I've never seen so many RVs in one place," Gillian said as they crossed Lone Star Trail and walked into the meadow now filled with two dozen motor homes. Though the sun had yet to set, the temperature had dropped, and she was glad she'd brought a hoodie.

TJ raised an eyebrow. As they'd walked, she had felt waves of tension emanating from him, and his replies, though courteous, had been curt. Now he smiled. It was just a casual smile, and yet it turned his face from ordinary to handsome.

This was twice that he'd seemed transformed. Gillian had almost not recognized TJ when he'd entered the dining room. She'd been expecting the scruffy biker with the ragged beard and long hair, not a clean-shaven man with curly hair that, despite the deplorable cut, gave him a boyish look. The new TJ was attractive, but the one who smiled at her now qualified as a heartbreaker.

"You obviously haven't gone camping," he said with another smile.

"That's true." It was silly the way her heart had begun to thud, all because TJ was smiling at her. Despite her father's admonitions, Gillian wasn't looking for romance. That wasn't why she'd come to Texas, and even though Kate had startled her with her declaration that Dupree, Texas, the Heart of the Hills, had three self-proclaimed matchmakers who would like nothing better than to find a husband for Gillian, she had no intention of asking for their help. All Gillian wanted was a chance to relax and reevaluate her life.

"My family didn't take many vacations," she said. There was no reason to tell TJ that—like teaching—camping was something a Hodge did not do. Her father had traveled occasionally, but other than the annual trip to Albany to celebrate George's birthday, he had not taken her with him. The live-in nanny had seen to Gillian's needs, ensuring that she was on time for her music lessons and did not neglect her practice.

"I was lucky, though. Kate and her grandparents used to invite me along on day trips to the beach or the falls or to one of the state or county parks. Having them live just three houses away was the best part of my childhood." The excursions might not have been as glamorous as her father's jaunts to Switzerland and New Zealand, but they'd been fun.

As a light breeze stirred the air, Gillian smiled, remembering the evenings she and Kate had run along the beach, kicking up damp sand as they raced toward the lifeguard's station. With her longer legs, Kate had normally won, making the few times Gillian had been the first to touch the tall wooden chair all the sweeter.

"Where was that?"

TJ's question brought her back to the present. "Buffalo, New York."

He nodded. "So the beach was Lake Erie, and the falls Niagara."

"Exactly. Have you been there?"

This time he shook his head. "No. I've been concentrating on the national parks, but I have to say I was impressed the first time I saw one of the Great Lakes. I couldn't imagine a lake so big that I couldn't see the opposite shore."

"That's why they call them great."

"Yeah."

As they approached the first row of RVs, TJ's posture changed, the tension Gillian had seen when they left Rainbow's End returning.

"Showtime," he muttered.

"Showtime?" That was a strange way to describe what they were about to do.

TJ nodded. "Teaching's a performing art. If you don't entertain the kids, you'll never get them to learn."

Gillian stared at TJ, trying to absorb what he'd just said. It was so different—180 degrees different—from her father's view that she wondered which one was correct. Right now, though, she needed to concentrate on helping TJ with whatever it was he was planning.

Though lights were on in most of the RVs, teenagers were milling around outside, their posture betraying the boredom Greg had described.

"You lookin' for someone?" A dark-haired boy approached

Gillian and TJ, his swagger declaring that he was King of the Hill or, in this case, the valley.

"Yeah, you. By the way, I'm TJ."

TJ's response seemed to take him aback, and there was a second of silence before the teen announced, "I'm Shane, and I'm in charge here. What do you want?"

"I figured we could build a fire."

This time it wasn't only Shane who seemed surprised. Gillian was too. She hadn't asked TJ about his plans, although now that she thought about the contents of the grocery bag, a fire seemed reasonable. The boy thought otherwise.

"You plainly ain't from around here," he said. "If you was, you'd know that fire's a four-letter word in Dupree. That's how we got here." Shane gestured toward the RVs. "Fire took out our old home."

TJ seemed unfazed. "A campfire's different. Besides, I brought adult supervision."

A blond boy had joined the dark-haired one while the others remained on the sidelines in two distinct groups. "Who?" The blond looked around, as if searching for an authority figure.

"This lovely lady is our designated adult," TJ said, gesturing toward Gillian. "She'll make sure no one complains about the fire or the noise."

Designated adult. Gillian suspected that was something like designated driver and wondered exactly what TJ intended to do that he wouldn't be playing that role.

"You serious?" Shane asked.

"Yep. What about you? Do you know how to build a safe fire?"

"Sure."

That the word was accompanied by a swagger and a threatening look at the blond told Gillian Shane had no idea what TJ meant. That didn't seem to bother TJ.

"Good. Let's get started. Call the others."

The next ten minutes could have turned into pandemonium,

but they didn't. Gillian stood on the sidelines, watching in amazement as TJ organized the boys into an effective fire-building team seemingly without doing anything more than pointing out what needed to be done. One group searched for wood while another gathered stones to build a fire ring. Still another cleared the ground of dried leaves and other combustibles.

Though TJ had not appointed team leaders, Shane took charge of wood gathering with three of what appeared to be his cronies and set his blond sidekick to finding stones with four others. The six who'd comprised the second group showed no intent of following Shane. Instead they shuffled their feet and gave exaggerated coughs until a skinny boy whose pale blond hair and light blue eyes hinted at a Scandinavian heritage cleared his throat.

"We need a rake." He looked around the group. "Jason, I think I saw one near your RV. Think your dad would let us borrow it?"

The teen nodded. "Sure, Todd."

"Who's got extra garbage bags?"

Another teen volunteered. And all the while, TJ simply observed.

"Todd's not just the class brainiac. He's also a born leader," TJ told Gillian. "The problem is Shane doesn't usually let him do anything."

Gillian wondered how TJ had learned all that in such a short time. Was it something teachers knew instinctively, or was it part of their training?

"What's going on?"

Gillian turned, not surprised to see half a dozen girls approaching. The noise level had increased to the point where even someone inside an RV would notice that something unusual was happening. Gillian looked for TJ, but he'd moved away and was now supervising the arrangement of wood inside the fire ring. Apparently dealing with the girls was part of Gillian's designated adult role.

"We're going to have a campfire," she said.

"Why?" the first girl asked. Perhaps an inch taller than Gillian's five foot four, the girl had dark brown hair and eyes and what would have been a pretty face had her makeup been more subtle. As it was, the heavy eyeliner and garish shadow made her resemble a clown. Her clothing, though, had nothing in common with a clown's baggy suit. The combination of a tight sweater with a deep vee neckline and an overly short skirt left no doubt that she had what was once called a pinup girl's figure.

"You have to wait and see, but an educated guess is that s'mores are involved. By the way, I'm Gillian."

The girl nodded. "I'm Brianna. Why do you think we're having s'mores?"

Gillian held out the grocery bag TJ had given her for safekeeping, revealing the contents. "I can't think of anything else to do with graham crackers, marshmallows, and chocolate. Can you?"

A second girl shook her head. "I'm Tracy." She gestured toward the other girls. "Are we invited?"

"Sure." The mission had been to entertain all the teens, not simply the boys. "You and anyone else who's interested in a s'more."

But TJ had more than s'mores in mind. Once the fire was built and the introductions made, he announced that it was illegal to have a campfire without telling stories around it. Remembering how powerful peer pressure and the worry of being embarrassed could be, Gillian wasn't surprised that no one volunteered. If TJ was disappointed by the lack of participation, he gave no sign of it; he simply launched into a tale of his travels around the country on his motorcycle.

The man was a born storyteller. Though Gillian doubted the actual events had been as amusing as TJ made them sound, there was no doubt that he'd gotten the kids' attention. They listened as intently as any group of teenagers she'd ever seen, and when he appeared to have finished, they asked for more.

"Maybe tomorrow," TJ said. No wonder he claimed that teaching was a performing art. TJ wasn't just a born storyteller, he was a great performer, recognizing the value of leaving an audience wanting more. "Right now," he said with a grin that was clearly visible in the light of the campfire, "my stomach wants a s'more. Who's going to roast the first marshmallow?"

Good-natured squabbling was the predictable result. Finally, TJ turned to Gillian. "What about you?"

She shook her head. "You must be kidding. After the supper I ate, I won't need another meal for a week."

Giving her a faux scowl, he said, "You can't disappoint the kids."

"Yeah," Shane agreed. "You're our adult supervision. You gotta eat some. Otherwise, how can you be sure it's really chocolate and not something bad?"

"That sounds like I'm the royal taster." Gillian couldn't help laughing. "It's the craziest argument I've ever heard, but okay."

She skewered a marshmallow and began to toast it. When it was perfectly browned, she slid it onto a graham cracker and topped it with a piece of chocolate and another graham. Taking a bite, she let the flavors of her childhood coat her tongue, then slide down her throat. "This is great!"

A half hour later, once the campfire had been extinguished, TJ and Gillian started back to Rainbow's End.

"You're really good with kids," she said when they were out of earshot of the group.

He shrugged. "It's been awhile since I was their age, but I still remember what it felt like. They're kids, but . . ."

He paused, his attention drawn to a couple standing in the shadows of a live oak. There was enough moonlight to reveal arms wrapped around each other and lips locked in a passionate kiss. Gillian wasn't surprised by the kiss. Teenagers, after all, were teenagers. What surprised her was the identity of the couple. She would never have pictured Brianna, with her heavy makeup, overly short skirt, and revealing sweater, with Todd, the nerd.

TJ shook his head. "Young love. It'll never last."

6

"So, how did it go?"

Gillian smiled. Though Kate had claimed she'd come to Gillian's cabin to make sure she had everything she needed, Gillian knew better. Her friend's curiosity about the trip to Firefly Valley was the real reason she'd knocked on the door.

"Really well, thanks to TJ. He was amazing with those kids."

Kate lowered herself onto one of the upholstered chairs, her smile as broad as Gillian's. "I'm not surprised. He was pretty amazing at supper—not at all what I expected after the way you described him. If I weren't a happily married woman expecting my first child, I might have entertained a fantasy or two about him."

"I'm shocked." Though Gillian's words were laced with sarcasm, there was a grain of truth to them. TJ was not the kind of man she would have expected to attract Kate.

"I was only kidding, Gillian. You know Greg's the only man for me. But I have to admit it was fun to see your reaction. For a woman who claims she has no interest in love and marriage, you looked just a tad upset by the thought of competition."

"You're mistaken, Kate. Sadly mistaken. Either that or matchmaking is contagious. Fortunately, I'm immune."

Kate shrugged. "So you say. But tell me, what did you learn about the oh so attractive TJ Benjamin? Is he married?"

"Do you really think I'd ask him that? In case you didn't notice, he was pretty uncomfortable when you asked him what he did for a living. I wasn't about to pry." But Gillian had noticed the absence of a wedding ring and that he had made no mention of a woman in his life. "If I had to guess, I'd say he's a confirmed bachelor having his midlife crisis a decade or so ahead of schedule."

"You could be right. That would explain why he's traveling instead of teaching."

But it did not explain the sadness Gillian had seen in his eyes. Though she'd told herself that it, like TJ's marital status, was none of her business, she couldn't help wondering what had caused it. And wasn't that silly? Though their paths had crossed, in another day or two, they'd diverge again. There was no reason—absolutely no reason—to be so concerned. It was time to change the subject.

"Have you and Greg picked out names for the baby?"

"Are you sure you don't mind driving me?"

Gillian shook her head, surprised by TJ's question. She thought they'd resolved that at breakfast when she'd mentioned going into town and had offered him a ride. Though he hadn't said anything, she suspected he was chafing at the forced inactivity while he waited for his bike to be repaired. Dupree was hardly a metropolis, but it might occupy TJ for an hour or so.

"Of course I don't mind." She opened the door to her rental car and slid behind the wheel. "You never can tell. I might decide to become a chauffeur." It was a joke, of course. Between her disability insurance and the income from the trust fund her father had established for her, she had no financial needs. What she needed was something to make her feel creative and productive.

Chuckling, TJ slung an obviously expensive camera around his neck and slid into the passenger's seat. "I'm trying to picture you in one of those chauffeur hats with the shiny brims, but the image won't come into focus."

"I guess that means I need to find something else to do." And that was the crux of the problem. Gillian had no idea what she wanted to do with her life now that she couldn't play the piano. All she knew was that she needed something to fill the void.

As she'd told Kate, music had been the most important thing in Gillian's life from the time she was five and a bored nanny had set her on the bench of the family's Steinway grand. That had been the beginning. The end had come on a Manhattan sidewalk last September, making her future an enigma.

Gillian knew she wasn't the only one with problems. The man in the passenger's seat had his share. As the car tires crunched on the gravel drive, TJ stared across the road at the RVs settled into Firefly Valley, his expression pensive, his shoulders as tense as they'd been last night when they'd approached the RV settlement.

Gillian didn't know what was bothering him, but something was, and her instincts told her this was different from the sorrow she'd seen in his eyes. This wasn't sorrow or pain; it was discomfort. Though it might be connected to TJ's cynical comment after they'd seen Brianna and Todd kissing last night, Gillian doubted that, since she'd noticed the discomfort before they'd met the teens. It almost seemed as if the sight of the motor homes had triggered it both last night and this morning.

For a second Gillian was tempted to scoff at the idea of an inanimate object causing fear until she remembered her reaction to TJ's motorcycle. Fears weren't rational. She knew that as well as anyone. She also knew that talking about them didn't always help, and so she decided to pretend she hadn't noticed TJ's uneasiness.

"So you don't think I'd make a good chauffeur," she said, hoping the silly speculation would distract him.

"I don't imagine there's a lot of call for chauffeurs in Dupree, anyway." TJ's voice held more than a note of amusement, telling Gillian he'd deliberately repressed whatever melancholy thoughts Firefly Valley generated. That was good. That was very good.

"That may be true now," she said, keeping her own voice light, "but you never can tell what will happen once Drew Carroll's web design company opens. Dupree could turn into a new boomtown." And pigs would fly. Though Kate had said that the town council was optimistic about the city's prospects, neither she nor Greg expected anything more than moderate growth, even with the addition of Greg's former partner's company.

"Are you a cockeyed optimist?"

Gillian turned to stare at TJ, startled by the question. "No, but the woman I'm going to visit is." Kate's grandmother Sally was both a self-confessed cockeyed optimist and a fan of *South Pacific*, and since Gillian had spent countless hours visiting Kate, she had more than a passing acquaintance with the songs from the Rodgers and Hammerstein musical.

Now happily married for the second time, Sally was a firm believer that every woman would have a "Some Enchanted Evening" moment when she met the man of her dreams. The best part of that was that Sally had never tried to push Gillian toward the altar. Thank goodness.

"What about you?" Gillian asked TJ. "Are you an optimist, cockeyed or otherwise?"

"Me?" He shook his head. "Why would a man who crashed his only form of transportation be optimistic?"

There it was again, the cynicism that clung to TJ like mud to Gillian's best suede shoes. She wouldn't pry, she reminded herself. TJ's expression left no doubt that he would not welcome meddling any more than she would welcome matchmaking. Besides, they'd be in Dupree in a minute. That was not enough time to start a serious discussion, and so Gillian said only, "Kate tells me Eric's the best. He'll have you back on the road in no time."

A grunt and a deliberate turn of his head toward the window were TJ's response. Gillian took the hint and remained silent until they passed the "Welcome to Dupree" sign.

"Where should I drop you?" she asked.

TJ shrugged. "Anywhere. And don't worry about driving me back. I can walk."

"It's three miles," she said, shuddering at the thought. It was one thing to walk that far on a treadmill, something quite different to climb Ranger Hill under the Texas sun. Even though it was only early April, what Gillian would have classified as summer had already come to Texas.

"Spoken like a city dweller," TJ said, a bit of scorn coloring his words. "It's not all that far."

Refusing to concede the point, Gillian glanced at her watch. "I'll pick you up at the Sit 'n' Sip in two hours. You can't miss it."

"If I'm not there, don't wait."

Gillian was still shaking her head at the man's stubborn streak when she pulled into Sally's driveway.

The small ranch-style home bore no resemblance to the two-story colonial where Sally had spent most of her life and where Kate and Gillian had shared countless secrets, but Gillian knew the same welcome was waiting inside.

"Come in, child." The woman who'd been as close to a grandmother as Gillian had ever known wrapped her in an embrace that smelled of talcum powder, strawberry shampoo, and dark-roast coffee. While so much of Gillian's life had changed, those scents had remained constant, a reminder of Sally's love.

"Where's Roy?" Gillian asked when Sally released her. Though she'd met Sally's second husband only briefly at Kate's wedding,

Gillian had formed an instant liking for the man who'd put the sparkle back in Sally's eyes, and she wondered whether he was responsible for Sally's new wardrobe. Growing up, Gillian had never seen Sally in anything other than skirts and dresses, but today she looked like a native Texan in jeans, a chambray shirt, and hand-tooled boots.

"Roy's playing golf with some friends." Sally laughed. "He told me we needed girls' time—not that I'm a girl anymore."

Wrinkles lined Sally's face; her tightly curled hair had been silver for decades; and her chin had lost its firm line years ago. While she wasn't a girl by anyone's definition, despite—or perhaps because of—the generations that separated them, she was one of Gillian's dearest friends.

"Come in," Sally repeated, ushering Gillian into the cool interior of the home she now shared with Roy. "Here's my new home sweet home."

To Gillian's surprise, it bore no resemblance to Sally's house in Buffalo. Instead of a formal floor plan with separate living and dining rooms and antique furniture, this one boasted a great room, and the only piece of furniture she recognized was the old upright piano.

"I couldn't leave that behind," Sally said, seeing the direction of Gillian's gaze. "I keep telling myself that one of these years I'll learn to play. Right now, though, let me get you some sweet tea."

They paused briefly in the kitchen while Sally loaded a tray with a pitcher, glasses, and a plate of fancy pastries before nodding at the French door. "It's too nice to stay inside." She led the way to a covered porch and settled onto a padded chaise longue. "Tell me about yourself," she said when she'd handed Gillian a glass of tea.

Gillian shook her head. "I'd rather talk about you. You look fabulous." If she hadn't known Sally had recently celebrated her seventy-fourth birthday, Gillian would have thought her no more than sixty-five. "Marriage is obviously agreeing with you."

A sweet smile crossed Sally's face. "God has been good to me," she agreed. "He gave me second chances at life and love. A year ago I had no idea what he had in store for Kate and me, but look at us now. We're both married and waiting for my first great-grandchild's arrival."

She gave the pastries a longing look, then cut one in two and placed the smaller piece on her plate. "After the scare with my heart, the doctor said I need to watch my diet." Sally wrinkled her nose. "You know doctors—they're so cautious. Speaking of which . . ." She reached over and picked up Gillian's right hand, inspecting it as if she could see beneath the skin to the once shattered bones and torn tendons. "They did a remarkable job."

"Yes, they did. I can do almost everything I did before."

Sally's eyes narrowed as she traced the scars. "But you can't play."

"Not at the professional level. Some days I can barely manage scales, but others are better. Those days I feel like a first-year student." Gillian shrugged, as if her failure to regain full use of her fingers was insignificant. "One thing's for sure: the days of concert stages are over."

"Fortunately, the future is limitless."

Gillian laughed and reached for the other half of the pastry. "I told TJ you were a cockeyed optimist, and you've proven me right."

She popped a bite of pastry into her mouth and savored the combination of pineapple and almonds on top of a flaky butter crust at the same time that she regretted mentioning TJ. Sally might not be a matchmaker, but as an incurable romantic, she was always interested in a good love story. That meant Gillian would be subjected to a series of questions about him.

"TJ. So there's a man in your life now."

It was time for Gillian to nip the speculation in the bud. "I hate to disappoint you, Sally, but TJ's a guest at Rainbow's End. He'll be gone in a couple days." And Gillian would be gone soon afterwards. A month from now, this trip and TJ Benjamin would be nothing more than memories.

Though Sally was obviously disappointed by the absence of wedding bells in Gillian's immediate future, she nodded as if she understood. "You're planning to stay until the baby's born, aren't you?"

Kate had asked the same question, insisting she and Greg were looking forward to having her as a long-term guest. Gillian gave Sally a regretful smile as she repeated what she'd told Kate. "I'm only going to be here for a week." The physical therapist had said Gillian shouldn't go any longer between sessions. Of course, the same therapist had told her she had achieved as much healing as she ever would, making her wonder why she would rush back for more therapy or even consider finding a therapist here if she decided to stay longer.

"Roy and I have two spare bedrooms," Sally said, ignoring Gillian's statement the same way she'd ignored protests in the past. "We talked about it last night, and we both agreed we'd love to have you stay with us. And don't try telling me that we're on our honeymoon. We're not teenagers. Besides, we've been married for close to a year."

Though Sally looked like the quintessential sweet little old lady, she did a good imitation of a steamroller when she wanted to convince someone.

"Thank you, but . . ."

Before Gillian could complete the sentence, Sally raised an eyebrow. "But what? Is there a special someone waiting for you up North?"

As Gillian shook her head, TJ's image flashed through her brain. How silly! She wasn't interested in him, at least not that way. If she were looking for a man—which she wasn't—it wouldn't be an unemployed motorcycle-riding teacher. The only reason TJ had even crossed her mind was that he was so different from the men she'd met at Juilliard and on concert tours.

None of those men had piqued her interest the way TJ did, and that was surprising. Those men were the kind of men she was expected to marry. TJ was not. It was true that he was no less educated, but he was definitely less polished than the perfectly dressed, perfectly coiffed men who'd been part of Gillian's life since she'd graduated. She couldn't picture him in a concert hall or a five-star restaurant, and she definitely couldn't imagine him being comfortable in the back of a stretch limo, yet somehow those differences made him intriguing. There were depths to TJ that she'd never seen in the men she'd dated. Perhaps that was the reason those dates had never been more than casual.

"I'm not planning to get married any time soon," she said, suddenly unsure whether she was convincing herself or Sally.

"I wasn't either, but look what happened to me." Sally refilled Gillian's glass. "I really think you should stay here, at least for a couple months. And don't roll your eyes at the idea of Dupree. It may be a lot smaller than New York and Chicago, but the town is changing. We've got Drew Carroll's web company coming in, and Marisa St. George—pardon me, Marisa Kendall—has opened a bookstore. The seniors are even planning to start a book club once we figure out where to meet."

Gillian wasn't certain why Sally thought those changes would affect her. Admittedly, Gillian relished a well-stocked bookstore, but that wasn't a reason to spend months in Dupree.

"Think about it, Gillian."

And, though it was the last thing she'd planned to do, Gillian nodded. "I will."

7

The town was more appealing than he'd expected. The business area, if you could call it that, was larger than he'd realized. There were more empty buildings than he'd like to see in a town this size, but Pecan Street boasted a number of small stores including what appeared to be a first-rate bootery and the shop that was the likely source of the quilts he'd seen at Rainbow's End.

One of the letter-named streets even had a decent barber, who'd managed to salvage TJ's hair after the crude hacking he'd given it. The fact that the man had made no comment other than that curly hair was a challenge earned him a healthy tip.

With his hair no longer sticking out in odd ways, TJ continued his tour of the town, discovering that Dupree was bookended with construction. An apartment complex was going up on the south side, while a sign on the north end showed an artist's rendition of the office building and cluster of duplex houses that were currently little more than cement foundations. Even when both were finished, Dupree would not be a boomtown. Still, it had more charm than TJ had expected.

He looked at the display on his camera, surprised that he'd

taken more than a hundred pictures. It wasn't as if he planned to remember his time in Dupree. As soon as Eric finished repairing his bike, TJ would be gone. And yet, something about the town intrigued him. Though he couldn't pinpoint the reason, he felt comfortable here.

Retracing his steps on Lone Star Trail toward the center of town, TJ studied the businesses lining the oddly named main street. Several of the buildings were empty. Others needed a good coat of paint. Still others needed their bricks repointed. But somehow this time the flaws didn't bother him the way they had the first time he'd noticed them. Instead, his mind began to whirl with ideas about how to renew the town. Odd. He'd never felt that way about a place, not even the suburb where he and Deb had spent their entire married life.

Glancing at his watch, TJ realized he had half an hour before he was supposed to meet Gillian. He might as well go into the Sit 'n' Sip and see what the town's premier—translation: only—eating establishment offered.

"Howdy, stranger. What can I get you?" The brown-haired, brown-eyed man gave him an appraising look as he handed TJ a laminated menu.

"Just a cup of coffee." Breakfast had been more substantial than TJ was accustomed to, making him suspect he'd be able to survive on the two meals a day that Rainbow's End provided. That would help him stretch his remaining cash until he decided what to do next.

"There you go," the man said as he slid a large mug in front of TJ, "and now that you have a cup of the finest java in Dupree, you're no longer a stranger." He extended his hand for a shake. "I'm Russ Walker, and this is my place."

"TJ Benjamin." As he returned the introduction, TJ took a sip of coffee, wincing when the overly strong and bitter brew slid down his throat. Hastily, he added cream and sugar to the beverage.

"You staying out at Rainbow's End or just passing through?" Russ Walker asked. It was more than casual conversation, TJ knew. This was quintessential small-town America at work. Residents looked after each other, and that included determining whether strangers were potential threats.

"I'll be at Rainbow's End for a couple days," TJ said as he explained what had brought him to the self-proclaimed Heart of the Hills.

The barely veiled suspicion in the man's eyes disappeared, replaced by sympathy. "It's a doggone shame about your bike, but Eric St. George is a good man. He'll do you right."

TJ nodded and took another sip of coffee. With the addition of what seemed like half a jar of sugar and a cup of cream, it was tolerable. "That's what everyone says." He could only hope the praise wasn't misplaced. "You said his name was St. George. Any relation to the St. George apartment building that's under construction?"

Russ Walker leaned on the counter, his smile announcing his delight at being the one to convey news. "You could say so. Fact is, the building was named for him, his wife, and his daughter. They all work at Rainbow's End now. Carmen's the cook, Marisa does the books, and from what I've heard, Eric does just about everything else."

"It's an unusual place." Though he had no intention of remaining once his bike was repaired, TJ had to admit that the combination of the beautiful location, excellent food, and comfortable bed was appealing. If it hadn't been for those RVs across the road, TJ might have said it was close to perfect.

Russ picked up the coffeepot and refilled TJ's mug. "I heard Gillian Hodge is out there. Did you happen to meet her?"

Though he was surprised that Russ knew Gillian's name, TJ suspected her connection to Kate and Greg might be the reason she was not a total stranger in town. Guessing that the Sit 'n' Sip's proprietor sought more news for the local grapevine, TJ nodded. "You could say that. She's the one who rescued me when I crashed my bike."

The man's eyes widened. "Is she as pretty as her pictures?"

Pictures? "I can't say. I never saw any pictures, but she's easy on the eyes." A pretty face, curves in all the right places, and hair that reminded him of a sunset. Yes, indeed, Gillian Hodge was easy on the eyes.

Russ nodded, as if he'd read TJ's thoughts. "I figured she would be. It sure is a pity what happened to her."

"I'm afraid you lost me there." But if TJ's suppositions about Russ's fondness for gossip were correct, he'd soon learn whatever had happened to Gillian.

Straightening his shoulders, Russ drew himself to his full height and puffed out his chest, clearly relishing his role of being in the know. "I'm surprised no one told you." He paused for effect. "She used to be a concert pianist. A pretty good one, from all accounts. Won some kind of fancy award."

A concert pianist. TJ's breath came out in a whoosh as the words registered. No wonder he'd found her so unapproachable when she'd stopped her car to rescue him. His first impression had been correct. They came from very different worlds. Gillian was probably used to caviar and chateaubriand, limos and luxury, where he was a barbecue and beans kind of guy.

TJ shook himself mentally. There was no reason Gillian's career should have shocked him. It wasn't as if they were more than casual acquaintances. He turned his attention back to Russ, whose expression had grown more sober.

"The way I hear it, she had one of those sky's-the-limit careers. Then she was in some kind of accident—hurt her hand pretty bad." Russ's mouth curved into a frown. "Rumor is she'll never play again."

8

Gillian pulled into one of the angled parking spots in front of the Sit 'n' Sip, wondering whether there was any point in going inside. TJ didn't strike her as the kind of man to wait patiently for a woman who was a quarter of an hour late. The time with Sally had passed quickly, and Gillian had been startled to realize she'd been gone longer than she'd planned. She had half expected to see TJ heading back to Rainbow's End or possibly standing on the curb, tapping his foot in annoyance. Instead, there was no sign of him. Unwilling to possibly abandon him, she climbed out of the car.

As she entered the small diner, she blinked to let her eyes adjust to the relative darkness, and as she did, a man called out, "Welcome to Dupree, Miss Hodge. I hope you'll sit a spell."

Gillian blinked again, this time at the novelty of being addressed as "Miss Hodge." It was true that reporters occasionally called her that, but this man was no reporter. His white apron and position behind the counter left no doubt that he worked here.

Before Gillian could respond, the man said, "I was just telling your friend here about your accident. Is it true you won't be playing again?"

He might not be a reporter, but he sounded like the ones who'd been waiting for her the day she'd been released from the hospital after the last round of surgery. Feeling as if she'd been ambushed, Gillian nodded. "That's what the doctors say."

She turned to TJ, who'd drained his cup and laid a couple bills on the counter. "Are you ready?" It might be rude, but Gillian had no intention of discussing either her medical history or her career with a complete stranger. Though Texans had a reputation for friendliness, there was a fine line between friendliness and prying. This man had stepped over the line.

"I'm sorry about that," TJ said as they pulled onto Lone Star Trail. When he ran a hand through his hair, Gillian noticed that the shaggy ends were gone. It appeared TJ had put his time in Dupree to good use.

"Russ was just being friendly," TJ said. "He was really impressed that a famous pianist came to Dupree."

"Former pianist," Gillian corrected him. Oddly, it didn't hurt as much as she'd expected to say that.

"That must be tough."

"It is." Though she had not wanted to talk to Russ whatever-his-last-name-was, Gillian had no such discomfort with TJ. The pain she'd seen in his eyes and his leaving his chosen career at least temporarily made her think he would understand.

"I feel rudderless," she admitted. "I had my life carefully planned, and now there's nothing. I have no idea what I'll do next, because the only thing I know is music."

Even though Kate had had no difficulty transitioning from a high-powered job in Manhattan to a totally different lifestyle as Greg's wife and the owner of a resort, Gillian could not imagine doing anything similar. There was no one like Greg in her life to make such a dramatic change seem appealing.

TJ stroked his chin, leaving Gillian to wonder if he missed

having a beard. "Have you thought about teaching? I'm not talking about a public school. You'd need certification for that, but what about private lessons? I imagine parents would pay well to have someone with your credentials teaching their kids."

Gillian shook her head. Her manager had suggested the same thing shortly before they parted company. She had refused then, and she was refusing now. "That's not for me."

Gillian wouldn't insult TJ by telling him her father would be horrified if she even entertained the idea. Admittedly, that was part of the reason she hadn't considered teaching, but it was only part. The primary reason was that she doubted she could establish the rapport with her pupils that would be needed to succeed. TJ seemed to have an instinctive bond with teens, while Gillian was ill at ease with children of any age, perhaps because she'd had so little experience with them. Though she had a nephew, Gabriel was twenty-four, only five years her junior.

"I'm not good with kids," she told TJ.

"Oh, I wouldn't say that. You held your own with those girls last night."

"But I felt uncomfortable every second we were there."

His skepticism obvious, TJ shook his head. "Then you ought to consider a career in acting. You didn't look uncomfortable."

"Well, I was. Teaching's not for me. The problem is, I don't know what I'm going to do next," Gillian said, hating the way her voice threatened to quaver. "What I do know is that I need a clean break. Music is my past."

TJ's lips thinned, and he stared out the windshield, his expression inscrutable. "I hear what you're saying, and I understand why you feel that way. I know you don't want advice—I didn't either—but if there's one thing I've learned, it's that you can't outrun your past."

TJ hated the way Gillian's face fell. It might have been kinder to say nothing, and yet he'd felt compelled to share the little he'd learned with her. When he'd embarked on what was beginning to feel like an odyssey, he'd believed it was what he needed to close a chapter of his life. At the time it had seemed like the right—perhaps the only—thing to do.

There'd been no deathbed promises, no tearful moments talking about Deb's still incomplete bucket list. Instead, during those final months they'd spoken of the places they'd seen, the adventures they'd had. It had seemed cruel to talk about a future here on Earth when Deb had none, and so TJ had kept them focused on the past.

Was that a mistake? Was he wrong in believing that finishing Deb's bucket list would bring him closure? TJ didn't know. All he knew was that the past still dominated his thoughts, and he had no idea what he would do once he checked off the final park.

A year ago he had thought that by now the future would be clear, but it was still as opaque as the Yellowstone mud pots that had fascinated Deb. TJ could only hope—he'd long since stopped praying—that Gillian would be more fortunate.

"I'd like to help you," he told her, "but one other thing I've learned is that you need to find your own answers." If only he could find his.

"That's all right. As you guessed, I've gotten my share of advice and don't really want any more." Gillian paused for a second, apparently concentrating on the road, before she said, "There is one thing you can do for me, though."

TJ looked at her, surprised there was anything he could do for her. "What's that?"

"Satisfy my curiosity. What does 'TJ' stand for?"

He laughed, remembering the number of times students had asked that. He'd always refused to answer, knowing how kids liked to ridicule names, but there was no reason not to tell Gillian.

"What do you think?"

"Thomas Jefferson."

TJ shook his head. "Not hardly."

"Timothy James."

"Nope." When she'd guessed three more names, all infinitely preferable to the one his parents had chosen, TJ took pity on her. "All right. I'll tell you, but only if you promise not to tell anyone, especially not the kids in Firefly Valley."

Gillian nodded her agreement. "You make it sound like it's something awful."

"Trust me. It is. How would you like to go through life saddled with Tobias Jeremiah?"

"Tobias Jeremiah." She rolled the name on her tongue. "I like it. You can tell your parents they chose well."

TJ shook his head. "That's no longer possible. My parents died ten years ago."

Gillian's eyes misted. "I'm sorry. Was it an accident?"

"Nope. One of those deadly viruses that are all too common in Africa. My parents went there as missionaries and never came back."

"That's awful."

It was, although nowhere nearly as awful as Deb's death had been. But TJ wouldn't talk about Deb. Trying to deflect attention from himself, he asked, "Are your parents both alive?"

Gillian shook her head. "My mother died when I was born."

TJ's surprise must have been evident, because Gillian continued. "Women dying in childbirth was supposed to have ended in the nineteenth century, but it seems no one told my mother or her doctor. They knew she was at higher risk just because of her age—I was a surprise baby—but no one expected that the delivery would have so many complications."

"Now I'm the one to say I'm sorry. Did your dad remarry?"

She shook her head again. "No. He's a one-woman man."

Like TJ.

9

When they reached Rainbow's End, as Gillian headed to her cabin, Eric St. George emerged from the building that served as the resort's garage and his workshop.

"We need to talk," the heavyset man with hair more gray than blond said as he ushered TJ inside.

Though Eric's tone of voice and his expression indicated that whatever he was going to say wasn't good news, TJ took a quick breath and smiled at the sight of his bike. There was nothing wrong here. In fact, everything was right. The crumpled fender and slashed tire were gone, and a closer inspection revealed that the repairs were invisible. If he hadn't known better, TJ would have said there'd been no accident.

"Wow! I heard you were good, but this is more than good. It's great."

"Thanks." Despite the compliment, Eric still looked uncomfortable. "I've had a fair amount of experience with body work, but engines are my real specialty." He pointed at TJ's bike. "That's why we need to talk. I didn't like the way yours sounded, so I took it apart. Someone did a lot of customization."

TJ nodded. "The last owner liked to tinker."

"I could tell." Eric patted the engine. "The problem is your crankshaft. It's more worn than I would have expected for the mileage. It could last another year, but it's just as likely to break in the next month or so. I don't have to tell you what that would mean if you were somewhere remote." Meeting TJ's gaze, Eric said, "The decision is yours, but I recommend you replace it."

No wonder Eric had seemed ill at ease. This was just what TJ didn't need: another major expense. "How much will that cost?" When Eric quoted a figure that seemed ridiculously low, TJ nodded. He could afford that, but he couldn't afford a breakdown in the middle of nowhere. "How long will it take?"

Eric frowned. "The installation is less than a day. The problem is getting the part. I called local suppliers, and no one's got one. I figure it'll be about a week. Is that okay?"

Two days ago, TJ would have shaken his head in frustration, but two days ago he hadn't known how intriguing Rainbow's End and a certain auburn-haired woman would be. Though he harbored no illusions that either one would be a permanent part of his life, he couldn't deny that the last twenty-four hours had been the most memorable since he'd begun his vagabond existence.

If he'd been allowed a redo, he certainly wouldn't have crashed his bike, but he had to admit that being at Rainbow's End had shifted his perspective, if only slightly. The location was one of the prettiest he'd seen. It wasn't spectacular like Yosemite or the Grand Canyon, and yet in its own quiet way, it touched him as much as they had.

As for Gillian, something about her piqued his interest. It wasn't a romantic interest. Far from it. When he'd lost Deb, TJ had known that his days of love and happily-ever-after were ended. TJ had had one chance, and he'd lost it. But he found himself thinking of Gillian more than he had any other woman besides Deb and wondering if they could be friends, at least for however long they were both at Rainbow's End.

Perhaps it was because she too had lost something important and was searching for her future. Perhaps it was because, although she projected a cool self-confidence, he'd seen the vulnerability beneath the outer shell. Perhaps it was simply that she had been his Good Samaritan. TJ didn't know the reason, but he did know that it would be no hardship to remain here.

He turned back to Eric and nodded. "The delay's okay."

* * *

"You look like a lady of leisure."

Startled by the sound of TJ's voice, Gillian let out a small gasp. She'd been sitting in one of the Adirondack chairs in front of the lodge, staring at the lake ever since she finished reading Janice Thompson's latest book. Her favorite author never failed to deliver a heartwarming story with more than one LOL moment, but today Gillian found herself wondering whether she'd ever find a happily-ever-after like Janice's characters. Though they might be confused at the beginning of the book, by the end, they'd found their direction in life, not to mention the perfect husband.

If only real life were as neat. All Gillian was looking for was a direction, but as it was, she felt as if her life had unraveled. Still, there was no reason to bore TJ with her problems. Gillian forced a light tone to her voice. "Is that a fancy way of saying I look lazy?"

TJ shook his head. Dressed in a plaid shirt and jeans, he was the picture of relaxation, and yet there was nothing relaxed about his gaze. He appeared to be studying her, almost as if she were some kind of specimen. Did he think former concert pianists were an exotic species? Gillian could assure him that they were not.

"Lazy is the way you're supposed to feel on vacation," he said.

"I wouldn't know about that. Vacations were never a big part of my life." Maybe that was the reason she had these moments of melancholy. Maybe she hadn't known what to expect.

This was Gillian's fourth day at Rainbow's End, and life had already settled into a pattern. After breakfast, she occupied herself with either a walk around the resort or an hour or so of reading while Kate handled the day's business. Most of the day was spent with Kate, but after supper Gillian accompanied TJ to Firefly Valley.

It was pleasant, and yet she felt an emptiness inside her that nothing seemed to fill. In the past, there'd always been a piece to practice, new music to consider adding to her repertoire, the next season's schedule to arrange. Even after the accident, her days had been full, with physical therapy replacing the hours she used to spend at the piano. Now there was a void.

TJ settled into the chair next to her and fixed his gaze on her. "That's a shame." For a second, she feared he had read her thoughts, but then she realized that he was speaking of vacations.

"There's nothing like heading out and not knowing exactly where you're going," he told her, his lips curving upward as if he were remembering a particularly pleasant excursion.

As a mockingbird flitted by, landing on one of the live oak trees, Gillian clenched and unclenched her hands, stopping only when she realized she no longer had a reason to keep her fingers limber.

"I can't imagine doing that." There'd been no spontaneity in her travels, only careful scheduling. Even her childhood trips with Kate's family had been planned. No spur-of-the-moment drives, no impromptu picnics. And once Gillian had won the Brooks, the planning had intensified. Nothing could be left to chance.

But the difference between her experiences and TJ's was more than a matter of planning. While Gillian had seen big cities, hotel rooms, and concert halls, TJ had explored small towns, national parks, and natural beauty. If something caught his fancy and he wanted to stay an extra day, he did. Gillian knew that from the tales he recounted around the campfire.

"You ought to try it. You never can tell what you might find at the end of the road."

The image of herself riding into the sunset with the man of her dreams—a man who looked a bit like TJ—was so appealing that Gillian caught her breath. She turned to TJ, a question in her eyes.

"As soon as my bike is fixed, I'll take you for a ride."

The bubble burst. "No." The word came out more forcefully than Gillian had planned, so she tempered it with a "thank you."

"Why not? Are you afraid of getting lost?"

"It's not that. I just don't ride motorcycles." She never had, and after her one experience with a bike, she knew she never would.

TJ seemed undaunted by her lack of enthusiasm. He leaned forward, his eyes shining with anticipation. "There's always a first time."

"Not for me." Gillian needed to change the subject. Though Kate and Sally knew the details of the accident, Gillian's manager had insisted the press release say only that Gillian Hodge had sustained an injury to her right hand. At the time, she hadn't worried about his motivation, and now it hardly mattered. She wasn't going to tell a man whose life centered on his motorcycle that one had destroyed her career. Instead, she said, "Speaking of motorcycles, how's yours coming?"

TJ flashed her a mischievous grin. "Are you trying to get rid of me?"

Rainbow's End without TJ. The thought was oddly disturbing. "Why would I do that? If you left, I'd have to go to Firefly Valley alone, and that would be a disaster. My stories can't compare to yours." Each night seemed easier, but Gillian knew she'd never have the easy rapport with the teens that TJ did.

"You underestimate yourself. I know you said you weren't good with kids, but that's not what I see. The way that group of girls was hanging around you last night, I'd have thought you were Scheherazade. What kind of tales were you telling them?"

Gillian smiled at the memory. "Don't laugh, but it was a dissertation on the fine art of applying blusher and eye shadow." When the girls had learned she had had professional makeup for some performances, they'd been fascinated and had asked her to share the techniques she'd learned.

To his credit, TJ did not laugh, although the corners of his mouth twitched upward. "Figures."

"What do you mean?" Did he think makeup was the only topic she could discuss?

"No need to be defensive. Boys want to hear about adventures because they're trying to appear brave. Girls want to be beautiful. There's nothing wrong with that."

As a gust of wind sent ripples across the lake and threatened to knock Gillian's hat off, she tightened the cord. "I feel sorry for the girls, especially Brianna."

"The brunette who dresses like a hooker?"

Gillian winced. "Unfortunately, that's an accurate description." Even by current standards, Brianna's clothes were extreme. Extremely short, extremely tight, extremely revealing. "She's being raised by a single mom who works at night. As far as I can tell, the mom isn't much of a role model."

Brianna had confided that she'd never met her father and that her mother dropped out of high school when she became pregnant. Though Gillian's parents had married fairly young so that Dad would be exempt from the Vietnam-era draft, by all accounts, they'd had a happy marriage, and George claimed they were good parents.

"Unfortunately, that's an all too common story." TJ stared at the lake for a few seconds. "What surprises me about Brianna is that she hangs out with Todd. They're one of the oddest couples I've seen, and believe me, I've seen my share of odd couples."

Gillian had to agree. There'd been girls like Brianna and boys like Todd at her school, but they'd tended to ignore each other. "I can't figure it out other than that Brianna's brighter than she wants people to believe. Maybe Todd sees that, or maybe he's just happy that a pretty girl is interested in him."

Shifting his weight, TJ leaned toward Gillian. "I've taught teenagers for almost a decade, and I still don't understand what makes them tick."

Though she didn't understand the reason, because at least from her perspective the man was brilliant with the Firefly Valley teens, Gillian heard a note of insecurity in TJ's voice and decided to combat it. "Now you're the one who's selling yourself short. The kids love your stories. You're reaching them, TJ. I know you are."

"I hope so."

10

"So, what do you think, Gillian?"

What Gillian thought was that the RV needed a good cleaning. Dirty clothes were strewn everywhere. The counters were lined with dishes bearing the caked-on remains of at least a week's meals. Crumpled movie magazines littered every other horizontal surface. No doubt about it: Brianna's home was well on its way to becoming a secondary landfill.

"Did I do it right?" the girl asked, staring into the bathroom mirror. She wanted Gillian's opinion of her makeup, not the cleanliness or lack thereof of her temporary home.

"It's very nice." Gillian leaned closer. After her discussion of makeup techniques, Gillian had offered to help the girls shop for cosmetics. Brianna and two of her friends had accepted the offer, but only Brianna had invited Gillian to her home to preview the results before the nightly campfire.

"The taupe shadow is just what you needed. It highlights your eyes." Not to mention that it was more flattering than the bright purple Brianna had previously caked onto her eyelids.

"You really like it?"

"Yes."

Brianna tipped her head from one side to the other, considering her reflection. "My mom doesn't like it. If she had her way, I wouldn't wear any makeup at all. She doesn't want boys to look at me. Especially not Todd." Brianna turned to face Gillian. "You know what, Gillian? I think Todd would like me even if I didn't wear makeup."

That was one discussion Gillian knew better than to encourage, and so she said only, "He seems like a very nice boy."

"He is." Brianna nodded vigorously, setting her hair to bouncing on her shoulders. "Some kids call him a nerd, but he's a great guy."

She looked at Gillian for a moment, her indecision obvious. Though Gillian didn't claim to be an expert on teenagers, she sensed that Brianna wanted to tell her something important but was debating whether Gillian could be trusted. After a few seconds, she said, "We're going to get married as soon as we're old enough. Then we won't have to live here."

Not wanting to get involved in such a sensitive subject, Gillian merely smiled and murmured, "You'll be a beautiful bride . . . someday." She glanced at her watch, grateful for an excuse to end this conversation. It was time to join the group around the campfire.

But Brianna wasn't giving up so easily. She blocked the door. Putting her hands on her hips, she stared at Gillian. "I don't understand you. You're still young. You're pretty. How come you're not married?"

Gillian was tempted to laugh. It seemed that the trio of middle-aged women Kate had called the Matchers had an apprentice. Though she suspected they would have phrased the question a bit more diplomatically, the meaning was the same: it was time for Gillian to marry. Even her father agreed.

"I haven't met the right man." Gillian gave Brianna the same answer she'd given her father, but tonight was different. As she pronounced the words, TJ's image floated through her mind. How strange.

The kids were in an odd mood tonight. TJ hadn't been kidding when he told Gillian that he still felt as if he didn't have a clue about teenagers. Oh, he'd read dozens of books and taken his share of psychology classes, but he wasn't the intuitive teacher Deb had been. She had had the empathy and the understanding that turned an ordinary teacher into a special one. TJ had never been more than average, and if he were being honest, that had bothered him. It certainly bothered him tonight.

Tonight the boys wanted to talk about wilderness survival and were disappointed to learn that a day hike was as far as he'd ventured into the back country. Fortunately, the lure of flames and marshmallows had kept them by the campfire, but TJ knew he'd have to come up with something different for tomorrow. As it was, the boys were clustered around the fire, waiting for the girls' arrival before they started roasting marshmallows.

And there they were. As Gillian emerged from one of the RVs with Brianna, the others joined them, forming a giggling group of girls. With all his heart, TJ hoped Gillian wouldn't leave Rainbow's End before he did. It was bad enough keeping the boys entertained. Half a dozen girls were beyond his skill.

"So, was she your girlfriend before, or did you just meet her?"

The boy's question startled him. He hadn't realized that Todd had remained at his side. Tonight the kid was one of the silent ones. Fortunately, he was only quiet, not sullen.

TJ spun around and faced him. "What do you mean?"

"Gillian." Todd's tone left no doubt that the answer should have been apparent. "She's your girlfriend, right?"

"Wrong." TJ wasn't looking for a girlfriend. Not now, and probably not ever.

"What's wrong?" Gillian asked as Kate handed her a cup of coffee before stirring sugar into her own mug of decaf. Gillian was the one who ought to look stressed after the mostly sleepless night she'd just spent, but it was Kate who seemed on edge. The silver lining to that was that her friend wouldn't ask why Gillian had circles under her eyes. And that was fortunate, because she didn't have an answer. Admittedly, she'd been disturbed by her conversation with Brianna and by how distant TJ seemed when they'd walked back to Rainbow's End, but that shouldn't have been enough to keep her from sleeping.

Kate laid the spoon on the table and looked up at Gillian. "Sorry. I didn't realize it was obvious. I'm a little nervous about one of the reservations that just came in."

That didn't sound like Kate. In all the years Gillian had known her, she hadn't been one to worry. Kate had always been a decisive, take-charge person. "Is it a big group? Do you need me to move out?"

Kate's reaction was instantaneous. "No, never! Isaiah's yours for as long as you want the cabin. The reservation I'm worried about is for one person."

Perhaps the shifting hormones of pregnancy were the reason for Kate's concern. "Then what's the problem? I know you're not full."

Kate let out a small sigh. "It's who that one person is that worries me. The name Mike Tarkett probably doesn't mean anything to you, but the Tarkett family is one of the most influential in the Hill Country. They practically own the town of Blytheville. And whether it's ranching, oil, gas, or wind energy, you'll find a Tarkett involved. I've even heard that they're planning to get into politics on the state level with a possible eye on Washington."

If the Tarketts had a résumé like that, Gillian would have thought Kate would be pleased to have a member of the family visit Rainbow's End. If Mike Tarkett was happy here—and

Gillian couldn't imagine that he would not be—he might recommend the resort to others. That kind of word-of-mouth advertising was something even Greg's money couldn't buy.

"I still don't understand the problem. You've had powerful people here before, not to mention that you're married to one."

Kate's small wince and the way she rubbed her belly told Gillian the baby was extra active this morning, perhaps in response to Kate's mood.

"It's not Mike himself that worries me. The problem is, I can't figure out why he wants to stay here. We're only half an hour away from his family home, and from everything I've heard, that home is a mansion on a huge estate."

"Maybe he's looking for a change of pace." That was part of what had brought Gillian here, that and the need to reevaluate her life.

Kate appeared dubious. "The only reason I can imagine is that Mike wants to buy a resort and is checking us out. The hospitality industry is just about the only thing the Tarkett clan doesn't have."

"But Rainbow's End isn't for sale." Kate had made it clear that she and Greg had no intention of leaving, although they'd discussed the possibility of building a home in Firefly Valley once the RVs were gone so they'd have more privacy and space when their baby became a toddler.

"That's true," Kate agreed, "but what if they build something similar and try to put us out of business?"

"They can't do that, can they?" Greg had very deep pockets, which was part of the reason Rainbow's End had a philanthropic arm, providing low or no-cost vacations for people who needed them.

"I don't know. Maybe I'm overreacting, but I can't help worrying."

Though Gillian suspected Kate was suffering from a major case of overreaction, there was no reason to say that. Instead she leaned forward and placed her hand on Kate's. "What can I do?"

"Stay another week." The answer came so quickly that Gillian knew it wasn't a casual request. "I need moral support while Mike Tarkett is here."

"Sure." As the answer slipped out, Gillian realized how right it felt. The vague malaise that had plagued her off and on all week had disappeared, replaced by a feeling of peace. The distant future might not be clear, but staying at Rainbow's End for the immediate future was the right decision. Gillian knew that as surely as she knew she'd do anything for her friend.

"In fact," she said slowly as she helped herself to a cinnamon roll, "if you're sure you don't need to rent out the cabin, I think I'll stay here until my godchild arrives."

"Really?" Kate's eyes shone with excitement.

"Really."

Kate leaned forward and wrapped her arms around Gillian. "Did I ever tell you that you're the best? Well, you are."

11

He ought to be glad, TJ told himself as he squirted shaving cream onto his fingertips. It was Sunday, his second day with no responsibilities. Greg had given him a reprieve from spending weekend evenings in Firefly Valley, claiming that most parents were home then and would spend time with their kids. That left TJ free to do whatever he wanted. Unfortunately, what he wanted to do today was to get on his motorcycle and clear his head with a fast and furious ride somewhere, anywhere, but that was impossible. Though Eric kept trying, he'd been unable to locate a crankshaft. It seemed there were disadvantages to owning a highly customized bike.

Like it or not, TJ was stuck at Rainbow's End. He picked up his razor and began to shave. The truth was, it wasn't a bad place. The food was excellent, and the company was good. He shook his head slightly. More than good, if he were being honest. Gillian Hodge was intriguing, perhaps because she was so different from Deb.

He wielded the razor carefully, not wanting to nick his skin just because his thoughts had turned turbulent. Deb had been loveable, lively, and occasionally mischievous, but until the final months when cancer wracked her body, she had not been sad. Even then, her sorrow had been for TJ and the fact that she was leaving him alone.

Though Gillian tried to hide it, there was a sadness deep inside her. It would be easy to blame it on the loss of her career. TJ didn't doubt that that weighed heavily on her, but his instincts, honed by years of counseling people in RV campgrounds from Acadia to Zion, told him something else was involved. If he had to guess, he would say it was her family.

Though she hadn't mentioned it again, he had to believe that never having known her mother would have left a void inside her. TJ had grieved when his parents had died, and he was still grieving the loss of Deb, but he had the memories of years with them. He couldn't imagine what it must have been like growing up without a mother.

Since he'd never heard Gillian mention siblings, he assumed she was an only child like him. That must have made her childhood lonely. TJ had hated that friends went home when playtime ended, but he'd had his parents—especially his mother—to help fill the empty hours.

Family. It was so important, and yet as TJ knew from experience, it was often difficult to talk about a family when it was less than perfect. Look at him. Though there had been opportunities, TJ had never once said "my wife." Instead, he'd let everyone believe he was a single man. That wasn't totally dishonest—he *was* single again—but it was splitting hairs on the honesty issue. The old TJ wouldn't have done that, but the old TJ was gone.

Fifteen minutes later, his hair almost dry after his shower, he entered the dining room. Though he'd expected it to be close to empty, as it normally was at this time, three tables were already filled. He glanced at his assigned table, smiling when Gillian waved at him.

She looked prettier than ever this morning, dressed in some kind of soft green blouse that highlighted her eyes, her hair left loose to fall in waves below her shoulders. Though she hadn't pulled her hair into the tight bun since the first day, she normally wore it in a ponytail or secured in one of those big clips. This was the first time TJ had seen it down. It suited her, or so he thought, but what did he know about women's hair?

His step a little lighter than it had been a minute earlier, TJ made his way through the buffet line in record time.

"I hoped you'd come," Gillian said as he pulled out the only empty chair at the table, one that just so happened to be next to her. "That's why I saved you this seat."

"Thanks." TJ laid the plate piled with pancakes, scrambled eggs, and sausage on the table. "Why's everyone here so early?" The other mornings, he and Gillian had been the only ones at this table. Although there was only one seating for supper, breakfast was less structured. The food was set out buffet style, with guests free to come anytime between 7:00 and 8:30.

Gillian waited until TJ picked up his fork before she replied. "Kate says it happens every Sunday and that there are two reasons. Some people are checking out and want to get an early start. Others are going to church."

"Which one are you?" Gillian had said she was only going to be here a week or two. If she were staying for a full week, she'd leave tomorrow, but TJ knew that some people preferred to travel on the weekend.

"The latter." She spread jam on a piece of toast as she added, "I guess I didn't tell you that I've decided to stay until Kate's baby is born."

The sausage he'd been chewing suddenly seemed even more delicious than it had a few seconds earlier. Perhaps it was foolish to care, but TJ couldn't ignore the relief coursing through him at the knowledge that Gillian wasn't leaving today. Waiting for the bike repairs would be decidedly easier with her here. And when the bike was ready, he'd convince the woman with hair the color of a desert sunrise to go for a ride.

He wouldn't tell her that now. Instead, he said, "I imagine Kate's happy about that."

Gillian nodded. "I am too. I hadn't expected it, but I'm enjoying the slower pace."

TJ could only guess what her life had been like before the accident, but he suspected there'd been little time for relaxation. "Do you miss performing?"

He could kick himself for asking such a stupid question. Of course she did. Even though teaching had not been his life calling, there were times when he missed the routine, the challenges, and—yes—the kids. He'd chosen to walk away from his job. Gillian had had no choice. Only an insensitive clod would remind her of all that she'd lost.

To TJ's surprise, Gillian did not appear angered by his question. She reached for the coffeepot and refilled her cup, then turned to look directly at him. "I'd be lying if I said no. Music has been the most important part of my life for just about my whole life. There were times when I felt as if it was consuming all my energy, but I didn't mind, because I loved what I was doing." Her hand tightened on the cup. "I always knew there would be a time when it would end, but I hadn't expected it to be so soon."

Taking a sip of coffee to hide the tightening of his lips, TJ realized that he could have said the same thing, substituting "Deb" for "music." Perhaps he'd been wrong about Gillian. At first he'd thought they had little in common because they'd come from such different worlds, but deep insidc they had the same pain, the same emptiness. "I probably shouldn't ask, but can you play at all?" When he'd talked to Gillian about teaching, TJ had assumed that she could. Though narrow scars crisscrossed her right hand, she appeared to have no trouble using it. But perhaps her being left-handed kept him from recognizing the extent of the damage. Since it was her non-dominant hand that had been injured, TJ hadn't had many opportunities to watch her using it.

"I can play," she admitted. "Just not well enough for a concert. My fingers don't have the same level of flexibility they did before. I can't stretch as far."

She held up both hands, extending the fingers as far as she could. Even TJ could see the difference between the two hands. And though he was no musician, he knew that the right hand was critical for a pianist. What a shame. What a terrible shame. Though he wanted to ask what had caused the accident, something in Gillian's expression stopped him. He'd already probed too deeply. What he needed to do was lighten the mood.

"I can't say that I was ever a fan of classical music, but I enjoyed your Carnegie Hall album."

Those green eyes that reminded him of spring grass widened. "You listened to it?"

TJ nodded. "I was in the gift shop yesterday." Pure boredom had led him there. "That's what they were playing. I'm no expert, but I can tell you that the music touched me in ways I hadn't expected." To his surprise, he'd found his heart pounding with anxiety, then soaring with joy as he listened to Gillian's rendition of what the clerk told him was a Beethoven concerto.

TJ had seen Gillian smile, but never before had he seen such a radiant smile. It appeared he'd done something right. Finally.

"Thank you," she said softly. "You have no idea how much that means to me. When I performed, it was always with the hope of touching someone's heart. I'm so glad that I did."

For the remainder of the meal, they spoke of trivial things, but it didn't matter. TJ knew they'd crossed a boundary, and though he'd feared his original question had reminded Gillian of her pain and loss, he now knew that his reaction to her playing had confirmed that she'd accomplished her dream.

Gillian's response left him feeling like a knight in shining armor who'd defeated the dragon and saved the princess. He wasn't a knight. Or if he was, his armor was tarnished, but still it was a heady sensation.

When she'd drained her coffee cup, Gillian glanced at her watch. "It's almost time to leave for church. Would you like a ride?"

The euphoria that had surrounded him popped like a soap bubble. "No thanks," TJ said more curtly than he'd intended. "That's not the place for me."

12

It had been more than twenty-four hours, and Gillian was still pondering TJ's reaction to her invitation to church. She had thought that, as the child of missionaries, he was a regular churchgoer, but it appeared she was wrong. Though she had wanted to tell him that God welcomed everyone into his house, TJ's frown had been so forbidding that she had said nothing. She didn't want to chide the man, but he was wrong. So very wrong.

And so were her father and her brother George. They viewed church attendance as a social obligation, part of being a pillar of the community. It had been Sally who'd shown Gillian the difference between sitting in church for an hour each Sunday and living a Christian life. That was one of the reasons Gillian was here rather than on a cruise with her father.

Biting back a sigh, she pulled out the laptop Kate had lent her and began to compose an email. The absence of cell service at Rainbow's End meant that vacationers here were free of electronic tethers, but there were times like this when Gillian was grateful for technology. Though she doubted she'd get more than a cursory response, since Dad was noted for the brevity of his written comments, she wanted him to know that she planned to remain at Rainbow's End until Kate's baby arrived.

So far, though he'd sent pictures of each port of call, there'd been no commentary other than the brief captions explaining the sights. Classic Dad. He was taking what many would consider the trip of a lifetime, a cruise around the world, and all he'd shared were photos of places he'd visited. No pictures of people, no indication of whether or not he was enjoying the cruise itself, the other passengers, or the sights he'd seen. But that was Dad, unwilling or maybe unable to express his feelings.

As she clicked "send," Gillian felt a sense of relief. She'd done her duty, and thanks to Kate, it had not been difficult. Though the other cabins had neither phones nor internet access, since Isaiah had been designed for staff, Kate and Greg had decided it should have the same connections as the office and their apartment.

Gillian rose and peered out the window. With Kate and Greg shopping in San Antonio and a light drizzle discouraging outdoor pastimes, she had spent the morning in her cabin. But now that the rain had stopped and cabin fever had set in, there was no reason not to go to the main lodge. TJ might be there, and if all else failed, she could chat with Carmen. The woman who provided such delicious meals had told Gillian she was always welcome in the kitchen.

Gillian was approaching the front entrance when a man blocked her way.

"Gillian Hodge!" The man doffed his Stetson in greeting. "If I'd known you were here, I would have come sooner."

He was a stranger. But what a handsome stranger. With classic features, sandy blond hair, china-blue eyes, and a height of an inch or two over six feet, he could have been a movie star, although Hollywood might have asked him to beef up a bit. The stranger was thinner than current fashion demanded. Dressed in what she had come to call the Texas uniform of jeans, a western shirt, boots, and hat, he looked like the quintessential cowboy, and yet he moved with such assurance that Gillian could picture him in a business suit or a tuxedo. It was no wonder Kate was worried. This man exuded charisma, and charisma combined with a healthy bankroll was extremely powerful.

"You must be Mike Tarkett."

"Guilty as charged, but how did you know?" Mike grinned and extended his hand for a quick shake. "I recognized you from the local paper's coverage of the grand reopening, but I doubt you subscribe to the *Blytheville Times* to know who I am."

His grip was firm, and if he held her hand a bit longer than courtesy demanded, Gillian wasn't complaining. There was something comforting, something almost familiar, about him. "No *Blytheville Times*," she agreed, "but I do subscribe to girlfriend gossip. Kate Vange told me you were arriving today. It didn't require Sherlock Holmes's skills to deduce that you were Mike Tarkett, since the other new guests are couples."

Mike wrinkled his nose. "I was afraid of that. I told Mom I'd be a fifth wheel here." He paused for a second before adding, "She's the one who insisted I spend a week doing what she calls recharging my batteries."

If he was telling the truth, the whole truth, and nothing but the truth, Kate had no reason to worry that the Tarkett family wanted to either buy or compete with Rainbow's End, but that was a big if. "This is a great place for battery recharging."

Mike wrinkled his nose again, making her wonder if that was a characteristic gesture. "It would be more fun with a companion. I don't want to sound presumptuous, especially since we've just met, but if you don't have any other plans for the afternoon, I wondered if you'd show me around the place. Maybe we can even play tennis. My mother said the court is supposed to be a good one."

He was being presumptuous, but Gillian didn't care. Spending time with Mike Tarkett might help her discover whether he and his family had any ulterior motives for his week at Rainbow's End. "It probably is a good court, but I can't play."

Though his hat shaded his eyes, Gillian detected a note of regret in Mike's voice as he said, "I should have realized you'd have something else planned."

"It's not that. I meant 'can't' literally. I've never played tennis."

"Oh." He paused, evidently digesting the idea. Based on what Kate had said, Mike was part of the country club set, where women were expected to be accomplished tennis players. Had Gillian not been a pianist, Dad would have insisted she learn to play, but music classes, her practice schedule, and the fear of falling and injuring her hands had kept her off the court.

Today was the first time Gillian wished she'd taken tennis lessons. A match or two might be a good way to pass the time. And a match with Mike would be fun. His smile was so warm and welcoming that Gillian suspected he wouldn't mind if her skill level was far below Wimbledon.

"Maybe we could do something else," he suggested.

Gillian looked at the now dry ground. Something else—anything else—sounded like a good idea. "My feet are in good working condition," she told him. "Once you've checked in, we can wander around the resort if you'd like."

Which was how she found herself strolling along the edge of Bluebonnet Lake with Mike Tarkett. Gillian had walked this way half a dozen times before, and each time she'd discovered something new. Today instead of natural beauty, she was discovering that Mike was unlike the other men she'd met.

On the surface, he resembled her manager and some of the other performers, but there were differences. Though he had the same careful grooming and obviously expensive haircut, Mike was more handsome than the other men. He was at least as confident as the others, but on Mike that confidence seemed natural, not tinged with arrogance. Best of all, there was no initial awkwardness between them. Instead, Gillian felt as if she'd known Mike for ages. It was an unexpectedly comfortable feeling.

"This place is even more beautiful than I'd heard," he said as they walked by the lakefront cottages. As far as Gillian could tell, there were no undertones to his statement, no hidden agendas. Mike appeared to be looking for nothing more than a vacation.

"It's obviously your first time here."

"Yeah." He paused and stared across the small lake. The light breeze had died down, leaving the water almost as smooth as glass. It was no wonder Kate and Greg stocked rowboats rather than catamarans.

Mike tipped his head to one side, reminding Gillian of a robin listening for a worm. She wouldn't tell him that, of course, for what man wanted to be compared to a worm-eating bird?

"I've lived in the Hill Country my whole life and must have driven by Dupree thousands of times, but I never bothered to turn off the highway." Mike shifted his weight and looked down at Gillian. "It was only after the reopening got so much press coverage that it hit my mother's radar screen." He chuckled. "Mom's going to gloat when I tell her she was right: this is the perfect place."

Gillian's antennae began to quiver, and she reconsidered her assessment of Mike's motives. Maybe he was looking for something more than a break in his routine. "Perfect for what?"

"For relaxing. What did you think I meant?"

There was nothing to be lost by being honest. "I wasn't sure. There's been speculation that your family might be expanding its horizons."

"It's true. We're talking about it." Mike gave her a self-deprecating smile. "To be more accurate, my parents are talking. I'm listening."

"Were they talking about a hotel or a resort?"

Surely the confusion Gillian saw in Mike's eyes wasn't counterfeit. "What do you . . . oh, I see." He chuckled. "The Vanges thought I was scoping out the competition. You can reassure them that we have no intention of entering the hospitality industry, at least not for the foreseeable future. It's politics that interests my father."

Picking up a small stone, Mike attempted to skip it across the water, frowning when it sank after only the second skip. "He wants me to run for mayor of Blytheville and use that as a stepping stone to state office. I think he has illusions—or delusions—of Washington." Mike's tone left no doubt about his opinion of those aspirations.

"You mean the big white house on Pennsylvania Avenue?"

Mike nodded. "No one ever claimed my father had small dreams."

That confirmed what Kate had said. Cal Tarkett was a shrewd and determined businessman who wanted the Tarkett name to be as familiar as Rockefeller and Carnegie were a century earlier.

Gillian looked at Mike, admiring the openness of his expression. Another man might have tried to hide his discomfort, but he did not. "You sound as if you're not sure those are your dreams."

"Was it that obvious?"

"Only to someone who's had her share of parental pressure."

Mike looked intrigued, or perhaps he was simply relieved that the conversation had shifted away from him. "Did they push you into music?"

"No, that was my dream. It's only been since the accident that my dad has started to pressure me into what he calls a 'suitable lifestyle.'"

"And that would be . . . ?"

Gillian paused. As comfortable as she felt with Mike—and that was strange, because she'd never felt so comfortable so quickly—they were venturing into highly personal territory. But she'd been the one to open the subject. She owed Mike an honest answer.

"The usual," she said as casually as she could. "I'm supposed to marry someone suitable, produce grandchildren—preferably girls since my brother has already given him a grandson—and live in a McMansion."

Mike's chuckle turned into a full-fledged laugh. "If you change 'live in a McMansion' to 'live in the White House,' that's my parents' dream." He grabbed both of Gillian's hands and smiled at her. "So, what do you think? Should we elope to Vegas and make everyone happy?"

13

"You don't have to worry." Gillian smiled at Kate as she accepted a cup of coffee and settled onto the comfortable couch in Kate and Greg's apartment. Though it had been the better part of a day since Mike had arrived, this was the first opportunity Gillian had had to talk privately with Kate, and she wanted to relay the good news. There'd been no time after supper, and when Gillian returned from Firefly Valley, she'd seen no lights in the apartment. Recalling Kate's saying that she was trying to schedule a date night with Greg, Gillian guessed they'd found a movie they both wanted to see.

Kate returned Gillian's smile. "That's what the doctor said. I wasn't worried, but she was a little concerned about my weight gain. She thought it might be the first sign of preeclampsia until I told her about Carmen's cooking." Kate gestured toward the plate of fruit in front of her and the tray of Danish pastries she'd pushed to the far side of the coffee table. "We both agreed I need to be more careful. Fruit instead of pastries and clear soup instead of tamales."

Though tamales had not been a big part of Kate's diet until she came to Rainbow's End, she'd soon developed a craving for them and had even served them at her wedding reception. "I'll bet you'd be allowed one."

Rolling her eyes, Kate reached for a piece of pineapple. "Come on, Gillian. You've tasted Carmen's tamales. You know they're like potato chips. Eating one is impossible. I don't have the heart to tell Carmen they're on my do-not-eat list. Fortunately, Marisa and Blake are due back from their honeymoon tomorrow, so Carmen will have something to think about besides what I am—or am not—eating. She'll be watching Marisa like a hawk, trying to figure out whether she's pregnant." Kate speared a strawberry and added it to her plate. "Carmen can't wait to be a grandparent."

"Like my father." Gillian sighed, remembering the last discussion she'd had with Dad. When Gillian had pointed out that George had already produced the Hodge heir, he simply pursed his lips and said, "What else are you going to do now that your career is over? It's time for you to be married and start raising a family."

Gillian had gritted her teeth and remained silent, though she'd been tempted to mention that at twenty-nine she was hardly over the hill and that while her father's generation may have thought women should marry as soon as they graduated, hers did not.

She'd been surprised when Dad had added, "I worry about you, Gillian. Who'll look after you when I'm gone?" Though he'd been quick to assure her that the doctor had pronounced him in excellent health, he'd given her a little hug as he'd said, "There's no ignoring the fact that I'm old enough to be your grandfather. Your mother and I were thrilled when we learned she was pregnant again, even though we knew it wouldn't be easy having a second child when we were that age. We never even considered that one of us would be doing the parenting alone."

He'd done his best—Gillian knew that—but there were times when she'd wished for a younger dad and more times than she could count that she'd longed for a mother rather than a succession of nannies.

"Marisa's lucky if her parents don't pressure her," Gillian told Kate. "You know my dad isn't exactly reticent where the subject of marriage and grandchildren is concerned."

"He just wants you to be happy."

That was Kate, the peacemaker. When they'd been growing up, Kate had tried to put a positive spin on everything. The day Gillian had been sobbing her eyes out because her father was heading for Australia, claiming Gillian was having her own vacation because she would be staying with Kate and her grandparents instead of at home with the nanny, Kate had pointed out that this would give Gillian the chance to try ice-skating.

Every time Gillian had asked for permission to join her classmates at the local rink, Dad had refused, claiming Gillian might fall and injure her hands. But he had never told Sally that Gillian wasn't supposed to skate.

"We'll have so much fun," Kate had declared.

And they did. Though Gillian had fallen countless times, she'd suffered nothing more than a few bruises as she learned to navigate the ice. For two glorious weeks, she'd felt like a normal kid, not Gillian Hodge, child prodigy.

"No matter what Dad says, I'm not going to marry the first man who asks me to run off to Vegas to be married by an Elvis impersonator."

As Gillian had expected, though she had no idea that Gillian had received a joking proposal to do exactly that, Kate laughed. "Think about your wedding album. Wouldn't that give him bragging rights?"

"Because Elvis would outshine the bride? No thanks. I'd rather have a small church wedding with the man of my dreams. If I ever find him, that is." Despite her father's claims, Gillian was certain there was another alternative for her besides marriage . . . if only she could figure out what it was.

Kate took a sip of her herbal tea before she said, "It might be just my imagination, but it certainly seemed as if Mike Tarkett couldn't keep his eyes off you last night."

"There are logical explanations," Gillian replied, glad that she'd managed to subdue her blush. Kate was her dearest friend, but that didn't mean she wanted her to know how much Mike's apparent attraction had affected her. She'd felt relaxed with him, and that had made the afternoon special. When she was with TJ, Gillian's senses were on high alert, but there was none of that hyperawareness with Mike. Instead, she felt comfortable. It might not be the "Some Enchanted Evening" moment Sally touted, but Gillian had found the afternoon unexpectedly enjoyable.

"So, just what are those logical explanations?" Kate made air quotes around the words. "The way I see it, a very eligible man finds you attractive."

Placing her now empty coffee cup on the table, Gillian said, "Number one: there were no other single women at the table. And number two: we spent the afternoon together. I gave him the grand tour of Rainbow's End."

When Kate raised an eyebrow as if to signal her skepticism, Gillian decided it was time to change the subject. "Remember how I said you didn't have to worry? I was talking about Mike. His family isn't planning to compete with you. He said they have no interest in hotels."

"And you believe him?"

"I do. I suppose I could be wrong, but Mike strikes me as an honest man. The reason he's here is that he's been working extra long hours since the beginning of the year. Apparently his mother decided he needed a vacation and practically forced him to come."

The way Kate smiled told Gillian she was both pleased and relieved. "That's good news," she said, "but I still think Mike views you as more than a convenient companion or a tour guide. The man looked positively smitten."

That guy looked at her the way someone who'd been stranded in the desert for a week would look at a cool glass of water. TJ gripped the oars and pulled for all he was worth. Maybe a good workout would help put the image out of his mind. Something had to. But as the oars plied the water, propelling him toward the small island on the other side of Bluebonnet Lake, the memories continued to roll.

Gillian had laughed at anything Mike Tarkett said, giving him those smiles that threatened to outshine the sun, while Mike had seemed as besotted as a teenager with his first love. It had all combined to make last night's supper feel endless. Oh, the food had been as delicious as ever, but TJ hadn't enjoyed it. How could he, when Gillian hardly spoke to him? Instead, she'd seemed as infatuated with Mike Tarkett as the business tycoon was with her.

TJ paused to wipe the sweat from his forehead. Why should he care? It wasn't as if he had any romantic interest in Gillian. He'd loved Deb. He still loved her, and he always would. And because he did, there was no room for another woman in his life or his heart.

TJ knew that. That was why he'd been surprised by how painful it had been to see Gillian and Mike together. He didn't understand it. He'd seen couples in love since Deb's death, and it had never bothered him, but for some reason, this was different.

If only his bike were fixed and he could leave! But Eric had delivered the bad news this morning. It would be another week before the parts arrived. That meant TJ had at least six more days with nothing to do other than watch Gillian and Mike Tarkett. The teenagers provided a welcome break in the evenings, but he needed something to do during the days.

He resumed the rhythmic rowing, focusing on the sound of the oars sliding through the water. When he'd first heard that the island was called Paintbrush, he'd pictured an artist with a palette and brush, but he now realized that the name came from the Indian paintbrush flowers that carpeted one side of the island. The island was beautiful and peaceful. His thoughts were not.

In the past TJ would have prayed for guidance, but he knew there was no point in doing that now. The only thing he could do was rely on himself and hope that all this rowing would leave him so tired and sore that he wouldn't notice the pain in his heart.

An hour later TJ returned to the dock, his shoulders and arms aching more than he'd thought possible but his head clearer than it had been in weeks. As he'd circled the small island and admired its beauty, he'd felt an unexpected peace settle over him.

He couldn't explain it any more than he could explain why the sight of Gillian and Mike together bothered him, but he wasn't arguing with the result. The turmoil deep inside him had subsided, and by the time he approached the dock, TJ had realized there were worse things than being stuck at Rainbow's End.

He didn't need Gillian's company to make the days enjoyable. He could do what Greg had advised: row a bit, run a bit, relax a bit. And in the evenings, he'd have the teenagers with their unbridled curiosity and raucous laughter to keep him company.

He was tying the boat to the dock when he heard footsteps.

"TJ, you're just the man I wanted to see," Greg announced as he stepped onto the dock. Dressed in the Rainbow's End uniform of khaki pants and a navy polo with the resort's logo, Greg was the epitome of casual living, though his expression was anything but casual. "An opportunity came up today." He settled onto one of the benches that lined the edge of the dock and nodded to the spot beside him, waiting until TJ was seated before he continued. "I'm not sure you'll be interested, but I told Jake Thomas I'd ask."

Though Greg kept his voice even, the glint in his eyes told TJ he was hoping TJ would avail himself of the opportunity, whatever it was. If TJ were lucky, this mysterious opportunity would provide a way for him to pass the time until his bike was repaired. There was only one way to know.

"Who's Jake Thomas, and what's the opportunity?"

Leaning back on his arms and feigning a nonchalant posture, Greg stared into the distance. "He's the school principal. The opportunity is to teach history for the rest of the school year." His posture might be relaxed, but Greg's speech was not. He spoke quickly, giving TJ no chance to interrupt. "The current history teacher, Mrs. Loring, had a massive stroke yesterday. She's still alive, but the doctor says she'll never teach again."

When TJ murmured his sympathy, Greg nodded. "Even though she was close to retirement, it's still a blow to everyone. Jake filled in today, but he can't keep doing that, and none of his regular subs want a full-time assignment." Greg turned, fixing his gaze on TJ. "Jake needs a permanent substitute for the rest of the term. When he remembered my saying that you used to teach history, he phoned to see if you'd be interested."

Was he interested? It had been less than two hours since TJ had wondered what he could do to keep painful thoughts at bay and how he would fill the days until his bike was repaired. Now this opportunity presented itself. A couple years ago, TJ might have called this the answer to prayer. Now he called it a coincidence.

"I'm not sure," he admitted. Though there was something surprisingly appealing about the idea of teaching the kids he saw each night at Firefly Valley, TJ wasn't convinced he should agree. "I had planned to go to Big Bend as soon as Eric finished the bike repairs."

It was the last item on Deb's bucket list, the last thing TJ wanted to accomplish before . . .

That was the problem: he didn't know how to finish the sentence. All he knew was that it wasn't returning to teaching, because teaching was one thing he and Deb had done together.

He'd spent a year trying to outrun his memories, failing more often than he succeeded. He couldn't count the times he'd seen something he wanted to share with Deb and had started to say, "Honey, look at that," only to realize she wasn't there, that no matter what he did, she wouldn't hear him.

Being on the bike rather than in an RV had helped, but returning to a classroom would be more difficult. It would be like ripping the scab off a barely healed wound. TJ wasn't ready to do that.

Greg nodded slowly, as if he'd expected TJ's response. "I won't pressure you," he assured him. "You need to do what feels right to you, but I can't help pointing out that the assignment is for less than two months. Big Bend will be there when school ends."

"Two months is longer than I've stayed anywhere in a while." TJ had deliberately chosen the itinerant life, not wanting to stop anywhere long enough to put down roots. He doubted he'd become rooted here in two months, but it could happen. And yet, how bad would that be? It wouldn't be the end of the world. He'd uprooted himself once. He could do it again.

TJ stared at the lake, picturing the teenagers he saw each evening. From what he could tell, few considered schooling more than a trial they were forced to endure. That was a shame.

It wouldn't be easy to walk into a school again, but maybe it wouldn't be as bad as he feared. After all, there were no memories of Deb here. No doubt about it: it would be a challenge, but maybe that was what he needed. And maybe, just maybe, he could help some of the kids realize just how important it was to understand history.

Greg waited until TJ looked at him again before he spoke. "If you're worried about overstaying your welcome here, that won't happen." He turned and gestured toward the cabins. "Moses is yours for as long as you want it. If you'll feel better paying for room and board once you're earning a salary, that's fine, but it's not necessary. The simple fact is, you'd be doing the town a favor if you agree to stay and teach." Greg leaned forward, his expression intense. "Dupree High's kids need you," he said firmly. "Only you can decide whether you need them."

TJ shifted his gaze to his boots. That was easier than letting Greg see his indecision. Stay and teach or leave and finish the bucket list? The decision ought to be simple, and yet it wasn't. TJ started to refuse, then stopped, remembering how peace had filled his heart as he'd returned to the dock. Even as he'd been waging his internal debate, the peace had remained.

Slowly, he nodded.

"I'll do it."

14

Could I interest you in a trip into Dupree?"

Gillian swiveled on the stool. When she'd spotted the piano in the main lodge her first day at Rainbow's End, she had told herself she would not touch it, but this afternoon she hadn't been able to resist seeing if anything had changed.

It hadn't. Though she was able to perform the basic warm-up scales and five-finger exercises that had been the beginning of her routine for years, she could not ignore the way her right hand hesitated. A casual listener might not notice the flaws, but to Gillian they were as distressing as wrong notes.

She smiled at Mike, grateful for the interruption. "I'll be glad to go, but I'm curious. What's the attraction in Dupree? Compared to Blytheville, it's a very, very small town."

Mike gave her one of his wrinkled nose smiles. "It may be small, but it has the best quilt shop in the area. I'm hoping to find something for my mother." Mike's grin widened. "I could tell you I wanted a woman's opinion, and I wouldn't be lying, but the truth is, I was looking for an excuse to spend more time with you. Does that satisfy your curiosity?"

It did. "Give me five minutes to get ready."

When she emerged from her cabin, Gillian found Mike waiting

in one of the most beautiful cars she'd ever seen. Long, low, and red, it practically shrieked power.

"What is it?" she asked as she slid into the leather seat that left her feeling pampered.

"A Ferrari."

Dad would approve. He was of the opinion that there was nothing wrong with flaunting wealth.

"Do you race?"

Mike shook his head. "Believe it or not, I rarely speed. I just like the way the car handles. It's a nice change from the trucks and ATVs I drive on the ranch."

"You mean you're a cowboy?" Gillian hadn't expected that.

"On occasion. My dad insisted that I learn every aspect of our businesses. I even had a stint waiting tables at Strawberry Chantilly. When it was clear I wasn't suited for carrying trays with carefully arranged food, I spent a month herding cattle."

Gillian chuckled, trying to picture Mike as a waiter.

"Do you have anything special in mind for your mother?" she asked as Mike parked in front of Hill Country Pieces.

Mike shrugged. "Not a clue. That's where you come in. I figured you could pick out something your mom would like."

This was not the time to explain that Gillian had never shopped for gifts for her mother. "I'm sure we'll find something." The quilts Lauren Ahrens, now Lauren Carroll, had made for Rainbow's End were exquisite. Gillian had no doubt they'd find a suitable gift for Mrs. Tarkett.

What they found were three women whose mouths dropped open as Gillian and Mike entered the quilt shop.

"Gillian Hodge," one said, recovering her composure at the same time that one of her companions said, "And Mike Tarkett."

The pretty brunette behind the counter appeared to be having trouble controlling her mirth. She stepped out and extended her hand in greeting. "Welcome to HCP. I'm Lauren." With a look that just missed being a wink, she gestured toward the three women. "Let me introduce you to Amelia, Debra, and Edie."

Though Gillian kept a polite smile fixed on her face, inwardly she was cringing. She'd just met the infamous Matchers.

"Is something wrong?" Though the day had been warmer than normal and the sun had just set, there was an unexpected chill in the air. Or perhaps it was only Gillian's imagination, triggered by the man at her side. TJ had seemed unusually quiet at supper. Several times she'd caught him staring into the distance, a pensive expression on his face, and he'd barely joined in the conversation. As they left Rainbow's End, though Gillian had been tempted to ask him if there was anything she could do to help, the almost forbidding set of his lips had held her back, and once they'd reached the RV town, there had been no opportunity for a private moment.

As soon as Gillian had arrived, Brianna had led her to her trailer, where the other girls had gathered for tonight's fashion lesson.

Gillian still had trouble believing she'd been able to develop a camaraderie with the girls so quickly, but she wasn't complaining. This was what Kate had hoped would happen, and the fact that it had reduced Kate's stress was good.

After she'd greeted the girls and listened to today's news, which centered on speculation over who would replace one of the teachers, Gillian pulled an assortment of scarves from her bag. When Brianna had read that French women changed the look of an outfit simply by the way they tied a scarf, the girls had been intrigued and had asked for Gillian's assistance in finding the most flattering way to wear a scarf.

They giggled as they experimented with the techniques Gillian demonstrated, seemingly impressed by her knowledge, never guessing she'd gleaned that knowledge from the internet rather than a fashion stylist. The source didn't matter. What mattered was that Gillian was helping them.

If only she could help TJ. But, unlike Mike, who seemed to have a sunny disposition, TJ was a brooder, a modern-day Heathcliff or Mr. Rochester with dark secrets. No matter how she wished there were something she could say or do, Gillian knew she had little hope of breaking through the barriers he'd built around himself.

By the time she and the girls joined the boys around the campfire, TJ seemed to be back to normal, and for the space of half an hour she was optimistic that whatever had bothered him was simply a passing mood. Now she wasn't so sure, for he appeared to be brooding again as they returned to Rainbow's End. That was why she'd posed the question.

Though Gillian wasn't certain he would respond, TJ slowed his pace and turned to meet her gaze. "I don't know whether it's wrong or not," he admitted, his eyes clearly troubled, "but I'm afraid I made a mistake."

Gillian could not imagine what that might be. As far as she knew, he hadn't left Rainbow's End today. "Do you want to talk about it?"

Once again TJ hesitated, but when they'd crossed the road and were approaching the gates of Rainbow's End, he stopped, leaning against the wrought-iron fence. "Yeah, I guess I do want to talk." He took a breath and exhaled before he began his explanation. "I agreed to teach for the rest of the school year."

"Here in Dupree?"

When he nodded, Gillian realized TJ must be the substitute teacher who'd triggered so much speculation among the girls. They'd be excited, and she . . . well, she was excited too. It might be silly to be so happy, but Gillian couldn't deny the pleasure she felt in knowing TJ would be here as long as she was. He no longer gave her pep talks when they walked to Firefly Valley, telling her she'd do a good job with the girls, but just having him at her side boosted her confidence.

"That's good, isn't it?" she asked.

He shrugged. "I'm not sure. It seemed like a good idea at the time, but now I don't know. I'm not convinced it'll be good for these kids." He turned and gestured back toward Firefly Valley.

"Why not? They already know you're a great teacher." The girls couldn't stop talking about the stories he told, and though the boys feigned nonchalance, Gillian had seen the way they listened to TJ. They were as fascinated by his adventures as she was.

"They don't know me as a teacher, and that's the problem. I'm a mentor to them. A grown-up friend. It'll be different if they have to sit in my classroom."

Though she didn't doubt that TJ was concerned, Gillian still didn't understand why. "I don't see a problem. If anything, the Firefly Valley kids will have an advantage over the other students, because you already know them."

"And they know me as TJ, not Mr. Benjamin."

The distinction sounded subtle, but Gillian suspected it was not. Maintaining discipline in a classroom was difficult enough without adding inappropriate familiarity to the equation. "I'm sure you'll find a way to deal with that. Your worries tell me you're a really good teacher. You're not thinking about yourself, only your students."

Gillian sighed, remembering her school days. She'd been thankful Sally had been able to convince her father of the benefits of public schools, the greatest of which was that she and Kate would be together, but there had been trade-offs. Though some of Gillian's teachers had been stellar, there had been others who'd exerted only the minimum effort in the classroom, then wondered why no one was enthusiastic about the subject.

"I wish all my teachers had been like you." Gillian laid a hand on TJ's arm, willing him to believe her. "The Dupree kids are lucky to have you."

And TJ was lucky to have found something meaningful to do.

Gillian had slept later than normal and had to rush to reach the dining room before the breakfast buffet was cleared away. After helping herself to a bowl of oatmeal with raisins and brown sugar, she added a piece of toast to her plate, then took a seat at her assigned table. When she'd convinced the two guests who volunteered to stay if she wanted company that she didn't mind being alone, Gillian spread peach jam on the toast and took a bite. The jam and homemade bread were delicious, and yet the flavors that normally tantalized her taste buds did nothing for her today.

Today marked ten days at Rainbow's End, ten days of a total change of pace. At first she had enjoyed the relaxation. It was wonderful seeing Kate every day, and there was no doubt the time she spent with TJ and Mike made days special, but TJ's announcement of the teaching position had opened the floodgates inside Gillian, filling her with regret that she had no similar announcement.

Never before had she gone so long without some form of work. Even during school vacations, she had practiced several hours a day, and once she graduated, there had been nothing more than brief holidays. This was the first time in her life she had been idle for so long. It felt wrong.

When she'd drained her coffee cup, Gillian rose and walked through the enclosed hallway toward the lobby. Although it took a few seconds longer than walking outdoors, she had made a habit of sticking her head into the kitchen each morning and complimenting Carmen on her cooking. Today the door next to the kitchen was open, and Kate was lounging against the doorframe, talking to a blonde. Though the woman looked familiar, Gillian could not place her.

Kate smiled and drew the other woman forward. "You remember Marisa, don't you, Gillian?"

Gillian did remember Marisa from Kate's wedding, but she hadn't been a blue-eyed blonde then. "I thought you were a brunette."

Marisa chuckled, taking no offense at the blunt comment. "I was, but this is my natural color." She touched her shoulder-length hair. "It's a long story, and I won't bore you with it, especially since this slave driver reminded me that I have work to do." She gave Kate's stomach a playful pat. "Mommy's cranky this morning," she told the baby bump. "She thinks I was gone too long."

Gillian looked from Marisa to Kate and then back to Marisa. "Is there anything I can help with? I wouldn't want slave driver Kate to have to crack the whip again. It might be bad for the baby."

Wrinkling her nose, Marisa shook her head. "I appreciate the offer, but it's mostly clerical work that piled up while I was gone."

"There are prices to be paid for a full month's honeymoon," Kate said with a teasing smile.

"I know, I know. But now I need to scan a gazillion invoices."

Gillian took a step inside the small office. "I can do that." Surely operating a scanner didn't require an MBA.

"Are you certain you want to?" Kate asked, stressing the word *want*. "You're a guest here."

"But not a paying one. I like the idea of earning my keep. Besides, it's either help Marisa or read another book. You know I love to read, but I also like to visit."

Though she had never minded the solitary hours she'd spent practicing, this was different. While Gillian wasn't lonely at Rainbow's End, she lacked direction. Scanning invoices might not be exciting, but it would give her something to do.

"No offense to Marisa," Kate said with a quick smile at her friend and employee, "but if you want company, Mike might be a better choice."

"I'm spending the afternoon with him." Gillian turned back to Marisa. "I can't promise expertise, but if you'd like an assistant, I'd be glad to help you this morning."

"Don't blame me if you're bored," Kate said, rubbing her stomach absentmindedly.

"I wouldn't dare." Gillian glanced at her watch. "Isn't it time for your conference call?" The regional innkeepers association supplemented their monthly meetings with weekly calls.

Kate nodded and turned to Marisa. "She's all yours."

"Thanks." As Kate left, Marisa smiled at Gillian. "Thank you too." She switched on her power strip. As electronic humming filled the room, Marisa gestured toward the door. "You'd better get a big cup of coffee. You'll need it."

When Gillian returned with caffeine for both of them, it took only a few minutes for Marisa to show her how to scan the documents and rename the files. While it was hardly challenging work, it was work that needed to be done, and being the person to do that work felt good.

"Who's Mike?" Marisa asked as she handed Gillian a second pile of invoices.

"Another guest. Mike Tarkett." Gillian was surprised Kate hadn't told Marisa about him. Even though Kate was no longer worried about his family competing with her and Greg, Mike was a noteworthy guest. Perhaps she hadn't had time to say anything.

"Mike Tarkett from the Blytheville Tarketts?" Marisa's voice rose a few notes.

"That's the one."

"Wow! I wonder what other things Kate forgot to tell me. What's a Tarkett doing here? But more importantly, is he as gorgeous in person as in his pictures?"

Gillian placed another invoice on the scanner bed, wondering why Rainbow's End didn't have an automatic sheet feeder. Surely a billionaire like Greg wouldn't begrudge a few extra dollars to simplify a tedious task.

"I haven't seen photos of him," she said, "but Mike's definitely good looking. I can imagine him on the cover of *GQ*."

Marisa took another slug of coffee, her eyes narrowing as she looked at Gillian. "And you're running a scanner rather than being with him? You're crazy, girl. Mike Tarkett is the most eligible bachelor in the Hill Country."

"Maybe so, but I'm not looking for a husband." No matter what Dad, Kate, the Matchers, and now Marisa thought, marriage was not the answer for Gillian.

"Maybe you should be."

15

Good morning, class. My name is Mr. Benjamin, and I'll be your teacher for the rest of the year." As TJ had expected, his introduction was greeted with some skeptical looks and a few barely muffled groans. Though the school was smaller than the one where he'd taught, the hallways and classrooms were almost exact duplicates. So too were the students' reaction to a sub.

TJ looked around the room, making eye contact with each student. "For those of you who were hoping for a permanent study hall, that's not going to happen. For those of you who were afraid you might fail the final, that's not going to happen either." Two boys in the back row exchanged glances that seemed to dispute TJ's assertion.

"How do you know?" the taller of the boys asked. "We could all be dummies."

"But you're not, Seth. I checked everyone's records. You're going to be my best class yet." TJ turned to write five words on the whiteboard. "Read this and take it to heart. I'm not kidding. Failure is not an option."

As he'd intended, the challenge got their attention. Though the rest of the day went as well as could be expected for a first day, by the time the final bell rang, TJ was exhausted. Not only was he out of practice dealing with teenagers for more than an hour at a time, but he'd forgotten how tiring it could be to try to keep ahead of five classes of active and sometimes combative students.

Rowing across the lake seemed like a beginner's exercise compared to this, not to mention that he still faced another long walk. The only good thing he could say was that he hadn't been blindsided by memories of Deb. It might have been because this was a different school, or it might have been the sheer busyness. Whatever the reason, TJ had gotten through the day without the overwhelming sorrow that so often accompanied activities he and Deb had shared. And now the school day had finally ended.

He loaded Mrs. Loring's lesson plan book and the class textbooks into his backpack, then headed toward Rainbow's End, promising himself a shower once he reached the resort. He was halfway up Ranger Hill when an SUV stopped alongside him.

"You look like you could use a ride," Greg said as he rolled down the passenger's window. "Hop in."

Only a fool would refuse, and TJ was no fool. "Thanks. It wasn't too bad this morning, but the day turned out to be hotter than I expected."

Greg slapped his palm against his forehead. "I should have realized you needed transportation. You sure don't need a three-mile walk on top of a day wrangling kids." He was silent for a second, as if considering options. "Eric could make an extra run with the van." That was how the Firefly Valley kids got to and from school each day. "That would work, but I've got a better idea. Why don't you use Kate's car until your bike is fixed?"

Though the thought was tempting, there was only one possible answer. TJ had run up more debts than he could repay. "I can't do that. You and Kate are already doing too much."

When they'd discussed payment for TJ's room, Greg had flatly refused to accept any money for the first ten days, claiming TJ's time at Firefly Valley paid for that, and when he'd quoted a sum for the rest of the school year, it was so low TJ knew he must have received a substantial discount over the long-term stay rate.

Greg's lips tightened, as if he'd expected but did not accept the refusal. "Believe it or not, you'd be doing me a favor. Kate and I had our first argument this morning. The doctor doesn't want her driving, and she's balking at giving up her independence. If I tell her you need the car to avoid heatstroke, she'll have a way to save face."

TJ raised an eyebrow as he looked at the man who'd left behind a lucrative career in Silicon Valley and wound up renovating a dying resort. Though the story of the doctor's edict sounded plausible, TJ wasn't certain he believed it. Still, he could hardly refuse to help Greg. "Are you always this devious?"

"I prefer the word *crafty*. The truth is, even before the doctor said anything, I worried about Kate overdoing things." Greg lowered his head to look at TJ over the top of his sunglasses. "You'll understand when you're in the same position."

Like that would ever happen.

"I told you I wasn't Wimbledon material." Gillian winced as she leaned back on the bench and glared at the site of her recent defeat. The clay tennis court might be state of the art as Kate claimed, but it could have been cracked asphalt for all the good it had done her.

"At least you hit the last ball."

"Right before I crashed into the net." Gillian uncapped the water bottle and took a swig. "I have a feeling I'm going to discover aches in muscles I didn't know I had."

Mike nodded. "That's why we're going to take a cool-down walk. If you ache tomorrow, we'll find something else to do." He tossed his empty bottle into his gym bag, then rose and extended a hand to Gillian. "We could go for a drive tomorrow. The bluebonnets are at their peak."

Wincing, Gillian stood and shook first one leg, then the other. "Kate and her grandmother keep raving about them, but the only ones I've seen are those that grow here." She waved her hand in the direction of the lake. "I told Kate it was deceptive advertising calling this Bluebonnet Lake when there are so few of them, but she just laughed. She claims she's not responsible for any of the names."

"She's right. It's been called Bluebonnet Lake for more than a century." As they emerged from the wooded area, Mike wrapped his arm around Gillian's shoulders and drew her close to him. "It would be a shame for you to miss Texas's pride and joy. Let's go bluebonnet hunting tomorrow."

As Gillian raised her head to smile at him, a car door slammed. "I'd like that."

Mike leaned forward and kissed the tip of her nose. "It's a date."

A date. TJ forced himself to unclench his fists. There was no reason to be so angry. Of course Mike wanted to take Gillian on a date. Why wouldn't he? Any red-blooded man would be interested in an attractive single woman like Gillian. It wasn't Mike's fault, or Gillian's either, that the thought of them together made TJ's blood boil.

Greg's footsteps crunched on the gravel as he matched his stride to TJ's. The two men had just exited the SUV when Gillian and Mike emerged from the woods, looking for all the world like a couple in love.

"Guess you've got some competition." Greg tipped his head in Mike's direction.

TJ frowned. "You're mistaken," he said firmly. "I'm not in the running."

"Why not?"

16

"I can't believe my week here is almost over."

Gillian smiled as Mike opened the door to usher her outside after breakfast. The week had gone more quickly than she'd expected. The addition of afternoons with Mike and her mornings helping Marisa to her evenings in Firefly Valley had meant that Gillian's days were full—and fun. As she'd told Kate yesterday when they'd gone to Ruby's Tresses to have their hair cut and styled, she felt as if she'd laughed more this week than she had in the past year.

All in all, it had been a good week. Gillian had kept so busy that she hadn't let her dad and George's failure to answer her emails bother her. Instead, she'd rejoiced that TJ was once again teaching. Though he'd said little at supper either Thursday or Friday night, the Firefly Valley girls had told her he'd been a success.

"I never saw the point of learning what happened before I was born," Brianna had confided, "but TJ—that is, Mr. Benjamin—showed us why it's important. I sure don't want to repeat some of the mistakes people made in the past."

It had been a good week for Mike as well as TJ. As each

day passed, it seemed that Mike's smiles grew wider, and he'd admitted his mother had known what she was doing when she insisted he come to Rainbow's End.

"I'll never forget this week," he said with a smile. "I can't remember the last time I went seven days without a single meeting."

As Mike feigned chagrin, Gillian laughed. Her smile broadened when she saw TJ approaching the dining room. Though he normally joined her for breakfast, there'd been no sign of him this morning. Gillian had told herself not to worry, and it appeared she was right. TJ must have overslept. The problem was, he didn't look rested. Instead, he seemed almost melancholy.

"Good morning, TJ." Gillian kept the smile on her face as she reported that the pancakes were particularly good this morning. "They're blueberry," she added, "and there's even blueberry syrup to go with them." Though the dinner menu did not vary from week to week, Carmen had confessed that she enjoyed experimenting with the breakfast buffet, especially on Sunday.

When TJ simply shrugged, Gillian tried not to frown. There was no reason to make a big deal out of his apparent bad mood. Sally would say he'd gotten out of bed on the wrong side and to give him a couple hours to snap out of it. Fortunately, the man at Gillian's side was less moody.

Mike had shared stories of his family, surprising her with the revelation that he was an only child. From his initial comments, Gillian had thought he was part of a large family. He was, but it turned out to be an extended family. His father was the oldest of six boys, each of whom had taken the command to be fruitful and multiply seriously, giving Mike more than a dozen cousins. "They're great," he confided, "but I would have liked a sibling."

Gillian had no trouble empathizing. Though she had a brother, because of the twenty years between them, George was more like an uncle than a sibling. But for the past week, she'd felt no longing for a brother. As she had told Kate, it had been a very good week.

Gillian took a deep breath of the fresh air, reveling in the prospect of not needing her jacket much longer. The day was warming quickly.

When Mike reached for her hand and suggested they take a quick walk along the lake, she glanced at her watch and agreed once she realized they had half an hour before they had to leave for church.

"You still have a few hours of your week," she told Mike. "If last week was any indication, Pastor Bill's sermon will be good, and then there's the best meal of the week. Carmen's ham is delicious, and her cherry pie is out of this world."

He shook his head. "I'm going to have to pass on all of that. My dad invited some potential supporters to the ranch today, and he wants me to meet them." Mike wrinkled his nose. "I'm afraid it's back to work for me. That's why I wanted this one last walk."

"I'm sorry."

"Does that mean you'll miss me when I'm gone?" The words were delivered with a smile, but Gillian heard the sincerity in Mike's tone.

She opened her mouth to respond, then stopped, startled by the sound of an owl hooting. Weren't they supposed to be nocturnal? She looked for the owl, grinning when she saw a mockingbird perched on a live oak branch. This was the second time one had fooled her. The day she and Mike had visited a field of bluebonnets, she'd thought she heard a bluebird warbling, only to discover that a mockingbird was imitating its call.

"Yes, I'll miss you," she told Mike. "I've enjoyed our walks, and while I wouldn't use the word *enjoy* in the same sentence as *tennis*, I'm glad I had a chance to try it. Now I can honestly say that tennis is not my game."

"But horseshoes are."

Gillian chuckled at the memory of the times they'd played what Mike had declared was a game for seniors, akin to shuffleboard.

After his disparaging remarks, she'd expected him to be as much of a novice as she was, but he'd displayed surprising skill, easily winning almost every game. "I can't believe I actually beat you once. Are you sure you didn't throw that game?"

"Of course not. Scout's honor."

Something in Mike's tone made her narrow her eyes as she gazed up at him. "Were you even a scout?" she demanded, remembering the number of movies and TV shows she'd seen where someone had said "scout's honor" and then done exactly what he'd vowed not to do, later announcing that he had never been a scout.

"You bet I was." Mike laced his fingers with hers and swung them lightly as they walked. "I'm the third generation of Tarkett males to be an Eagle Scout."

"I'm suitably impressed." And she was. "This has been a fun week." Gillian continued to be surprised at how comfortable she was in Mike's presence. It was a far cry from being with TJ, whose prickly edges kept her wondering which TJ she would see next: the happy, joking man or the brooding one.

Mike was consistent. Consistently upbeat, consistently friendly. Perhaps more than friendly. Though he wasn't one to flirt, there was no denying that the interest Gillian had seen in his eyes was more than friendly. It might be an exaggeration to say Mike was smitten, as Kate had alleged, but Gillian would have had to be blind not to have seen the appreciative glances he'd given her.

"I'm so glad you showed me the bluebonnets," she told him. "They were spectacular."

"So are you."

Gillian swallowed, not sure how to respond. She had assumed whatever attraction Mike felt for her was like a shipboard romance and would fade as soon as he left Rainbow's End. Now he was acting as if he expected it to last.

"Don't look so surprised, Gillian. You must know I'm interested in you, and not just as someone to play horseshoes with."

Mike faced her and reached for her other hand. His touch was warm and comforting, and if there were none of the sparks Kate claimed she felt every time Greg touched her, Gillian didn't care. She wasn't looking for romance. Besides, sparks were highly overrated.

Mike's eyes turned tender as he said, "You're the most fascinating woman I've ever met. I have no intention of letting you slip away."

"That's very flattering, but . . ."

"No buts." He shook his head. "I have to go home today, but I can promise you this is not the end. I want to see you again, and if there's one thing I've learned from my family, it's not to give up on anything important. You're important." He gave her a smile designed to melt her heart. "I want to see you again and learn whether what I'm feeling is real. Don't say no."

Gillian did not.

What was wrong with him? TJ scowled at his plate. There was nothing wrong with the blueberry pancakes. As Gillian had said, they were excellent. What was wrong was TJ himself. He'd overslept, which rarely happened. Even worse, just before he'd awoken, he'd been dreaming of Deb. They'd been inside their RV, making breakfast together the way they used to every Sunday, and she'd been laughing.

"There's something I need to tell you," she'd said, a secretive smile lifting her lips. But before Deb could finish the thought, TJ had been jolted awake by the sound of a car door slamming, feeling as out of sorts as the proverbial bear whose hibernation had been interrupted.

Nothing, not even a hot shower, had dissipated his melancholy. And then he'd practically snapped at Gillian. She hadn't deserved that. It wasn't her fault that he felt so alone, that the dream had reminded him how wonderful it had been to be part of a couple. He'd hurt her, and that was inexcusable. Gillian deserved far better. She deserved a man like . . .

TJ refused to complete the sentence.

If the church had assigned pews, this would be the Rainbow's End pew. Marisa and her husband Blake had filed in first, followed by Greg and Kate, Gillian, then Sally and Roy. It was a tight fit, but if TJ had come, Gillian knew they would have made room for him. Sadly, there was no sign of TJ.

Once again Gillian found herself wondering what had caused him to turn away from faith. Though she'd seen sorrow in his eyes on far too many occasions, when he'd refused her invitation to church last week, he'd appeared angry. Why would the thought of attending a worship service make a man angry?

Speculating accomplished nothing, for TJ offered very little personal information. Gillian knew he had taught somewhere in Texas but had no idea where that might have been. As for other family and friends, she'd never heard him mention either. Perhaps he'd always been a loner. He certainly was now. And yet, though she couldn't explain why, Gillian's instincts told her TJ had not always been alone.

When the first hymn began, she focused her thoughts on the service, and as she did, Gillian felt a familiar peace settle over her. Being in God's house normally helped her put her life in perspective. While problems didn't disappear, worship gave her the strength to deal with them. She wished TJ were here to receive the same comfort.

An hour later, when Pastor Bill had pronounced the benediction and the congregation began to file outside, Marisa touched Gillian's shoulder. Today the lovely blonde wore a blue dress that highlighted her eyes.

"Do you have a minute? I don't like to work on Sunday, but there's something I want to discuss with you."

"Sure." Once they were outside, enjoying the shade of a spreading live oak, Gillian turned to Marisa. "What's up?"

Marisa twisted her wedding ring in an unconscious gesture Gillian had noticed when they'd worked together. It was, she suspected, the result of still not being accustomed to wearing a wide band on her left hand.

"I really appreciated your helping with the invoices. It made a big difference for me." Marisa smiled and touched Gillian's hand. "I hope I'm not being presumptuous, but I know you said you wanted something to do while you were at Rainbow's End and that you love to read."

"Correct on both accounts." Though she'd enjoyed helping Marisa with her paperwork and getting to know her better, Gillian knew there was at most one more day's work for her.

"Did Kate tell you that Blake and I own Hill Country Pages?"

"She did. We were going to stop in when we had our hair done, but we ran out of time." Though Gillian wasn't certain where this was heading, she was intrigued. From the outside, Hill Country Pages looked like a bookstore where she'd enjoy browsing.

"Did Kate also tell you I've been having a terrible time finding staff?"

Gillian shook her head. "That's one thing she did not share with me."

Marisa resumed her fiddling with her ring. "Well, I am. It won't be a problem during the summer, because I can hire teenagers, but right now I don't have enough people to run the store while I'm at Rainbow's End. I'm there the three evenings we're open and on Saturday, but Monday through Friday from ten to five is a problem. The woman who used to be full time just had a baby, and the others only want to work a few hours a week." Marisa took a shallow breath and exhaled. "Would you consider helping me?"

"Sure."

"Sure, as in you'd consider it?"

"Sure, as in I'll do it." How hard could working in a bookstore be? "When do you want me to start?"

"Tomorrow."

17

It had been easier than she'd expected, Gillian reflected as she took a sip of the milk shake that was serving as her lunch. Carmen would frown, but after the breakfast she'd eaten, Gillian hadn't needed a full meal at noon. She had closed the store for ten minutes and had walked to the Sit 'n' Sip, spending a couple minutes chatting with Russ Walker while he made her shake.

TJ was right. Russ hadn't meant to pry into Gillian's personal life; he was simply a friendly man who liked to be in the know. Today he'd shared the news that the teenagers seemed to like their new history teacher. Gillian planned to pass that tidbit on to TJ at supper tonight. But first she had to finish her workday.

There had been a steady stream of customers all morning, most of whom made at least a small purchase, but fortunately there had been no rush that would have taxed Gillian's skills. Equally as fortunate, the computer system and cash register had been easy to operate. All in all, it had been an enjoyable morning.

She looked up as two women entered. Of similar heights, both had the tightly curled gray hair Gillian associated with women in their eighties. They both wore loose fitting jeans, western shirts, and running shoes that probably had not experienced more than a moderately paced walk. The primary difference appeared to be that one woman's hair was silver, while the other's resembled gun metal.

"It's nice to see a new face," the silver-haired woman said as she closed the door behind her companion.

"It's nice to see the store still open," Gun Metal added. "We were worried, because we heard Marisa was having trouble finding help."

"She even asked us. Can you imagine?" Silver feigned horror. "Linda and I are more than eighty."

"But young at heart." As if to prove her point, the woman named Linda did a little two-step, then winced.

"Hearts are one thing, but you still need good knees to work in a store like this. Speaking for myself, these knees have seen better years."

Since neither woman appeared to expect Gillian to respond, she suspected they'd continue talking indefinitely if she didn't interrupt them. "Is there anything special you're looking for?" she asked. Marisa had told Gillian to expect browsers and not to be concerned if she made no sales, but that wasn't good enough for Gillian. She wanted to turn every browser into a buyer.

Silver nodded. "We want something set in olden times, but no smut, if you know what I mean."

Gillian matched the older woman's nod. "I understand." She walked to one of the shelves and pulled out a book. "You might like Jane Kirkpatrick. She's won all kinds of awards for her writing."

Linda read the back cover copy. "Let's try this. If we like it, we can recommend it to the book club."

Gillian's ears perked up. "Is Sally Fuller, that is, Sally Gordon," she corrected herself, "in your club?" Though it seemed unlikely that a town the size of Dupree would boast two book clubs for seniors, Gillian didn't want to make any assumptions.

"She is," Silver confirmed. "We're all looking forward to it once we settle on a place to meet. At least then there'll be something for us to do here." She fixed her gaze on Gillian, as if willing her to understand. "Don't get me wrong. Dupree's a nice town, but it seems to me everyone's so busy planning activities for the kids that they forget about us older folks."

Linda put a hand on Silver's arm. "Let's just pay for the book and leave. I'm sure this young lady doesn't want to hear about our problems. There's nothing she can do."

* * *

He shouldn't be so happy that the man was gone. After all, that meant less revenue for Rainbow's End, and while Greg Vange didn't need the money to survive, TJ was certain a full resort pleased both him and Kate. But, though he told himself it was wrong, TJ couldn't help but be glad that Mike Tarkett had returned to Blytheville and was no longer sharing walks, tennis matches, and who knew what else with Gillian. And if that wasn't meanspirited of him, TJ didn't know what was. Still, there was no denying that meals had been more pleasant without Mike at the same table, monopolizing Gillian.

TJ grabbed the bag of groceries and headed out of the lodge. Though he'd suggested a change of menu, the teens had insisted that s'mores should remain their nightly fare, and so each night he loaded graham crackers, chocolate, and marshmallows into a bag.

"I hear you're a working woman now," he said as Gillian emerged from her cabin, a smaller bag tucked under her arm. He wasn't sure what aspect of fashion she was discussing tonight and wouldn't ask. There were things a man didn't need to know. What he did know was that she looked especially pretty tonight.

If it hadn't been for the specter of Mike Tarkett, TJ might have told her that, but he didn't want to appear to be like Mike, flirting with her. It might give her the wrong idea. That's why TJ hadn't gone so far as to compliment Gillian, though he'd noticed that the green sweater she'd knotted around her shoulders made her eyes look closer to emerald than grass green.

She laughed, that silvery tinkle of a laugh that made him wish he knew how to coax it out of her more often. There had never been a problem getting Deb to laugh, but Gillian was very different from Deb.

"If you can call five hours of fun employment, then I'm a working woman."

"Fun?" TJ focused on the word that sounded like an anomaly. Though he had to admit that returning to the classroom had proven to be better than he'd feared, he would not have described it as fun.

Gillian nodded. "I thought it might be fun, but it definitely exceeded my expectations."

TJ couldn't help staring at her. Here was a world-renowned pianist, a woman who'd had standing ovations from coast to coast. She probably had enough money to go anywhere and do anything, yet she described working in a small bookstore as fun. Amazing. That was Gillian Hodge—amazing.

She didn't appear to expect a response, because she continued, "The day didn't feel too busy, but Marisa said she'd never had so many customers on a Monday."

As they left the pavement, TJ's and Gillian's shoes crunched on the gravel of the temporary entrance road to Firefly Valley. Though Greg had not wanted to pave anything, since he and Kate had not yet decided where they would build their future home, they'd provided a crude gravel drive for the residents, saying it was the least they could do for those who'd lost so much. Typical Greg, TJ reflected, giving generously, yet never demanding recognition for his kindness. Gillian was like that too.

"I'm not surprised you had so many customers," he told her. "Folks wanted to meet a celebrity." TJ hoped he wasn't bursting any bubbles with his statement.

"You mean me?" Gillian laughed again, her voice so filled with mirth that TJ couldn't help smiling in response. "I doubt that. No one even mentioned music."

"But they knew your name, didn't they?" When she nodded, TJ continued. "This is a small town, Gillian. There are no secrets here." Except his.

Jake Thomas had learned about Deb when he'd done his reference checks, but when TJ had said he preferred not to have that be common knowledge, Jake had respected his desire for privacy. As for the rest of his life, there was no reason anyone in Dupree would connect TJ Benjamin, history teacher, with the man who'd been known as the RV Reverend.

He slowed his pace, wanting to finish this conversation before they were interrupted by the teenagers. "Everyone knows that a famous pianist is staying at Rainbow's End and that she was helping out at the bookstore today."

"Oh." Gillian appeared to be digesting his words. "I hadn't thought about that. Even if folks just came out of curiosity, I had fun talking to them, and Marisa benefited from the sales. A classic win-win. Plus, I got to spend the day surrounded by books."

Other than history books, of which he'd once had a sizeable collection, books had not been a major part of TJ's life. Gillian was different. He'd heard her discussing virtually every fiction genre with a librarian who'd shared their supper table the first week they'd been at Rainbow's End.

"You really like to read, don't you?" Without waiting for her response, TJ said, "Maybe we can get the Firefly Valley kids more interested in reading." He was surprised they hadn't grown bored by the campfire stories and s'mores routine by now. A new activity might be just what they needed.

"A campfire book club?"

"Something like that."

But when TJ suggested the idea, the boys scoffed.

"You talking about fiction?" Shane asked, his swagger more pronounced as he added another log to the pile. "We got no need to read when we got you telling us tall tales every night."

"Tall tales?"

"Yeah. You don't expect us to believe you've been to all those places, do you?"

TJ hadn't thought anything the kids would say could surprise him, but this did. They believed he was inventing or at least embellishing his stories, and that couldn't be further from the truth. Admittedly, he'd chosen to dramatize the most interesting parts of his travels, but the results were not fiction.

"Not only have I been there, but I have proof," he announced. Raising his voice so that everyone could hear, he continued, "Meet me outside the lodge tomorrow night, and I'll give you proof."

Gillian had never seen the teens so excited. They'd arrived earlier than the designated time and were milling around the lodge, bickering less than normal.

"What do you think TJ meant by proof?" Brianna asked.

Though she knew what he planned to do, Gillian merely smiled. "You'll have to wait and see."

"Todd believes he's telling the truth."

"So do I." Gillian's smile broadened as she looked at the girl whose wardrobe had taken a definitely conservative turn over the past few days. Though she'd said nothing to Brianna about what she'd considered inappropriate clothing, the girl seemed to have begun to emulate Gillian's choices. Today she wore jeans and a shirt. Although they were tighter than any Gillian owned, they were also at least two sizes larger than the clothes Brianna had been wearing the first day they'd met.

Brianna's smile turned coy. "You gotta believe TJ. After all, he's your boyfriend."

There was no point in protesting. Brianna wouldn't believe TJ and Gillian were just friends, and so Gillian merely pointed toward TJ, who'd raised a hand for silence. "It looks like we're ready."

TJ waited until the teens were gathered around him and as quiet as a group of teens could be before he spoke. "I know we've got some doubting Thomases here, so . . ."

"What's a doubting Thomas?"

Smiling, TJ began his explanation. "He was one of Jesus's disciples who wouldn't believe Jesus had risen from the dead until he touched the scars."

"Oh." The boy looked around, his expression clearly asking whether he was the only one who hadn't known the story. Though Gillian suspected he wasn't alone, no one else admitted their ignorance.

As if he recognized the teen's embarrassment, TJ continued speaking. "Anyway, I'm going to give you proof of my travels, but before I do that, I want you to see one thing." He led the way to the resort's garage and opened the door. Switching on a light, he pointed to his motorcycle. "That's my bike."

Shane gave out a low whistle. "Cool."

"Yeah, it is."

"So, how come you're showing us this?" Once again, Shane was dominating the group. Gillian wondered why Todd said nothing until she saw him whispering something to Brianna. He might not even be listening to TJ.

TJ shrugged. "You'll see. Let's go inside."

The lodge had been transformed, its windows covered with blackout curtains, the furniture moved to the perimeter, leaving the center of the room empty. It was there that TJ directed the teens to sit facing the large screen he'd placed next to one wall. When everyone was settled, TJ dimmed the lights and turned on the projector. For the next twenty minutes, he displayed pictures from his travels.

It took only a few seconds for Gillian to understand why he'd shown the teens his motorcycle. The photos were so good that they might have thought they were stock pictures if it hadn't been for the presence of the bike in some of them. That added authenticity to the entire slide show and left no doubt that TJ had not been telling tall tales. He had indeed visited the parks and other sights he'd described in his nightly stories.

Tonight as he took them on a photographic tour of the country, it was clear the kids were fascinated.

"I've saved my favorite park for last," TJ said as a picture of Old Faithful flashed onto the screen, followed by a solitary bison apparently strolling along the edge of the road. "Geysers, wildlife, waterfalls—Yellowstone has it all. But to my mind, there's nothing quite like the mud pots."

Gillian stared at the picture of a tall woman with sandy blonde hair and a bright smile standing by the railing, gazing raptly at what appeared to be a witch's cauldron of bubbling mud. She wasn't beautiful by any standard, but there was something so engaging about her smile that Gillian wanted to meet her, to ask what made her so happy.

"Hey, man, who's the chick?" one of the boys demanded.

"My wife."

18

His wife? Gillian felt the blood drain from her face. She'd known TJ had secrets and that those secrets were painful, but she hadn't expected this. She took a deep breath, trying to recover from the shock of learning that TJ had been—perhaps still was—married.

There was no reason that thought should have wrenched her heart, she told herself, though that very same heart continued to pound with what seemed like twice its normal force. Plenty of people married and divorced. Some separated, needing time apart to determine whether that was better than remaining together. Whatever the situation, it was TJ's life. If he'd wanted Gillian's advice or her help, he would have asked.

It was silly—downright silly—to be hurt that he hadn't confided in her. Though Gillian thought they'd become friends, friends didn't necessarily tell each other everything. Gillian had never told Kate that, despite all the statistics to the contrary, she worried that Kate's pregnancy might end the way her mother's had. Nothing good would come from sharing that fear with Kate. Perhaps TJ felt the same way about his wife.

"You're married?" one of the boys asked, his voice filled with skepticism, perhaps because TJ wore no wedding ring.

"Was. She died." TJ tapped a key, revealing a new slide. "And now, if you look at these mud pots, you'll see there's some color to them. That's why they're sometimes called paint pots." His tone left no doubt that he was changing the subject as well as the picture. The low murmur his revelation had provoked diminished as TJ showed them pictures of hot pools and explained the different types of geysers.

Though Gillian said nothing, her mind continued to whirl. It was no wonder she'd seen such sorrow in TJ's eyes, no wonder he hadn't wanted to discuss family. He was a private person, and this was a private tragedy.

Judging from the pain she'd seen in his expression, TJ's marriage had been a happy one. If not, he wouldn't be experiencing such sorrow. Leaving his job to travel the country began to make sense. It wasn't an early midlife crisis. TJ was trying to deal with what had to be overwhelming grief.

Half an hour later, when the last of the teens had left, having devoured doughnuts and cider tonight instead of s'mores, Gillian touched TJ's arm, then settled onto one of the couches. She wasn't sure whether he'd accept her unspoken invitation to join her, but when he took the seat next to her, she turned so she was facing him.

"I'm sorry about your wife." Though the words seemed inadequate, they were all she could find. "If you want to talk, I've been told I'm a good listener."

She'd debated saying anything, reminding herself that TJ had never asked for help. Desire to respect his privacy warred with the belief that healing came only after a wound was opened and cleansed. Talking and praying were the only ways Gillian knew to heal inner pain, and since TJ had made no bones about not being a man of faith, that left talking.

He was silent for a long moment, as if he were trying to decide what, if anything, to say. At last he nodded shortly. "I probably should have said something earlier, but as you've guessed, this story doesn't have a happy ending. There's really not a lot to tell. I met Deb the first week of college at one of those freshman mixers that everyone's supposed to attend, and I knew right then she was the only one for me."

If Sally were here, she'd be nodding, claiming this was proof that "Some Enchanted Evening" moments were real, that it was possible to meet someone and know instantly that was the person you were meant to marry. Gillian had never felt that way, and even Kate admitted that when she first met Greg, marriage was the furthest thing from her mind. But TJ had been fortunate, at least for a while.

He stared into the distance, his expression solemn. "We dated all through college, got married right after graduation, and had six wonderful years together until . . ." His voice trailed off, as if the memories were too painful to share with anyone.

Though she considered saying nothing, once again Gillian's instincts told her TJ needed to talk. He wouldn't have told her this much if he hadn't wanted to, but the way he'd begun to speak about his wife signaled that this was the right time for him to speak of his past. "What happened?"

He swallowed deeply, then looked directly at Gillian, his brown eyes filled with anguish. "She was diagnosed with cancer. A particularly aggressive form of breast cancer." TJ closed his eyes briefly, and she wondered if he was remembering a specific day.

Though the moment of her accident was indelibly etched on her memory, the most painful day had been the one when the surgeon announced he'd done all he could and that it would take a miracle for her to ever again play on a concert stage.

Gillian suspected TJ had had at least one of those days when everything seemed hopeless. Was that the reason his faith had faltered? If he and his wife had prayed for and not received a miracle, that might explain why he no longer attended church services.

"The cancer had already metastasized by the time the doctors discovered it. We tried everything—chemo, radiation, stem cell replacement—but nothing worked."

And now TJ was alone. Half of what had once been a couple, a man who'd lost his faith. Gillian could feel herself starting to tear up as she thought of the sorrow he had endured. Her injury, as bad as it was, had only been life-changing. What had happened to TJ's wife had been life-ending. And even though Gillian knew there was life after death, she also knew how painful the parting was for those left behind. Look at her father. It had been almost thirty years and he hadn't fully recovered from his wife's death.

"I'm so sorry." Once again Gillian wished for more eloquent words. "I won't say I understand how you feel, because I don't. I've never lost anyone close to me." She'd been shocked and saddened when Kate's grandfather had died, but Grandpa Larry's death hadn't changed her life as the loss of a spouse would have. And while she had felt—and still did—the absence of a mother, it wasn't the same kind of sorrow she would have had if she'd known and then lost her mother.

Gillian said a silent prayer, searching for words that might comfort TJ. "I won't tell you to be thankful for the time you had together. I'm sure you've heard that far too many times. All I can say is that I'm sorry."

Though she tried to blink it away, a tear slid down her cheek. TJ stared at her for a moment, his expression inscrutable. Then the corners of his lips curved upward, and he reached forward, drying the tear with his fingertip.

"Thank you," he said softly.

* * *

"Oh, Sally, I didn't know what to say when he told me his wife died." Gillian leaned forward on the breakfast bar, cupping the coffee mug. When she'd accepted Sally's invitation to stop in for coffee before she went to the bookstore, Gillian hadn't expected to be baring her heart to the older woman.

She had wanted to tell Kate what she'd learned about TJ, but Kate had been unusually emotional yesterday, crying over a dead mouse she'd seen along one of the walks. A few minutes later she had laughed, blaming her tears on her pregnancy, but that had been enough to convince Gillian her friend did not need to hear anything that might upset her emotional equilibrium. Now, though it hadn't been her intent, she was confiding in Sally.

"I feel like the most ungrateful person alive. I've been feeling sorry for myself because my career is over, but that's nothing. I'm still alive. I have second and third chances. TJ and Deb don't."

Sally swiveled her stool so she could pat Gillian's back the way she'd done so often when Gillian was growing up. When Dad would leave on another trip, Gillian would race to Kate's house, shed a few tears over what sometimes felt like abandonment, then surrender to the comfort of Sally's embrace.

"Sometimes there's nothing you can say," Sally told her. "Sometimes silent sympathy is what's needed."

Thinking back, Gillian realized that Sally had rarely spoken when Gillian had been upset. Instead, she had simply held Gillian until her tears subsided.

Gillian took a sip of coffee, wondering if she'd taken the wrong approach with TJ. "I wasn't exactly silent. In fact, it felt like I was babbling."

Shaking her head, Sally continued to trace circles on Gillian's back. "You, my dear, are not a babbler. I imagine that whatever you said—or didn't say—helped TJ with his healing." Dropping her hand and picking up her own mug, Sally continued, "I wouldn't be surprised if that was why God put you in TJ's path the day he crashed his bike. He knew you both needed to heal. Maybe you're meant to help each other."

There was no question that Gillian needed to heal, and now

she knew what had caused TJ's wounds. The question was whether they could help each other.

She laid her right hand on the counter and stared at it. "Each day is better," she admitted. "There's no change in my fingers, but I worry about them less every day." Gillian felt as if she was gradually letting go of the past and enjoying the present. Though she still had no plans for the future, she hoped those would come with the next phase of healing.

"The rumor mill says you've been too busy to worry," Sally said with a chuckle. "And I'm not just talking about working at Hill Country Pages. I heard you caught the eye of the most eligible bachelor in the Hill Country."

"Did Kate tell you that?"

"Who needs Kate?" Sally scoffed. "I've got better sources."

Gillian wouldn't bother asking which of the gossipmongers had linked her name with Mike's. Though the Matchers were an obvious choice, since they'd made no secret of their curiosity and had visited the bookstore both days Gillian had been there, asking when Mike would return, others had seen Gillian with him. As TJ had said, Dupree was a small town, and small towns had few if any secrets.

"I enjoyed Mike's company when he was at Rainbow's End," she admitted, "but it's not as if we have a relationship. This was a shipboard romance, minus the ship and minus the romance."

Sally's raised eyebrow said she wasn't buying that story.

"Really, Sally, there's nothing between us. I'm not looking for a husband."

"Perhaps you should be. I'll admit that marriage isn't for everyone, but you'd be a wonderful wife and mother."

Gillian swallowed the last of her coffee and prepared to leave. "Even if I were interested in Mike—and note that I said 'if'—he isn't interested in me. He told me he'd call, but he hasn't."

Sally shrugged. "He will. Don't you fret."

Gillian wasn't fretting, she told herself two hours later during a lull between customers. It was true that she'd wondered why Mike hadn't called and that she'd been mildly disappointed, but those thoughts were overshadowed by two things closer to home: TJ and the seniors. Though TJ was the more important, she doubted there was anything she could do to help him.

The seniors were different. Linda and Silver had come in again today, this time to buy one of Serena Miller's books, and once again they'd bemoaned the absence of activities for them. Despite what Linda had said on Monday, there had to be something Gillian could do. She simply had to find it.

TJ hated study halls. They were supposed to give teachers a break, but what they gave him was too much time to think. Thoughts had been roiling through his mind ever since he and Gillian had talked. Predictably, he hadn't fallen asleep until late last night. As a result, for the second time since he'd arrived at Rainbow's End, he'd overslept, making him so late that he'd missed breakfast. Maybe if he had had a chance to see Gillian again he might not be so preoccupied now, but as it was, nothing he did stopped his thoughts from racing in what seemed like circles.

As one of the students crumpled a piece of paper and prepared to attempt a hoop shot into the wastebasket from the back of the room, TJ frowned. That was enough to stop the boy. It did not stop his thoughts.

He probably shouldn't have included Deb's picture in last night's show. He'd debated about it when he'd been assembling the slides and had included it at the last minute, because it was the best shot he had of the mud pots. He'd justified his decision by telling himself there was no reason for the kids to comment on her. After all, there were tourists in other pictures. But somehow the teens had realized that Deb wasn't a person who just happened to be in the frame. She was special.

He could have lied, claiming he didn't know the woman's identity, but lies had never come easily to TJ, and so he'd blurted out the truth. And that had led to his conversation with Gillian.

Though he'd been able to squelch the kids' questions, discouraging them as easily as he'd stopped the would-be basketball player, Gillian was different. As soon as the words had popped out of his mouth, he'd known she would ask about Deb. What TJ hadn't expected was his reaction to Gillian's response.

In the past, talking about Deb had only deepened his pain and stoked his anger, reminding him of all he'd lost. That was the reason he'd made a point of never even hinting that he'd once been married. He didn't want pity, because it only made him feel worse.

Last night had been different. Gillian's soft words and that solitary tear that had touched him in ways mere words could not had been like a soothing balm. For the first time, it had felt right to be speaking of Deb. And for the first time, memories had brought peace rather than regret.

He'd lain awake last night with memories of Deb whirling through his brain, changing like the patterns of a kaleidoscope, and interspersed with images of Deb smiling at the sight of a moose emerging from a willow thicket, long strands of grass dripping from its mouth, was the memory of Gillian's tear. For the first time, TJ felt as if the healing had begun.

19

"How's Junior or Juniorette or whatever you're calling the baby this morning?" Gillian stirred a spoonful of sugar into her coffee as she took her favorite seat in Kate's apartment.

Though Kate had told her that a colleague and her husband referred to their unborn child as Peanut, Kate and Greg hadn't chosen a nickname for theirs. And, since they'd chosen not to know the gender, they alternated between "he" and "she" when referring to it.

"Rambunctious," Kate replied with a wry smile. "She's decided that the middle of the night is playtime, which means Mommy doesn't get much sleep." Kate patted her baby bump, her lips curving into a smile of pure delight as the baby kicked again. "I can't believe I still have seven weeks to go. I can only imagine how big I'll be by then."

"But you're loving every minute of it." Gillian had never seen Kate so happy, and though she'd heard some expectant mothers described as radiant, this was the first time she had ever seen one. Kate was definitely radiant, glowing, and any number of other positive adjectives.

"I didn't love morning sickness, and I miss caffeine," she said with a frown at her cup of herbal tea, "but other than that, it's been an amazing experience. You'll see when it's your turn."

Gillian feigned indignation. "Now you're sounding like the Matchers. Even Sally appears to be climbing on their bandwagon. She seems to believe that since Rainbow's End brought both you and Marisa a happily-ever-after, I should be the next bride. Next thing I know, one of you will be picking out a husband for me."

"C'mon, Gillian." Kate pushed the plate of muffins toward Gillian as a peace offering. "You know me better than that. It's true I hope you find a man who'll make you as happy as Greg has made me, but I'm not going to push you." She paused for a beat before adding, "Too hard."

When Gillian chuckled, Kate said, "I'm not sure you need a push," and for a second Gillian wondered whether Kate had somehow realized how often Gillian's thoughts turned to TJ.

She'd told herself it was only natural that she would worry about a man who'd lost so much, but that did not explain why she dreamt about him last night. In her dream, TJ had seemed carefree as they'd waited in line to board the Maid of the Mist, and when the boat had taken them to the foot of Niagara Falls, he'd laughed. The laughter had been wonderful, but it was what happened next that haunted Gillian's thoughts. TJ had wrapped his arms around her shoulders, drawing her close and tipping her face toward his. She'd been certain he was going to kiss her, but before their lips touched, the alarm clock had jolted her awake.

As she felt her cheeks redden at the memory, Gillian took another sip of coffee, trying to hide her reaction to the dream. It was only a dream, she told herself. It meant nothing.

Kate's chuckle deepened. "If I'm not mistaken, there's some extra color on your cheeks and a twinkle in your eye this morning. Should I guess who put them there?"

Kate might be her best friend, but there was no way Gillian

was going to tell her about that silly dream. "You can try, but I think you'll be surprised."

"Be surprised by what?" Marisa asked as she hurried into the apartment, glancing at her watch.

"I'm speculating on the reason Gillian looks so happy today. At first I thought it was Mike Tarkett, but now I'm beginning to suspect it's related to the reason she asked me to invite you here for coffee."

Thankful that the redirection had worked, Gillian waited until Marisa poured herself a cup of coffee and settled into one of the overstuffed chairs before she spoke. "You're right, Kate. If there's a twinkle in my eye, it was caused by two women—Linda and a woman whose name I don't know. I just think of her as Silver." Even though she'd never dreamt about them, when she was awake, Gillian's thoughts turned toward the two women almost as often as they did toward TJ.

"The second one must be Sheila." Marisa nodded knowingly. "They're sisters-in-law and do almost everything together."

"They came into the store twice this week." Gillian smiled at Marisa as she said, "They bought a couple books, but what got me started thinking were their comments—more like complaints—that there's nothing for seniors to do in Dupree."

Kate turned to Marisa. "Sally hasn't said anything to me, so I haven't given it much thought. I know she's excited about the idea of a book club."

"Because that's the only activity available."

Kate seemed surprised by Gillian's comment. "What do you think, Marisa? Is that true?"

"Probably. Some people play golf, but that's the only other thing I can think of."

And that was the problem. A once-a-month book club or an occasional golf game wasn't enough, especially since some seniors didn't enjoy reading or golf. The thought of people being stuck at home with little to do other than watch TV bothered Gillian.

"What if there were a place where they could gather?" she asked. "Not the church fellowship hall or a room at the library but something special for them."

"A senior center." Kate looked pensive as she sipped her tea.

"Exactly. I keep thinking it's like *Field of Dreams*. You know the line about if you build it, they will come. The good thing about Dupree is we don't have to build it. There are plenty of empty stores just waiting for someone to use them. Why not the seniors?"

"I think it's a great idea." Marisa punctuated her sentence with an enthusiastic two thumbs-up.

"I agree." Kate rubbed her belly as she said, "Greg and I can help with funding, but I'm afraid I can't offer much else. The doctor doesn't want me to drive or do much of anything other than wait for the baby to make his appearance."

Marisa nodded slowly. "I can't offer the kind of money Kate can, but I can show you what I had to do to get Hill Country Pages ready for business. It's not too hard to start a business in Dupree, and nonprofits are even easier, but it never hurts to have someone show you the ropes."

Their approval was exactly what Gillian had hoped for. She'd tossed the concept around in her mind, trying to find reasons why it wouldn't work, but all the thinking she'd done had merely solidified her belief that a senior center was a good idea. "So you think we should do this?"

"We?" Kate raised a skeptical eyebrow. "I think *you* should do it. Correct me if I'm wrong, but I believe you came up here with plans almost done and what you wanted from Marisa and me was confirmation that it's a good idea. Am I right?"

"You are."

Gillian had spent the lulls between customers thinking about Marisa's explanation of the business permitting process. She'd updated her list and made two new ones, and all the while, her eyes kept returning to the empty store directly across the street from Hill Country Pages.

It was no different from half a dozen other vacant buildings, but the location appealed to Gillian. It was close to the bookstore and Hill Country Pieces, the town's quilt shop, both of which drew women to this part of Pecan Street. And it was next door to Sam's Bootery.

Though Gillian doubted they all needed new boots, she'd seen a number of older men enter the store and remain for an hour or so. What they did inside was a mystery, which was part of the reason Gillian headed for the bootery as soon as she turned Hill Country Pages over to the teenager who'd arrived for the second shift.

"How can I help you?"

Gillian blinked as her eyes adjusted to the relative darkness of the store. The smells of leather and polish competed with the fragrance from a large bouquet of hyacinths on one corner of the counter, but what caught Gillian's attention was that the person behind the counter was a beautiful young woman, not the grizzled man she'd expected. Though Gillian had seen the woman's face on the boot advertising the store, she had assumed the woman was a model, not someone who worked there.

Extending her hand, she said, "I'm Gillian Hodge and I'm looking for Sam Dexter."

The woman smiled. "You're in the right place. I'm Sam Dexter. Samantha, actually. My dad's the original Sam, but the business is mine now."

"Now I see why so many men come here." Gillian would have thought that Samantha's combination of light brown hair, blue eyes, and classic features made her a candidate for a modeling career rather than running a bootery in a small Texas town.

"Older men?" Samantha raised a carefully shaped eyebrow. "If you think they come to see me, you're mistaken. They're looking for a game of chess or checkers." She gestured toward the back of the store. "Dad has a table set up most of the time."

It was the perfect segue. "That's really what I wanted to talk to you about. I'm hoping to start a senior center in Dupree. At this point, nothing's decided, but I envision a place for chess and checkers and lots of other activities."

Gillian gestured in the direction of the empty store next door. "That location seemed ideal to me, but now I'm not so sure. If you have plans to expand or if your father doesn't want anything to compete with his games, I'll look for another spot."

"A senior center." Samantha nodded slowly. "I wonder why no one thought of that before. Dupree could definitely use one."

She tipped her head to one side, listening to the sound of men's voices emerging from the back of the store. "To tell you the truth, I suspect Dad would be just as happy if the men had another place to play. My mom thinks he ought to be spending more time with her now that he's retired, but he hates to disappoint his buddies. Half the time Dad doesn't play—just watches the other guys."

"So a different location would help him."

"Definitely." Samantha gave Gillian a conspiratorial grin. "Me too. They're nice guys, but sometimes they're a little, shall we say, nosy."

Gillian had no trouble imagining that. "What about the store next door? Do you have any plans for that?"

Samantha shook her head. "Business is great, but we have no need to expand. So I say, go ahead. It's a good idea."

As relief washed over Gillian, she realized how much she'd wanted that particular location. While it was true, as she'd told Kate and Marisa, that there were many empty stores from which to choose, this one had caught her eye and her imagination and had refused to let go.

"Do you happen to know who owns the building?" Given the town's size, Gillian would have been surprised if Samantha did not.

A laugh was her response. "I sure do." She turned toward the back room and called out, "Dad, Gillian Hodge wants to talk to you about turning the store next door into a senior center."

"What's this about a senior center?" The man who emerged from the back followed by the two men Gillian had seen entering the store an hour ago had Samantha's blue eyes, but his hair had turned gun-metal gray, and his shoulders were slightly slumped, perhaps from years of hunching over a work table.

When Gillian completed her explanation, she said, "I wondered if you'd be willing to rent it out."

Sam Senior turned to the other men. "Seems to me you guys have a chess game to finish while this lady and I tend to business."

Recognizing the dismissal, the men headed to the back room. Sam lowered his voice as he addressed Gillian. "If you start a senior center, will my buddies have a place to play chess?" His expression gave no indication of whether he favored the idea.

"I understand that they already do."

"An official place with room for more than one game?" This was beginning to sound like an interrogation.

Gillian nodded. "Chess, checkers, and other things. Some of the women are interested in starting a book club, and the center would give them a place to meet. If I can find an instructor, I thought we might offer yoga and tai chi. We'd have to charge for those separately from the monthly membership fee, but I don't think the classes would be too expensive."

Gillian had spent several hours online learning what services other senior centers offered. While some of them involved more equipment than she envisioned, at least initially, she liked the idea of courses like tai chi that could help seniors avoid falls.

"How about dances?" Sam Dexter waggled an eyebrow as if the thought intrigued him.

"Ballroom or modern?" Since she suspected Sam had already made up his mind, Gillian decided to answer his question with one of her own.

"Both."

It was what she'd expected. He was testing her. She shrugged. "I don't see why not, if there's interest."

Sam studied her for a moment before saying, "Okay. You can have the building. Now, about the rent. How does a dollar a month sound?"

Gillian stared at the man, not certain he was serious. But there was nothing in his expression to indicate that he was joking. "That sounds incredibly generous."

He gave his daughter a fond look. "Let's see what she says after she's seen the inside." Turning back to Gillian, Sam said, "I don't think it needs any structural work, but it sure does need paint."

It did indeed. Cobwebs, dirt, and dingy paint made the former showroom unappealing, but the building had what Gillian had heard described as good bones. The large front room would accommodate twenty or thirty people, which she suspected would be more than adequate. The back of the store boasted a small kitchen and an even smaller bathroom, which was, to Gillian's delighted amazement, ADA compliant.

"So, what do you think?"

Gillian smiled at Sam. "It's perfect."

20

It was a good thing no one could hear her, Gillian reflected as she sang along with the radio on her drive back to Rainbow's End. Her vocal instructors had said her musical talents did not extend to singing, but the way she felt practically demanded a song. How else could she express her pleasure that the senior center project was turning out to be so simple and so much fun?

Gillian had never done anything like this. A year ago if she'd been asked if she possessed an entrepreneurial spirit and organizational talents, she would have shaken her head. Now she felt as if she had at least a smidgen of both. It was a heady feeling, but even that could not compare to the feeling that helping the seniors was what she was meant to be doing.

Though she hadn't been able to meet with the building inspector who would have to approve the plans for the center, her assistant had told Gillian there should be no problem. As Gillian had expected, the town council was happy to have one less empty store, and as it turned out, Sam Dexter was equally happy to have his second building occupied.

There would be work involved in getting the center ready. Even though the changes she wanted to make were strictly cosmetic, Gillian did not underestimate the effort involved. And, as much as she hated to disappoint Marisa, she was going to have to work fewer hours at the bookstore if she was going to get the center running before she left Dupree.

The phone was ringing as she entered her cabin. Gillian sprinted to the kitchen, not wanting the call to go to voice mail.

"Gillian?"

There was no mistaking that voice. Gillian's face broke out in a smile. "Hi, Mike." It was vanity, pure feminine vanity, but Gillian couldn't help being flattered that the area's most eligible bachelor hadn't forgotten her. This was the perfect ending to an already good day.

"I'm glad I caught you." She could hear the smile in his voice, a smile that matched hers. "I'm sorry it's taken me so long to call, but this week has been beyond busy. I've had back-to-back meetings every day and then meetings with my family that lasted way too long." His smile turned into a soft chuckle. "I didn't think you'd appreciate a call at 3:00 a.m."

"You're right about that. I need my beauty sleep, especially now that I'm once again a working woman."

"What?"

"I'm working at Hill Country Pages, the local bookstore. It's only part time, but it's been fun."

"I want to hear all about this new job of yours when I see you," Mike said. "That's why I'm calling. I know it's short notice, but I've managed to clear my calendar and I wondered if you'd like to have dinner with me tomorrow night. I can guarantee a good table at Strawberry Chantilly."

"Because your family owns it?" Gillian thought that was the name of the upscale restaurant the Tarkett family operated in Blytheville.

"Precisely. I may have been a failure as a waiter and busboy, but I know how to reserve a table." Before Gillian could tell him she doubted he'd been a failure, Mike continued,

"The food is actually very good. Not that I'm prejudiced or anything."

"There's nothing wrong with being prejudiced, especially when the critics agree. And, unlike you, I don't have an over-scheduled calendar."

Tomorrow night was free except for going to Firefly Valley with TJ. Though Gillian hated to miss that, she wasn't about to refuse Mike's invitation. She had no doubt that she'd enjoy the dinner, but more importantly, time with Mike might dislodge the memory of the dream she'd had about TJ.

Even when she'd been helping customers in the bookstore and working on plans for the senior center, the thought of that almost-kiss had lingered in the back of her brain, tantalizing her with the possibilities. That was ridiculous. It wasn't as if they had a future together, at least not one that included romance. The expression in TJ's eyes when he'd spoken of Deb was the same one her father had when he spoke of his wife. Like Dad, TJ was a one-woman man. He and the teens could get along without her for one night.

"Yes, Mike, I'd like to have dinner with you."

*

TJ hadn't thought it possible, but Gillian looked more beautiful than ever tonight. Her cheeks were flushed with what appeared to be pleasure, and her eyes had turned a deeper green than usual.

"Did something special happen today?" he asked as he handed the platter of chicken cutlets to her. The chicken was delicious, but in TJ's opinion, the side dishes outshone the main course. He particularly enjoyed the casserole of onions, tomatoes, and green beans Carmen served with the chicken.

"As a matter of fact, it was a special day," Gillian told him. "I'm curious. What made you ask?"

"Because you look happier than I've ever seen you." More beautiful too, but he wasn't going to say that. If he did, she might get the wrong idea. She might think he was interested in her romantically when he wasn't.

Admittedly, his thoughts turned to Gillian far more often than he'd expected, and there were times when he even pictured the two of them on his bike, heading for some unknown destination. If that wasn't ridiculous, TJ didn't know what was. He wasn't the man to take her anywhere. He'd given his heart to Deb, leaving nothing for Gillian or any other woman.

"So, what happened?" he asked, deliberately pushing the thought of Gillian on his bike to the dark recesses of his brain.

"Remember the women I told you about who came into the store on Monday?"

"Linda and Silver?"

"Yes, although it turns out that Silver's name is Sheila. I kept thinking about what they'd said about how there's nothing for seniors to do in Dupree and wondering how I could help them."

TJ wasn't surprised. Gillian was one of the most giving people he knew.

"And you figured out a way."

"I did." She spooned a piece of molded salad onto her plate. "The bottom line is, I'm going to try to organize a senior center."

TJ thought back to the day he'd walked around Dupree, snapping pictures. Though the town had the usual amenities, there was nothing specific for seniors. Leave it to Gillian to recognize the need and try to fill it. "That's a great idea."

The flush in her cheeks deepened as she glanced around the table, as if wondering whether anyone was listening to them. Though the round tables lent themselves to group discussions, tonight the other guests were involved in what appeared to be their own private conversations.

"You really think so?" The incredulity in Gillian's voice made it seem like she was unaccustomed to praise. That couldn't be the case. This was the woman who used to receive standing ovations.

"I know so. Why should kids be the only ones with planned activities? So, what have you done so far?"

When Gillian finished her explanation, TJ let out a soft whistle. She must have been a human dynamo to accomplish that much. "All that in one day? You're incredible."

She shook her head. "I wouldn't say that, but I am excited. I can't remember the last time I felt this energized. Right now, everything about the project seems wonderful." A shrug accompanied her next sentence. "I may change my mind when I start the cleanup, but at this particular moment, I can't wait to get started. Bring on the buckets, soap, and sponges."

That sounded like Gillian, charging forward, determined to be the first to cross the finish line. But this wasn't a solo sport. Surely she knew that. Even though she'd played many piano solos, there were just as many times when she'd had a symphony orchestra accompanying her.

"You don't plan to do it all yourself, do you?" Though none of the stores in Dupree was huge, cleaning one was still a massive undertaking.

Gillian nodded, as if what she had in mind was trivial. She took a sip of iced tea, then reached for a biscuit as she said, "Kate and Marisa would help if they could, but they have too many other things going on."

And she hadn't thought beyond her girlfriends. Regret and something else—perhaps wounded pride—stabbed TJ as he realized that Gillian hadn't even considered asking him for help.

"Gillian, Gillian, Gillian." When her eyes widened at his slightly scolding tone, TJ continued. "There's a whole section of the workforce you haven't considered."

"And who would that be, besides you?"

So she had thought of him. Though his pride no longer felt as if it had been trampled, TJ wondered why she hadn't asked.

Perhaps he'd been mistaken. Perhaps she'd wanted his assistance but hadn't wanted to presume. Perhaps the reason she was telling him about the project was that she hoped he'd volunteer.

"Of course I'll help," he told her, "but if you're going to finish this in a reasonable amount of time, you need more resources. The Firefly Valley kids could make short work of this."

In response to Gillian's skeptical look, TJ said, "Trust me. They'll come. We'll call it a work party and promise them all the pizza they can eat. I'm sure some will volunteer right away, and once the leaders do, the rest will fall in line." TJ pictured Shane swaggering around the campfire, ordering his minions to sign on the dotted line.

Recalling the work plans the principal of his last school had drafted when the school decided to adopt a section of highway and enlisted the students' help in keeping it free of litter, TJ said, "We'll need to get the parents' permission, but that shouldn't be too hard. If you have access to a computer, we can have permission forms ready to take tonight. That gives you tomorrow to assemble all the supplies so we can work on Saturday."

"This Saturday?" Gillian's eyes lit with excitement. Though she'd been prepared to do the work alone, she appeared surprised by the idea that they could begin so quickly.

"Why not? It'll be fun."

As she laughed and clinked her glass to his in a toast to their future success, TJ realized it wasn't only Gillian who was enthusiastic about the project. It must be contagious.

21

Gillian glanced at her watch. She'd awakened earlier than normal this morning, perhaps because she was still excited about the plans for the senior center, and even after a leisurely breakfast, she had a few minutes before she had to leave for her shift at the bookstore. That should give her enough time to meet Brianna's mother and have her sign the permission slip. The other kids' parents had been home last night and had joined the group around the campfire long enough to hear what was planned and to grant their children permission to participate.

Gillian had heard several of them say they thought it was a good idea that their kids would be helping others, especially since they'd been given so much. When their apartment complex had burned, complete strangers had offered the former apartment dwellers the RVs free of charge for as long as they needed them. As if that weren't enough, Marisa and her husband were equipping the new apartments with the latest in appliances and state-of-the-art smoke detectors, meaning that the Firefly Valley residents' new homes would be more modern and safer than the old ones.

The adults were approving, the teens excited. Only Brianna

was unhappy. Her mother had been at work last night, and Brianna had admitted she wasn't certain she would have signed her permission slip, even if she'd been home.

"She doesn't want me to do anything," Brianna groused.

Though Gillian suspected that might be an exaggeration, she couldn't be certain without meeting Brianna's mother. And so here she was, approaching Firefly Valley, paperwork in hand.

When he'd first mentioned it, Gillian had wondered at TJ's insistence that the parents come in person to sign the release forms. When she had been in school, the teachers had simply sent the forms home, and she'd returned them the next day.

"Times have changed," TJ had said, pointing out that he didn't recognize all the teens' signatures and wouldn't know if they'd forged the documents. "There are a lot more lawsuits these days, so we need to be extra careful," he'd told Gillian, and she'd agreed. As it was, since the senior center wouldn't have liability insurance in effect for a few more days, Greg had called his agent and gotten a rider added to the Rainbow's End policy for tomorrow's event. He'd also volunteered to pay the center's utility bills for the first six months. By then, Gillian expected enough people would have joined that their monthly dues would cover basic expenses. She had already established a fee schedule for meals and special classes but, in what Kate called a loss leader, had decided not to charge a membership fee this first month.

Gillian knocked on the door to Brianna's trailer.

"Good morning," a woman said as she opened the door. "What can I do for you?"

Gillian tried to mask her surprise. The woman had the same coloring, the same features, the same Barbie doll figure as Brianna, but she was much younger than Gillian had expected. Gillian doubted Brianna's mother was much older than Gillian herself.

"Good morning, Mrs. Carter."

The woman who looked so much like her daughter shook her

head. "Just call me Natalie, but for the record, it's Ms. Carter. Brianna's father split before she was born and before he could put a ring on my finger."

Unsure what response Natalie expected, Gillian settled for giving her a noncommittal nod and saying, "I'm Gillian. Gillian Hodge." When the woman's eyes registered familiarity with her name, Gillian continued. "I don't know whether Brianna told you about it, but some of the kids are going to help get the new senior center building ready. I came to see if you'd allow Brianna to be part of the work party. It's all day tomorrow."

Natalie tugged the hem of her T-shirt, perhaps to cover the small rip in her shorts. The clothing, though obviously not new, was far more modest than the outfits Brianna had worn the first few times Gillian had seen her.

"She told me about it. In fact, it was all she could talk about at breakfast." Giving Gillian a sharply appraising look, Natalie narrowed her eyes. "Tell me, Gillian. Will there be adult supervision?"

"Of course. I'll be there, and so will TJ Benjamin. He's the one who's been running the campfires here every night."

Natalie nodded, confirming her familiarity with both TJ's name and the nightly entertainment.

"I wouldn't be surprised if some of the other teachers come tomorrow, but even if they don't, TJ and I will serve as chaperones, if that's what you're worried about."

"It is," Natalie admitted. "I'm sure you know Brianna fancies herself in love with Todd."

It was Gillian's turn to nod. "He seems like a good guy. Pretty sensible."

"I agree that he's basically what my mother would have called a straight arrow. The problem is, he and Brianna are only fifteen, and at that age, being sensible isn't what kids do." Natalie lowered her eyes and appeared to be examining her pedicure. "I should know. I was fifteen when I had Brianna."

Gillian tried not to let her surprise show. She'd been correct in assuming that Natalie was close to her age. For her part, Gillian could not imagine being a mother at fifteen. How had Natalie done it when she was little more than a child herself?

"I don't want Brianna to make the same mistakes I did," Natalie said, her voice fierce. "My daughter deserves a better life than mine."

The intensity of the woman's emotion touched chords deep inside Gillian. Was this how her mother had felt when George was born? Had she had the same depth of maternal love for Gillian, even as her own life had slipped away? Now was not the time to think about the mother she had never known. Gillian was here to convince Natalie to sign the permission slip.

"I understand your concerns." Gillian wanted to reassure this woman whose life had been so different from her own. Gillian had had the financial, social, and educational advantages that had been denied to Natalie, and yet Natalie had accomplished far more than Gillian had, for she was raising a daughter, lavishing her with maternal love.

Brushing aside those thoughts, she smiled at Natalie. "I can't promise to keep them apart, but I can promise that if you let her come, Brianna and Todd will spend tomorrow working."

Natalie stared at Gillian for a moment before nodding. "Okay. I trust you."

TJ wasn't certain who was more anxious for school to end: the students or himself. In addition to the usual TGIF syndrome with its predictably reduced attention spans, the kids were excited about tomorrow's work party. This was probably the first time those who lived in Firefly Valley were involved in something that wasn't being offered to the others, and they were taking full advantage of feeling special. To TJ's amusement, the teens were strutting around as if being asked to sweep and mop floors and wash windows and walls was an adventure.

TJ had every intention of making sure that it was. He'd already decided to harness the kids' competitive spirit and planned to divide them into two teams. They'd be awarded points for how quickly and completely they accomplished each task, with the winning team receiving a prize.

Though he had a few ideas, TJ hadn't decided what the prize would be. Somehow it didn't seem right to make that decision without Gillian. It was, after all, her project, and though he had more experience with teenagers in general, she had developed a good rapport with this particular group. She might have ideas that had not occurred to him.

The work party wasn't the only reason TJ was looking forward to the final bell of the day. In fact, it wasn't even the most important reason. He felt adrenaline surge each time he thought of what was waiting for him at Rainbow's End. Eric had told him his bike would be finished by midafternoon.

All day long, he'd pictured himself taking it for a spin, riding up Ranger Hill and straight down Lone Star Trail to the highway. Once there, he'd see which direction beckoned him. The sun and wind in his face, the roar of the engine in his ears—there was nothing like being on a bike. And this time he wouldn't be alone. Gillian would be sitting behind him. It would be the perfect ending to the day.

*

As she left the bookstore and headed for her car, Gillian glanced at her phone. Though she hadn't expected it, she had email. Most of her friends preferred to text, but since she was frequently out of cell range, the number of texts had declined substantially since she'd come to Rainbow's End. Maybe a friend had decided to email her.

Gillian tapped the icon and smiled. This was better than she'd expected. Dad had responded to her note about the senior center. Eagerly, she opened the message, her smile fading as she read. *"The senior center is a bad idea. How will you find a husband if you spend all your time with old people? Write a check and let someone else do the work."*

No greeting, no closing, nothing but disapproval.

Gillian cringed, feeling the way she had the one time she had come in second in a competition. Dad had made no secret of his disappointment, telling her she could do better. And she had.

A second later, anger replaced her sorrow. Would she never learn? Dad was accustomed to getting what he wanted, and right now he wanted Gillian to marry. She should have anticipated his reaction and simply not told him what she was doing. She had made a mistake, but it was one she would not repeat.

She was back. Though he hadn't wanted to admit how impatient he'd been, TJ had glanced at his watch what felt like a million times during the last half hour. When he'd returned from school and had inspected the bike, he'd taken a quick spin around the resort, just to verify that the engine sounded as good as Eric claimed it did. The man might not be a miracle worker, but he came pretty close. Not only was it impossible to tell that the bike had been crashed, but it sounded better than it ever had, at least while TJ had owned it.

His fingers itched to touch the throttle, his feet to feel the smooth shifting as he climbed hills, then swooped down the other side. And he'd do that, once Gillian arrived. Though the wait seemed endless, it was over now. She had arrived.

"Do you have a minute?" TJ asked as she exited her car. A ride would take more than a minute, but he was going to do this one step at a time. He hadn't forgotten that she'd never ridden a bike and that she'd claimed she never would, but surely he could convince her otherwise. "I want to show you something."

Gillian nodded. Though she'd seemed unusually somber when she'd stepped away from her car, her face brightened as she looked at him. He took a quick glance at her clothing. The skirt and knit top were pretty, but she'd need something different for the bike. Though others might ride with their arms and legs unprotected, TJ did not, and he most definitely would not let Gillian run the risk of road rash on that soft skin. Once he explained where they were going, he'd suggest jeans and a jacket.

Gillian's smile made him wonder whether she knew what he had in store for her. "You look like you've had a good day."

"I have," TJ said as he led the way to the garage, "and this is part of the reason why." He flung the door open, letting daylight stream into the closest bay. "My bike is done." He patted the engine. "Eric did a great job. It's good as new now."

"That's nice." Surely it was TJ's imagination that her voice held no enthusiasm. Perhaps she was tired. A quick ride would take care of that. There was nothing like being on a bike to chase away fatigue. That was one of the things he wanted to show her.

TJ stepped back from the bike. "I'm glad you're back, because I was hoping you'd take a ride with me to celebrate." He'd even bought a second helmet for her to wear.

The blood drained from Gillian's face, and she looked as if he'd suggested a free fall from the top of the Empire State Building.

"Me, ride a bike?" She shook her head vehemently as she backed toward the door. "I will never, ever, ever get on one of those things."

He'd expected a little resistance, but not this much. TJ stared at Gillian, wondering why she'd had such an over-the-top response to his invitation. Although, thinking back, he remembered that she'd been almost this upset when they'd met. At the time he'd thought it was because she feared he'd been seriously injured, but perhaps he'd been wrong. Perhaps the bike was the cause.

"Why don't you like motorcycles?" he asked as calmly as he could.

Gillian took another step backward, as if she feared the bike might somehow propel itself toward her. "I don't just dislike motorcycles." Blood had returned to her face, and now she appeared flushed rather than pale. "I hate them." The venom in her voice left no doubt that she meant every word.

"Help me, Gillian," TJ said, joining her outside the garage and closing the door so she wouldn't have to look at his bike. "I'm trying to understand. Why would you hate an inanimate object?"

"Because a motorcycle—a bright red motorcycle, to be precise—is the reason I'm no longer a concert pianist."

The pieces were starting to come together. "A motorcycle was involved in your accident?"

"'Involved' is one way to describe it. 'Caused' is another." She took a deep breath, exhaling slowly before she continued. "I was coming out of a recording studio when the rider lost control. He skidded on a patch of oil, jumped the curb, knocked me down, and rode over my hand," she said, shuddering slightly as she recounted the events of that day. "He wasn't hurt, but my hand was shattered. The doctors say it's a miracle that I've regained this much mobility." Gillian stared at her right hand with its tracery of scars.

"I'm sorry." When she'd said those words, they'd comforted him, but they didn't seem to be having the same effect on Gillian. Her color was still high, her breathing ragged.

"It wasn't your fault." The words sounded perfunctory, as if she knew she was expected to say them.

"It wasn't the motorcycle's fault, either." Perhaps it was foolish, but TJ felt the need to convince her that a motorcycle was more than an instrument of destruction. He'd spent many, many pleasurable hours on his, and he wanted to share that pleasure with her.

Gillian sighed. "My head knows that, but that doesn't mean my heart does. I know it's irrational, TJ, but I don't want to so much as touch a motorcycle. As for riding one, that'll never happen."

She sounded so determined that TJ knew better than to try to persuade her. It was obvious Gillian needed more time to heal. Still, he couldn't stop himself from saying, "I wish there were something I could do to change your mind."

"Believe me, there isn't."

"I'm starting to believe the male of the species is trying to drive me crazy."

Kate raised an eyebrow as she tossed a bottle of sparkling water to Gillian. "Take a deep breath and a sip of water. Then tell me what happened." She paused as Gillian opened the bottle. "I hope this doesn't mean Mike cancelled your date."

"Not so far." Gillian took a long drink. "It's my dad and TJ."

When she told Kate about the email, her friend nodded. "Your dad's always been that way. Sally said he was a little more mellow before your mom died. Her theory is that he didn't know the first thing about raising girls and was afraid of making a mistake." Kate rubbed her baby bump, her expression serious. "I can identify with that. I don't know how I'd raise this baby alone, especially if it turns out to be a boy. I don't know anything about little boys."

"But you wouldn't tell them something they really wanted to do was a bad idea."

"I sure hope I wouldn't, but there are no guarantees. Did you tell your dad how excited you were about the project?"

Gillian thought back to the email she'd sent and shook her head. "I don't think I did. I was in a hurry that day." She frowned, wondering if Dad's response might have been different if he'd known how dear to her heart the center was. Now she'd never know.

"So, what did TJ do to get you all hot and bothered?"

"He thought I'd ride his motorcycle. I know he's right that the bike wasn't responsible for the accident, that it was the rider, but I can't help it. Every time I even think about a motorcycle, I start to relive that day. I can't do it, Kate. I can't ride one."

Kate reached over to squeeze Gillian's hand. "You don't have to." After a quick glance at the clock, she said, "What you have to do is get ready for your date with Mike. I can pretty much guarantee he won't be riding a motorcycle."

So that was why she didn't come to supper. TJ watched as Gillian, decked out in a fancy dress and some of those mile-high shoes that women seemed to like, climbed into a long, low sports car. TJ frowned as he recognized the dancing horse on the hood. A Ferrari. A red Ferrari. It figured.

At first he'd thought Gillian was skipping supper because she'd been upset about the bike, but now he knew the real reason. She had a date with Mike Tarkett. No wonder she'd appeared relieved yesterday when he'd told the teens they wouldn't have a campfire meeting tonight. She wouldn't have been there anyway. Instead, she was off with Mr. Rich Guy.

Gillian was going in style, in an expensive sports car instead of on a bike with more than its share of miles. Instead of a ride to who knows where and a possible ice-cream cone along the way, she'd be having dinner at some fancy restaurant. Instead of being with a schoolteacher who just managed to survive, she was with one of the wealthiest men in the area.

Mike Tarkett could offer her things TJ had never even dreamt of. Mike could . . . *Stop it, TJ*, he admonished himself. Those were foolish thoughts, the thoughts of a man who still believed in love, romance, and happily-ever-after. Those days were over.

22

It was a night to remember, a welcome respite after the turmoil of the afternoon. From the moment she'd settled into the Ferrari, Gillian had felt as if she had slipped back into her old life. For a few hours she could pretend that the accident had never happened, that she was still Gillian Hodge, concert pianist. And it was all because of Mike.

Gillian had ridden in luxury cars before. She'd been to elegant restaurants before. She'd dated eligible men before. But never before had she done those things with Mike Tarkett.

She smiled as she gazed at him across the table. He was so handsome in his jacket and tie, looking like the successful young entrepreneur he was. But Mike's appeal was more than his good looks and worldly success. There was something special about him, something that warmed Gillian's heart and made her grateful they were spending this time together.

Mike would never challenge her the way TJ did. He would never suggest much less insist that she ride a motorcycle. Mike was a gentleman, and a gentleman would never make a lady feel uncomfortable, while TJ . . . Gillian forced thoughts of

TJ aside. Mike was her date for the evening. Mike was the one who'd brought her to this beautiful restaurant.

Strawberry Chantilly couldn't have been nicer. With formally clad waiters, fine linens and china, and tables set far enough apart to ensure privacy, it was the perfect spot for either a romantic evening or an important business meeting. Plush carpet and heavy draperies muffled the other guests' conversations, while soft music added to the atmosphere.

As Gillian had expected since Mike's family owned Strawberry Chantilly, they'd been given the best table in the house, and the service was superb. The waitstaff anticipated their needs, filling water goblets before they were empty, replenishing the basket of rolls well before they needed more, and bringing fresh plates of the restaurant's signature butter pats, carefully pressed into the shape of strawberries.

The service and setting were enough to make Gillian relax, but what she enjoyed most was Mike's company. It felt so good—so right—to be with him. They'd talked about everything from wildflowers to Mike's plan to run for mayor, and throughout it, Gillian had felt comfortable.

She wouldn't use the tired analogy of "as comfortable as an old shoe." Mike was more like a custom-made shoe, or since this was Texas, a custom-made boot like the ones Samantha Dexter and her father created. TJ, on the other hand, was a running shoe, one that had seen many miles but still had more to go. He was . . . Gillian bit the inside of her cheek, trying to halt her errant thoughts. She would not, would not, would not think about TJ tonight.

"Are you sure it's what you want to do?" she asked when Mike finished explaining his plans for the mayoral campaign. Though he'd appeared animated when he'd described the process, Gillian still wondered whether this was his decision or the result of parental pressure.

He took a sip of water before he answered. "I gave it a lot of soul-searching—a lot of prayer too—and I believe it's the right move." His gaze met hers, and this time Gillian had no doubt of his sincerity. "My parents are happy, of course, but what's important is that I feel it's what God has in mind for me."

Gillian smiled, her heart leaping at the realization that Mike had a good relationship with God. Unlike TJ. *Stop it.* She gave herself a mental shake. She needed to stop thinking about TJ. It wasn't fair to Mike. This was his evening, not TJ's.

"What will your platform be?" she asked, determined to keep her thoughts firmly focused on Mike.

"Wooden?" He gave her a look that was meant to be angelic but failed. "I suspect that wasn't the kind of platform you meant. And, yes, I have thought about the other kind."

He cut a piece of his steak, then looked up. "I believe Blytheville needs sustainable growth. I've seen a number of cities expand too rapidly. It's easy to build houses, but the infrastructure is much harder. That needs to be planned before the expansion occurs."

Gillian nodded her approval. "I'm a firm believer in plans." She had spent the afternoon putting together detailed plans for tomorrow's work party, everything from lists of the materials she needed and the tasks that had to be done to the order they should tackle those tasks. There was no point in mopping the floor until the ceiling, walls, and windows were done.

"As for infrastructure, believe it or not, I learned about that as a kid." When Mike lifted an eyebrow, as if he thought she was exaggerating, Gillian continued. "My father was in real estate. He was one of those people who said the three most important things in real estate were location, location, and location. I don't think I was more than six or seven when I heard him say that for the first time, but I remember asking him what it meant."

Gillian suspected the reason the memory of that particular conversation was still fresh was that it was one of the few times she could remember her father talking to her for more than a few minutes when she was a child. That afternoon he'd taken her into his home office and shown her plans for a condo complex.

"Dad didn't use the word *infrastructure*, but that's what he meant: schools, shops, roads, public transportation."

Mike speared another piece of meat. "It's funny you should mention public transportation. The man who's going to run against me wants to start a bus line in Blytheville."

"And you don't agree." It was an ordinary conversation, nothing earthshaking, and yet Gillian found herself enjoying it more than she would have expected. Perhaps it was because of the warmth she saw in Mike's eyes. He was looking at her as if he cared—really cared—about her. Was Kate right that he was interested in her romantically? Whatever the reason, Mike's approval made Gillian's heart beat a little faster.

"A fleet of busses wouldn't be cost effective. My opponent is right that we need some form of public transportation, especially for seniors who no longer drive and are still living in their homes, but a bus that seats fifty would be major overkill."

Though Mike hadn't said so, Gillian suspected this was one of the subjects that had kept him working late each night. "So, what are you proposing?"

"Minivans. They're a lot less expensive than busses."

As she savored the lobster tail portion of her surf and turf, Gillian wondered whether Dupree needed something similar. It would be foolish to create a senior center if people couldn't get there. She made a mental note to find out how many seniors might need transportation.

"I see what you mean by sensible growth," Gillian said as she dipped another piece of lobster into the drawn butter. "You'd have my vote if I lived here."

"Thanks." Mike grinned as the waiter replenished their glasses. "Enough about me," he said when they were once again alone. "Tell me about your job."

"Which one?"

He blinked, his surprise obvious. "Now you've done it. You've shocked me. What's going on? I knew that you were helping out at the bookstore, but this sounds like you're doing something else too."

"I am. It actually came as a result of working at Hill Country Pages." Gillian finished her explanation by saying, "The next month or so will be hectic, but then everything will slow down. Marisa has teenagers scheduled to work at the bookstore, and once the center opens, I won't be needed there. After Kate's baby arrives, I expect to leave."

Simply pronouncing the words made Gillian's heart sink. She'd been in Texas less than three weeks, and it had already begun to feel more like home than her apartment in Chicago ever had.

"Unless I convince you to stay," Mike countered as he leaned across the table, laying his hand on hers. "I'm giving you fair warning that I plan to do exactly that. And in case you haven't figured it out, I'm not used to losing."

It was a heady sensation, having a man like Mike Tarkett so obviously interested in her. Gillian put down her knife and fork, signifying she had finished eating.

"I hope you're not planning to refuse dessert," Mike said with another of his irresistible smiles. "I've had the pastry chef working all day on a sampler platter for you."

Gillian raised her eyebrows, not believing what she'd heard. "A dessert made just for me?"

Mike nodded. "I was hoping you'd share it with me, but it's your decision. Everything on the platter was prepared specifically for you."

Gillian felt the way she had the day she received her first standing ovation: honored, overwhelmed, and undeserving. "I don't know what to say. You're making me feel like a pampered princess."

Mike smiled and squeezed her hand. "That was the idea."

23

Gillian did not feel pampered the next afternoon. Far from it. She was grimy and disheveled with sore muscles and aching tendons, and yet she had a sense of satisfaction every bit as great as the night she'd won the Brooks Competition. That night she'd been awarded a cash prize, a management contract, two years of guaranteed concert bookings, even a new wardrobe for performances. Today she had a building that was slowly being transformed. While her father might not have considered that a significant accomplishment, Gillian couldn't help grinning every time she looked at the progress.

She flexed her fingers, getting the kinks out of them. Though the teens were doing all the work in the main room, she and TJ had arrived early and spent two hours making the kitchen clean enough for them to serve food there. That alone had been a bigger job than she'd anticipated, underscoring TJ's wisdom in enlisting help. If Gillian had had to do all the work alone, it would have taken weeks, not a single day, to get the center ready for paint.

As it was, thanks to TJ and peer pressure, they'd made amazing progress. To Gillian's amusement, when the teens had discovered that TJ had gotten two sets of T-shirts—one lime green, the other purple—and issued them to the team members so there was no question who was on which team, there'd been a major debate over which was the better color.

Gillian had been even more amused when TJ had presented her with a green and purple striped shirt that matched his, a clear statement of impartiality. The colors weren't ones she would have chosen, particularly with her hair, but she'd gamely slipped the shirt over her head. Today was all about the teens and teamwork.

"Watch that ladder!" TJ's voice filled the room, quieting the chattering teenagers and attracting the attention of the boy who was ignoring the "do not stand above this level" warning and was about to climb on top of the ladder. "Remember the rules. Any injury, even a minor cut, counts against your team."

The sheep-faced teen returned to the second step from the top, stretching to reach the ceiling.

"What a clever way to keep them thinking about safety," Gillian said, referring to TJ's inclusion of demerits for accidents and injuries on the score cards. As they'd both expected, the teens had been enthusiastic about having a competition, and while some of them groaned when they heard the rules, the majority had abided by them, not wanting to lower their chances of winning.

"You can thank my father for the safety messages," TJ said, leaning against the door frame. "Before he and Mom quit their jobs to become part of our church's missionary team, Dad worked in a plant that put safety first." TJ continued his explanation. "He said you couldn't go anywhere without seeing some reminder of safe procedures. That carried over to home."

There had been a single safety message in the Hodge household: protect Gillian's hands.

"Does that mean you never jumped off a shed roof or climbed onto the wrong tree limb?" she asked, remembering some of her friends' antics.

"I didn't say that. I got into all the normal scrapes," TJ admitted. "The difference was, I knew I was taking a chance. When I climbed the tree, I knew to stop before I was so high that a fall would mean broken bones." He gave her a wry smile. "Bruises were okay. They were badges of honor."

"You had all that safety training and yet you ride a motorcycle." The mere thought made Gillian shudder. Though the counselors had assured her that her fears would fade, that had yet to happen.

"I ride safely, and I have the best helmet money can buy." TJ paused to inspect the wall Shane's team had finished washing. When he'd nodded his approval and checked it off the list, he returned to his post next to Gillian. "The helmet I bought for you is just as good as mine," he said, acting as if there'd been no interruption.

Gillian hated the idea of his wasting money. "If you really bought it only for me, I hope you can return it. I wasn't kidding when I said I would never ride."

"A man can still hope."

TJ's bittersweet expression made her think he was remembering his wife. No wonder he had been wandering around the country. Fortunately for Gillian, he had found his way to Dupree and was here, for at least two more months, helping her turn her new dream into reality.

He glanced at his watch. "Break time," he called out. "This one means food." When she'd scheduled the day, Gillian had included ten-minute breaks every hour, figuring that the teens would need them if only as a change of pace from the unaccustomed physical labor. Scrubbing walls and ceilings was different from shooting a basketball or jogging up Ranger Hill. And, knowing how many calories work consumed, she had planned snack breaks in the middle of the morning and afternoon in addition to a substantial lunch. As she had expected, a round of cheers greeted TJ's announcement. Gillian was tempted to join them in their cheers. The food was nothing like the gourmet fare she'd had at Strawberry Chantilly, and the company was certainly very different, but she wouldn't have traded this day for anything.

"What's on the menu this time?" Brianna asked as she and Todd got into line. As had happened during each of the breaks, they were holding hands and looking as if they couldn't wait to be alone together.

Gillian tried not to sigh. Though there were other couples, Brianna and Todd seemed more infatuated than the others. It was no wonder Natalie Carter worried about her daughter.

"Fruit and veggies." The morning break had included doughnuts, muffins, and—for the more health-conscious—granola bars.

Brianna's expression left no doubt that she was less than thrilled. "Nothing but healthy food," she scoffed.

Since it wasn't like Brianna to be peevish, Gillian suspected something other than food was responsible. This was neither the time nor the place to deal with teenage insecurities, and so she said only, "The fruit and veggies may be healthy, but the dips aren't. We have chocolate and caramel for the fruit. The vegetables get guacamole and something that appears to have a couple pounds of bacon in it."

Grinning, Todd stared at the food. "So, what's everyone else going to eat? That bowl of chocolate looks like a single serving to me."

Her good mood restored in one of those rapid changes so common among kids her age, Brianna gave Todd's arm a playful punch. "Be careful. Gillian might cut you off from everything if she thinks you're serious."

As they went through the line, piling food on their plates, one of the other boys tapped Todd on the shoulder, his body language saying he wanted to talk to him, and so once they reached the end of the line, Brianna and Todd separated.

To Gillian's surprise, Brianna approached her. "Thanks for talking to my mom," she said softly. "She worries too much."

Gillian smiled, as much at the assortment of previously disdained fruits and vegetables on Brianna's plate as at her comment. "I think that's part of the job description. Mothers worry." Or so she'd heard. "Your mom loves you."

Brianna nodded. "I know that. I just wish she understood how much I want to get married."

"She does." That was the problem.

"It looked like you were doing some counseling on the side," TJ said a few minutes later when the break ended and the teens resumed work.

"You mean Brianna?" When he nodded, Gillian shrugged her shoulders. "I'm hardly one to give her advice about mother-daughter relationships."

"Maybe that makes you exactly the right person to help Brianna. If your life had been perfect, you wouldn't understand her angst. Your situations are different, but pain is pain."

"I hadn't considered that."

Gillian touched TJ's arm, grateful for his opinion. While it didn't change the past, it made her regard it in a different light. Maybe Sally had been right when she'd told Gillian that scar tissue was strong and that the scars themselves—both visible and invisible—were reminders of battles fought and survived.

Gillian smiled at the man who'd opened her eyes. "Thanks, TJ. You're the best."

He wasn't, of course, TJ told himself four hours later when he returned to his cabin. He wasn't the best at anything, and yet he couldn't help being pleased that the furrows between Gillian's eyes had disappeared and that her smile had returned.

There'd been a lot of smiling today. Even when the kids had

grumbled, it had been a good-natured grumbling accompanied by a smile. And by the end of the day, Gillian's smile had been radiant, for the formerly grimy room was now ready for its first coat of paint.

TJ pulled off his boots, smiling as he set them on the closet floor. Gillian might claim she was going to do all the painting herself, but he had every intention of helping her. While he didn't doubt she could paint the room alone, there was no reason she had to.

As he settled into one of the comfortable chairs, he picked up his camera and started looking through the pictures he'd taken. TJ smiled again. Gillian was a fascinating woman—warm and caring despite a less than perfect childhood.

Though he'd wanted to hug her and tell her just how amazing she was, a room filled with teens was hardly the place for even a casual hug, and so TJ had done nothing more than utter a few words. He hadn't expected those words to resonate with Gillian the way they obviously had. *The best*, she'd said. Far from it, and yet somehow he'd been able to touch her heart. That was almost as amazing as Gillian herself.

TJ had the impression that although she had never had financial worries, Gillian had worked hard for everything she'd achieved. He'd Googled her and discovered she'd had very stiff competition for the Brooks Award. The articles claimed that year's contestants displayed more talent than any of the previous years, yet she'd won and handily, if the scores were to be believed.

And now, while she could be lying on a beach somewhere, doing nothing, she was helping both the teens and the seniors in a small Texas town. Not many women with her background and resources would do that, but Gillian was different.

TJ scrolled through the pix, deleting a few with cutoff heads and unpleasant expressions, marking the ones he liked the best. Though he hadn't had a plan in mind when he'd started taking them, as the day had progressed, he'd decided to have a few shots printed and framed to hang on the center's walls. The seniors would enjoy seeing how their center had taken shape, and the kids would get some recognition for the hard work they'd done.

TJ laughed as he saw one of the last shots he'd taken of Gillian. Though it captured the happiness in her eyes and the pride in what the group had accomplished, TJ doubted she would be happy to have it put on display. Dirt smudged one cheek, her lipstick had worn off, and the striped shirt clashed with that glorious red hair. This was a far cry from the glamour shots he'd seen online, and yet this was Gillian too. Perhaps it was even the real Gillian.

Later that night as he was setting the alarm, TJ sank onto the bed. Was it possible? He stared at the clock, shocked by what had—or more precisely, what hadn't—happened. It had been a full day, and he hadn't thought of Deb once. Not once.

Guilt swept through him, but to his surprise, it was followed by a glimmer of relief. He couldn't explain why it had happened; he wouldn't even try. All he knew was that today had been the best day since Deb had died.

24

There was no logical reason to be here. TJ frowned as he saw where his footsteps had taken him. While it was true that he wanted to invite Gillian to spend the afternoon with him, there was no reason to have come here. He would have asked her at breakfast, but he'd gotten so caught up in telling Greg about the work party that he'd been late again and had missed her.

That was hardly his last chance. He would see her at noon for Rainbow's End's special Sunday meal. He could casually ask whether she had plans for the afternoon and, if she did not, tell her what he had in mind. There was no reason, no reason at all, to be walking by the church and even less reason to be standing so close to the open window that he could hear the minister begin his sermon.

"Today I want us to ponder the words of Joshua 1:5," Pastor Bill said in a voice that carried without amplification. "And today instead of a modern translation, I want us to hear this message in the formal words of the King James Version. 'There shall not any man be able to stand before thee all the days of thy life: as I was with Moses, so I will be with thee: I will not fail thee, nor forsake thee.'"

The minister paused for a moment, letting the congregation absorb the verse. TJ couldn't count the times he'd used deliberate pauses like that. They were one of the most effective tools a minister had at his disposal.

"The message seems simple," Pastor Bill continued, "and yet I wonder how often we heed it. Do we really accept that no one person can lead us or be with us for our entire life? Our parents filled that role when we were young. Later we might look to siblings, friends, mentors, or spouses, but none of them will walk the whole path with us. Only one will, and that's God."

The pause was shorter this time. "Not only will he be with us, but he gives us a wonderful promise: he will not fail or forsake us. Others can promise that, but inevitably they will fail, simply because they're human. Only God can and will deliver on his promise 100 percent of the time." When Pastor Bill resumed, his voice had the deeper resonance of a closing statement. "If that's not worthy of praise, I don't know what is."

TJ turned away, clenching and unclenching his fists as he tried to slow his heartbeat. The late April morning was beautiful, as filled with promise as the minister's sermon, yet neither assuaged the pain deep inside. The emptiness, the horrible hollow feeling, had returned this morning, reminding him of all he'd lost: his parents, Deb, the assurance that he was doing what God had planned for him.

The promise God had given Joshua was wonderful, but Joshua had deserved it. TJ did not.

Realizing he was in no mood to talk to anyone, TJ strode away from the church. When he reached his motorcycle, he shoved the helmet onto his head, then climbed onto the bike. He wouldn't think about the sermon and shattered dreams. Instead, he'd take a ride to clear his head and make himself fit for human company. Only then would he issue his invitation.

Gillian might laugh. She might refuse. After all, what he was going to propose could hardly compare to dinner at a fancy restaurant. But then again, she might accept. There was only one way to find out which answer she would give him.

It must be her imagination that TJ seemed a bit nervous. He hadn't acted like this yesterday at the senior center or when they'd met for supper after the work party. But now as he pushed the last bite of cherry pie onto his fork, he seemed distinctly ill at ease.

Gillian waited until they'd left the dining room before she asked, "Is something wrong?"

Her question seemed to startle him. "No," he said so quickly that she knew her assumption had been correct. TJ might deny it, but she'd touched a sensitive chord. "Why did you ask?"

"You seemed quiet at dinner."

He shrugged, but the gesture seemed forced, once again telling Gillian there was more than he wanted to admit. "Who could get in a word with the Palmer sisters at our table?"

Perhaps she had been mistaken. The three middle-aged women had dominated the conversation. "You've got a point there." Gillian feigned a look of chagrin. "It's bad of me, but I kept thinking of them as the Magpie Sisters, always chattering."

Something about her response pleased TJ, because she saw his shoulders begin to relax. "Do you like birds?" he asked.

The question seemed to come from out of the blue. "I suppose so," she said. "No one's ever asked me that before. Does it matter?"

He nodded. "It might. I wondered if you'd like to go birdwatching with me this afternoon. Greg told me April is a great time to see some rare species including golden-cheeked warblers and black-capped vireos."

If TJ had expected her to recognize those species, he was

mistaken. Gillian could identify common birds like robins, cardinals, and bluebirds, but she'd never even heard of the two he'd mentioned.

"I don't want to disappoint you, but I wouldn't know either of those birds unless they landed on my arm and announced their names."

Holding out his arm as if he expected a bird to perch on it, TJ chuckled. "The truth is, I wouldn't either, but Greg lent me a field guide. My plan was to snap pictures of every bird I saw and sort them out later."

Though Gillian suspected true birders would be horrified by that approach, she thought it had a lot of merit. "That sounds like my idea of bird-watching."

"So you'll go?" The surprise in TJ's voice made Gillian wonder if this was the reason he'd seemed ill at ease before. It seemed he'd been unsure of her response, and yet she couldn't imagine why. They'd spent so much time together that he surely must know she enjoyed his company. Perhaps it was because this would be the first time they'd done something on their own, something that might be construed as a date.

As a flush stole its way to her cheeks, Gillian hoped TJ would not notice. She was acting like a schoolgirl, blushing at the thought of a date with a handsome man. This wasn't a date, she told herself firmly. It was two friends spending time together. Nothing more.

She gave TJ a bright smile. "I'd love to go, as long as I can drive. You know how I feel about your bike." It hadn't been her imagination. Her acceptance made him relax.

"Fair enough. How soon can you be ready?"

"Give me ten minutes to change clothes." High heels and a skirt were standard church garb, but they were definitely not what she wanted to wear to look for whatever those birds were called.

Nine and a half minutes later she approached her car, dressed in jeans, a long-sleeved shirt, a broad-brimmed hat, and boots, carrying a cooler in her left hand.

"What's in that?" TJ asked with a look at the cooler. Like Gillian, he'd changed into casual clothes and a Stetson.

"Sustenance. When Carmen heard what we were doing, she insisted on packing us a snack."

Gillian wouldn't admit that she'd called Carmen to see if she had anything they could take with them. Unsure of both how long they'd be gone and the state of TJ's finances, Gillian didn't want him to feel obligated to buy a meal. The T-shirts he'd bought for the work party had not been cheap, but when she'd offered to share the cost, TJ had refused, saying he wasn't on poverty row yet.

He hefted the cooler and grinned at the weight. "Knowing Carmen, there's enough in here for four."

"At least." With the cooler in the trunk and TJ's camera equipment on the backseat, Gillian settled behind the steering wheel. "Which way are we headed?" she asked as she backed out of the parking area.

"North and then west. I read that Lost Maples is one of the best places to see golden-cheeked warblers, but Greg said it's liable to be crowded on a weekend. That's why he told me about a rancher who lets a few birders onto his property. Apparently the rancher and his wife even have a bird feeder that's supposed to attract its share of the rarer species."

"Once again, that sounds like my kind of bird-watching." Gillian had heard birders spent a lot of time in insect-laden swampy areas, standing motionless to avoid disturbing the birds. Sitting by a feeder would be much easier, especially for a confirmed city dweller like Gillian.

Less than half an hour later, she pulled into the drive that led to James and Andrea Kulak's ranch and found the middle-aged couple waiting on their front porch. Both were dressed in jeans, Western shirts, wide-brimmed hats, and hand-tooled boots. Wide smiles completed their outfits.

"Welcome!" Andrea called as Gillian and TJ climbed out of the car. "Greg said you're novices, so if there's anything you want to know, just ask." She nodded with approval when she saw TJ's field guide and the water bottles Gillian attached to her fanny pack. "Looks like you're well prepared."

James led the way to the back of the ranch house and pointed toward what appeared to be a three-sided shed behind the bird feeder. "We built the blind so the birds would be less likely to be spooked by visitors. They're used to us, but you never know about strangers."

He showed them the built-in benches inside the small structure and the viewing holes cut at different heights to accommodate both children and adults. "Sometimes the kids get so excited that they scare the birds away, but most of them come back."

While James was talking, TJ's camera was clicking as he took a few pictures of both the blind and the Kulaks.

"If you want to be more adventuresome," Andrea said as they walked back outside, "that path leads to a thicket where we've had good luck. James put a bench in the best spot."

Gillian was impressed with the care they lavished on strangers. "Thank you."

"Just make yourselves at home, and don't rush. I always tell folks that bird-watching is a lesson in patience." James hooked his arm in his wife's and turned toward the house.

Gillian smiled at the sight of the couple's obvious affection. "Thanks again. This looks like fun."

And it was. She and TJ spent half an hour in the blind, not talking but communicating with gentle touches as they spotted a new bird. When activity at the feeder diminished, they ventured into the thicket, taking advantage of the Kulaks' bench. Though they saw no birds with golden cheeks, she and TJ spotted several varieties of woodpeckers, a number of Swainson's hawks soaring as they searched for food, and more dragonflies than Gillian could count.

"So, what's the tally?" she asked when two hours had passed.

"Number of birds or species?" TJ turned, focusing the camera on her. When she gave him an exaggerated frown, he took several shots in quick succession.

"Neither. I was curious about how many pictures you'd taken."

He glanced at his camera. "Two hundred and seventeen."

"You can delete the last few." Though she'd had her portrait taken dozens of times, Gillian had never been comfortable with casual shots. "Are you ready for a break?"

"Any time you are. In fact, I'm ready to head back if you are."

Gillian nodded. "I thought we might share the snack I brought with the Kulaks. A small thank-you for letting us come."

The older couple seemed pleased by the invitation to join them. Andrea brought out what she called proper plates and glasses, while James looked at a few of the pictures TJ had taken, identifying the birds.

"That's a pretty bird," James said with a chuckle. "You caught her essence."

"Let me see." Andrea's laugh blended with her husband's. "I have a feeling you're going to be in the doghouse over this, TJ, but I like it." She turned to Gillian. "That little pout is absolutely adorable."

She turned the camera so Gillian could see the picture of herself feigning a pout. While she would not call it adorable, Gillian had to admit that TJ had captured something she hadn't expected to see on her face: peace. While she and TJ had been looking for birds, Gillian had been so focused on the moment that she had thought of nothing other than the pleasure of being outdoors in a particularly beautiful location.

"Like I said, a pretty bird." James clapped TJ on the shoulder. "You're a first-rate photographer. Ever think about selling your pictures?"

It was a question Gillian had wanted to ask the night TJ

had shown his pictures of the national parks, but it had been forgotten after the revelation that he was a widower.

He nodded. "My wife used to tell me I should, but I haven't done anything about it. Too busy taking the pictures to think about marketing them." He looked from James to Andrea. "If you show me which ones you'd like, I'd be happy to send you prints."

"That's very generous of you," Andrea said with a warm smile, "but I wonder if you'd send us electronic files instead. James bought me one of those electronic picture frames. I was hoping to make a slide show of all of our birds." She glanced at the camera in TJ's hands. "Your pictures are better than the ones I've taken."

Though TJ said nothing, Gillian noticed that his shoulders straightened and he held his head a bit higher. Was it possible he didn't realize the extent of his talent? She found that hard to believe, and yet his reaction seemed as if he weren't accustomed to praise. That was a shame. Gillian knew firsthand how important recognition was and resolved to make a special effort to let TJ know just how special he was.

While Andrea and James scrolled through the pictures, making notes of the ones they'd like, they sampled the bar cookies, lemonade, and sweet tea Gillian had brought. Carmen had included an assortment of blondies, chocolate chip squares, and Gillian's favorite, oatmeal raisin bars.

"These are especially good," Andrea said, pointing to the oatmeal raisin bars. "Did you make them?"

Gillian shook her head, noting that the men seemed to prefer the chocolate chip squares. "I'd like to take credit, but they're Carmen St. George's work. She's an extraordinary cook. Carmen tweaks an ordinary recipe a little and turns it into something special."

Gillian made a mental note to send Andrea a copy of the Rainbow's End cookbook. She'd already purchased half a dozen copies to share with some of her college friends.

TJ and James exchanged looks before shrugging. "All I know is that these chocolate things taste mighty good," James said. "You're welcome to come back anytime."

Andrea gave her husband's arm a playful swat. "Now, James, you're making it sound like they need to bring food." She turned toward Gillian and TJ. "You're welcome anytime. No strings attached."

When they'd eaten the last of the cookies and emptied the thermoses, TJ and Gillian said their farewells and climbed back into the car.

"That was fun," Gillian said as they bumped down the rutted drive. "Thanks for inviting me."

"I thought you might like a rest after yesterday."

"That was fun too, just a different kind of fun."

TJ tapped his fingers on the armrest, keeping time to the music. When he'd asked if she minded if he played the radio, Gillian hadn't protested, although she was thankful he hadn't chosen classical music. It was easier to listen to something that didn't bring back memories of her former life.

"The senior center is a great idea," TJ said. "I hope you're proud of the way it's turning out."

She was. "It fills a need, and that makes it important to me. It would be nice if my dad approved, but that's not going to happen." Why had she shared that with TJ? There was no reason for him to know how Dad had reacted when she told him what she was doing.

TJ turned and stared at Gillian, not trying to hide his surprise. "Why wouldn't he approve? Doesn't he believe in philanthropy?"

"Oh, he does indeed, just a different variety. Dad and my brother serve on the boards of charitable foundations, and every time there's a charity gala, they're there. For them, philanthropy is about writing checks, not getting your hands dirty." And then there was Dad's insistence that she should spend her time with younger people, searching for a husband.

TJ's expression said he didn't understand. "Every endeavor needs both."

"You don't need to convince me." Though she'd been tired last night, she'd also been filled with satisfaction. Not only was the senior center taking shape, but she and TJ had given the Firefly Valley kids a chance to contribute to the town. It had been a good day. A very good day, even if Dad did not agree.

"I'm sorry to have dumped that on you. I guess no family is perfect."

"I still can't believe your dad wouldn't approve. You're finding a new direction for your life."

Gillian sighed. That was part of the problem. She wasn't going in the direction Dad wanted. "I wish that were true. Everything I'm doing here in Texas feels good, but I know it's temporary. I'm not sure what I'll do when I leave."

Unbidden, the image of herself holding a baby in her arms flitted through Gillian's mind. Where had that come from? Surely it wasn't because she knew that was the one sure way to gain Dad's approval. Nor could it be because of the dreams she'd had of herself and TJ sharing tender moments. There was only one logical explanation: she had been spending so much time with Kate.

25

So, what do you think, Marisa? Am I right?" Kate shifted in her chair, the smile that followed her quick grimace telling Gillian the baby's latest kick had been harder than expected. When Gillian saw Kate enter Marisa's office after breakfast, she'd joined them, wanting to give them both a quick update on her plans for the center.

"Are you right about what?" she asked.

Kate shook her head slowly. "You always did have the worst timing. Or maybe your ears were burning and you knew we were talking about you. Before you so rudely interrupted us, I was asking Marisa if she saw the same things I did. I think you look—and act—like a woman in love."

Gillian stared at her best friend. Not once in the more than twenty years she'd known Kate had she made that accusation.

"Me? In love? I don't think so." It was true that she'd enjoyed her time with Mike and that she'd had a silly dream about TJ, but that wasn't love. That was the kind of thing that could be blamed on eating too many s'mores too close to her bedtime.

"You're definitely mistaken," Gillian said, her voice a little louder than she'd planned. It was ridiculous to be so flustered by Kate's speculation.

Marisa nodded. "Shakespeare was right. The lady doth protest too much."

"She's always been slow to recognize her own feelings."

"I thought you two were my friends." Gillian looked from Kate to Marisa and back. "I wanted to discuss the center, not my nonexistent love life."

Kate exchanged a conspiratorial glance with Marisa. "All right. Tell us how you're turning it from dingy to dynamite."

As Gillian started to explain, she heard a cough and the sound of footsteps outside Marisa's office. "Should I close the door?"

Marisa, who'd had a clear view of whoever had passed by, seemed to be struggling to contain a smile. "No need. Now tell us . . ."

Thankful to be on familiar ground, Gillian did.

It was six hours later, and though she knew anyone who heard her would cringe, Gillian couldn't help humming while she painted. So what if she couldn't carry a tune when she sang or hummed? Days like this simply demanded a way to express her joy.

Once she'd diverted Kate and Marisa from the subject of romance, she'd had an exceptionally good morning. Not only was there a steady stream of customers at the bookstore, many of whom wanted to discuss the senior center, but Sheila and Linda had volunteered to babysit so the woman who used to run the store during the day could come in for the rest of the week. That meant Gillian could devote herself to getting the center ready.

"We told Marisa it's the least we can do since you're doing so much for us," Linda had announced when she and Sheila stopped by the store, telling her to expect Alexa. "Besides, we love little Nathan, and Alexa needs a break."

And so Gillian had changed into her oldest jeans and an inexpensive shirt, arranged her hair in a bun, and covered it with what had to be the ugliest hat she'd ever seen. She would have taken her chances with paint speckles, but she couldn't disappoint Linda.

When she'd presented Gillian with the hat, Linda had insisted it was perfect for painting. Now, three hours later, Gillian stared at the ceiling, searching for any spots she might have missed. Though she suspected her face was as paint-speckled as her hands, her hair was protected, and the ceiling was a beautiful uniform shade of eggshell.

When she'd consulted them, both Kate and Marisa had agreed an eggshell ceiling would complement the light ecru walls she envisioned and would make the room seem light, no matter the time of day. Situated on the west side of the street, the building received morning sun but, thankfully, not the brunt of the afternoon heat.

Convinced she hadn't missed any spots, Gillian placed the roller in the pan and began to climb down the ladder.

"Ms. Hodge?"

Gillian turned, her heart pounding at the unexpected greeting. "I'm sorry. I didn't hear you."

The woman who'd entered the building so quietly stood a good half foot taller than Gillian. Her sister-in-law would have declared her features coarse, her frame large-boned, and her hair carrot-red rather than a becoming shade of auburn, but Lisa wasn't here. What Gillian saw was intelligent gray eyes and a friendly smile.

"I didn't want to disturb you while you were on the ladder," the woman said, extending her hand. "I'm Emma Ingersoll, Dupree's building inspector."

Gillian frowned as she glanced at her right hand. "I don't think you really want to shake my hand right now. Let me clean up a bit and we can talk." A couple minutes later, she emerged from the bathroom, her hands now free of paint, the ugly hat left behind.

"I'm glad to meet you," Gillian said, giving Emma Ingersoll's hand a firm shake. "Your assistant said you'd be coming by to inspect."

Emma nodded. "I read your application for a permit, and everything seems to be in order. The electrician will be in tomorrow to check the wiring and smoke alarms, but I doubt there'll be a problem. Sam had this building brought up to code when he upgraded the bootery."

For what felt like the hundredth time, Gillian gave thanks for Sam Dexter's foresight. He'd saved the center a substantial amount of time and money.

Emma walked around the room, keying notes into her tablet. "You've made remarkable progress," she said when she'd completed the circuit.

"I had a lot of help."

"So I heard." When she smiled, Emma was almost pretty. "Folks are excited about what's happening. They feel more involved with this than either the new apartment complex or Drew Carroll's buildings."

"This is a much smaller project." The others were major new construction, neither of which lent itself to amateur workers. And because they were big projects, their time frames were substantially longer. It was more difficult to maintain enthusiasm for a project that was a year from completion than one that would last only a week or two.

"True." Emma opened the door to the bathroom and looked around. "You're fortunate this is ADA compliant."

Gillian nodded. "I couldn't believe my luck with that. More than almost any place in town, we need to be able to accommodate walkers and wheelchairs." She made a mental note that the center's van had to be fitted with a wheelchair lift.

When they'd met this morning, Kate had said she and Greg

had discussed Gillian's idea of providing door-to-door transportation and wanted to buy at least one van for the center.

"If you need a second one, we'll pay for that too," Kate had said. "Just make sure you buy only the best." Like Linda and Sheila, Kate had claimed it was the least she and Greg could do to support a project that would benefit the town.

"Besides, Sally will get a kick out of riding in the van. She hasn't driven since she moved to Texas—claims she likes being chauffeured."

Both Kate and Gillian had chuckled at the idea of feisty, independent Sally pretending to be a lady of leisure.

"You'll see plenty of walkers," Emma agreed. "A few of our seniors have motorized carts, but they're no wider than a standard wheelchair, so you shouldn't have a problem once you get the ramp installed."

Though the front door was only a single step above the sidewalk, that was one step too many for a person in a wheelchair. When she'd heard which building Gillian had chosen, Marisa had enlisted her father's help, and Eric—who seemed to be a wiz at everything from motors to ramps—had begun constructing a barrier-free entrance to the senior center.

"What are you planning to do here?" Emma asked as she and Gillian entered the kitchen. For the first time, the inspector appeared concerned.

"I thought we'd provide snacks and the midday meal, maybe an occasional dinner if we have a special evening event."

The frown lines around Emma's mouth deepened, and she shook her head. "I'm afraid you won't be doing that without a lot of work." She gestured, encompassing the whole room. "This doesn't meet the restaurant code. I don't want to discourage you, Gillian, but that's a big deal."

She tapped her tablet and brought up a lengthy document. "If you want to provide meals, here's the list of what you can and cannot do."

Though she knew Emma was only doing her job, Gillian felt as if someone had punched her solar plexus. "I really want to be able to serve food. You know it's hard for some people to get around. If they have to leave when they're hungry, they might not come back."

In talking to the managers of other senior centers, Gillian had learned that some members spent the whole day there, using it as a substitute for the jobs that had once occupied their time. Others, particularly those who lived alone, came each day at noon for the camaraderie as well as the meal.

"I understand." Emma scrutinized the kitchen before shaking her head again. "Unfortunately, this is not an area where I can be flexible. You cannot prepare food here."

She looked around, frowning at the outdated appliances. "My guess is that you're looking at a substantial investment and at least two months' delay to bring this up to code."

The money was not as much of a problem as the delay. Gillian knew Kate and Greg would pay for the renovation, but she didn't want to delay the opening by two months. In two months, neither she nor TJ would still be here.

There had to be a solution. As she replayed Emma's words, a glimmer of hope lodged inside Gillian. "Could I serve food," she asked, stressing the verb, "if it was prepared elsewhere?"

Pursing her lips, Emma scrolled through the document. When she finished, she looked up at Gillian, a smile lighting her gray eyes. "That could work. Anyone who handles food will need to wear aprons, gloves, and hairnets; there can't be any overnight storage of perishables, and you shouldn't let anyone other than the servers use the kitchen. If you can live with that, I don't see a problem with serving meals. Of course, there's still the issue of proper preparation."

Relief settled over Gillian, soothing her like yesterday's bird-watching adventure. "What you've outlined sounds reasonable. I'll hire someone who's already licensed to prepare the food."

"Other than Carmen St. George, there's only one person in Dupree."

"Russ Walker." Gillian completed the sentence.

"Exactly."

"That's who I had in mind. I think I'll pay him a visit. I wanted a milk shake, anyway. Can I interest you in one?"

Emma shook her head, switched off her tablet, and headed out the door. "Have fun with Russ."

Gillian did. The milk shake was as delicious as the last one, and when Gillian told Russ what she had in mind, the man's face glowed as if she'd turned on a light somewhere inside him. It didn't take long to discover the reason.

"I've got a list of people who're looking for work," he told her. "It's no secret that I couldn't afford to hire them, but now . . ." He poured the last of the shake into Gillian's glass. "Based on everything I've heard—and believe, me I've heard a lot—you'll have at least a dozen folks there every day, especially if they know they'll be getting a hot meal." His smile widened. "I think I'll hire two part-timers. That way I'll have backup. So, when do you want to start?"

"Monday." When Russ didn't react, Gillian added, "A week from today."

"That soon?"

She shrugged and gave him a wide grin. "Why not? I'll want food for the opening ceremony—enough to feed most of the town—and then a meal for the seniors at noon. Can you do all that?"

Matching her grin, he slapped a hand on the counter. "I can't think of a single reason why not." When they'd finished their discussion of the type of food to serve, he said, "I'll have those positions filled before the day ends, and by next week, the new staff will be trained. No problem. No problem at all."

While Gillian sipped her shake, Russ entertained her with stories of Dupree's past, acting as if he were one of the founding fathers rather than a man only in his midthirties. Church socials, Fourth of July picnics, Christmas parades—nothing was too big or too small to have escaped Russ's notice. Gillian suspected he could—and would—continue talking until closing time, but she had other things to do.

"This was superb," she said as she drained the last drop of milk shake. "May I have my bill?"

He shook his head. "Absolutely not. That's on the house. It's the least I can do."

Smiling at the number of times she'd heard that particular phrase today, Gillian left the small diner. She'd taken only a few steps toward the senior center when she heard a man calling her name. Turning, she saw Pastor Bill approaching.

"Do you have a minute?" he asked. "There's something I want to discuss with you."

Gillian glanced at her watch. "Can we do it walking? TJ's going to be at the center any minute, and I don't want to keep him waiting."

"TJ, the RV—" The minister broke off abruptly and nodded. "Yes, of course we can walk and talk." He matched his pace to Gillian's. "I'm glad you have help with the center. It's a fine thing you're doing for Dupree."

"It's a fine thing for me too. I'm enjoying being busy."

Pastor Bill greeted two of his parishioners as they headed for the diner, then turned back to Gillian. "It's good you like being busy, because that's what I wanted to talk to you about. Mrs. Bautz—she's the church organist—has a new grandson in Dallas. She left today to visit him and won't be back for a week." He paused for a second. "I was going to come up with some fancy appeal to convince you, but I might as well cut to the chase. Will you take her place on Sunday?"

The milk shake that had tasted so delicious only minutes ago began to curdle in her stomach. How could Pastor Bill even ask her to do that? He knew her career was over.

Though Gillian wanted to shout her refusal, she forced herself to take a deep breath. Perhaps that would slow the pounding of her heart and help her give a more measured response. If she'd learned anything from her father, it was the importance of being polite.

"I haven't played in public since my accident," she said when her heart had resumed its normal rhythm. "The truth is, I haven't played very much at all. My right hand will never be the way it was a year ago."

She looked at the scars that were the only visible reminders of the accident. The badly shattered bones had healed better than anyone had thought possible that first day. Unfortunately, her tendons had not recovered as well.

"I'm no longer a professional musician."

Pastor Bill looked as if he'd expected that answer. His expression was warm and friendly, not judgmental. "This isn't Carnegie Hall," he said mildly.

"True, but . . ." Gillian looked down at her hands, wondering if the right one would betray her if she tried to play a hymn.

The first time she'd tried some simple five-finger dexterity exercises, her index and ring fingers had refused to cooperate, and she'd pushed the bench away from the piano as tears had streamed down her cheeks. Though therapy had helped, she had had to face the reality that what had once been second nature to her would now always be a struggle and that on bad days she would sound like a first-year student.

Gillian was about to give the minister an unconditional refusal when the memory of yesterday's service flashed through her mind. The hymns had been joyous musical offerings of praise. While the congregation could have sung a cappella, it wouldn't have been the same. They might have struggled to stay on key, and even if they had managed to follow the melody, the hymns would not have sounded as beautiful without the organ.

If she refused, Gillian knew that she would be disappointing more than Pastor Bill and the congregation. She would also be disappointing God. He'd given her a talent, and now he was giving her another chance to use it.

"All right," she said, feeling her spirits rise as she pronounced the words. "I'll do it."

The minister grinned. "Thank you. You won't regret it."

26

"This looks good if I say so myself." Gillian smiled as TJ gestured toward the newly painted walls of the senior center. He'd come as soon as the school day had ended, intending to help her, and had been surprised that she was almost finished with the last wall.

"I agree." Though this was only the primer, the improvement was dramatic. The formerly blotchy walls were now a uniform white. Though she was as paint-speckled as she'd been when she worked on the ceiling, Gillian didn't mind. Paint was an occupational hazard and one that was easily remedied.

She headed for the kitchen, gave her hands a quick scrub, and opened the small refrigerator. "One more day and we should be done. The furniture is scheduled to be delivered on Friday."

Marisa had ordered that, saying she and Blake wanted to be part of the project. While his pockets weren't as deep as Greg's, Blake's bestselling novels had given him and Marisa financial security. "Then all that's left will be the finishing touches."

Accepting the soda Gillian offered him, TJ asked, "Like what?" He popped open the can and took a long swig.

She led the way back into the main room. "I'm still debating over whether to have curtains or shades, but I definitely want some artwork for the walls."

Though she hadn't expected a reaction from him, TJ seemed pleased by her answer. "I've got an idea for that—the artwork, that is. The curtains are all yours." He took another drink of soda in what Gillian suspected was a deliberate attempt to increase suspense. She'd watched him tell stories often enough to recognize what she'd heard described as a pregnant pause.

After yet another sip, TJ said, "I wondered if you'd like prints of some of the pictures I took at the work party. I thought the seniors might enjoy seeing the change from dingy to dynamite."

It was a good idea, much better than the travel posters she'd considered. "I like the idea, but I have to tell you that you sound just like Kate. Dingy to dynamite was the way she described the work we're doing."

A mischievous grin lit TJ's face. "I might have overheard her say that."

Gillian felt blood rush to her face as she remembered the footsteps she'd heard outside Marisa's office. How much had TJ heard? She wouldn't ask.

"Which pictures did you have in mind?" Gillian asked, determined to pretend that she wasn't concerned by what TJ might or might not have overheard. If he'd just been walking by Marisa's office, he'd probably caught only the tail end of the discussion. There was no reason to think he'd overheard Kate's assertion that Gillian was in love.

"I thought you should select them." TJ glanced at his watch, apparently focused on nothing other than artwork. Excellent. "If we pick them out tonight, I can order the prints and have them framed by Saturday. There's a place in Blytheville that's supposed to be first rate. One of their claims to fame is having a great selection of frames."

Relieved by the innocuous direction of the conversation, Gillian studied the walls, trying to imagine them with pictures hanging on them. "How many do you think we should have and what size?"

She and TJ were discussing the pros and cons of fewer but larger pictures when Gillian's phone rang. She glanced at the caller ID, intending to let it go to voice mail, but when she saw the caller was Mike, she excused herself and walked to the corner of the room. He deserved better than voice mail.

"Hi, Mike. Can I call you back? I'm in the middle of something." Though their last call had been brief, Gillian didn't want to make the assumption that this one would be equally short, nor did she want to leave TJ standing around while she talked to Mike. That would be rude.

"I'll make it quick," Mike promised. "The problem with a callback is I'm going to be hard to reach. This is turning into another one of those weeks when there's not even time to sleep."

His voice was warm, friendly, and filled with more than a hint of frustration. "I was calling to invite you to spend Sunday with me and my family. I think you'd like them, and I really want them to meet you."

Gillian blinked. Dinner at a fancy restaurant was one thing, but an invitation to spend a day with his family was taking their relationship to a new level. *He's smitten.* Kate's words echoed through Gillian's brain. Was she right? And if she was, how did Gillian feel about that? Though her brain was whirling, she was unable to answer either question.

"The whole family goes to church together," Mike continued, "and then Mom fixes a big meal. After that, we just hang out."

Still unsure of her feelings, Gillian realized she had a valid reason for refusing. "That sounds like fun, but I'm afraid I can't. I've agreed to play the organ here next Sunday."

"That's not a problem." Mike wasn't accepting the excuse. "I'll pick you up afterwards. In fact, maybe I'll come early and attend your service. Maybe I'll even bring the family along. I'm sure they'd enjoy hearing you play."

The thought of Mike's family coming to Dupree simply to hear her at the organ bothered Gillian. Though the evening at Strawberry Chantilly had felt like a flashback to her former life, the simple fact was that she was no longer Gillian Hodge, renowned pianist. On Sunday she would be nothing more than a substitute organist.

"I'd rather you didn't." Sensing Mike wouldn't give up easily, Gillian made a quick decision. "Getting together later would be nice."

When she'd ended the call, she turned back to TJ, who'd been staring at the far wall as if fascinated by the primer. "Sorry about that."

As he turned, she saw that he had clenched his fists and wondered why. Surely he didn't mind her talking to Mike.

"I couldn't help overhearing," TJ said, his voice betraying no chagrin that he'd been an eavesdropper. "You're going to play the organ?"

Feeling oddly disappointed that he was bothered by that rather than her date with Mike, Gillian nodded. "Yes. Do you think it's a bad idea?" The clenched fists and stiff posture seemed to indicate that he did.

TJ unclenched his fists. "Not at all. I'm just surprised. I didn't think you were giving public performances."

"It's not a performance," Gillian protested. "Pastor Bill needed a substitute organist and asked me."

"I thought you were a pianist."

Gillian nodded. "That was my primary instrument, but I also studied the organ when I was at Juilliard. The flute and violin too, although I certainly didn't excel at either of those."

TJ did not look convinced. "Be that as it may, once word gets out—and it will, because everyone will be speculating on who's going to replace the regular organist—the church will be packed. After all, it's not every day people get to hear Gillian Hodge in person."

Though Mike hadn't used those exact words, the thought had been the same, making Gillian wonder if she'd made a mistake in agreeing to be Mrs. Bautz's substitute.

"This isn't a concert," she said. "It's a church service. People will come to worship."

TJ didn't look convinced. "Maybe, and maybe not."

"Does that mean you'll come?" If her playing brought TJ back to church, Gillian would have no reservations.

He stared at her, his expression firm. "Sorry, but no. Not even for you."

"You look like you could use some company," Greg said as he joined TJ on his cabin's porch. Ever since he'd returned from Firefly Valley, TJ had been sitting on the porch, staring into the distance. He shouldn't care—he didn't care, he told himself—that Gillian had another date with Mike or that her best friend was convinced she was in love. Gillian was a beautiful, loving woman, and Mike Tarkett was the kind of man she would be attracted to.

"I'm afraid I'm not very good company right now." Perhaps Greg would take the hint and leave.

No such luck. "A problem with the Firefly Valley kids?" he asked as he settled onto the second Adirondack chair.

"No. The problem's me."

"My guess is it's something to do with Gillian."

Though he hadn't planned to respond, hoping Greg would tire of silence and leave TJ alone, he found himself saying, "Why do you say that?"

"Because you look the way I do when Kate and I have a falling out. I've seen the way you look at Gillian, and it's clear she's more than a friend."

Anger bubbled up from deep inside TJ. Anger that he hadn't

been able to hide his feelings. Anger that Greg, a man he'd known for only a few weeks, had been able to read him so easily. Anger that his life hadn't turned out the way he'd expected. "She's just a friend. She can't be anything more." And he was a fool to wish it could be otherwise.

"Because of Mike Tarkett?"

It was true TJ didn't like Gillian having another date with Mike, but that wasn't the crux of the problem. Even if Mike were out of the picture, TJ couldn't do anything about the tender feelings he harbored for Gillian. It was wrong to even admit how often he thought of her, how he wished he had something to offer her.

"Mike's not the problem." TJ shook his head. "I am. Deb was the love of my life." With her gone, he was only half a man. The good part of him, the heart of him, had been buried along with his wife. Like Gillian's father, he was a one-woman man.

Greg leaned forward, resting his hands on his knees. "And you don't think God gives us second chances at love?"

"God's given me what I deserve, and there are no second chances included in that." The words burst out of TJ with more venom than he'd intended. He thought of apologizing but couldn't force the words past his lips. That would only prolong a conversation he didn't want to be having.

Greg was silent for a long moment. "I see." He let out what sounded like a sigh. "So, tell me this: if you'd been the one to die, would you have wanted Deb to spend the rest of her life alone if she met someone she could love?"

"Of course not." The idea was preposterous. "I'd want her to be happy."

"Then why do you think she wouldn't want the same thing for you?"

27

"I think I should call you Wonder Woman."

Gillian turned at the sound of his voice, her pulse beginning to race at the sight of TJ standing in the doorway of the center. How silly. She wasn't a schoolgirl in the throes of a crush.

"I thought I was going to spend the afternoon painting," he said, "but it's obvious I'm too late. Again." He shook his head in mock dismay. "When the staff meeting was cancelled, I was sure I'd get here in time to help."

Gillian shrugged, trying to feign nonchalance when all the while her heart was pounding. Though she'd been pleased to finish the painting before school ended, pride had nothing to do with the dance her heart was performing. "I had a whole day without interruptions."

Stepping inside, TJ settled his fists on his hips as if he were exasperated. "Are you calling me an interruption? I thought you were glad to see me yesterday." The mocking tone of voice belied his belligerent posture.

"No and yes." When he said nothing, Gillian continued. "No, I wasn't calling you an interruption. Emma Ingersoll was here for the better part of half an hour yesterday, and I spent time at the Sit 'n' Sip. Those were interruptions." She flashed TJ a smile that said she knew he had only been kidding. "Yes, I was glad to see you yesterday, and I'm glad to see you today."

Gillian was babbling, something she rarely did, but the sight of TJ had sent her into a tizzy. She was overreacting, probably the result of Kate's continued assertion that she was in love. As if that weren't enough, one of the Matchers had stopped her as she was unlocking the center and had asked about Mike. But it wasn't Mike who Gillian was thinking about now.

She'd lain awake last night, replaying the day. Though she still had concerns about being the organist on Sunday based on both Mike and TJ's reactions, the image that whirled through her brain and kept her from sleeping was the expression on TJ's face when they'd returned from Firefly Valley and had sorted through the pictures he'd taken.

Nothing in his voice had seemed different as they'd chosen a dozen photos to hang on the walls, but twice Gillian had caught him looking at her, his eyes filled with what appeared to be wonder, as if he were seeing her differently. Though she couldn't imagine what had caused the difference, Gillian had found herself responding with brighter than normal smiles. Now he was here, sending tingles through her body.

"You don't need me today." TJ gestured toward the walls with their drying paint.

"Maybe not to paint, but I could use a cheer team." It was only an excuse. The reality was, Gillian wanted a reason for TJ to stay. She wanted to explore these new feelings and see if they were something more than a passing fancy. She nodded at the walls. "How do you think they turned out?"

"Now who's being insecure? You've been breathing too many paint fumes if you think this looks anything other than phenomenal."

TJ walked around the room slowly, apparently inspecting every square inch she'd covered with paint. "I couldn't have done better myself. Of course," he said with a self-deprecating smile when the circuit was complete, "that's not saying much. After the time I tipped over a full gallon of paint, my mother wouldn't let me near a brush or roller. I was the one-man cleanup crew, but you haven't even left that for me."

His eyes narrowed, and the grin changed to a mischievous smile. "I spoke too soon." Leaning forward, he scraped the bridge of Gillian's nose with his fingernail.

"Ouch."

"Sorry, but you missed a spot. I didn't mean to hurt you, but I doubted you'd want to go out in public looking anything less than perfect."

Gillian smiled at the idea of anyone considering her perfect. She wasn't. Far from it.

Her eyes widened as TJ kissed the tips of his index and middle fingers, then pressed them to her nose. It was hardly a romantic gesture, and yet it caused her pulse to accelerate again. It seemed as if mere proximity to TJ was enough to put her senses on high alert.

"Better now?" he asked. "That was my mother's cure for cuts and scrapes once I turned seven or eight. She knew I didn't want her to kiss me, so she figured that touching me with fingers she'd kissed was the next best thing."

Gillian wasn't like the boy TJ had been. She wouldn't have minded being kissed, not even if it was only the tip of her nose, so long as TJ was the one doing the kissing. But it seemed he wasn't interested. She must have been mistaken in believing something had changed and that he'd seen her as a woman, not simply a friend, last night.

"Thanks," Gillian said as calmly as she could when a lump the size of Texas had settled in her throat. "Do I look presentable now?" Thankfully, as far as she could tell, her face had not flushed despite the turmoil inside her.

"You do indeed, Wonder Woman. I think we should celebrate

your accomplishment. What do you say to a congratulatory milk shake?"

"That sounds perfect!"

She and TJ were halfway to the Sit 'n' Sip when a couple emerged from the diner. At first Gillian paid them little attention. School was over, and it was not uncommon to see teenage couples in town. But when the couple descended the two shallow steps to the sidewalk, Gillian stopped abruptly and stared, shocked by the identity of the couple.

She touched TJ's arm to get his attention. "That's obviously Brianna, but who's the guy? I've never seen him before." And that bothered Gillian. Why was Brianna, who'd declared her intention of marrying Todd, with someone else?

This man—for he was a man rather than a teenage boy—bore no resemblance to Todd. He had brown hair instead of blond, was a couple inches taller than Todd, and a good fifty pounds heavier with muscles straining at the seams of his T-shirt.

TJ glanced at the couple before nodding slowly. "His name is Pete Darlington. He's part of a new construction crew that's working on Drew Carroll's complex. One reason you haven't seen him in town is they only started here last week."

Gillian felt her eyes widen in amazement. Her question about the man's identity had been a rhetorical one. "How'd you learn all that?" She had expected TJ to be as clueless about the strange man's identity as she was.

TJ tipped his hat to the three women who were approaching before he responded. "I took my bike on a spin around town. When I got to the Carroll site, Pete was one of a group of men who wanted to talk about bikes." As if anticipating Gillian's next question, TJ continued. "He seems okay. A little rough around the edges. Not a bad guy, but definitely too old for Brianna."

"I agree. He's got to be in his midtwenties."

The couple were heading for what Gillian assumed was Pete's truck. Even from a distance, Gillian could see the way Brianna appeared to be hanging on Pete Darlington's every word. Questions spiraled through her brain. Where had Brianna met Pete? Why was she attracted to him? And, most of all, what had happened to Todd?

"They probably had a fight."

Despite the concern she couldn't dismiss, laughter bubbled up inside Gillian. "Are you a mind reader? That's twice you've answered questions before I could ask them."

"There are times I wish I could read minds," TJ admitted. "It sure would make teaching easier. But in this case, the answer is simpler. I figured you were wondering the same thing I was: why Todd was no longer in the picture."

"Last week Brianna was ready to marry him."

TJ gave Gillian a knowing smile. "But a week is forever for a teenager. My guess is that Todd did something to annoy Brianna, and now her head's turned by Pete's attention. Besides the obvious appeal of having an older man interested, she's probably using Pete to make Todd jealous."

"That sounds dangerous to me. I know it's a cliché, but Brianna could be playing with fire."

TJ nodded. "Someone needs to set Pete straight."

As the truck bearing Brianna and her new crush raced away, Gillian looked at TJ. "Are you volunteering?"

"Yeah."

"It sounds like infatuation to me." Kate rested her hands on her baby bump and made a visible effort to relax. Though Gillian had thought she was joking about how nervous she was in the obstetrician's waiting room, the pallor of Kate's face as they'd entered the medical arts building had told her it was no joke. For some reason, normally unflappable Kate did not like even routine visits like today's. Gillian hoped it had nothing to do with what happened to her mother, but she wouldn't ask, because that might heighten Kate's anxiety. She was nervous enough as it was.

Normally Greg accompanied Kate and held her hand both literally and figuratively, but today he was in San Antonio at a meeting of area hoteliers. That was why Gillian had asked Linda and Sheila to babysit and Alexa to work at Hill Country Pages so she could accompany Kate.

"Once TJ talks to Pete, it'll be over," Kate continued. "Pete will leave her alone, and Brianna will go back to Todd."

Though she had doubts, Gillian hoped TJ and Kate were right. There had been definite undercurrents at Firefly Valley last night. Brianna and Todd had joined the group, but they'd sat on opposite sides of the campfire, and though Todd's gaze had drifted toward his former girlfriend, Brianna had kept her attention focused on either TJ or the girls at her side.

"How do you know the difference between infatuation and love?" Gillian asked. If she was lucky, Kate would think her question was precipitated by Brianna's situation, not more personal concerns.

Kate closed her eyes for a second as she caressed the bump. "I can't claim to be an expert on either one."

"But you dated a couple guys seriously before you married Greg." And that made Kate an expert compared to Gillian, who'd never progressed to the seriously dating stage.

"You would bring that up, wouldn't you?" The twist of Kate's lips told Gillian she didn't appreciate the direction the conversation had headed. "I loved them, but now I realize I wasn't in love with them."

She uncapped her water bottle and took a sip. "It's a critical difference. I enjoyed being with them, but I wasn't willing to commit when they started talking about marriage." Her brown eyes were warm with mirth as she said, "It's supposed to be the guys who get cold feet, isn't it? Leave it to me to do things differently. I couldn't explain it at the time, and I'm not sure I can even now, but something was holding me back."

Gillian thought about the years Kate had been dating. "Is that the reason I never met them? I was in New York enough times that you could have arranged for us to get together, but you never did." Kate had talked about the two men and had shown Gillian their pictures, but she'd never done more than speak casually about Gillian's meeting either man.

Kate's eyebrows rose, and a flush stained her cheeks. "I hadn't thought you'd be upset by that. I guess I just didn't want to share the time you and I had together with anyone." Her expression turned thoughtful. "That should have been my clue. When I met Greg, I wanted you to meet him. Not to check him out and give your approval but because I wanted my best friend to know the man I love. I wanted you to be friends."

And they were. Before Gillian could do more than nod, the nurse entered the waiting room and nodded at Kate. "The doctor's ready for you."

Kate rose, her previous nervousness apparently gone as she followed the nurse. "This won't take long. Twenty minutes tops."

But that was more time than Gillian needed to ponder Mike's invitation to spend Sunday with his family. Sally had told her when men were serious about a woman, they took her home to meet their mothers. At the time, Gillian had believed that to be an old-fashioned custom. No one did that anymore, or did they? Though Gillian had vague memories of being the flower girl at George's wedding, she had no idea how her brother had approached courtship and when Lisa had first met her future father-in-law.

All that had happened more than twenty years ago. Times had changed. As if that weren't enough, this was Texas, a state noted for its friendliness. In all likelihood, Mike was simply being friendly, offering Gillian a chance for a home-cooked meal and a change of scenery. She had no reason to imagine other motives behind the invitation.

Gillian took a deep breath and switched on her e-reader. Perhaps Patricia Bradley's latest suspense novel would keep her from worrying about Mike and his invitation.

She shouldn't worry. The truth was, she was looking forward to Sunday. If the rest of the Tarkett family was like Mike, it would be a pleasant day. Gillian imagined she'd feel both welcomed and at home with his parents and the aunts, uncles, and cousins who continued the tradition of spending Sunday together. She already knew she enjoyed being with Mike. They had a camaraderie that made her look forward to their time together.

Gillian sighed as her brain refused to concentrate on the words she was trying to read. It was more than silly; it was downright annoying the way her thoughts kept drifting to TJ and the time they spent together.

Why did her heart leap every time she saw TJ? He'd made it clear they had no future. Gillian had never been one to chase after lost causes or pine for something she could not have, but this was different. Though she told her brain there was no reason to cherish every moment she was with TJ, her heart was not listening.

Infatuation. That must be the answer. What she felt was infatuation. Definitely not love.

"Hey, dude, whatcha doing here today?" Pete Darlington called as TJ pulled into the job site. The muscular man was standing next to the construction trailer, a cold soda in his hand. "You gonna let me ride your bike?"

TJ shook his head. "Nope. I wanted to talk to you about Brianna." Though TJ rarely left school during his lunch break, he'd made an exception today, wanting to be certain he saw Pete before Brianna's classes ended.

"Brianna Carter?" The man's innocent air did nothing to reassure TJ.

"I heard you two are seeing a lot of each other."

"So what if we are? There's no law against being friends."

"There is if it goes beyond friendship. She's a minor."

The way Pete blanched confirmed TJ's fear that the man had more than simple friendship in mind.

"You're kidding. She looks . . ."

TJ shook his head. "I wouldn't kid about something like that. She's definitely underage."

Pete held up his hands in surrender. "Hey, man, I don't plan to get into trouble."

As he returned to school, TJ couldn't help noticing that Pete's concern had been for himself and not Brianna.

*

"Do you want to talk about it?" Gillian asked when she entered Brianna's trailer and found the girl with a tear-stained face. Though Brianna had seemed distant last night, she'd attended the campfire. Tonight she'd been conspicuously absent, and that had worried Gillian enough that she'd come looking for her.

"Nope." Brianna shook her head to emphasize her response. "There's nothing you can do. Nothing anybody can do."

Recognizing the despair as a call for help, Gillian settled onto the couch. "Sometimes it helps to talk."

There was a moment of silence before Brianna gave a grudging nod. "Promise you won't tell my mom?"

It was Gillian's turn to shake her head. "I can't make that promise. If I think your life or someone else's is in danger, I'd have to do something."

"It's not my life. It's my heart." Brianna swiped a tear from her cheek. "I love him, but I don't think he loves me anymore."

"Todd?" The boy had looked lovelorn the last time Gillian had seen him.

"Todd?" Brianna spat the name as if it were a curse. "That's over. Todd's a boy. Pete's a man." Brianna's face softened as she looked at Gillian. "I love Pete. He's everything I ever wanted in a man. He's even got a truck."

A truck and a driver's license were an almost irresistible combination for a girl Brianna's age. Add to that the appeal of having caught an older man's attention and it didn't take a genius to understand why Brianna was infatuated with Pete Darlington.

"I'm probably going to sound like your mom, but what do you know about him?"

"I know that he's big and strong and handsome and he makes me feel like I'm the most beautiful woman in the world."

"But he's kind of old, isn't he?" Gillian tried to mute her concern, not wanting to discourage Brianna from confiding in her.

Brianna shook her head again. "He's not old. He's grown up. Oh, Gillian, I want to marry him. He's not like Todd." She wrinkled her nose in disgust. "I wanted to get married this summer, but Todd said we had to wait."

And that, Gillian suspected, was the reason for the rift between them.

Brianna gestured toward the table with its heavy load of magazines and the dust bunny convention underneath. "Pete will take me away from this dump and give me a nice home and we'll be so happy."

But that wouldn't happen, because Natalie would never agree to the marriage, and—thanks to TJ's conversation with him this afternoon—Pete now knew Brianna was far younger than she appeared.

"Then, why are you crying?"

"Because he says we can't do anything until I'm older. Oh, Gillian, I don't want to wait."

TJ smiled at the muted roar of his bike engine. It didn't have the same deep-throated sound as a Harley, but he liked it, in part because the modifications the previous owner had made gave it a distinctive sound. His bike was one of a kind, like Gillian.

His smile faded, and he gripped the handlebars tighter than necessary. This was becoming absurd. Though he was a grown man who knew better, he was acting like one of his students, being distracted by a pretty face. He frowned and shook his head. Gillian was more than a pretty face. She was an intelligent, talented, caring woman. A woman with many depths. A woman any man would be proud to have by his side.

TJ leaned to the right as he rounded a corner a bit faster than he might have had he not been so obsessed with Gillian. Obsessed was a strong word, and yet he couldn't deny that it fit. No matter how he tried to stop it, he found himself daydreaming about her, trying to understand every facet of the woman who'd become such an important part of his life.

Gillian had an intense loyalty to Kate and her grandmother, but there was more to her than that. She obviously cared deeply about complete strangers. Why else would she devote so much energy to the senior center? And look how she'd taken Brianna under her wing. Others might have been put off by the girl's appearance, but Gillian had seen beneath that and was doing everything she could to make sure the girl had a good future.

She was brave too. TJ was certain it had taken a lot of courage to agree to play the church organ, knowing everyone was expecting perfection and that she might not be able to deliver it. A lesser woman would have found an excuse to refuse, but Gillian had not. She'd accepted the challenge, and if TJ was right, she would meet it.

And then there was her giving nature. Though she was a woman of obvious means, she was willing to contribute sweat equity rather than simply writing a check. Even more importantly, she seemed to gain an inordinate amount of pleasure from that sweat equity, almost as if she had been proving something to herself as she painted those walls. Perhaps she had been.

Though he'd planned to stop by the senior center to see if there was anything else Gillian needed, TJ headed for the highway. He needed a couple miles of open road to clear his head. Somehow, some way, he needed to make sense of his thoughts.

He wouldn't deny that Gillian was a woman of contrasts, a woman who fascinated him. He also wouldn't deny that he wanted to spend every day with her. But as Shakespeare said, there was the rub. No matter how he felt about Gillian, TJ knew he had little to offer her.

Mike Tarkett had money, prestige, and social prominence. On top of that, he was a genuinely nice guy who obviously cared for her. He could give Gillian everything she deserved with no strings attached. Mike was the kind of man she should marry.

What did TJ have? Not even a whole heart. Slowly, ever so slowly, he was coming to accept that what Greg had said was true. Deb wouldn't want him to give up a chance at happiness. But that didn't mean TJ was ready to open his heart to another woman, not when all he could give her was a tiny sliver of that heart.

Logic said he should back off, that he should limit their time together to supper and the evenings at Firefly Valley. TJ knew that. But his heart said something quite different.

28

"I can't believe it." Gillian leaned forward, her eyes fixed on the arena. If she minded being at the top of the grandstands, she gave no sign. If this wasn't the way she'd expected to spend a Saturday afternoon, again she gave no sign. Instead, she seemed fascinated by everything going on below. It was TJ who had second thoughts.

He'd told himself to keep his distance. He'd told himself they could be nothing more than friends. He'd even told himself it didn't bother him that Gillian would be spending most of tomorrow with Mike Tarkett and his family. None of those admonitions had had any effect, which was why TJ was seated next to Gillian on what could only be called a date.

Coming here had been a last-minute decision, which was why they had seats in the nosebleed section. Though TJ was not normally impulsive, when he'd seen the ad for a rodeo less than an hour's drive from Dupree, he'd found himself imagining it through Gillian's eyes.

To his surprise, she hadn't needed much persuasion. When he'd mentioned it, a bright smile had lit her face, and she'd confirmed what he'd suspected: she'd never been to a rodeo.

Her obvious eagerness to experience this quintessential western event had told TJ it wasn't a mistake, no matter how his heart might ache. If today brought Gillian pleasure, that was all that mattered.

So far she seemed to be enjoying the day. Gillian had asked about the events during the drive, but once they'd arrived she'd seemed content to simply look around. They'd watched cattle being herded into pens behind the chutes, the arena being groomed by tractors pulling huge spiked rollers, and the stands filling with people wearing everything from jeans and Stetsons to long flowing skirts and flower-bedecked hats that TJ suspected were a fashion faux pas.

Like him, Gillian had worn jeans, a Western shirt with pearl snaps, and a wide-brimmed cowboy-style hat. The difference was, she was wearing boots that looked like they'd come from Sam's Bootery while his were mass-produced. TJ doubted anyone would recognize her as Gillian Hodge, renowned concert pianist. Today she was simply a woman attending her first rodeo.

Her smile left no doubt that she was having fun. "Those guys look just like cowboys from those old Westerns Sally used to watch." Not only were the men clad in regulation cowboy garb, but they were seated on intricately carved saddles atop some of the finest horseflesh TJ had seen. Though this wasn't a major stop on the rodeo circuit, it drew its share of top-ranked contestants.

"Only one problem: the guys from *Bonanza* didn't have cell phones." TJ pointed toward the man engrossed in a conversation.

"I'm going to pretend I don't see that. That way, I can tell myself I'm back in the Wild West."

TJ had never understood why filmmakers and some authors glamorized that period of American history. He'd heard of families taking vacations in covered wagons, forgetting the fact that most of the pioneers on the Oregon Trail had walked beside those wagons rather than riding in the dubious comfort of a Conestoga.

"I assure you this is a twenty-first-century rodeo. If the cell phones aren't enough proof, check out that electronic scoreboard." TJ pointed to the large sign displaying sponsors' products, then smiled at the woman seated next to him. His reservations had been misplaced.

"Ladies and gentlemen," the announcer's voice boomed throughout the arena, "please rise for the presentation of colors."

Two riders entered the arena, one carrying the United States flag, the other the Texas lone star. When they reached the center, the announcer led the audience in the pledge of allegiance followed by a singing of "The Star Spangled Banner." As they took their seats again, TJ noticed Gillian blinking rapidly.

"That's one of those moments that make me proud to be an American," she said, wiping a tear from the corner of her eye.

"I know what you mean. The national anthem never fails to send chills down my spine." Without conscious thought, he reached over and clasped her hand. It felt good—so very good—to be touching her like this, and when she smiled, TJ felt his heart leap. Today was not a mistake. Far from it. Coming here was the best move he'd made in a long time.

As the tie-down roping began, TJ kept Gillian's hand in his. Though her attention was focused on the arena, his gaze rotated between the event and the woman next to him. Watching Gillian watch the calf emerge from the chute and look around as if puzzled over why it was there, was even more fun than staring at the animal. As the audience began to laugh at the calf's indecision, it moved forward another foot. An instant later the cowboy burst from his chute and headed for the calf.

Though the calf ran, it was no match for the cowboy and his well-trained horse. Within seconds, the calf had a rope around its neck. The rider leapt from his horse, picked up the calf, dropped it on its side, tied three legs together, then threw his hands into the air, telling the timekeeper he was done.

"Wow!" Gillian stared at the man and the calf, then at the scoreboard. "What are they waiting for?"

"There's a six-second delay," TJ explained. "If the calf frees itself, the rider is disqualified." But the calf remained on the ground, his legs trussed, and the cowboy garnered the best score yet.

"I can't believe they do all that so quickly," Gillian said, her voice filled with enthusiasm after they'd watched a few more entrants successfully rope their calves.

"Not everyone does." As if on cue, the next rider failed to rope the calf, leading the announcer to call out, "No time."

"There's nothing a contestant hates more than to get a 'no time,'" TJ explained.

Gillian looked down at the line of cowboys waiting for their turn in the chutes. "Why do they do it?"

"You mean other than for sport? They can earn some impressive purses if they're good enough, and there are always the bragging rights. But if you're asking why anyone would want to tie a calf's legs, tie-down roping is like many of the rodeo events. It has its background in ranching. The same skills you just saw are important on a ranch or a cattle drive. A cowboy needs to be able to catch and restrain a calf for branding and even doctoring."

"I hadn't thought about that." Gillian turned toward TJ, her face lit with a mischievous smile. "All right. I'll admit it. Before today I never thought about cattle ranching. I eat steaks and own my share of leather goods, but I never thought about how those things were produced." She gave her new boots a look that told TJ she had a different perspective on cowhide.

"It's a business, always has been," TJ said. "Technology has changed some things, but you're still dealing with animals, and they can be unpredictable. Like this one." He pointed toward the calf running in a zigzag pattern, trying to elude the cowboy. "He doesn't want to be roped." But he was.

Gillian's hand moved within his grip, her fingers lacing with his. "How do you know all this?"

"I'm a Texan."

As he'd hoped, she chuckled. "Don't tell me they teach Rodeo 101 in school."

"Okay. I won't."

Her chuckle turned into a full-fledged laugh.

"This is really fun," she said while the arena was being groomed between events. "I'm so glad you invited me."

They both rose as the family that had been next to them returned carrying paper trays laden with hot dogs, fries, and sodas. When they were once again seated, Gillian's smile broadened. "I mean it, TJ. This is the most fun I've had in years."

Before he knew what was happening, she moved closer, her head tipping to the side as she kissed his cheek. "Thanks."

For a second TJ was too startled to do anything but stare at Gillian. When he'd thought about the day, kisses—even casual ones like this—had not been part of it. Though he'd suffered hugs at the funeral, even the most demonstrative women had seemed to realize he would not welcome a kiss. His wife's lips had been the last to touch him, but now Gillian had changed all that by doing the unexpected.

TJ wasn't certain how long it took him to find his voice and manage to stammer out, "I'm glad you're enjoying the rodeo." It was probably only a second or two, but as he pronounced the last word, he knew he'd done something wrong. Though the change was subtle, TJ saw the light in Gillian's eyes dim ever so little. Somehow he'd hurt her, when that was the last thing he'd intended. He wanted to say something—anything—to restore the gleam, but his brain refused to think of anything other than how good it had felt to have Gillian's lips on his cheek.

Why had she done that? Gillian wished she could rewind the tape and eliminate that foolishly impulsive kiss. She knew TJ wasn't looking for a romantic relationship. They were friends—just friends—and while it was true that hugs and kisses on the cheeks were common among friends, it was obvious she had made TJ uncomfortable. Oh, he'd done his best to hide it, but there was no ignoring the way he'd turned into a stone statue the moment her lips had touched his cheek.

Gillian took a deep breath, trying to convince herself this was a minor glitch, not an earth-shattering event. Though she was sorry she'd embarrassed him, she could not regret the kiss itself. Her lips could still feel the faint whisker stubble, and she could still smell soap and sunblock, ordinary fragrances that combined with the scent that was uniquely TJ to create something unforgettable.

She knew she'd remember the moment her lips had touched his cheek. Perhaps she'd even dream of it. But one thing she would not do was talk about it. Not to TJ, not to anyone.

Settling back in her seat, Gillian searched for a subject to put him at ease. "Did you ever dream of being a rodeo star?" she asked. That seemed likely for a boy growing up in a state with so many champions.

He shook his head. "My dream was owning a motorcycle."

"And now you do."

"Yeah. Next month marks a year."

He said it casually, and yet the simple statement surprised Gillian. "I assumed you'd had it much longer. I don't know much about bikes, but I thought it was older than a year."

"It is. I had my eye on it for ten years, but my wife didn't like motorcycles."

"Smart woman." Though she would not have introduced the subject, now that TJ had, Gillian was grateful for the opportunity to learn more about the woman who still owned TJ's heart. At times Gillian had believed TJ was healing, that his grief was lessening, but his reaction to her kiss had proven how wrong she was. TJ wasn't ready to move on. Perhaps he never would be.

"Deb was a smart woman." He nodded to emphasize his words. "You would have liked her. She wasn't a fancy person, but she had a real knack for getting along with people."

Though TJ stared into the distance for a moment, Gillian knew he wasn't seeing the other side of the arena or the scoreboard. His thoughts were focused on the woman who'd been his wife.

"Everyone who met Deb liked her, even her worst students."

"She was a teacher like you?" Gillian wasn't certain why, but she was surprised. When he'd spoken of his wife before, TJ had focused on her illness, not what she'd done with her life.

"She was a teacher, but not like me." He corrected Gillian's assumption. "Deb was much better. She was born to teach. It came naturally to her, while I always had to work at it. And I didn't always succeed. She did."

Gillian couldn't say whether she heard pride or awe in TJ's voice, but she knew that his wife's teaching skill had had a major impact on him. Perhaps believing he couldn't match her was part of the reason he'd given up teaching.

"Were you both at the same school?"

"Yeah. Deb taught elementary. I was junior high, then high school." TJ stared at his boots as if fascinated by the pattern on their toes before he said, "We did everything together."

"Including rodeos."

"No. Deb never wanted to go." TJ paused for a moment, then turned his gaze toward Gillian. "You're the only woman I've taken to a rodeo."

It was a simple statement, hardly a declaration of love, and yet the warmth welling up inside her surprised Gillian with its intensity. "I feel special," she said softly.

"You are."

Gillian hadn't been this nervous in years. She took a deep breath as she told herself there was no reason for a case of nerves. To her surprise, she'd slept well last night, and if she'd dreamed, she hadn't remembered it. When she'd met TJ for breakfast, he'd been his normal friendly self, telling her he was confident she would play flawlessly but assuring her no one would notice if she made a mistake. It had been a classic pep talk, one she appreciated because it came from TJ, the man who pulled no punches.

Gillian took another deep breath, reminding herself that she'd practiced a few days earlier and was familiar with the organ. It wasn't even as if people would be staring at her while she played. The organ was in the rear of the church as part of a choir loft. Pastor Bill had told her that after considerable debate over the location, the congregation had chosen by the narrowest of margins—one vote—to place the organ and choir out of sight.

"The majority believed our focus should be on the altar and the cross," he told her. "That's the reason we come to this building."

Taking another deep breath, Gillian said a silent prayer that her music would please the One who gave his Son for her.

"Are you ready?"

Her eyes flew open at the sound of the minister's voice. When he'd reviewed the schedule for the morning, he hadn't mentioned that she would see him before the service.

"I am now." The prayer, though brief, had restored her confidence and filled her with peace.

"Good. I saw the first people pulling into the parking lot, so any time you want to start is fine."

Glancing at her watch, Gillian realized this was a full ten minutes before the congregation normally arrived. It was no wonder Pastor Bill had come over to talk to her.

"All right." She placed her fingers on the keyboard and began. Within seconds, she was lost in the beauty of the music.

"You looked like you belonged there," Sally told her an hour and a half later when the church was once more empty. Gillian had switched off the organ and hurried outside, planning to make a quick exit so she'd be ready when Mike came for her.

"How do you know what I looked like?" she asked. "I was behind you."

Sally merely grinned. "You weren't invisible. I imagine almost everyone did what I did and snuck a peek at you." Sally gave Gillian a hug. "The music was wonderful. I'd even go so far as to say it sounded inspired."

"It was." That was the only way Gillian could explain the feeling that had come over her as she'd played and that not once had her damaged fingers betrayed her.

"That's what I thought. This is where you're meant to be." Sally took a shallow breath, smiling at her husband as he made his way toward her. "Gillian, don't laugh, but I believe God intends you to spend your life in a church."

"As an organist?" Though the idea wasn't as foreign as it might have been two days earlier, it didn't feel quite right to Gillian.

"No. As a minister's wife."

This time Gillian did laugh. "I'm sorry, Sally. You told me not to laugh, but I couldn't help it. It's bad enough that the Matchers want to see me married this summer, but did you have to join their ranks? Even if I were interested in your idea—which I am not—there are several problems, starting with the fact that I don't know any single ministers."

Undaunted, Sally shrugged. "Don't forget that all things are possible for God. He'll provide."

Gillian was still shaking her head as she walked toward Mike's Ferrari. This was without a doubt the craziest idea Sally had ever had.

29

You look great!"

Though there was no denying the enthusiasm in Mike's voice, Gillian felt more than a twinge of concern. "I hope it's not too fancy."

She'd worn a full-skirted sundress with its matching jacket to church and had a big floppy hat in her hand, in case the afternoon involved a lot of time outdoors. Both could be considered sensible. Her shoes were not. They consisted of nothing more than a few narrow straps and the highest heels she owned. Perhaps it was silly, but Gillian was always conscious that Mike was at least ten inches taller and didn't want him towering over her today.

She looked down at her shoes, suddenly aware that although TJ was almost as tall as Mike, she hadn't worried about height when she'd dressed for the rodeo or, for that matter, for anything else they did together. She'd chosen whatever clothing best suited the occasion. Perhaps that was because with the exception of the rodeo, she had never felt as if they were going on a date. They were friends spending time together. But the rodeo had changed all that, and when TJ had told her she was special . . .

"It's perfect," Mike said.

For a second Gillian was confused until she realized that Mike was referring to her outfit, not to anything TJ might have said. Resolving that she would not think about TJ for the rest of the day, Gillian gave Mike her warmest smile. He was her date today, and that was the least he deserved.

"My family tends to dress up on the Lord's day," Mike added with a casual gesture at his own clothing. The perfect fit of his dark suit told Gillian it had been custom-made, and his shoes looked as if they'd come straight from Italy. The only concession he'd made to the warmth of the day was a loosened tie.

"Do I dare ask how your stint at the organ went?" he asked as he opened the car door for Gillian and waited until she'd arranged her skirt before he closed it. The man was chivalry personified.

Gillian smiled again, remembering how peaceful she had felt in the choir loft and how she had not hit a single wrong note. The hymns she'd played were nowhere near as challenging as concert music, but she'd still been surprised at how easy it had been. "It went amazingly well. I shouldn't have worried."

"I'm not surprised. Was the church crowded?" Mike put the car in gear and pulled away from the curb, the Ferrari's low-throated rumble attracting the attention of several teenage boys.

Gillian nodded. "I was warned it probably would be full, and it was. When I looked down, I couldn't see a single empty spot." The thought that at least some of those people might have come only to hear her play still bothered her.

"That's good." It was almost as if Mike had read her thoughts, because he continued, "You provided a reason for the C&E Christians to come to church."

"What do you mean by C&E Christians?" she asked as they headed east on Lone Star Trail. It was the perfect day for a drive. The clouds that had obscured the sun and threatened rain at the end of the rodeo were gone, replaced by a brilliant blue sky.

"Christmas and Easter."

"Of course." Though she hadn't heard the term, Gillian knew many people who attended church services only twice a year.

"Think about it, Gillian. Who knows how many of them were touched by today's service?"

Settling back in the seat, Gillian enjoyed the sensation of being cocooned in fine leather. "I hadn't considered that." Pastor Bill's sermon about God's hand being visible in even the smallest of actions had resonated with her and had made her determined to view everything she did through that lens. If others in the congregation had had the same reaction, anything was possible.

"But now tell me about your week."

"It was boring and exciting at the same time." Mike tapped the controls on the steering column, switching radio stations until he found one with praise music.

When he'd lowered the volume so they could converse, Gillian raised an eyebrow. "How did you manage that? I would have thought boring and exciting were mutually exclusive."

Mike shrugged, as if the answer should be obvious. "The meetings were boring. We were working out the details of the campaign: where to hold fundraisers, where and when to make public appearances." Mike turned to gaze at Gillian, his lips curving into a wry smile. "Boring."

"If the meetings were boring, what was exciting?"

"The idea of making a difference. I can picture Blytheville five or ten years from now, and I like what I believe can happen. We'll keep the town's charm but move it firmly into the twenty-first century with gradual but sensible changes."

Though sunglasses hid his eyes, nothing could hide Mike's enthusiasm. This was what he wanted to do, what he felt called to do. This was the kind of infectious enthusiasm Gillian had seen in TJ's expression on a few occasions. He'd looked that way when he'd talked about the rodeo and his motorcycle but never when he spoke of teaching.

She bit the inside of her cheek at the realization that while teaching had been the way TJ earned his living, it was not his passion. How sad. Gillian's career might have ended too soon, but at least she had had a few years to do what she loved. She couldn't help wishing TJ had been as fortunate.

"You really want to win," she said, turning her attention back to Mike. It wasn't fair to him that her thoughts kept drifting toward TJ. She had resolved to make today Mike's day, but so far she'd been unsuccessful in keeping that resolution.

"I do. I think I'm the right mayor for Blytheville right now, but let's talk about you. How did you spend your week?"

"Painting, hanging pictures, arranging furniture, and going to a rodeo."

"Really? I never pictured you as a rodeo gal."

Gillian smiled, remembering the way the aromas of hot dogs, fries, and sunblock had assailed her when she'd entered the arena. "It was my first time, but I enjoyed it . . . all except for the time a steer was injured."

"They have some pretty good vets on the circuit."

"That's what TJ said." He'd told her not to watch if she didn't want to, but she'd been fascinated by the speed with which the cowboys had brought in a sled, raised its sides, and carried the injured animal out of the arena.

"TJ?" To Gillian's surprise, Mike's voice held a note of disapproval.

She nodded. "You remember him, don't you? He's been helping me with the senior center, and he took me to the rodeo yesterday."

"I see." This time there was no doubt. Mike didn't approve. The tightening of his lips told Gillian that. A second later, his face was back to normal and he smiled as he said, "It might not be as exciting as a rodeo, but I have tickets for the symphony in Austin next Friday evening. I was hoping I could convince you to be my date."

His voice was warm and persuasive, that of the consummate

politician. "There's a new restaurant in Austin that's supposed to be pretty good. I thought we could have dinner there, then go to the concert."

Though she was flattered to be invited, Gillian's instincts told her to refuse. As much as she loved music, she wasn't certain she was ready to watch others perform. It was one thing to listen to a recording, quite another to attend a live performance. In the past, Gillian had been the one on the stage. But the way Mike phrased the invitation made it clear this was important to him.

"I'd love to."

"Wonderful." The smile that accompanied his response told Gillian she had made the right decision.

"We're almost there," Mike said twenty minutes later as he turned onto a gravel drive.

The time had gone quickly, with them talking about everything from his campaign to Gillian's senior center. Now they were on the outskirts of Blytheville, bumping along a road better suited for trucks than low-slung sports cars. With trees and shrubs lining the drive, it felt like the private road it was, and though they traveled no more than half a mile, Gillian had the sensation of entering a different country, one of cattle ranches and old money.

As the road took a bend to the left, emerging into an open area, Gillian inhaled sharply. Mike's parents' home was not what she'd expected. Knowing the family was one of the wealthiest in the area and having heard others refer to their home as a mansion, she'd expected an elaborate building, perhaps constructed of native limestone. Instead, it appeared to be a log cabin.

As the thought formed, Gillian dismissed it. Cabin was a misnomer for a building this large. Constructed of red-stained logs with one of the green metal roofs so common in this part of Texas, the house looked as if it had been there for generations. The majority of it was only one story high, although the A-line roof in the center suggested a second floor or at least a loft. Two

Adirondack chairs and half a dozen simple wooden rockers lined the porch that appeared to wrap around the entire house.

Far from being a mansion flaunting its owners' wealth, this building seemed to whisper a welcome. Without setting foot inside, Gillian was convinced this house was truly a home, a place where family lived and loved.

As the car rolled to a stop, a middle-aged couple emerged from the house, wearing smiles that underscored Gillian's sense of welcome.

"We're so glad you could come," Mrs. Tarkett said as she hugged Gillian. Unlike her husband and son, Mike's mother was average height. A brunette with dark brown eyes, she seemed to have contributed little other than her patrician nose to Mike, who had his father's lighter coloring and his strong jaw. When the older woman smiled again, Gillian revised her assessment. Mike had his mother's smile.

Though his greeting was more restrained than his wife's, Mr. Tarkett echoed her sentiments, giving Gillian a soft pat on the shoulder before he wrapped his arm around his wife's waist and kissed the nape of her neck.

Gillian stared, startled by the obvious love Mike's parents shared. She'd expected a Southern version of her brother and his wife, two people who respected each other and were comfortable in their marriage, not a couple who looked as much in love as newlyweds.

"Thank you for inviting me, Mrs. Tarkett."

Mike's mother shook her head. "None of this Mr. and Mrs. Tarkett stuff. We're Stacy and Cal."

As soon as the introductions were complete, Cal Tarkett clapped Mike on the shoulder. "C'mon, son. The grill's ready for those steaks. Let's leave the women to their work." In that moment, he sounded exactly like George and his old-fashioned ideas of gender-appropriate tasks.

Wrinkling her nose as if she knew her husband was kidding,

Stacy led the way into the house. "Cal's all bluff," she said, pausing only briefly as Gillian admired the soaring ceiling and the double-sided fireplace that separated the living room from the dining area. "The house suits us," she said. And it did. Spacious without being overwhelming, the interior was as welcoming as its exterior.

"How can I help you?" Gillian asked when they reached a kitchen that, while small, was equipped with restaurant-grade appliances.

"You can help me by relaxing," Stacy said. "You're our guest." She pulled a pitcher from the refrigerator and set it on the breakfast bar along with two glasses. "Sweet tea with a touch of lavender."

When Gillian had perched on the stool she indicated, Stacy filled the glasses and took a sip from hers. "I'm glad you were able to come today. Cal and I've been looking forward to meeting you."

The nervousness that had plagued Gillian dissipated under the force of Stacy's smile. "I'm glad to be here. But please, let me do something to help you. It can't be easy to cook for a crowd."

Stacy shrugged as she washed two tomatoes and began to dice them. "Four's not a crowd."

"Four?" Gillian was confused. "Mike said the whole family was coming."

Looking up from the tomato she was chopping, Stacy shook her head. "Not today. I didn't want you to be overwhelmed on your first visit. Don't get me wrong, Gillian. I love Cal's family, but they can be a bit exuberant, if you know what I mean."

Exuberant was not a word Gillian would have applied to her own family. Her father, George and Lisa, even her nephew Gabriel were restrained.

"They tend to steamroll people," Stacy continued. "But I imagine most families are like that."

"Mine isn't." The words were out before Gillian knew what was happening.

"Really? Tell me about them."

And so, though she had never before confided in a virtual stranger, Gillian found herself telling Mike's mother about her father's hands-off style of child rearing and how George had always seemed more avuncular than brotherly. When she finished, Stacy opened her arms and drew Gillian into them.

"You poor dear. Now I see why Mike wanted to bring you here. You need a family. A real family."

It seemed as if the entire town of Dupree had come for the grand opening. Gillian had deliberately scheduled it for seven in the morning so people could come before work or school, and since seniors were notoriously early risers, they'd be ready for a full day of activities once the ribbon was cut and the speeches delivered.

"You should be the one doing this. It's your center," Linda said as Gillian handed her one of the two oversized pairs of scissors.

"Nonsense." Gillian gave the other pair to Sheila. "This would still be a vacant building if you two hadn't given me the idea. Now let's let the mayor do his thing. I can see everyone eyeing the coffee and muffins."

Two long tables laden with food and morning beverages were arranged between the ceremonial ribbon and the storefront, and the aromas were filling the air, making Gillian as hungry as the rest of the crowd.

To her delight, the mayor's speech was mercifully short. After thanking Gillian and TJ for helping what he referred to as the town's old-timers, he turned to Sheila and Linda, urging them to wield their shears. Seconds later, Dupree's senior center was officially open.

Though some people entered the building to admire all that had been done, most remained outside, enjoying the food Russ Walker and his staff had prepared. Gillian didn't blame them. Food was always a big attraction.

"I'd call this a resounding success," TJ said as he stood inside the doorway, snapping pictures of people inspecting the photographs on the walls, shuffling cards at one of the bridge tables, and chatting with each other.

Two women were even seated on the bench to what used to be Sally's piano, leafing through the sheet music, though neither had opened the fallboard, perhaps because they didn't relish an audience.

Though Gillian had been surprised when Sally had insisted on donating the piano to the center, she couldn't argue with the logic. "It's just collecting dust in my house," Sally explained. "At least there, someone will use it."

Gillian hadn't disagreed with Sally, and she didn't disagree with TJ's assessment of the center's success.

"I couldn't have done it without you," she told him.

TJ shook his head as he framed another shot. "Sure you could have. It might have taken longer, but you'd have gotten it done." He looked up, his brown eyes serious. "Haven't you figured out yet that you can do anything you set your mind to?"

That was so far from the truth that Gillian wanted to laugh. She couldn't even figure out what she wanted to do with the rest of her life.

The thought of spending more time with Mike, perhaps exploring a permanent relationship, was appealing, especially after yesterday. Though she'd expected to feel welcome at the Tarketts' ranch, Gillian hadn't expected to feel as if she were part of the family, but that was exactly what had happened.

She'd shared more than two meals and an afternoon with them. She'd shared part of their life.

Both Stacy and Cal had entertained her with amusing stories of Mike's childhood, and when the discussion had turned to his mayoral campaign, they'd asked her opinion about several key platform planks, acting as if she were a member of the inner circle. Gillian couldn't remember the last time she'd felt so stimulated yet relaxed at the same time. If this was what being part of a family meant, the only thing she could say was that she liked it. She liked it a lot.

But no matter how much she had enjoyed her time at the ranch and no matter how often she'd found herself wishing Cal and Stacy were her parents, Gillian knew it was too soon to be thinking about marriage. When she married—if she married—she had to be certain she was making the right decision. There could be no doubts, no lingering thoughts of another man.

That was something she had no intention of sharing with TJ, and so she said, "I appreciate the vote of confidence, even if it's exaggerated. I'm just thankful we've gotten this far with the center."

TJ followed Gillian into the kitchen, where she'd stashed a couple dozen muffins and a plate of doughnuts for midmorning snacks. "What's next?"

Gillian opened the refrigerator to check the supply of orange and cranberry juice. That was something she could do. Predicting the future was far more difficult. "I don't know."

And that bothered her. The center was done and would be functioning on its own within the week. Sheila and Linda had volunteered to be co-managers; the first set of instructors had been hired; Russ Walker had his standing order for food. Though she knew she'd be welcome any time she walked through the door, Gillian also knew she wasn't necessary. It was time to find something else to do. The question was, what?

"It's good to see the town so excited." Pastor Bill snagged TJ's arm as he headed for school. "You and Gillian did a great job on this."

It wasn't only the town that was excited. So was TJ, though his excitement had little to do with the senior center and everything to do with the woman who'd created it. It had been more than thirty-six hours since they'd left the rodeo grounds, but the memory of Gillian pressing her lips to his cheek had not faded. He could still recall the rush of pleasure that had flooded through him, the way his nerve endings had tingled. All because of a kiss that had lasted no more than a second.

It had been a special day, and as he'd told her, Gillian was a special woman. But he wasn't going to tell Pastor Bill that any more than he would take credit he didn't deserve. "It was Gillian's idea. All I did was some grunt work."

Pastor Bill released his grip on TJ's arm as he shook his head. "I wouldn't call those pictures grunt work. They're outstanding. You're a truly talented man."

Uncomfortable with the praise, TJ looked at his boot tips. "The camera does most of the work."

"Maybe for focusing and setting the exposure, but it takes an artistic eye to frame the shot. Don't shortchange yourself, TJ. God has given you many talents. And I'm not just talking about photography."

The minister looked directly at TJ, his brown eyes serious. "If you ever feel the calling, you're welcome in my pulpit any Sunday. I know the congregation would welcome the RV Reverend."

Feeling the blood drain from his face, TJ stared at the man who'd delivered the bombshell. "How did you find out?" The day Deb had died had been the day the RV Reverend had retired.

Pastor Bill kept his eyes fixed on TJ, willing him not to break the contact. "Someone blogged about you a couple years ago. What he said impressed me so much that I bookmarked the post. When you first came to town, I thought you looked familiar, but

I couldn't figure out why." He laid his hand on TJ's shoulder, perhaps to keep him from bolting.

"I was cleaning up my bookmarks a week or so ago, saw your picture, and the pieces fell into place."

TJ said nothing, unsure what to do now that his past had come to haunt him.

"You don't need to make any decisions today," Pastor Bill continued. "You're always welcome in our church family, either as part of the congregation or as a minister. Just think about it. That's all I ask."

31

"Will you show us around?"

Gillian turned, her eyes widening at the sight of Stacy and Cal in the doorway.

"Mike wanted to come," Stacy continued, "but there was a problem at one of our oil fields in West Texas, so he had to fly out there. Cal told me to wait a day or two until the excitement died down, but I couldn't. I know how important this is to you, and I just had to be here."

Gillian smiled—who wouldn't smile at Stacy's obvious enthusiasm?—and returned the hug the older woman offered. "It was awfully nice of you to come, especially since the grand tour will take less than a minute."

She ushered Cal and Stacy into the room. "Here it is—Dupree's senior center." The two men she'd met at the bootery the day she'd arranged to rent the building were playing chess in one corner, their silent contemplation of the board in direct contrast to the animated discussion taking place at the table next to them. Gillian had watched the four women who were allegedly playing bridge and had decided that the ratio of conversation to card playing was three to one.

"With the exception of the piano and those chairs," she said, pointing to a grouping of four upholstered club chairs, "everything folds. That way we can move stuff to the edges and have room for dancing, exercise classes, and anything else we dream up."

"Great idea." Cal's nod underscored his approval. "We could use something like this in Blytheville."

Gillian didn't try to hide her surprise. "From what Mike said, I thought you had plenty of activities for seniors."

"Oh, there are activities," Cal agreed. "A couple of the churches have active senior groups, and the Y offers classes and pool time, but things are scattered." He looked around the room, obviously assessing it. "This is what we need—on a bigger scale, of course. What would it take to get you to do this in Blytheville?"

Surprise turned to shock. Surely he wasn't serious.

Stacy laid a hand on her husband's arm. "Shame on you, Cal. You know better than to pressure her." She gave Gillian a commiserating look. "When he gets an idea, my husband has a tendency to become a steamroller. I'm just as impressed as he is with what you've accomplished, but I know you need some time to make sure everything's running properly here before you consider another venture." She took a step forward and hugged Gillian. "Just think about it, okay?"

By three o'clock Gillian was exhausted. She could understand the physical fatigue. After all, the past few weeks had been busy. What she couldn't understand was why she felt so drained, why all she wanted to do was return to her cabin and cry. She wasn't a crier. Dad had told her tears accomplished nothing, and he was right. But the way she felt right now, she could sob for hours and still not be done.

That was ridiculous. She wasn't going to cry; she wasn't going to pound her fists against a wall. Gillian wasn't a toddler having a tantrum. She was a grown woman who ought to be celebrating what everyone agreed was a highly successful achievement.

What she needed was a good listener, and only one person fit that bill. Gillian grabbed her bag and headed out, determined to reach the school before classes ended. If TJ couldn't help her, no one could.

The last thing TJ expected to see when he left school was Gillian standing near his bike. She wasn't sitting on it, of course, and was in fact a few feet away, but he had no doubt that she was waiting for him. A strange day had just turned even stranger.

With Pastor Bill's challenge to think about preaching ringing in his ears, TJ had had trouble concentrating on his classes. A year ago when his own faith had crumbled under the force of anger and despair, he had realized he was the last person worthy of helping others find comfort in God's Word. That day he had sworn he'd never again try, but today was different. Though TJ hadn't expected it, Pastor Bill's words had caused him to waver as memories of the times he'd counseled fellow campers and had shown them God's hand in their lives had lodged in his brain. For the first time since Deb's death, those memories had not made him feel like the worst of hypocrites.

He had spent the day counting the minutes until school ended, intending to take a long ride to clear his head. But now Gillian was here, looking as troubled as he felt.

"What's wrong?" he asked as he approached her. Those lovely green eyes were filled with confusion.

"Was it that obvious?" Though she tried to laugh, the sound was mirthless.

TJ shook his head. "Only if you know what to look for."

And he did. He'd seen the same expression on his own face too many times to count. "Do you want to talk?"

"Yeah."

He looked around. The faculty parking lot was hardly the place for a serious discussion. "Why don't we try the park?" It was only a block away from the school grounds, and though it was a popular spot on weekends and evenings, it was normally close to empty at this time of day.

When they were seated on one of the wrought-iron benches under a large oak tree, he cupped both ears in an attempt to lighten Gillian's mood. "I'm listening," he told her.

She was silent for a moment, blinking rapidly as if she were trying not to cry. Oh, how TJ hoped she wouldn't cry. He'd never known what to say when faced with a woman's tears.

But Gillian did not cry. Instead she said, "I don't understand it. I ought to be happy. The senior center opening was a huge success. Everything went perfectly, and I didn't hear a single complaint. I should be thrilled, but all I want to do is cry."

Though he'd never actually dissolved into tears, TJ knew the feeling. "That's normal. You've been running on an adrenaline high, and now that the center's open, it's wearing off. It's not unusual to feel drained." He was glad he had an answer. Though he expected Gillian to nod, she did not.

"It's more than being drained. I feel totally empty, as if there's this enormous void inside me. I've had that feeling before, but never to this extent. I hate it, TJ. I hate feeling like this."

Though he wanted nothing more than to gather her into his arms, TJ wouldn't do that. She had come to him as a friend; he would respond like one. He searched his brain, looking for words to help fill the void. He could tell her he knew how she felt, for he did, but Gillian needed more than that.

Help me, Lord, he prayed, surprised at how natural it felt to speak to God again. *Give me the words I need*. As the plea left his mind, a memory surfaced.

"You've seen *The Sound of Music*, haven't you?"

Gillian nodded. "Who hasn't? But please don't expect me to sing one of the songs, because I don't have a very good voice."

"No singing required. Remember the line about how the Reverend Mother claims that when God closes a door, he opens a window?"

Gillian tipped her head to the side, her interest apparent. "Doesn't Maria say that to the Captain?"

"Exactly. What she doesn't tell him is that it takes more courage to climb through a window than to walk through a door. You and I are in the same boat. You lost your career; I lost Deb. We're both looking for that window."

"And the courage to climb through it."

Though her words were solemn, the way Gillian's expression seemed to have lightened ignited a spark deep inside TJ. Perhaps he'd been wrong and Pastor Bill was right. Perhaps God would forgive him for his anger and his doubts. Perhaps this was what TJ was meant to do.

32

The truck looked like a dozen others in Dupree—big, black, with darkened windows. TJ paid no attention to it until it stopped next to his bike and the driver rolled down his window.

"Got a minute?" Mike Tarkett asked.

"That depends." TJ had been planning on a long ride. While he couldn't regret the way he'd spent his after-school time yesterday, he still wanted an hour with the wind in his face to clear his head while he processed Pastor Bill's challenge.

Seemingly unconcerned that he hadn't gotten a more positive response, Mike switched off the engine and climbed out, then leaned against the side of the truck. "We need to talk."

Though his posture appeared casual, the gleam in Mike's eyes left TJ no doubt that this was a conversation he did not want to have. TJ had only one thing in common with the Tarkett heir, and he had no desire to discuss her.

"I heard you took Gillian to the rodeo."

TJ tried not to bristle. It was possible Mike didn't intend to sound either confrontational or condescending, even though that was the way his words came across. "So what if I did? She had a good time." *And she kissed me.* Not that that was any of this guy's business.

Mike crossed his arms, his displeasure evident. "You're wasting your time. Gillian deserves the finer things in life."

"And I suppose you plan to give them to her."

"Exactly." Mike stood up straight and glared at TJ. "I'm taking her to the symphony this week, and next week . . ."

If he was supposed to be impressed, TJ was not. He also had no intention of listening to Mike's plans. "You think that's what she wants." He made it a statement, not a question. Though Mike was not an arrogant man, his self-assurance grated on TJ.

Mike nodded. "It's what she deserves. I can't do anything about what happened to her career, but I can give her the life she's meant to have."

TJ waved as two of his co-workers exited the building, waiting until they were out of earshot before he spoke. This was one conversation that did not need to be overheard.

"I see." He infused his words with every ounce of sarcasm he possessed. "It's all very altruistic of you. The fact that having Gillian Hodge at your side would help your campaign never crossed your mind, did it?" When Mike looked as if he wanted to respond, TJ shook his head. He was on a roll, and nothing was going to stop him. "My guess is that Mommy and Daddy planned everything. They decided you needed a wife or at least a beautiful woman to attend fundraisers and other events with you. It wasn't coincidence that you came to Rainbow's End when Gillian was there, was it?"

Mike blanched, and for the first time, that self-assured veneer cracked. Was it possible he hadn't considered his parents' motives?

"You're wrong," he announced, his composure sliding back in place.

"Am I? Everyone knows your family gets what it wants." Though they'd never been accused of underhanded dealings, the Tarkett clan hadn't gotten to their position of prominence by being soft with competitors.

"You're right. We do get what we want, and what I want is Gillian. She's a mighty special woman." Though Mike's voice was firm, the look he gave TJ was almost conciliatory. "I don't need to tell you that. Let's be frank about this. I can give her the kind of life she deserves."

And TJ couldn't. The implication was clear. TJ was tempted to punch his fist into Mike's face, but he didn't. It might make him feel better temporarily, but he knew how Gillian would react.

"That's three times you've talked about what Gillian deserves," he said as calmly as he could. "What about what she wants? Doesn't she get a say in this?"

Mike flinched as if TJ had hit him. "You're twisting my words."

"Am I?"

There was a second of silence before Mike straightened his shoulders and shot another glare at TJ. "Look, TJ." The voice that might have caused competitors to reconsider their position had no effect on TJ other than to increase his anger. "I only came here to tell you my intentions. I've done that. Just so you can't twist my words, let me say it one more time: I care about Gillian and I plan to do everything in my power to convince her to marry me, so back off."

"Not a chance."

* * *

"Hey, stranger." Gillian smiled when she saw Brianna emerging from Hill Country Pieces as she was leaving the bookstore. It wasn't coincidence that Marisa had decided to locate Hill Country Pages across the street from her friend Lauren's quilt shop, any more than the choice of names had been coincidental.

Marisa had explained that she and Lauren always referred

to the quilt shop by its initials and that she wanted her store to have those initials in common with her best friend's establishment. As for the location, both women knew there would be synergies—a fancy term for the fact that many of Dupree's women shopped for both books and quilting supplies. Today that proximity benefited Gillian.

As she crossed the street, she continued talking to Brianna. "I missed you last night." And the night before. Though she hadn't wanted to ask the other teens what had happened, Gillian had been concerned when neither Brianna nor Todd had attended the campfire gatherings the past two evenings and when there'd been no answer to her knock on Brianna's trailer. She had believed Brianna had bounced back from Pete's declaration that she was too young, but something had caused a relapse. Now she'd have a chance to learn the reason.

A scowl marred Brianna's pretty face. "Campfire stories are for kids."

Biting her tongue, lest she point out that Brianna was the same age as many of the people she was referring to as kids, Gillian said only, "I thought you enjoyed them."

"Yeah, well . . ." Brianna stared down the street, as if searching for someone, then frowned as she pulled out her cell phone to check the time. "I've got better things to do now."

Though she wished she were wrong, Gillian suspected Brianna was once again waiting for Pete Darlington and that he was late.

Her disappointment obvious, Brianna glanced at the shopping bag in her hand. "I bought this for my mom for Mother's Day," she said, opening the bag so Gillian could look inside. "Do you think she'll like it?"

The quilted messenger bag with Natalie Carter's initials in the center of an intricate design was one of the most beautiful and practical things Gillian had seen. "It's gorgeous. I'm sure she'll love it."

Gillian tamped down the wistful feeling whose intensity surprised her. It had been years since she and Kate had gone Mother's Day shopping together, trying to find the perfect gift for Sally. After they'd decided on a designer handbag, Kate's eyes had filled with tears. "I still remember my mom," she said. Gillian had no such memories. Her mother was the woman in the photographs that covered one wall of her father's bedroom.

Forcing a smile, Gillian added, "I know I'd enjoy having something like this." And she would enjoy buying one for someone. Though Stacy Tarkett's face popped into her mind, Gillian knew it would be presumptuous to give Mike's mother a gift on Mother's Day.

Fortunately, Brianna seemed oblivious to Gillian's descent into melancholy. She gave the street another quick look, her frown turning into a pout when there was no sign of Pete. "You'd have to wait awhile if you wanted your initials on one, but Lauren's got others ready-made. They're pretty nice."

They were indeed. Gillian looked at the bag again, wondering whether Lauren had something similar for Kate to use as a diaper bag. "Thanks for the suggestion. Do you want to help me pick out something for Kate's baby?" The baby wouldn't appreciate the exquisite design, but his or her mother would.

Though her eyes lit with enthusiasm, as if she were unaccustomed to being asked for advice, Brianna shook her head. "I can't. Pete'll be here any minute." The tug on her cropped top covered a bit more of Brianna's midriff but revealed more of her generous curves. "He's gonna take me for a ride."

I'll bet. Gillian wouldn't say that. Instead, she placed a hand on Brianna's arm. "I thought you two broke up."

Brianna wasn't listening. Her face wreathed with a smile, she pointed toward a dented and dirty black truck with a faded flag decal on its left rear bumper. "There he is." Though all the parking on Pecan was angled, Pete didn't bother to park. Instead he pulled close to the curb, taking up three spots.

It was clear Brianna had forgotten Gillian's existence. Gripping the shopping bag in one hand, she climbed into the truck and slid across the seat toward Pete, then flung her arms around him.

Gillian wasn't surprised when Pete cupped Brianna's head to draw her closer. She wasn't surprised by the long, lingering kiss. What did surprise her was that as soon as he'd broken the kiss, Pete looked directly at Gillian and winked.

What was that all about?

Think about it, Pastor Bill had said. TJ frowned as he closed the cabin door behind him and headed for the dining room. He felt as if he'd done nothing but think since the minister had issued his invitation on Monday. It was Wednesday evening now, and TJ still wasn't certain.

He'd thought about being in a pulpit, preaching the Good News, and though he hadn't expected it, there had been an undeniable appeal to the thought, especially when coupled with the satisfaction he'd found at being able to ease Gillian's pain. For the rest of the day, he'd felt an inner glow that reminded him of the years he'd been known as the RV Reverend. The glow had faded by the next morning, replaced by the old familiar doubts.

Pastor Bill was mistaken if he believed TJ had anything to offer his congregation. He didn't. There had been a time when he'd been confident—some might even have called him cocky—about the messages he delivered, but he'd been forced to face reality. He was a fraud. Though he'd spouted platitudes like "God will never forsake you," the emptiness TJ had felt when Deb died left him with no doubt that he'd been forsaken. Anger had filled the empty spaces for a while, but then the emptiness returned and with it the realization that he had no right to call himself a minister. A man whose faith was as weak as TJ's was the last person who should try to help others find peace in God's messages. He would never again counsel or preach.

TJ had kept his vow for over a year, but when Gillian had so obviously needed help, he had slipped back into the role that had once felt so comfortable. Perhaps it had been coincidence that he had remembered the *Sound of Music* quote immediately after his silent prayer, but TJ doubted it. Though he wasn't worthy, God had given him the words to comfort Gillian. Was that enough? TJ didn't know. No matter what Pastor Bill thought, no matter how appealing the prospect had been for that split second, TJ feared he was not meant to be a minister again.

Dismissing ideas of the ministry had not settled his thoughts. It had only sent them in different, equally painful directions. As happened so often, he found himself thinking about Gillian, but instead of remembering the good times they'd shared, thanks to his conversation with Mike, he focused on how little he had to offer her.

There had been moments when he thought they might have a future together—moments like the rodeo, the time they'd spent working on the senior center, the hour in the park—but those were overshadowed by the reality of TJ's future, or more precisely, the lack thereof. He still hadn't found the window, much less the courage to climb through it.

When he'd joined Gillian for supper on Monday, she had regaled Kate with stories of her time at the Tarkett ranch and how kind Cal and Stacy had been to come for the senior center's opening. It was a casual conversation, but the happiness in Gillian's expression left no doubt of how much she had enjoyed her time with the older Tarketts—especially Stacy. It didn't take a genius to know Gillian was looking for a substitute mother and that she might have found one in Stacy Tarkett. A mother was one more thing TJ could not give Gillian.

Mike could give her everything she wanted: a close-knit family, a comfortable lifestyle, a bright future. Gillian deserved a man like that, not one with half a heart and an uncertain future. He paused, struck by the realization that he'd used the same word he'd criticized Mike for using: deserve. He had no right to make assumptions about what Gillian wanted.

"Is something wrong?" she asked when TJ entered the dining room and took the seat next to her. It must be his imagination that she looked prettier than usual tonight. She'd pulled her hair back in a ponytail. Though the severe style didn't suit some women, it highlighted Gillian's features and drew attention to those deep green eyes. Right now those eyes betrayed concern. Somehow she'd sensed TJ's troubled state.

"Nothing more than usual," he lied. "The kids were antsy today. They're definitely ready for school to end. What about you?"

Though he'd expected a lighthearted recounting of the people who'd come into the bookstore this morning, Gillian's expression was serious. "I saw Brianna this afternoon. She was with Pete again. She told me she and Todd broke up. That's why we haven't seen them at night."

TJ had suspected that, rather than have to explain how he'd been rejected, Todd had decided to avoid the nightly gatherings, but he hadn't expected Pete to resume his friendship—or whatever it was—with Brianna.

"Pete? I told him to back off."

"Well, he didn't, and Brianna's thrilled." Gillian didn't sound any happier about it than TJ was. "She's acting like a girl in love, or at least in infatuation."

TJ didn't want to think about love, because thoughts of love made him wonder just what it was Gillian felt for Mike. That was one question he didn't want answered. But he needed to do whatever he could to reassure Gillian and protect Brianna.

"I guess it's time for another talk with Pete."

"I hope he listens this time." Gillian sounded as dubious as TJ felt.

As they ate, her mood seemed to improve. She engaged the others at the table in conversation for a few minutes before turning back to TJ. "Tell me what you have planned for Firefly Valley tonight."

When he'd finished his explanation, Gillian nodded. "That sounds good. I think I can get the girls interested. I wanted to tell you, though, that I won't be able to help on Friday."

"A hot date?" Though he forced a light tone, TJ's gut wrenched at the thought of her with Mike.

"If you call dinner in Austin and a night at the symphony a hot date, then I guess it is." Her tone of voice gave him no clue whether she was looking forward to the evening.

TJ nodded. A five-course dinner prepared by a celebrity chef and a concert, probably enjoyed from box seats, might be what Gillian wanted. Not hot dogs and soda at a rodeo.

"Have fun," he said, wishing he meant it.

Kate poured herself another cup of herbal tea and lowered herself to the chair across from Gillian, declaring that sitting down was starting to feel like trying to turn the Titanic.

"Sally told me she's decided you're meant to marry a minister," she said with a smile. "Where did she come up with that idea?"

"You're asking me? She's your grandmother." Gillian took a bite of pastry, chewing carefully before she added, "I have no idea what's behind that unless Sally's been spending too much time in the sun. Maybe the gray matter is getting fried."

"I suspect she just wants you to move to Texas."

"And do what? That's the problem I'm having. I'm not sure what I want to do next." Or what she was meant to do. Though she'd prayed for direction each day, she had heard no answers. She hated to disappoint Stacy, because she had said she wanted to be involved, but Gillian wasn't convinced creating a senior center in Blytheville was the right move for her. Perhaps it was because it hadn't been her idea. Perhaps it was because the need didn't seem as great. Perhaps it was only because she'd already done it and wanted a new challenge. All Gillian knew for certain was that the prospect of organizing another senior center wasn't the open window she'd been searching for.

"You could always get married, settle down, and have two point five children." Kate rubbed her baby bump as she pronounced the final words.

"Now you sound like the Matchers. Amelia made a special trip to the bookstore today to offer her services."

"What did you do?"

Gillian raised both hands in the classic gesture of hopelessness. "What could I do? I thanked her nicely and told her I had no intention of marrying."

"And she was horrified."

"You could say that. I was afraid she might go into cardiac arrest, so I told her I was only kidding. But seriously, Kate, marriage isn't the answer to every problem." Even though Brianna thought it was.

Kate took another sip of tea. "I didn't say it was. I was simply pointing out the possibilities. Not every woman has two men interested in her."

"Two?"

"Sure. Mike and TJ."

Though the thought of TJ considering her more than a friend brought a flush of color to Gillian's cheeks, she shook her head. "You must have been spending as much time in the sun as Sally if you think TJ is interested in marriage. He may be forty years younger, but this is one area he's just like my father. He believes love is a once-in-a-lifetime event."

Kate gave Gillian one of those "trust me, I know what I'm saying" looks. "I wouldn't be so sure about that if I were you. I know how much you hate it, but you'd better get ready for me to say 'I told you so.'"

"You again." Pete Darlington practically snarled. "What do you want?"

Though he hated confrontations, TJ had once again foregone his lunch break to come to the construction site. Like Gillian, he was concerned about the man's continued pursuit of Brianna, knowing nothing good could come from it.

"Dupree's a small town," he said as he took another step toward Pete. There was no point in shouting. "Folks look out for each other. A bunch of us are concerned about Brianna."

"Why? Just because she and I took a little ride in the country? There's no law against that."

"True. But she's still a kid, so there are laws against other things."

Pete smirked. "Trust me, man, I'm not looking to spend time in prison. I know she's young. You told me, and so did she."

"Did she tell you exactly how underage she is?"

"Yep. And nothing's gonna happen until that magic birthday. Now, unless you're planning to let me ride that bike, get out of here."

33

Gillian was glad she'd gone shopping in San Antonio. She'd wanted a new dress for tonight, and judging from the expression in Mike's eyes, she'd chosen well. Admittedly, she'd been skeptical when the clerk had pulled what had looked like a shapeless piece of green silk off the rack, but when she'd tried it on, the designer's genius was apparent.

The silk flowed, hinting at Gillian's curves, ending in a flirty hem that grazed the top of her knees. What made the gown special was the asymmetrical bodice. While her right shoulder was covered with a cap sleeve, there was no matching sleeve on the other side. Instead, the neckline extended into a bow over Gillian's left shoulder. Simple and yet elegant, it was worth the hefty price tag.

Crinkles formed at the corner of Mike's eyes as he grinned. "Politicians aren't supposed to be speechless, but I don't know what to say other than 'wow.'"

"I wasn't sure whether the restaurant had a dress code, but I saw some pictures of Austin symphony performances and realized that jeans and boots might be a tad casual."

Mike shrugged as he opened the car door for her. "You might

be surprised at what you'll see tonight, but I assure you that you're perfect."

Though his words sounded sincere, the compliment made Gillian uncomfortable. "The dress may be, but not me."

"Oh, I don't know. You charmed my parents. That hasn't happened before."

That sounded as if Mike had had a parade of women at the ranch. Gillian kept a smile firmly fixed on her face. She shouldn't have been surprised. After all, he was an eligible bachelor, and he'd admitted his parents were urging him to marry.

"You have a wonderful family," she told Mike, meaning every word. The hours she'd spent with them had reminded her of her childhood and the time she'd spent with Kate and her grandparents. When her father had traveled, he'd given Gillian the choice of staying at home with the nanny or moving into Kate's home. That had been the classic no-brainer. The nanny had enjoyed the time off, and Gillian had relished being part of a normal family, one with both a mother and a father.

That Sally and her husband had actually been Kate's grandparents hadn't bothered Gillian. What she'd appreciated was that both Sally and Larry had been more demonstrative than her father, freely dispensing hugs. It had felt good to experience the same warmth at the Tarkett ranch.

"When your dad gets back from his cruise, I hope you'll introduce me to him."

Gillian felt her eyes widen in surprise, and she realized that although she'd enjoyed meeting Mike's family, she wasn't ready for him to meet her father or brother. Dad would welcome him—at least on the surface—but there was no way to predict George's reaction. If he decided he didn't like Mike's political views, he might be brutally sarcastic. While Gillian did not doubt that Mike could defend himself, she hated the idea that he might be put on the spot.

"The cruise doesn't end until mid-October, and by then I imagine you'll be spending every minute you can campaigning."

Mike raised an eyebrow. "I hadn't realized he was going to be gone so long."

"It takes awhile to travel around the world, especially when you stop at every port of call. To tell you the truth, I'm still amazed that Dad's doing it. He used to say a two-week vacation was the perfect length—long enough to relax but not so long that you got bored."

"It's been more than two weeks. Is he bored yet?"

Gillian shook her head. "Not that I can tell. His emails are full of pictures of the things he's seeing. He doesn't say a lot, but that's my dad. He never was one for the written word." She told herself that was the only reason he hadn't responded to her email describing the successful launch of the senior center. "Still, I can tell he's having a good time."

And that made Gillian happy. If the cruise kept Dad as busy as it seemed, he'd have less time to worry about his daughter. At least he hadn't bombarded her with suggestions of how to attract a husband. Other than the comment about the folly of surrounding herself with seniors, he'd been silent on the subject.

"Maybe you can convince him to come to the ranch for Thanksgiving," Mike suggested. "The election will be over by then, and it would be the perfect time for our families to meet. Your brother's welcome too."

Whoa. Mike was moving too fast. Way too fast. "We'll see," Gillian said as noncommittally as she could. "I'm not sure where I'll be then. I told Kate I'd stay until the baby's born, but after that I'm not sure what I'll do."

Mike chuckled. "In case you haven't figured it out, I've made it my mission to convince you to stay here. But I can see you're not comfortable with that idea yet, so let's talk about the senior center. I'm still trying to imagine my grandmother doing martial arts."

Gillian couldn't help laughing as Mike took his hands from the steering wheel and feigned a karate chop. "Tai chi isn't karate," she said when she stopped laughing.

"Then tell me what it is."

Grateful for the reprieve, Gillian did, with the result that the rest of the drive proved pleasant and relaxing, reminding her of how much she enjoyed Mike's company.

When they arrived at the restaurant, Gillian discovered it was even more elegant than Strawberry Chantilly, its décor reminding her of a French chateau. The food was superb, the service impeccable, her conversation with Mike once more comfortable.

"So, what did you think?" she asked as they waited for the valet to bring the car.

Mike gave her a puzzled look. "What do you mean?"

"About the restaurant. Did you get any ideas for Strawberry Chantilly?"

Puzzlement turned to chagrin. "Was I that obvious?"

"Only to me. There were times when I thought you were taking mental notes." Though brief, she'd noticed occasions when Mike's eyes had glazed and he'd appeared to be lost in thought.

"Guilty as charged. I'm sorry. That was rude." Mike's expression reminded her of a chastened schoolboy.

"There's no need to apologize. I do the same thing when I hear someone else playing the piano." Gillian smiled at Mike as he opened the car door for her. "It's only natural. Call it an occupational hazard."

He slid behind the wheel and was silent for a moment as he pulled out of the parking lot. "I should have realized that. It's true I was curious about the restaurant and wanted to see how it compared to Strawberry Chantilly, but I hadn't thought about the concert. Would you rather we not go? This was supposed to be a relaxing evening for you, not work."

Gillian shook her head. "It'll be fine."

But it wasn't. Though she tried to keep her expression serene,

Gillian's stomach knotted as the first notes sounded, and she found herself staring at her right hand rather than gazing at the orchestra or closing her eyes to let the music envelop her. Memories of all the times those same sounds had filled her with anticipation washed over her, reminding her of the joy of performing, of being part of an orchestra, of bringing music alive to a new audience.

She clenched her hand, trying to stop the memories from flowing. It wasn't the first time she'd been a spectator. She'd sat in the audience before the accident, and each time she had enjoyed the performance. As Gillian had told Mike, work had mingled with pleasure. In the past she'd listened with a critical ear, but tonight was different. Tonight the music did not soothe her. Instead it served as a painful reminder that she would never again sit on a concert stage.

"They were good, weren't they?" Mike asked when the final bow had been taken and the audience began to file out of the hall.

"Yes, they were excellent." Gillian forced enthusiasm into her voice. She wouldn't spoil Mike's evening by telling him how she'd reacted to the orchestra. It wasn't his fault. He'd offered her an escape route when he'd realized there might be a problem. Gillian was the one who'd refused to take it.

"The cellist was particularly fine," she added.

As they made their way to the exit, Mike kept his hand on the small of her back, guiding her through the crowd, nodding at acquaintances, greeting those who were close enough for casual conversation. Texas might be a big state, but at least in this part, Mike Tarkett was a familiar face.

To Gillian's relief, no one seemed to recognize her. She had no desire for the limelight, especially tonight when her emotions were so fragile. All that changed the instant they stepped outside. They were greeted by the glare of flashes and the whir of cameras. A second later a reporter shoved a microphone in Mike's face.

"Is it true that being mayor of Blytheville is only the first step in your political aspirations?" the reporter probed. Her voice was well modulated, her appearance glamorous yet businesslike at the same time.

Mike gave her a practiced smile. "I'm not mayor yet," he reminded her, "but if the citizens of Blytheville elect me, I plan to spend the next four years doing everything I can to honor their trust in me." It was the perfect politician's response, sounding positive but not answering the question.

The reporter turned her attention and her microphone to Gillian. "What do you think of Mike's plans?"

Grateful that no one had recognized her as anything more than Mike's date, Gillian smiled. "I think he'll be a terrific mayor."

The questions continued as they waited for the car, with Mike fielding them as easily as if he were born to do this. Perhaps he was. As she'd watched Mike respond, Gillian had been struck by the realization that his parents hadn't exaggerated when they'd told him he would shine in politics.

"Thank you all," Mike said as the valet opened the door to the Ferrari for Gillian. Another barrage of flashes marked their departure, but within seconds they were pulling away from the concert hall.

"I'm sorry," he said for the second time that evening. "I didn't expect that."

"Chalk it up to another occupational hazard." Fortunately it had been Mike's career and not her own that had been the reporters' focus.

TJ closed the cabin door behind him and descended the steps. He couldn't explain his restlessness. The time at Firefly Valley had gone well, despite Gillian's absence. The teens had finally started telling stories themselves rather than relying on TJ to entertain them, which made his evenings easier. Unfortunately, tonight it had also given him too much time to picture Gillian and Mike sitting in that fancy Italian sports car of his, having a dinner that cost more than TJ earned in a week, attending a concert surrounded by the rich and famous crowd.

TJ didn't begrudge her any of that. That was Gillian's world before her accident. It was only natural that she would enjoy being there again. TJ wasn't jealous of Mike. Even if he could, he wouldn't change places with him. All that money meant Mike lived in the public eye, and a fishbowl existence had never appealed to TJ.

There was no reason he should be worried about Gillian, and yet he couldn't dismiss the feeling that something was wrong. She had filled his thoughts tonight and set his nerves on edge. Perhaps it was only because he felt so empty inside that he was projecting his feelings onto Gillian.

TJ walked slowly along the edge of the lake, trying to concentrate on the way the stars reflected on the almost still water. It was a beautiful spring evening with a crescent moon rising over the horizon, the lightest of breezes wafting the scent of cedars through the air. It was an evening to rejoice, but TJ wasn't rejoicing. He hadn't rejoiced in a long time, just as he hadn't felt complete in a long time.

He kicked a pebble, smiling when it landed in the water with a satisfying plop. That was good. What wasn't good was being unable to remember the last time he'd wakened without that horribly sickening feeling of emptiness inside him. Teaching hadn't filled it. As he'd told Gillian, TJ knew he was a good but not a great teacher. Even marriage hadn't satisfied everything. Being married to Deb had been wonderful and had filled many of the empty spaces, but even then TJ had had a sense that something was still missing.

He stopped and stared at the lake, as if the answers were

hidden in the ripples, and as he did, memories flashed before him. Life had changed when he and Deb began to spend their summer vacations traveling in an RV. They'd both enjoyed the adventure of discovering new places, of meeting new people, but the turning point had come the day TJ had led a Sunday worship service. That day he'd felt as if the last empty space had been filled. But now . . . now he was once again empty, and it was worse than ever, because he could remember what it had felt like to be fulfilled.

He walked slowly, his feet moving without conscious thought. When he reached the end of the Rainbow's End property, he turned around, intending to return to his cabin. But though he couldn't explain why, he did not turn down the small path to his front porch. Instead, he continued along the lake's edge, paying little attention as he passed the main lodge. It was only when the dock came into sight that he paused. There, sitting on the small bench, her shoulders slumped, was Gillian.

TJ stared at her, his heart aching at the sight of her obvious distress. Should he approach her? He might be intruding, and yet he could no more bear the thought of her unhappiness than he could stop his feet from moving toward her.

"Bad night?"

34

Gillian turned, startled by the sound of TJ's voice. "I didn't hear you coming."

She hadn't expected anyone else to be out, or she wouldn't have come to the dock. When Mike had dropped her off by her cabin, her only thought had been to climb into bed and bury her head beneath the blankets, but instead she'd changed into jeans and a shirt and had walked to the dock.

As a child she'd found the rhythm of Lake Erie's waves relaxing. Bluebonnet Lake had no waves, nothing more than ripples, and yet there was something mesmerizing about watching those ripples form and vanish. She'd been staring into the distance, trying to make her mind a blank, when TJ arrived.

"I'm not sure you would have heard me even if I'd been on my bike. You looked lost in thought." He came closer but didn't take a seat on the bench until she nodded.

"Just lost is more like it." Gillian wasn't certain why she'd admitted that. Though she'd tried to pretend nothing was wrong on the drive back from Austin, she wasn't certain she'd convinced

Mike. And when she'd practically sprinted from the car to her cabin door, giving him no chance for a good-night kiss, she knew she'd disappointed him. But now she was telling TJ more than she'd intended.

"Do you want to talk about it?"

"I'm not sure." On Monday she had known that talking—some would call it venting—was the only way to ease the pain. Tonight she was not so certain. Though Gillian had considered knocking on the door to Kate and Greg's apartment, she had reconsidered. Kate would listen. Gillian knew that. But she also knew that her friend needed more sleep and fewer worries. She wouldn't burden her, and she had no intention of asking TJ again. Twice in less than a week was too much.

"Sometimes it helps."

Gillian looked at TJ. Though he was dressed as casually as ever, something about him seemed different. Perhaps it was only her imagination, but she thought she saw uncertainty in his eyes. It hadn't been there on Monday.

"You're right," she said softly. "Sometimes it helps. It did on Monday, but sometimes it doesn't."

He nodded. "You won't know which one this is unless you try." He cupped his ears again, reminding her of the almost playful gesture he'd used in the park. "I'm ready to listen."

Gillian was silent for a moment, considering. TJ had opened the door, his question and gentle persuasion announcing that she wouldn't be burdening him with her revelations. Remembering how much he'd helped, she nodded.

"Once again you're right. What you called my hot date turned out to be a mistake."

"Did Mike . . . ?" TJ broke off, as if he feared his question might be too personal.

"It wasn't Mike's fault," Gillian said quickly. "If I didn't realize how difficult it would be, how could he?"

"Where did you go?"

Gillian wasn't certain why he was asking, because she'd mentioned her plans the previous day. "We went to dinner in Austin, then to the symphony."

TJ nodded. "And you weren't ready to be reminded of the times when you were one of the performers, not a part of the audience." It was a statement, not a question.

"Exactly, but how did you know? I had a few misgivings when Mike first invited me, but I didn't expect it to be so bad." She turned to face TJ directly. "You nailed it on your first guess. How'd you do that? And how did you know just what to say when I was so upset on Monday?"

She wasn't sure he'd answer, but as an owl hooted and a small rodent scurried through the grass, TJ began to speak. What he said surprised Gillian.

"Over the years, I've spent a lot of time watching people, trying to figure out what made them tick and what their problems were, then working with them to solve those problems."

Simple words, and yet the way he uttered them told Gillian there was a story behind them. "I can't help noticing that you used the past tense. Why did you stop being a counselor?" Knowing this part of his past made her understand why he was so good with the teens. It wasn't simply his teaching background. He did more than impart knowledge of historical facts and dates to his students; he helped them understand themselves.

"I wasn't a counselor per se." TJ's voice held a melancholy note. "I never had any formal training." And he regretted that. She could hear it in his voice.

Gillian was determined not to let the conversation die. "It sounds like you counseled anyway. When was that?"

"Summers." TJ's fingers gripped the edge of the bench, as if the memories were painful. "You know Deb and I used to travel. We rented an RV, which meant we stayed in campgrounds. Lots of people there with lots of problems. I tried to help." He shook his head slowly, making Gillian wonder if he was trying to shake the memories loose. "One thing led to another, and before I knew it, I wasn't just counseling. I was holding informal church services each Sunday, trying to share God's Word with the other campers. Folks started calling me the RV Reverend."

As blood drained from her face, Gillian gulped in surprise. That wasn't just counseling. It was much more. "You were a minister?" The man who said a church wasn't the place for him had once been a preacher?

"I wasn't ordained. I was just a man who tried to help folks through their hard times." Though he made it sound simple, Gillian knew it wasn't. There was more to his past than TJ wanted to admit.

"But you were really good at it."

"Why do you say that?"

"I've seen you with the teenagers. You've gained their respect, and that's not an easy thing to do. You've also set a good example for them. The first day we were in Firefly Valley, I heard a lot of profanity and crude language. Someone else might have ordered the kids to clean up their language, but you didn't. Though you never said a thing, it's stopped. All you had to do was look at them, and they knew you were disappointed. And because they didn't want to disappoint you, they stopped swearing."

"I didn't even think about it."

Gillian wasn't surprised. "It must be instinctive." She paused to stare at the water, then returned her gaze to TJ. "Why did you stop being the RV Reverend?" Though she believed the reason was his wife's death, she wanted him to say the words. As he'd proven to her just a few minutes earlier, there was something cathartic about voicing thoughts.

"Why? Because I wasn't willing to be a fraud. I thought my faith was as strong as a rock, but it wasn't."

"Because of how you felt when your wife died." If TJ wouldn't say it, she would.

"Yeah. All I felt was emptiness and anger."

TJ stared into the distance, the set of his lips telling Gillian how deep the hurt was. "People kept reminding me of Jeremiah 29:11. I don't know how many times I preached from that passage. At the time, I thought I was giving people comfort, but when Deb died, I realized I didn't believe it anymore. I didn't see any good things happening."

The anger and bitterness in his voice made Gillian's heart ache. *Help me*, she prayed. *Help me find the right words to comfort TJ*. She took a breath, searching deep inside herself for something to say.

"You were angry. Maybe you even still are. After all, anger's a normal part of the grieving process." Gillian remembered the sessions she'd had with the psychologist. "Believe me, I know all about anger. At first I was angry with the motorcyclist for hitting me, but then I started being angry with myself. I kept telling myself I should have seen him coming, I should have moved more quickly. And when people started quoting Jeremiah to me, I felt the way you did," she said, hoping she was on the right track. "I still do at times. So many people reminded me of that verse that I started to hate it. One even embroidered it on a little pillow. I can't count the number of times I was tempted to throw that pillow into the garbage. To this day, I can't tell you why I didn't."

Gillian watched as TJ swallowed, shifting so he faced her. Surely that was a good sign. He wasn't tuning her out. Instead, he looked as if he cared about what she was saying.

She took a deep breath to calm her nerves, then continued. "When I felt as if I'd reached the end of the rope, I Googled Jeremiah 29:11, trying to find every translation. I was sure I'd missed something, and I had." Gillian kept her eyes fixed on TJ, wanting to ensure that he was still listening.

"Some of the translations say God has plans to give us prosperity and good things, but some—including the King James Version—take the approach that what he promised us was peace."

TJ's lips tightened momentarily, as if she'd touched a sensitive chord, before returning to their neutral state.

Gillian kept her voice low but firm. "It took me awhile to realize that peace didn't mean there would be no suffering, but once I accepted that, my anger began to fade. Many days I feel as if I'm still waiting for the peace; others I feel as if I've found it. You helped me regain part of that peace on Monday."

Now that she knew he'd devoted his summers to helping others, Gillian understood how TJ had been able to reach through her pain and touch her heart. Perhaps knowing how he'd helped her would show him he was still the RV Reverend, someone who could touch people's hearts.

TJ said nothing, and his expression remained impassive. Had she reached him? Gillian didn't know.

"I feel like a fool telling you all that," she said when the silence grew oppressive. "You're the one who used to be a preacher."

He shifted on the bench to face her again. "*Used to be* being the operative words. How can I even think about preaching when my faith is so weak?"

She heard the anguish in his voice. "Do you think you're the only one whose faith has faltered? What about the apostle Peter? He was confident he would never deny his Lord, but he did exactly that—not once but three times—yet Jesus called him a rock."

"I'm no rock."

"Aren't you? You shored me up twice this week."

TJ was silent for a long moment, as if he were trying to digest all Gillian had said. Finally he rose, then reached forward to pull her to her feet. "It's too cold for us to be out here. Let's get you back to your cabin."

He slid his arm around her waist, drawing her closer, and as he looked down at her, his eyes were somber. "I came out here hoping to help you, but you're the one who comforted me. To be honest, I didn't know that was possible. I didn't think anyone could help me, but you did. Thank you, Gillian."

She started to respond, but before she could, TJ's lips curved into a smile. "You're a very special woman," he said softly. And then, before Gillian knew what he intended, he lowered his head to kiss her.

It started as the lightest brush of lips, a touch as soft as a butterfly's wings, but within seconds it intensified. TJ's hand moved to the nape of her neck, bringing her face closer to his while his lips tantalized her, feathering kisses on her eyelids, her cheeks, the corners of her mouth before recapturing her lips.

Gillian had been kissed before, but never—not even in her dreams—had there been a kiss like this. She entwined her arms around TJ's neck, savoring the sweetness of his lips and the shivers of excitement the touch of his hand on her neck sent down her spine. Her pulse raced and her heart began to pound, all because of this man and a kiss that was sweet and tender at the same time that it was deeply passionate. If dreams came true, this moment would never end.

Closing her eyes, Gillian etched the memory of each sensation onto her brain and into her heart. Then, without a warning, TJ stepped away.

"I'm sorry, Gillian. That was a mistake."

35

It wasn't a mistake. Gillian frowned as she ran the brush through her hair, trying to tame the tangles that somehow managed to appear overnight. The kiss she and TJ had shared was *not* a mistake.

Admittedly, the evening had not turned out the way she'd expected. When she'd shopped for the dress and later when she'd applied her makeup and styled her hair, she'd thought about how the evening might end. She'd expected a kiss. More than one, actually. She'd expected a romantic interlude with sweet words and even sweeter kisses. What she hadn't expected was that it would be TJ who gave her that kiss and that the interlude preceding it would be far from romantic.

The way the evening ended had been unexpected, and yet Gillian could not regret it. TJ might not believe in Jeremiah 29:11, but she did. It and Romans 8:28 were among her favorite Bible verses. Although she had yet to discover the good behind her accident, and though she was still struggling to imagine what the future might hold in store for her, Gillian knew that God did work things out for the best.

Last night was a good example. If she hadn't been distressed by the concert, she would not have gone to the dock. If she hadn't gone to the dock, she wouldn't have met TJ there. And if she hadn't met TJ, she wouldn't have received—and given—comfort. That was all part of God's plan, and so was the kiss. It had stirred her senses, but more importantly, it had shown her that TJ was beginning to heal.

As they'd walked beneath one of the resort's lights, Gillian had seen the difference in his eyes. The pain that had dominated his life had lessened. It might have been their conversation. It might have been the kiss. The cause didn't matter. What mattered was the result. That was not a mistake.

And the way she felt this morning was not a mistake, either. Though she'd lain awake for hours, replaying her time with TJ and the unforgettable kiss, Gillian had wakened feeling energized, as if TJ wasn't the only one who was healing.

She frowned again as she glanced at the clock and realized she'd missed breakfast. That hadn't been her intention, but perhaps it was for the best. She needed more time before she saw TJ again.

Ten minutes later Gillian climbed the stairs to Kate's apartment, hoping her friend wasn't going to grill her about her date with Mike but recognizing the unlikelihood of that. At least Kate didn't know what had happened on the dock. Even if she had been looking out one of her windows, none of them overlooked the dock.

"Do you and Mike have any plans for today or are you still recovering from your big night?" Kate asked when she'd offered Gillian a cup of coffee. She settled back in her chair, glancing at the laptop on the table in front of them. "You certainly caught the paparazzi's attention. I had half a dozen Google alerts this morning."

Kate tapped the screen to wake it and read, "'Has Mike Tarkett found the woman of his dreams?' Only you can answer that. Here's another one. 'A noteable match?' They spelled it wrong and even put a musical note next to it in case readers didn't catch the pun. 'Renowned pianist and Hill Country heir spotted together.' You get the idea."

Gillian tried not to wince. "I didn't think anyone recognized me."

"You, my friend, were dreaming if you believed that." Kate slid the plate of pastries closer to Gillian, encouraging her to take one. Though Gillian's hunger had faded with the realization that she was once again a news item, she knew she needed to eat something before she went to the center.

"Reporters are trained to ferret out names," Kate continued, "and when that name is as famous as yours, there's no chance of anonymity. I wouldn't be surprised if a couple paparazzi showed up here today."

"Would you mind?"

Kate shook her head. "You know better than that. Every marketing manager loves free publicity."

Gillian wouldn't be at Rainbow's End if they arrived, but knowing Kate, she'd charm the reporters so much that they might wind up doing a feature about the resort's renaissance rather than the former pianist who was a guest. And if they discovered that Gillian worked at Hill Country Pages, Marisa's shop might see a boost in sales.

"That only leaves Mike to worry about," Gillian said after she'd washed down the pastry with a slug of coffee. "I hope all this buzz doesn't hurt him."

Kate looked puzzled. "How could it?"

"I don't know." Though the press that had covered her career had been mostly benign, one reporter had believed he could boost his ratings by being the first to report a scandal in Gillian's past. When he'd found nothing, he'd resorted to innuendos that, while ungrounded, had made her manager cringe and insist on a retraction. Gillian hoped nothing similar would happen to Mike.

"All I know is that I don't want to do anything to hurt his chances of being elected."

Kate smiled as she rubbed her ever-expanding baby bump. "If you really want to help Mike, you'll say yes when he asks that very special question."

The question TJ would never ask. As color triggered by the memory of the kiss they'd shared flooded to Gillian's cheeks, she forced a light tone to her voice. "You're getting ahead of yourself, aren't you?"

"Am I?" Kate's eyes took in the telltale blush. "It doesn't look like it from where I'm sitting."

"It's not what you think." And, though she shared most things with her dearest friend, Gillian had no intention of telling her what had happened on the dock or how often her thoughts turned to the man who'd loved so deeply that he would not let himself love again.

"To answer your original question, I thought I'd spend some time at the senior center." Since it was Saturday, Gillian was not scheduled to work at the bookstore. "Want to join me?"

Kate shook her head. "Greg and I are going to San Antonio to do some shopping. I can't believe it, but my husband has discovered he was born with a shopping gene after all, at least where the baby's concerned. He wants to kick the tires on a stroller for Junior. Apparently this one has running lights like some of the trucks."

Gillian couldn't help smiling at the image. "I've heard about men and their toys, but I didn't know that strollers fell into the man-toy category."

"That's because Greg's not your average man."

And neither was TJ.

Was she right? TJ had spent a virtually sleepless night asking himself that question. Now he was rowing around Bluebonnet

Lake for the umpteenth time, trying to answer it. Was anger what had distanced him from God?

His arms ached, but that pain was nothing compared to the ache in his heart. He'd spent more than a year without the peace Gillian had described, and that had taken its toll on him. Though he'd traveled thousands of miles and had seen some of the country's most beautiful spots, nothing he'd done had filled the emptiness inside. It wasn't only the loss of Deb that had weighed on him. The greater anguish had come from losing the closeness he had once felt to his Lord, the knowledge that God was watching over him, guiding him. How had that happened?

When he reached the far side of the lake, TJ laid the oars aside and stared at the small island. Though he'd circled it numerous times, he'd never set foot on it. Perhaps he would some other day. Today he was content to simply look at the spot that had captured so many people's fancy. It was beautiful, as beautiful as Deb had been. Even when cancer had deprived her of her hair, she'd still been beautiful to TJ, because her beauty had been more than superficial. She'd had a beautiful spirit, and that had shone through eyes that had endured overwhelming pain.

Deb had been strong. He was not. While Deb was alive, TJ had believed his faith was as strong as his parents'. That was one of the reasons serving as the RV Reverend had felt so right. But when the moment of testing had come, he'd failed.

Gillian was right: TJ had been angry. He'd been angry that Deb suffered. If he could have, he would gladly have borne that suffering so she could be spared. But the real anger was at himself. In those dark moments after her funeral, he'd told himself that if only his faith had been strong enough, God would have healed Deb the way Jesus had healed the centurion's servant.

TJ couldn't count the number of times he'd read that story, marveling at the Roman's faith. There had been times when he'd thought his own faith was equally strong, but he was wrong. Totally wrong. TJ's faith had wavered, and when it did, he'd failed Deb, he'd failed himself, he'd failed his Lord.

As anguish clenched his heart, he leaned forward, clasping his hands around his knees and resting his head on them. "I'm sorry, Lord," he sobbed. "Please forgive me."

TJ had no idea how long he remained there, but when he raised his head, a ray of sunshine broke through the trees, the sight filling his heart with peace.

Gillian was halfway to Dupree when her cell phone rang. She'd turned it on when she'd left Rainbow's End, and now that she'd reached the top of Ranger Hill, she was once more in cell range. Glancing at the display and seeing Mike's picture, she pulled over and answered the call.

"How are you this morning?" he asked without preamble.

"Fine. I'm on my way to the senior center. Today's the first tai chi class, and I wanted to see how it goes."

"I still can't quite picture seniors doing tai chi." A faint chuckle accompanied Mike's words. "But that's not the reason I called. I was worried about you. Actually, I'm worried that I did something wrong last night."

Gillian hated having caused this wonderful man even a moment of worry. If she were permitted a do-over, she wouldn't have run away without an explanation, but the combination of the concert and the reporters had left her so badly shaken that she hadn't been thinking clearly.

"It's nothing you did," she said quickly, wanting to reassure him. "I just wasn't ready to be part of the music scene. It was harder than I'd expected."

"I thought it might be something like that. I spent the night kicking myself for taking you to the concert." Once again, Mike was being the perfect gentleman, kind and sensitive. He was one man in a million, a twenty-first-century Prince Charming.

"It's over. No harm done." To the contrary, though she wouldn't share the details with Mike, some very good things had resulted from her time at the concert.

"It wasn't the evening I wanted for you. Let me make it up to you."

Gillian waved at Kate and Greg as they drove by on their way to big city shopping. "What did you have in mind?" she asked Mike. She wasn't going to spend the rest of her life pining for a man who would never love her, a man who called the sweetest of kisses a mistake. Only a stupid woman would do that, and Gillian was not stupid. Mike was a wonderful man with a wonderful family, and—unlike TJ—he didn't need time to heal.

"I was hoping you'd have dinner with me on Tuesday." Gillian heard the smile in Mike's voice and knew she'd said the right thing. "What I had in mind was a barbecue joint that I've been to dozens of times. It's absolutely no competition for Strawberry Chantilly, so you don't have to worry that I'll be thinking about anything other than you."

"And the food." Gillian added the way Mike was able to poke fun at himself to the list of his admirable qualities.

He chuckled. "Well, that too. It's pretty amazing food. You have your choice of beef or pork or both, and if you like fries, they serve regular and sweet potato fries along with onion rings and the best slaw in the county."

"It's a good thing we're not on video chat, because I'm practically drooling." Gillian leaned back in her seat, enjoying the gentle banter she and Mike were sharing. Other than last night, she could not recall a time when she hadn't been comfortable with him.

"Now that's something I can't picture—the elegant Gillian Hodge drooling. Fortunately, there shouldn't be any paparazzi there, although my campaign manager wouldn't mind if there were. He's grateful for all the free publicity we got last night."

It was Gillian's turn to sigh with relief. "I'm glad to hear that. I wasn't sure whether it was good or bad."

"Definitely good." Mike echoed Kate's assertion that any notice from the media was good. "Dinner on Tuesday would be even better. Will you go with me?"

"That sounds wonderful."

* * *

When she arrived at the senior center, half a dozen women including Sally were waiting for the tai chi instructor. Though Gillian greeted them, pleased that she recognized most of them and remembered their names, she remained on the sidelines once the instructor arrived. It was amazing to see how quickly the women moved from the natural awkwardness of unfamiliar positions to something that resembled the instructor's movements. By the end of the class, everyone was laughing, leaving Gillian no doubt that putting tai chi on the schedule had been a good idea. Her only regret was that TJ was not here to capture the students' progress in pictures.

"That was fun!" Sally declared as she snagged a doughnut and sank into a chair next to Gillian. "I'm going to try to convince Roy to come next time and bring some of his buddies. We need to show Dupree that real men do tai chi."

"Shall I alert the media?"

"Why not? I saw you got your share last night."

Gillian wrinkled her nose. "Is there anyone who hasn't seen those pictures?"

"In Dupree? Probably not. Our grapevine is the fastest in the state." Sally took a bite of doughnut, savoring what was supposed to be a forbidden treat. "I haven't met Mike, but from everything I've heard, he's a good guy. It's just too bad that he's not a minister. If he was, I'd know he was the one for you."

"Oh, Sally, you never give up, do you?"

"No, and you shouldn't either. You need to keep looking for the preacher man."

What would Sally say if she knew Gillian had found one?

He was an idiot. TJ downshifted to climb the hill, frowning as he thought about what he'd done. Kissing Gillian Hodge was the dumbest, most idiotic thing he'd done in years. It was true that he'd felt closer to her last night than he had to anyone since Deb had died. It was true that he'd wanted to comfort Gillian when he'd seen how distressed she was. It was true that Gillian had helped him sort out his thoughts and that, thanks to her, he had begun to restore his relationship with God, but none of those were reasons to kiss her. The worst part was, even though he'd told her it was a mistake, TJ did not regret the kiss.

He took a deep breath as he crested Ranger Hill and descended into Dupree. It had felt so good, so right, to hold Gillian in his arms, to feel the softness of her lips, to inhale the sweet yet spicy scent of her perfume. His fingers could still remember how her hair felt like silk, how her skin was as smooth as satin, and when he'd heard her soft sigh, it had sent tremors down his spine, reminding him of an earthquake's aftershock.

The kiss had been wonderful. It had been unforgettable. It had also been wrong. Gillian had been vulnerable. So had he, for that matter, but the fact was, he'd taken advantage of Gillian's vulnerability. He'd kissed her when her defenses were down, when he should have offered nothing more than words. Even though the kiss had confirmed the depth of his feelings for her, it was too soon. He needed to continue his conversation with God, to learn what he had in store for TJ. Until he settled his future, TJ had no right to take his relationship with Gillian to the next level. But he had let himself kiss her, and that definitely made him an idiot.

Gillian slid her sunglasses down from their perch on top of her head. The sun was overhead and bright enough to burn unprotected skin in just a few minutes, making her regret that she hadn't worn a long-sleeved shirt or slathered sunblock on her arms. If she hurried, she'd be inside the car before her skin turned pink. Though there had been an open spot on Pecan Street, she'd parked around the corner on Avenue J to leave the closer spots for the seniors.

She rounded the corner, her stride faltering at the sight of the couple leaning against the big black truck, lost in a passionate embrace. Brianna and Pete. Gillian took a deep breath, trying to quell the uneasiness that filled her whenever she thought about those two together. According to TJ, Pete was well aware of Brianna's age. Admittedly, there was nothing illegal about kissing, but it still bothered Gillian.

A quick glance at her watch told her it was a quarter past noon. Though she'd planned to fill up her gas tank before having lunch at the Sit 'n' Sip, this was more important. She climbed into the car and headed back toward Rainbow's End, hoping she wouldn't appear to be a busybody.

When she arrived in Firefly Valley, Gillian felt relief flow through her at the sight of a car parked next to the Carters' RV. As she'd hoped, Natalie was still at home. This was not a conversation she wanted to have at the supermarket where Natalie worked.

"I didn't expect to see you today," the attractive woman said when she opened the door. "You got another permission slip for Brianna?"

"No." Gillian looked around, noticing a couple neighbors within earshot. "Could I come in for a few minutes? I want to talk to you."

"Sure." Natalie shoved a pile of magazines off the couch to make room for Gillian. "What's going on?"

Now that she was here, Gillian wasn't certain how to begin. Perhaps this whole trip had been a mistake. Perhaps Natalie would think she was intruding into what wasn't her business. But she was here.

"I'm a little worried about Brianna," she said carefully. "I wanted to be certain you were okay with the guy she's dating."

"Pete Darlington?" Natalie spat the name as if it had poisoned her tongue.

"Mm-hmm. I didn't want to interfere, but I wasn't sure you knew about him."

"I know about him all right." Natalie's frown left no doubt of her disapproval. "He's all Brianna can talk about. Pete this. Pete that." Her frown deepened. "Just because I know my daughter's seeing him don't mean I approve. I don't. I told Brianna she couldn't see him again, but the fact that you're here tells me she's doing just that." Pain filled Natalie's dark eyes. "She is, isn't she?"

"I'm afraid so. I saw them in town. They were . . ."

"Kissing. Maybe even more." Natalie completed the sentence. "Brianna's making the same mistake I did. She's letting her head get turned by fancy words and a truck. She thinks she's in love. Fact is, what she really loves is the idea of an older man being interested in her. Pete has a job, so he can give her things like that scarf she was wearing the other day. I'm afraid she's gonna wind up like me, a single mother before she finishes high school."

Natalie reached out to Gillian and grabbed her hands. "I don't know what to do. I can't lock her inside here when I'm gone, but I gotta do something. You got any ideas how to control her?"

Gillian nodded. "TJ's talked to Pete—twice, in fact—so he knows Brianna's a minor. That doesn't seem to have stopped him, though. Maybe you should talk to the police."

Natalie shook her head. "It won't work. My mama tried that with me. It just made me more determined to marry Earl. There's gotta be another way."

Unfortunately, Gillian couldn't think of one.

36

Hey, Mr. B. Got a minute?"

TJ grinned. He was still getting used to his new name. In the past, students had always referred to him as Mr. Benjamin, at least within his hearing, but Todd had started the abbreviation, and others had followed his example.

The slight hesitation in Todd's voice made TJ suspect his question was not related to the latest homework assignment. "Sure. What's going on?" It had been a week since Todd had come to the evening gatherings at Firefly Valley, and he'd been unusually silent during class, giving TJ little clue to what he was thinking. In all likelihood, Brianna was the reason for both Todd's absence and his uncharacteristic reticence, but TJ knew better than to rely on assumptions.

Todd looked around the rapidly emptying classroom. "It's private."

"Of course." As soon as the last student left the room, TJ closed the door and returned to the front. That way if someone did enter, they'd be less likely to overhear him and Todd. Perching on the edge of his desk and hoping his casual position would put the boy at ease, TJ raised an eyebrow before he repeated his question. "What's going on?"

Apparently unwilling to meet his gaze, Todd stared out the window. "It's what isn't going on that's the problem. We used to be a couple, but now Brianna's seeing that older guy, Pete Something-or-other."

"Darlington. He's part of the crew working on the Carroll complex." Todd might as well know who his rival was.

"So what do I do? How do I get her back?" This time Todd looked directly at TJ. Though he kept his voice even, the tick at the corner of his eye revealed his stress.

"Have you tried talking to her?" TJ doubted that would have any effect at this point in Brianna's infatuation with Pete, but it might be worth a try.

"Yeah." Todd was back to staring, this time at the floor. "She won't listen. I left notes in her locker the way we always do, but she won't answer them. I even asked my dad what to do."

Remembering how hard it had been to admit that he needed advice when he was Todd's age, TJ figured the boy must have been desperate to have done that. "What did he say?"

"That I deserve better than someone who'd dump me and I need to move on." The advice was sound and was in fact what TJ would have suggested, but he knew it wasn't what Todd wanted to hear. "That's easy for him to say." Todd scuffed the floor with his boot. "He doesn't know how I feel. My mom wouldn't be any help, 'cuz she's a girl, but you understand."

When TJ raised an eyebrow, startled by Todd's assertion, the teen continued. "I know you understand. You have to, 'cuz you're in the same situation. The girl you love is dating another guy."

"I don't . . ." TJ broke off the sentence. Though he'd started to deny that he loved Gillian, he couldn't, not without lying to both himself and Todd. The truth was, he did love her. He'd been brushing the memories of the kiss and the feelings they'd uncovered aside, trying to tell himself what he felt was nothing more than caring, one step above friendship but a mile away from love. He'd been deluding himself. Just as Gillian's discussion of anger had forced TJ to examine his behavior and ask for God's forgiveness, Todd's simple statement had forced him to accept the truth about her. He loved Gillian. It might not be the same kind of love he'd felt for Deb, but that didn't make it any less real.

TJ gripped the edge of the desk as he tried to make sense of his feelings. Though he knew many widowed and divorced men found a second chance at love, he hadn't expected that to happen to him. He'd believed he was like Gillian's father—a one-woman man. How wrong could a man be? He loved Gillian, loved her deeply. The reason it had taken him so long to admit it was that he'd believed he was betraying his love for Deb. Now he realized that his love for Gillian wasn't wrong, even though it was very different from what he'd shared with Deb.

TJ had heard one of the seniors talking about her second husband, claiming one had been like silver, the other like gold. At the time, he'd paid little attention, but now he realized how poor the analogy was. Silver had less value than gold. Surely the woman didn't mean that one husband was less loved than the other. In thinking about Deb and Gillian, TJ decided it was more accurate to say that one was like a peony, the other a lilac. They were two very different women, but each was special in her own way.

"Is something wrong, Mr. B? You look like you saw a ghost."

TJ shook his head. "It's more like I saw the light," he told the boy.

"Does that mean you know what I should do to get Brianna back?"

Once again TJ shook his head. Though he hated to disappoint Todd, he was the last person to be giving advice to the lovelorn. "I'd like to tell you I had a better answer than your dad did, but I don't." TJ slid his feet to the floor and clapped

Todd on the shoulder. "I guess we both have to wait and see how this turns out."

Gillian tipped her head to one side, holding the position as she tried to ease the tension in her neck and shoulders. Though it was only mid-afternoon, she was exhausted. She hadn't slept well for the last few nights, ever since the kiss that she still had not been able to put out of her mind. The exhilaration she'd felt the first morning had faded. Now she was torn between wanting to talk to TJ about not just the kiss but everything they'd shared that night and fearing what he might say.

Frowning, Gillian repeated the neck stretch on the other side. As it turned out, she'd had no opportunity to speak with TJ. He'd missed supper Saturday night and had excused himself as soon as he'd eaten the last bite of dessert on Sunday. The message was clear: he didn't want to talk, at least not to Gillian. He'd seemed preoccupied, and while he hadn't ignored Gillian, he hadn't confided in her. That was what had kept her tossing and turning for most of the night.

She didn't understand what had changed. It was one thing for TJ to say the kiss had been a mistake. Though she didn't agree with him, Gillian understood why he hadn't wanted her to believe they had any future together. No matter how she felt, TJ was like her dad and could give his heart to only one woman. But that didn't explain why he'd backed away from her. Gillian had thought they were friends—good friends.

She straightened her neck, then curled it forward, thankful for the momentary lull between customers. When she'd wakened feeling as if she'd had no more than two hours of sleep, she'd promised herself a nap this afternoon. Unfortunately, that plan had failed when the woman who was supposed to work from two until closing called in sick.

Unwilling to close the store, especially since Mondays were one of the busiest days, Gillian had agreed to stay until Marisa could wrap up things at Rainbow's End and relieve her. In the meantime, she kept a smile on her face as she helped customers find everything from cookbooks to the latest bestsellers.

The store phone rang, interrupting Gillian's yoga-inspired exercises.

"I'm on my way," Marisa said. "I can't thank you enough for staying."

"It's what friends do." As she hung up the phone, Gillian nodded. Marisa had become a friend, as had Lauren. Perhaps that was the reason she felt so comfortable in Dupree: she had friends who liked her for who she was, not because she'd once graced a concert stage.

The pace was slower here than in the big cities, and while that sometimes frustrated her, Gillian had to admit that for the most part she enjoyed it. And though the grapevine occasionally felt intrusive, the overall friendliness of the townspeople warmed her heart more than she'd thought possible. No doubt about it, life in Dupree was good.

Taking advantage of the continuing lull, Gillian pulled out her cell phone. No missed calls or voice mail messages, but the email icon told her she had at least one note. Curious, she opened the app and was surprised to see a message from her father with the subject line "good work."

The rush of pleasure surging through her overcame her fatigue, and she smiled. This was truly a case of better late than never. It might have taken him awhile, but Dad was finally acknowledging her work on the senior center, and that was sweet. So sweet.

Gillian opened the note, her pleasure evaporating as she read, "Saw the news. Good work, Gillian. Mike Tarkett is the kind of man you ought to marry." Disappointment mingled with anger, and anger won, shocking her with its intensity. She hadn't realized how much she'd wanted her father's approval of the center or how delusional she'd been trying to convince herself that his silence was nothing more than his unwillingness to express his thoughts any way but verbally. But here was the proof. What Dad approved of was Gillian's appearance on the arm of an eligible bachelor, not the effort she had put into the center.

"Do you have a copy of . . ."

Once more TJ had startled her with his almost silent approach. Gillian looked up. Just minutes earlier she'd wanted to talk to him, hoping they could renew their friendship, but right now she was not fit company for anyone.

She tried to feign a polite smile but obviously failed, for TJ's smile faded.

"What's wrong?" he asked, coming closer to the counter. "I probably shouldn't say this, but your face is almost as red as your hair."

Gillian nodded, not surprised by his observation. Her fair skin had always betrayed her emotions, particularly anger.

"I know he loves me," she said, hearing the resignation in her voice. "I shouldn't let it bother me, but it does."

"Something your father did."

Gillian shook her head. "More like what he didn't do. He didn't comment on all we accomplished with the center, but one picture of me with a man he considers appropriate son-in-law material and he sends me an email with the subject line 'good work.' He's acting like I was on a campaign to snag a husband. I wasn't doing that, TJ. I wasn't." Gillian hated the way her voice broke, but there was nothing she could do about it.

"I know." To Gillian's surprise, TJ looked as if the thought of her hunting for a husband bothered him. Silently he reached for her hand and led her to one of the comfortable chairs the store offered to customers. When she was seated, he took the chair next to her. "It's only natural to want your parents' approval. I know I did."

Though he'd dropped her hand, TJ was looking at her the way he had Friday night, as if she was more—much more—than a casual acquaintance. The thought helped quell the anger that had caused her stomach to clench and her throat to constrict.

"I wish I could take away the hurt," TJ continued, "but I can't do that. Only you can let it go." He leaned over and captured her hand again, cradling it between both of his. "I apologize if I sound like the RV Reverend now, but there's a verse in Galatians that talks about needing to please God, not men. There are times when we can please both, but I don't have to tell you which is more important."

Gillian thought for a moment, reviewing the Bible verses she had memorized over the years. "Galatians 1:10. I know the verse."

She remembered being in college and having the minister challenge each member of his congregation to answer the question of whether their chosen careers would honor God. At the time, Gillian had believed hers would, but now she wasn't certain. Perhaps she had been so caught up in pleasing her father that she had lost sight of God's will.

"I thought I was doing that. Now I don't know. It shouldn't be, but sometimes it's hard to tell the difference."

"Of course it is." TJ gave her a reassuring smile. "It's especially difficult where parents are concerned. We're taught to honor them, but there are times we need to step back and realize they're not perfect."

Gillian knew that. She'd believed she'd long since accepted both her and her father's imperfections, but today she felt as if she'd been ambushed. Perhaps it was merely because she was so tired that Dad's note bothered her so much. Perhaps it was because his reaction had been so different from Cal and Stacy's. Or perhaps it was simply because the center was the first thing that had fired her imagination since the accident and she wanted him to share her excitement. Gillian wasn't certain why it had happened, but she knew she'd overreacted.

"How'd you get to be so wise?" she asked TJ.

"Me wise? You're the one who set me on the right path. Thanks to you, I'm mending my relationship with God."

Nothing he could have said would have pleased her more.

37

The phone woke Gillian from the first deep sleep she'd had in days.

"Hello?" She switched on the light as she picked up the receiver, frowning at the red numbers on the alarm clock. Three a.m. was no time for a call. "Who's this?"

"Kate Vange. Best friend and expectant mother." Kate's voice held a note of amusement as well as something else, something Gillian couldn't identify. "Remember when I told you Junior was anxious to be born?" Gillian nodded, recalling the conversation they'd had only yesterday. "It seems I was right. I'm in labor."

The last vestiges of sleep fled from Gillian's brain as she realized the element she could not identify in Kate's voice was strain. "Labor? Really?" The fear Gillian had tried to control flooded through her. "You're not due for another month."

History wouldn't repeat itself, she told herself firmly. Kate and her baby would be fine.

Oblivious to Gillian's distress, Kate chuckled. "Junior didn't get the message. Greg and I are on our way to the hospital now. If the doctor agrees that it's not false labor, would you bring Sally? Roy left last night for a golf tournament in El Paso."

When Kate finished giving her directions, she said, "I'll call you in an hour or so. Ooh! Here it comes. Sorry."

Gillian heard Kate's intake of breath as another contraction hit her. "Call me later," she said and hung up the phone. There'd be no more sleep for any of them tonight.

Two hours later, Gillian was headed toward San Antonio with Sally in the passenger seat. Though otherwise she appeared relaxed, Gillian noticed that Sally gripped the armrest.

"I'm glad you're driving," she said as Gillian swung onto the freeway. "City traffic and I don't get along." And there was the fact that Sally hadn't driven in over a year. Gillian hoped that was the reason for Sally's tension and that she wasn't remembering another premature birth and its tragic ending.

Gillian merged into the surprisingly heavy stream of cars and nodded. "I wouldn't miss this for anything. It's not every day I get to watch you become a great-grandmother."

Keeping her eyes moving from the windshield to the rearview and side mirrors and back again, Gillian forced herself to smile. She would do nothing to upset the woman who'd been the closest thing to a mother she'd known. "It's still hard for me to realize Kate's about to be a mother."

"She'll be a good one. She and Greg are meant to be parents."

"But it'll be a big change."

Sally nodded. "Another one. I can hardly believe how much our lives have changed in the last year."

Most of those changes had been happy ones, with Gillian's accident being the notable exception. "At least you and Kate are settled. I'm still trying to figure out what I'm supposed to do next."

"Besides marry a minister?"

After a tractor trailer merged into traffic ahead of Gillian, she glanced at her passenger. "I wasn't joking, Sally. I believe God has something good in mind for me, but I haven't been able to figure out what it is." Dad was sure that marriage was the answer, but though Gillian wouldn't discount the possibility, she believed it was only a part of the plan.

"Have you considered that could be your problem?" The traces of mirth had left Sally's voice. "You think you should do all the work. Why not try the LGLG method?"

Gillian tightened her grip on the steering wheel as traffic increased and cars whizzed by her on both sides. "LGLG? What's that?"

"Let go and let God. Surely you've heard of that."

"I know the phrase but not the acronym." What Sally said was a variation on TJ's advice from yesterday. Surrender. Accept God's will. Seek only his approval. Gillian knew it was good advice, but while the concepts sounded easy, applying them wasn't. She knew because she'd tried. Though she'd told herself that was what she wanted to do, Gillian had discovered a barrier between her thoughts and her deeds. And a moving car in rush traffic was hardly the place to try again.

Half an hour later they reached the hospital and found Kate still in labor. Though she smiled to reassure Gillian and Sally, Kate's face left no doubt of the strain she'd been under, and Gillian said a silent prayer for both Kate and her baby.

"The doc tells me it's going to be a few more hours," Kate said with an exaggerated frown. "Junior's not in as much of a rush as I thought." She pointed at her husband, who looked even worse than she did, perhaps because he could do nothing more than coach Kate. "Greg has to stay here. That's part of our deal, but you two can relax. The coffee shop is very nice," she told Sally, turning her attention to Gillian as she said, "So is the chapel."

"Have you been talking to Sally?" Gillian demanded when Sally reluctantly agreed she could use a cup of coffee.

"Nope. I just looked at your face. You look like you could use some quiet time. I spent my share of time in the chapel last year and can vouch that it's a special place."

And so Gillian found herself in the hospital chapel. It was a simple room, as quiet as Kate had promised. Though it could accommodate thirty or forty people, Gillian was the only one there. If she was going to LGLG, this might be the right place.

She knelt, folded her hands, and bowed her head, not sure where to start. She needed words, but none were forthcoming. Instead Gillian pictured the first painting she had seen of Jesus, one that had hung in the Sunday school she'd attended as a child. Even then she had known there was something special about that painting.

Jesus's eyes had seemed to be looking directly at her, and though she now knew they were nothing more than an artist's representation, created with a dab of oil paint and a brush, at the time she'd felt as if the love she'd seen in those eyes was able to touch her. Jesus didn't need a halo to tell viewers he was holy. He possessed infinite love, infinite power, infinite wisdom, and all of them shone from the painting.

Her father loved her. Like Jesus, he wanted only the best for her. Had her mother lived, she would have lavished love on Gillian. But their love, as strong as it was, could not compare to the love of her heavenly father. His was the only love that knew no boundaries.

Gillian nodded slowly. God would lead her. He might have closed a door, but he would show her the way to the open window, if only she would let him. She rose and unfolded her hands. Facing the stained glass window, she slowly extended her hands, turning them so her empty palms faced upward.

"I have nothing to offer," she said softly, "but I put my life in your hands. Lead me, Lord."

There was no answer, and yet as she stood there, Gillian felt the tension drain from her, and in its place, she found peace.

"Thank you, Lord."

38

"If you're looking for Gillian, she's at the hospital."

Fear sliced through TJ, destroying both his appetite and the anticipation he'd felt about spending the evening with Gillian. He'd missed her at breakfast but hadn't worried, because her schedule had been erratic recently. When a faculty meeting had kept him later than usual, he'd been annoyed but had told himself it was only a couple hours before supper. He'd see Gillian then. Or so he'd thought, until Kevin, one of the teenage waitstaff, had turned anticipation into dread.

TJ tried not to shudder at the thought of Gillian in a hospital. Though Kevin sounded almost nonchalant, TJ associated hospitals with suffering and death.

"What happened?" Gillian had to be all right. She simply had to. TJ didn't know what he'd do if yet another person he loved were taken from him. Surely God wouldn't do that, especially now that TJ was finding his way back to him.

He took a deep breath, trying to vanquish the fears that threatened to smother him. Gillian had occupied his thoughts even more than normal today as he'd come to grips with the fact that he loved her, that he wanted her to be a permanent part of his life. It had been a bittersweet realization as he'd struggled with the knowledge that he had little to offer her—no home, no full-time employment, not even the large extended family she longed for. The truth was, TJ had nothing that would make this wonderful woman want to share her life with him. And now she was lying in some hospital somewhere.

Kevin looked up from the tray he was unloading onto the lazy Susan, his expression remarkably calm for someone who'd just delivered a bombshell. "Gillian's fine. She's staying with Kate and Greg for a while." As TJ tried to absorb his words, Kevin gave him a sympathetic look. "I guess you didn't hear the news. Kate had a baby an hour or so ago. It was all anyone could talk about in the office."

But TJ had bypassed the reception area. "That's good news." Doubly good news. As relief chased the adrenaline from his bloodstream, TJ felt himself relax. In a minute or so, other guests would fill the table. It was an ordinary evening at Rainbow's End except for the arrival of Baby Vange. There had been no reason to panic. Gillian was safe.

TJ blinked in surprise as images danced through his brain. The picture of himself holding an infant in his arms morphed into one of him standing in front of a congregation next to a young couple and their baby. TJ had never baptized anyone. He'd never married a couple. He'd never presided at a funeral. In the past, counseling people, sharing God's Word with them as he tried to assuage their pain and their fears, had been enough. But though he could not explain what had caused the change, today was different. He felt as if something seismic had shifted his life focus. The role he'd played in the past no longer seemed adequate. He wanted more. Much more. Perhaps that was his answer.

How could one person feel totally drained and exhilarated at the same time? Gillian clenched the steering wheel as she backed out of Sally's driveway and headed to Rainbow's End. The day had been tiring, both physically and emotionally. Though it was only 8:00 p.m., she'd been awake since 3:00 a.m. It had been a long, unforgettable day as many of Gillian's prayers had been answered.

Kate and her baby were safe. Junior, who now bore the name of John Jacob Vange, had made his arrival at 5:37 after sixteen hours of labor. Though premature, he weighed over five pounds and was healthy enough that he'd be released tomorrow.

There had been no complications in the delivery, no father grieving the loss of his wife. Instead, when Sally and Gillian had been allowed back into Kate's room, they'd discovered a couple whose happiness bordered on euphoria. The strain that had creased Kate's face during labor had disappeared the instant she'd heard her son's first cry and had cradled him to her breast.

"He's perfect," she announced. Never before had Gillian heard that note of wonder in her friend's voice. Never before had she seen such joy on Kate's face.

"Do you want to hold him?" Kate offered when great-grandma Sally relinquished the now sleeping baby.

Of course she did. Gillian reached for the almost impossibly tiny bundle. John was wearing the blue knit cap the hospital provided and the blue onesie that Kate had brought along with a matching pink one just in case Junior had turned out to be Juniorette. His fists were clenched, and his mouth was scrunched into what Gillian would have described as a scowl, though she'd never tell his proud parents that. They thought he was perfect, and he was—perfectly healthy.

Gillian smiled at the child who, despite Sally's claims to the contrary, resembled Greg far more than Kate. She had expected a sense of awe as she cradled her best friend's firstborn, but she had not expected to be filled with a longing so deep it was almost physical.

In that instant, Gillian had pictured herself holding her own baby. She wasn't certain whether she carried a boy or a girl, but she knew that the man standing behind her, his arm wrapped around her waist, was her husband and that his smile was as joyful as her own. In her mind, she turned to see his face, but though she tried, Gillian could not bring it into focus. Ever since, the image had been gnawing at her, leaving her feeling as if she'd caught a glimpse of happiness only to have it snatched away.

Sighing deeply, she pulled into Rainbow's End and headed for her parking spot, her eyes widening in surprise at the sight of Mike's Ferrari parked in the visitor's slot.

"Mike!" she called as she switched off the engine and hopped out of the car. He was seated on the front steps of her cabin, obviously waiting for her. "What are you doing here?"

He rose, and in the light from the streetlamp, she saw a hint of amusement mingled with something else—perhaps frustration, perhaps boredom. "It's Tuesday," he said, his drawl more pronounced than normal. "We were going to have barbecue together."

Embarrassment and regret swept over Gillian. Tonight was supposed to be the night she proved to herself she'd overcome the discomfort she had experienced at the symphony. It was supposed to be a night of good food and good conversation, a chance to put the symphony and the paparazzi behind them. Instead, Gillian had left Mike sitting here for more than two hours without so much as a call.

A call. She reached into her purse, chagrined to realize she hadn't turned her phone back on. She'd switched it off when she'd entered the chapel, and that had been the last time she'd thought of it.

"I'm so sorry." Gillian held out her hands, hoping Mike would accept her apology. "It's not a good excuse, but with all the excitement, I completely forgot about our date."

She would let him think the excitement had been over the

arrival of Kate and Greg's son, though that was only a small part of the reason Gillian had forgotten both their date and her phone. What had happened in the chapel was so new, so deeply personal, that she had told no one, not even Sally.

Apparently unfazed by her forgetfulness, Mike nodded and clasped her hands. His were warm and strong, reminding Gillian of how they'd felt when he'd touched the back of her waist leaving the symphony hall and how she'd felt safe and protected when he'd wrapped an arm around her shoulders as they'd dodged the paparazzi.

"I figured that's what happened. When you weren't here, I checked inside. The guy at the front desk told me about Kate's baby. I didn't want to leave without seeing you, so I went into Dupree, found cell service, and did some work." He shrugged. "There's no shortage of that. But tell me about the baby. Is everyone healthy?"

"Very. Happy too. The only one who isn't happy is me. I'm not happy that I forgot about our date. I should have called you." Gillian thought quickly, searching for a way to salvage the evening. "Have you eaten?"

Mike shook his head. "I was waiting for you."

"I can't promise you barbecue—Tuesday's spaghetti night at Rainbow's End—but if you give me a few minutes, I should be able to come up with something to curb those hunger pangs." As her stomach growled, Gillian chuckled. "Mine too."

Mike insisted on accompanying her to the kitchen and entertaining her with stories of his day as she raided the refrigerator and prepared a plate of roast beef sandwiches with tossed and molded salads on the side. There were even two pieces of Carmen's famous chocolate pound cake left for their dessert.

"Where would you like to eat?" Though no one would mind if they used the dining room, being there raised the possibility of interruptions by guests in search of Rainbow's End's signature evening treats: milk and cookies. Though Mike had been good-natured about the change of plans, Gillian doubted he'd appreciate that.

He tipped his head to one side, obviously considering her question. "How about the gazebo, or is it too much trouble to take the food out there?"

"It'll be perfect." Gillian opened one of the lower cabinets and retrieved a large tray. "That's why trays were invented."

Within minutes, she and Mike were seated inside the gazebo, balancing plates on their laps. It might not be barbecue, but Carmen's food was always delicious.

"Have you made plans for Memorial Day?" Mike asked when he'd finished his first sandwich and had helped himself to a second along with a refill of iced tea.

"Not yet." Kate had been so focused on her pregnancy that if she and Greg had special plans for Rainbow's End, she hadn't mentioned them to Gillian, and no one at the senior center had talked about the holiday. "I imagine Dupree has some kind of celebration, but I don't know what's involved."

Mike nodded as if her reply pleased him. "I was hoping you'd spend the day with me. I won't mislead you. It's a family event. All the aunts, uncles, and cousins are invited, so it can be a bit chaotic, but I think you'd enjoy the parade and the fireworks." Mike took a slug of tea, his eyes serious as he continued. "I'm probably prejudiced, but I believe Blytheville does a good job of helping people remember the reason for the holiday. It's not just about barbecues."

That sounded like a refreshing change from the usual commercial focus. And having the whole family involved was a definite plus. Though both Stacy and Mike had issued mild warnings, Gillian was looking forward to meeting the rest of the Tarkett clan. "Thanks. I'd like that."

She took another bite of her sandwich. While she might not be as hungry as Mike, she was enjoying the simple meal and the chance to relax after an undeniably eventful day. "Now, tell me how your campaign is going."

Mike did, making even the planning meetings seem entertaining. "You're really enjoying it, aren't you?" He'd spoken for close to five minutes, enough time for Gillian to finish her meal and set her plate aside.

"Yeah." He nodded when Gillian offered to refill his glass. "Of course it helps that the family is behind me."

"That doesn't surprise me. If there was one thing I learned the first time I met them, it's that your parents are determined to make you Blytheville's next mayor. My impression is that when they want something, they get it."

Mike nodded. "You'd be right about that." He drained his glass, then laid it and his plate on the bench beside him. "I almost forgot. Mom asked me to give you something."

"She did?" Gillian couldn't imagine what that might be.

"Yes, this." Mike leaned toward her and pressed a kiss on her cheek. It was brief and brotherly, the kind of kiss George had given Gillian on numerous occasions. She smiled at Mike, acknowledging the kiss.

Though she'd expected Mike to resume their conversation, he rose and tugged Gillian to her feet. "That was from my mother. This is from me."

Moving slowly but surely, Mike drew Gillian into his arms and lowered his lips to hers. There was nothing tentative about the kiss. Mike kissed as masterfully as he did everything else. His lips were firm, the kiss somehow familiar, as if they'd done this before. His hands were warm and comforting as he stroked her back, drawing her closer to him. It was a kiss that touched Gillian's heart and stirred her senses, the perfect ending to the day. And yet as they drew apart, it was not Mike who filled her thoughts.

39

She ought to be back by now. TJ glanced at his watch. When he and Deb had visited friends with newborns, the staff at the hospital had suggested they leave fairly early to give the new family time alone. Even factoring in the drive back from San Antonio, Gillian should have returned. TJ looked at his watch again. The question was whether he ought to disturb her.

He'd stayed later than normal in Firefly Valley, talking to Todd and Shane about the end-of-school party. TJ wasn't certain what surprised him more—the teens planning something almost a month in advance or Todd and Shane working together. In any event, the discussion had taken almost half an hour, and it was now close to ten. That was hardly late, but TJ had learned that Gillian had left Rainbow's End very early this morning. Even if she was still awake, she might be too tired to appreciate a visit.

Gravel crunched beneath his feet as he stepped onto the Rainbow's End driveway. A wise man would wait until tomorrow, he told himself. What he wanted to discuss with Gillian was too important to leave to chance. He needed to plan the right way to explain what he felt called to do. He needed time to find the words to tell her all he'd learned about himself and how he felt about her. He wasn't ready.

He ought to wait, and yet TJ did not want to. He wanted—no, he needed—to be with Gillian, to tell her he loved her, to see if she shared his dream of a future together. He couldn't wait another hour.

Seemingly of their own volition, his feet increased their pace, propelling him along the driveway toward Gillian. And then he heard it. The unmistakable, deep-throated rumble of an expensive sports car. Seconds later, the Ferrari's headlights blinded TJ. Shielding his eyes, he jumped to the side.

"Sorry, buddy," Mike Tarkett called through the open window. "I didn't think anyone would be on the road. I wasn't watching where I was going. Sorry."

TJ shook his head. "No harm done."

Other than to his heart. It felt as if someone had taken an ice pick to it. Gillian hadn't told him she was seeing Mike tonight, so it must have been a spur of the moment thing. The way the scene played out in TJ's mind, Gillian had called Mike with the news of Kate's baby and wanted to celebrate with him. And that's what hurt. TJ had thought they were friends, but instead of him, she'd chosen to share the news of her best friend's baby with Mike.

TJ strode toward his cabin, clenching and unclenching his fists. The game wasn't over. Far from it. He wasn't going to give up without a fight. But before he told Gillian how his heart had opened and that she was the reason he'd begun dreaming of second chances, he was going to get his ducks in a row. He needed to have his future planned before he asked her to share it. That meant that for the next few weeks they would be friends, nothing more.

Gillian narrowed her eyes, studying TJ. "You look different," she said when they met for breakfast the next morning. After

Mike had left, she'd tumbled into bed and fallen asleep, waking this morning with the overwhelming need to tell TJ what had happened. A quick call to the hospital had confirmed that Kate and John were doing well and that Kate and Greg were eagerly awaiting the doctor's arrival to sign the release papers.

Though Gillian wanted to share that news with TJ, she was hoping for some private time to tell him about her experience in the chapel. Fortunately, none of the other guests who shared their table had entered the dining room. That left her with TJ, a TJ who seemed to be changed.

Gillian wondered at the reason. It had been thirty-six hours since she'd seen him, but time alone could not account for the changes. Though she felt different and suspected her face bore testimony to the revelation she'd experienced, it was unlikely TJ had also had an epiphany yesterday. What were the odds of that?

But something had definitely changed. TJ's hair was the same. He hadn't decided to let his beard grow. As she looked more closely, Gillian decided the difference was his eyes. The pain and indecision she'd seen there so often were gone. In their place she saw peace and something else, something she couldn't identify.

"You think I look different?" he asked, breaking a piece of bacon into bite-sized pieces. "I could say the same thing about you. What happened?" That was vintage TJ, responding to a question with one of his own.

She smiled, thinking of everything that had occurred yesterday. There'd been Mike's kiss and Kate's baby, both of which had caused Gillian to look at the world a bit differently, but the most important thing had been the decision she'd made in the chapel.

"I took your advice and Sally's, and I turned my problems over to God," she told TJ as she poured milk on her cereal. The simple words only hinted at the magnitude of her act. "It feels nice not carrying those burdens." More than nice. Though she hadn't thought it possible, Gillian felt like a different person.

TJ met her gaze, his smile leaving no doubt of his approval. "Have you discovered what's next for you?"

"Nothing other than that I'm staying here for a while. I want to spend time with Kate and her son, but there's another reason." This morning while she'd prepared for the day, Gillian's thoughts had focused on the teenagers, particularly Brianna, and she'd known she couldn't simply walk away. "It may sound strange, but even with all the excitement of Kate's baby yesterday, I missed the time in Firefly Valley. I've decided to stay here long enough to see those kids settled in their new homes."

Once again TJ's expression radiated approval. "The last I heard, the builder is hoping to have the apartments finished by mid-August so everyone'll be moved even if they're not fully settled in before school starts."

"I guess that means another three months in Dupree." Gillian smiled as she took a spoonful of cereal, enjoying the blend of grains, fruits, and nuts that Carmen had turned into granola. How wonderful it would be if she could spend those months with TJ. It had been several weeks since he'd spoken of his trip to Big Bend, leading her to wonder whether he'd changed his mind and might remain here.

TJ raised an eyebrow. "Far be it from me to discourage you, but are you sure you're ready for June, July, and August in Texas? There are plenty of days when going outside makes you think you've walked into an oven."

Gillian nodded. "Kate warned me about that. The way I figure it, that's why they invented air conditioning."

As he refilled his mug, TJ gave her an approving look. "Exactly. We may have to figure out something different to do with the kids when it's so hot. Campfires lose their appeal in the summer."

We. He'd said *we*. Her heart soaring over TJ's use of the plural pronoun, as if he were planning to stay at least as long as she was, Gillian smiled. "S'mores never lose their appeal, but we could always ask the kids what they'd like to do."

Though it was possible they had summer activities that would keep them too busy for nightly gatherings, she doubted it. From what Kate had said, activities were scarce, which was part of the reason she and Greg had offered the Firefly Valley kids the use of the resort's tennis court and rowboats.

"Are you sure you want to do that?" TJ's expression telegraphed his skepticism. "If we ask them, half will say they want to learn to ride a motorcycle."

Gillian's shudder was only slightly exaggerated. Many things had changed yesterday, but her fear of motorcycles had not. "That's not a good idea," she said as calmly as she could. "Besides the fact that the kids aren't old enough, there are obvious safety issues."

TJ laid his mug back on the table and turned to face her, a hint of a smile teasing his lips. "I understand why you feel the way you do about motorcycles, but I still wish you'd ride one. You might be surprised at how much you enjoy it."

Gillian shook her head. "You can wish all you want, but it's not going to happen. Subject closed. On a happier note, it sounds as if you've decided to stay. Is that why you look more relaxed?"

TJ dropped his gaze to his plate in what Gillian suspected was a deliberate effort to keep her from reading his expression. "I haven't made any decisions other than that—like you—I want to be here for the kids this summer. I'm also reevaluating my future, but I'm not ready to talk about that yet."

Classic TJ, preferring to keep his life private. Some things would never change.

40

What's going on with TJ?" Kate pushed the button, smiling when the mobile Gillian had bought for John began to revolve. When she'd seen the Noah's ark toy, Gillian had been unable to resist. Now the animals—in pairs, of course—moved slowly in circles along with the rainbow-topped ark.

"What do you mean?" she asked, trying to buy time. She'd believed she was the only one who'd noticed how TJ seemed to smile more often and how there were times when he looked at her with a warmth that hinted at more than simple friendship.

"The man is obsessed with something," Kate said. "He told Greg he needed to do some online research and asked if he could use one of our computers after hours. You know Greg. Of course he agreed. Ever since, TJ's been spending four to six hours a night doing something on the internet." Kate turned to Gillian. "I don't suppose you have any idea what's going on."

"He said something about reevaluating his future. Maybe it's related to that." But in typical TJ fashion, he'd shared none of the details with Gillian.

When John's gurgles turned into the slow and even breathing

of sleep, Kate took a seat near Gillian. "Looks to me like you and Mike are working on your future. For a man who's supposed to be getting ready for an election, I hear he's spending a lot of time in Dupree."

"That's hardly a secret. I told you we had lunch together."

Kate lifted an eyebrow. "You neglected to mention that that was a daily occurrence."

"He missed last Wednesday."

"But his mother came instead."

Gillian raised her hands in surrender. "If you know all that, why are you making such a big deal about it?"

"Because it's so much fun to tease you. I've waited a long time to see you date a man like Mike." Kate leaned forward and laid her hand on Gillian's. "So, tell me. Is he the one?"

Gillian sighed. "I don't know. And, no, I'm not being coy. It's great spending time with Mike. I don't know how to explain it other than to say I'm more comfortable with him than I've ever been with a man. His family's incredible too. When I'm with them, I feel as if I'm another Tarkett."

Kate nodded slowly. "I'm probably out of line saying this, but sometimes I wonder if the attraction is Mike or his family. You talk about Stacy and Cal almost as much as Mike."

Did she? Gillian wasn't aware of that. "They're all pretty wonderful."

"So when Mike proposes—you'll notice that I said 'when' and not 'if'—you'll accept."

Turning her hand over, Gillian laced her fingers through Kate's the way she'd done so many times when they were growing up. "I don't know. I wish I did, but I'm just not sure."

"Why? What's holding you back?"

"Nothing. Everything."

Kate's eyes narrowed. "TJ?"

Unwilling to admit the truth, Gillian countered with another question. "What made you say that?"

"I'm not blind, Gillian. I've seen the way you look at him. You can deny it all you want, but you care for him."

"I do. He's a friend. A good friend, but that's all it'll ever be. TJ's like my dad. He's a one-woman man." To Gillian's dismay, she burst into tears.

It was awful. Not even in her kindest moments would she call the sounds coming from the center "music." Whoever was attempting to play the piano was torturing it. For the past three days, each time she'd left the bookstore, Gillian had heard the noise. Butchered scales, chords that would make Beethoven grateful for his deafness, mangled arpeggios. Today it was worse than ever. Though Gillian couldn't be certain, it sounded as if two people were attempting a duet. Surely it was better for Sally's piano to gather dust than to be abused like this.

Though she'd deliberately ignored the sounds the other days, she could ignore them no more. She crossed the street and entered the senior center. As she'd thought, two women were seated on the piano bench, banging keys as if the sheer noise would make up for hitting all the wrong notes.

"Ladies, what's going on?" Gillian raised her voice to be heard over the cacophony.

Amelia and Edie, two of the Matchers, turned, their expressions radiating innocence. "We were trying to play 'Chopsticks.'"

Gillian tried not to cringe. The notes they'd hit bore no resemblance to the simple tune. If she hadn't known better, she would have said they were deliberately pressing the wrong keys, but surely no one would do that.

"Why don't we try a prettier song?" she said, reaching for the pile of sheet music someone had left on top of the piano.

"I can read music," Amelia told her, "but I've never had formal lessons."

"We both want to be able to play Christmas carols this year." Edie gave Gillian a look that was little short of beseeching. "Can you help us?"

And so Gillian found herself agreeing to give piano lessons each afternoon when she finished work at the bookstore.

To her surprise, the women weren't as inept as the noise that had emanated from the center had led her to believe. All three Matchers displayed basic competence. It was Sally who found the stretch required for octaves to be a challenge. But, though she admitted that her hands hurt when the lessons were over, she persisted.

"She's a real trouper," Gillian told Kate a week later, "but she's making progress."

"What about you? Are you enjoying it?"

Gillian nodded. "I never expected to. You know how my dad is about teaching. After years of listening to him carry on about how I was meant for better things, I never even considered it."

She smiled at Kate as she tickled little John's nose. "I should have listened to TJ when he told me I ought to try teaching. He was right."

The ache in Gillian's heart that never completely disappeared deepened. Somehow everything came back to TJ.

* * *

Today was the final test. TJ swung his left leg backward, retracting the kickstand, then nodded as the bike moved forward. He'd expected to feel nervous, but to his surprise, he didn't. It was time. It had been almost two weeks since he'd realized what he wanted his future to be.

He took a deep breath as he turned onto Lone Star Trail, heading for Dupree. There had been two parts to his vision of the future, and he was close to settling the first. That was the reason the past two weeks had been so busy. In addition to his teaching responsibilities and the time he spent with Gillian—breakfast, supper, and evenings at Firefly Valley—TJ had stayed up late each night researching his choices.

There had been more options than he'd expected. He'd briefly considered lay ministry, but that didn't feel like the right answer for him. It seemed definite that God wanted him to make the commitment of attending a seminary and being trained as a minister.

When he reached the top of Ranger Hill, TJ glanced in his rearview mirror. The panorama spreading out behind him never failed to touch him with its beauty. Against all odds, he'd found peace in a place that included an RV village and a Christian resort. Two months ago he would have believed that impossible, but two months ago he hadn't known Gillian.

TJ's smile faded as he considered the woman who'd captured his fancy in so many ways. Ordinary moments spent with Gillian seemed extraordinary. Just walking together toward Firefly Valley, their hands occasionally brushing, was enough to stir TJ's blood. But he'd done nothing about his feelings, because he knew it wasn't time. Not yet.

Meanwhile, Mike Tarkett was courting Gillian. Todd had told TJ that Mike's Ferrari was parked in front of Hill Country Pages each day at one, leaving an hour later. TJ couldn't imagine that lunch in a bookstore where customers could arrive at any moment was romantic, but Mike's taking time away from both work and his campaign told TJ how serious he was.

He also knew Mike and Gillian had gone on what TJ would classify as real dates the last two Saturdays, because Gillian had mentioned that she wouldn't be at supper those nights. He hadn't asked for details. There were some things a man didn't need to know. What he needed to know was whether he was right in believing God intended him to be a minister, not just the itinerant RV Reverend, but a fully ordained minister with a church of his own.

Two minutes later he parked his bike in the lot next to the church. It was time to find the answers to his questions.

TJ walked confidently up the stairs. When he entered the narthex, one of the men he'd seen at the senior center gave him a warm smile and the church bulletin. "It's good to see you, TJ."

"It's good to be here." Though the words were a polite reply, TJ realized he meant them. As he'd walked through the doors, he'd felt welcomed and not simply by the greeter. He took a seat in the last row, not wanting to draw any more attention to himself. Gillian was seated toward the front with Kate, Greg, and their baby along with Kate's grandmother and her husband. TJ knew they'd be happy for him to join them. Perhaps he'd do that next week, but today he needed to be alone.

He closed his eyes, offering a silent prayer for direction. Afterward, TJ could not have told anyone which hymns were sung, which Scripture readings had been chosen, or what the sermon had been. But when Pastor Bill pronounced the benediction and the congregation began to file out of the church, TJ had his answer. This was where he was meant to be.

41

I heard you came to church today," Gillian said as she slid a piece of ham onto her plate. Though she attempted to keep her voice neutral, when Kate had reported that TJ had been seen in the last pew, happiness had surged through Gillian. Surely this meant TJ had continued to mend his relationship with God, and for that she gave a silent prayer of thanks. Once again the Lord had answered one of her prayers.

Gillian didn't claim to be an expert, but if the way he'd comforted her was indicative of his ministry—and Gillian believed it was—TJ was meant to be a pastor. Her heart filled with joy that he was moving in that direction.

TJ nodded. "I figured the grapevine wouldn't waste much time in spreading the word. I ducked out as soon as I could, but I wasn't able to avoid everyone."

"You sound like a teenager breaking curfew."

A smile crossed TJ's face. "More like the prodigal son, although I didn't see any fatted calves."

"Carmen could arrange that. And for the record, you could have sat with us." Though if he had, Gillian wasn't certain she would have heard much of the sermon. As it was, she wondered what had brought him to church this morning. Since there was nothing special about today's service, she had to believe it was simply the right time for him.

"I know you'd have welcomed me," TJ said as he took a spoonful of peas before replacing the bowl on the lazy Susan, "but the back of the church seemed like a better idea."

"In case there were lightning bolts?"

The question was meant to be facetious, but TJ seemed to take it seriously. "Something like that."

"I didn't notice any."

This time he smiled. "No, and before you ask, yes, this was part of my plan for the future."

That was wonderful news. Gillian laid her hand on TJ's. "I'm glad."

"It was time." TJ reached for a roll. "When I was in town yesterday, everyone was talking about tomorrow's Memorial Day celebration," he said, obviously changing the subject. "I heard the seniors are planning to carry a flag to the cemetery and stop at each veteran's grave. They asked me to take some pictures." He broke the roll open and buttered one piece. "I'd offer you a ride, but I know how you feel about my bike. I'll just meet you there." Amusement tinged his words.

Gillian shook her head. "Actually, I won't be here." There was no reason to feel so awkward telling TJ about her dates with Mike. Still, she tried to avoid any mention of Mike. Somehow, though she couldn't quite explain it, it seemed wrong to tell TJ she'd be spending the day with the man who'd made it no secret that he was interested in being more than a friend.

"I'm going to Blytheville's celebration," she said quickly. There. It was out in the open.

For a second, TJ's expression was unguarded, and Gillian thought she saw both anger and disappointment in his eyes. It happened so fast that she might have been mistaken, because a second later he shrugged. "Oh . . . of course."

The weather was perfect, the sky a vivid blue with a few puffy cumulus clouds drifting across it, a light breeze keeping the day from being too hot. Gillian looked around as she and Mike drove into Blytheville. It seemed as if everyone in town had come out for the ceremony. Though she'd referred to it as a celebration, that was a misnomer. Instead, it was a solemn reminder of those who'd given their lives for freedom.

As she studied the people who'd begun to line the parade route, Gillian was grateful Mike had told her about the unwritten dress code. Almost everyone wore red, white, and blue. The majority were dressed in jeans with red gingham shirts, but a few women wore red shorts, blue chambray shirts, and white hats. Gillian had chosen a white skirt with a red and white striped shirt. A wide navy belt and the navy boots Samantha had made for her added the blue to Gillian's ensemble.

She was in full patriotic dress, but Mike was not. When he had arrived to pick her up, Gillian had been surprised to see that, though he wore jeans and a white shirt, there was no red in his outfit.

"Where's your red?" she asked as she slid into the passenger seat.

He gestured toward the shiny red Ferrari. "Isn't the car enough?" When Gillian shook her head, pointing out that he wasn't wearing the car, nor was he driving it in the parade, he relented. "You'll have to wait until we arrive, but trust me. This mayoral candidate has no intention of breaking with tradition."

Though Gillian speculated that he was planning to wear a red vest or that he had red boots like Kate's, Mike refused to confirm or deny her guesses, simply saying "maybe" and "possibly."

When they parked behind Strawberry Chantilly in what appeared to be the staging area for several floats, he turned to Gillian. "You want red? Here it comes."

He covered the distance to one of the floats in a couple quick strides. Reaching inside, he pulled out a red cowboy hat and plunked it on his head.

"A red hat?" Gillian studied the man standing in front of her. Though she'd seen a few red hats in the crowd, they'd been either ball caps or the fancy creations some over-fifty women wore to club meetings. Not one had been a cowboy hat. The look was distinctive, and yet . . .

"I thought the good guys always wore white."

Mike adjusted the angle. "I imagine that's what my opponent is wearing. My campaign manager suggested I try something less predictable."

Not only was it less predictable, but the hat made the statement that Mike wasn't afraid of change. He hadn't flouted tradition; he'd merely given it a fresh spin.

"If someone takes a picture of you holding the hat in front of you for the national anthem and the pledge of allegiance, you've got the perfect campaign photo."

"Have you been talking to my mother? That's what she said." Raised eyebrows accompanied Mike's response.

"You know what they say about great minds."

Glancing behind him when he heard the rumble of a truck, he grinned. "Here comes the other great mind."

Stacy hopped out of the truck and hurried toward Gillian, leaving her husband to follow at a more decorous pace. "I'm so glad you could come." A warm hug accompanied her words, and for the seconds she was in the other woman's embrace, Gillian felt like part of the family.

There was no question about it. Being with the Tarketts—all of them—was wonderful. Moments like these filled Gillian with happiness and made her wonder if this was the future God had in store for her. The appeal of being part of a loving family and living near Kate and Sally grew with every hour Gillian spent with Mike.

"So, what do you think of the Tarkett uniform?" Stacy demanded as she took a step backward and gestured toward her jean skirt, white shirt, and red hat. The feminine version of Mike's outfit flattered her and announced that she was one of Mike's supporters.

"It's great. Very distinctive. My friend Kate would approve." Pulling her phone from her bag, Gillian gestured toward Mike and his mother. "Let me send her a picture."

As soon as Gillian had snapped the picture, Stacy reached for her phone. "And let me take one of you and Blytheville's future mayor." When Mike wrapped his arm around Gillian's shoulders and she looked up, smiling into his eyes, Stacy took a couple shots. "Nice."

"It is indeed," Cal said as he approached the trio. Like his wife and son, he was dressed in jeans, a white shirt, and a red hat. "There's only one problem. Where's Gillian's hat?"

Stacy gave his arm a playful swat. "Now, Cal, don't pressure her. Gillian's already in red, white, and blue."

"But it's not the same." Cal feigned a scowl.

"C'mon, guys. I think you've said enough." Mike reached into the float and pulled out another red hat, extending it toward Gillian. "I wasn't sure you'd want to wear one, but even if you don't, I was hoping you'd ride on our float."

At the moment, there was nothing Gillian wanted more. "Yes to both." As she settled the hat onto her hair, she grinned. "I'm happy to be an honorary Tarkett."

Though Stacy looked as if she wanted to say something, the arrival of half a dozen trucks bearing the rest of the Tarkett clan distracted her. Within a minute, the parking lot was filled with two generations of Tarketts, all sporting the distinctive red hats of Mike's campaign.

"All right. Let's get started." Cal helped his wife onto the float, then gestured toward Mike and Gillian.

"Just a second. I want a better look." Before she climbed into the float, Gillian walked around it, studying it from all angles.

"You seem surprised," Mike said when she'd completed the circuit.

"I am. I was expecting something more elaborate and a 'vote for Mike' sign," she admitted. The Tarkett float was identical to the other two in the parking lot, nothing more than a farm trailer draped in red, white, and blue bunting.

"Not today. One of the town's traditions is that all floats in this parade are the same. There's no one-upmanship on Memorial Day. Instead, we're commemorating others. It's kind of like those candlelight vigils where the important thing is just being there."

"But there are no restrictions for the Fourth of July." One of Mike's cousins rolled her eyes. "Everything is big and gaudy and fun. You should see what my brother and I have in mind for Mike's float."

Mike wrinkled his nose in faux disgust. "I can see you and I are going to have to have a long, serious discussion."

"Discuss away, cousin. You know you'll cave in the end."

"Now, children." Stacy shook her head and turned to her husband. "What did we do that they turned out this way?"

"Showed them that life should be fun?" he offered, giving Stacy's nose a light tweak followed by a kiss.

Gillian smiled at the playful banter. If she'd been asked to define the perfect family, it would be this one. Though she'd known that Sally and Grandpa Larry loved each other, they'd never been as demonstrative as Cal and Stacy were. It was refreshing, and yes, heartwarming, to see the love Mike's parents shared.

Gillian knew she'd never forget either that love or the way Blytheville celebrated the day. The parade wound through the streets, the bunting-draped floats interspersed with marching bands playing patriotic songs.

When they reached the center of town, Gillian thought they would stop in front of the courthouse. The large square bordered by Blytheville's most impressive buildings seemed the perfect location for speeches, but the parade did not slow until they reached the cemetery. Once there, everyone disembarked from the floats and gathered around the small platform that had been erected in the center of the graveyard.

When the last person had arrived, one of the town's ministers climbed onto the platform and offered a prayer, asking God to bless the memory of the men and women who'd served their country so faithfully. He was followed by the current mayor, who made a brief speech. Mike's opponent was the next to step behind the microphone.

Gillian sized him up. He was as tall as Mike and equally distinguished. And, as Mike had predicted, he wore a white hat with a red, white, and blue hatband and a large button pin that Gillian suspected was one of his campaign buttons. To Gillian's surprise, the man began his speech with a reference to his service in Afghanistan. At her side, Stacy hissed, then nudged Cal. Apparently the other man had broken one of the unwritten rules.

Mike said nothing, and when it was his turn to speak, he gave a simple tribute to fallen heroes with no mention of himself. The round of applause after his speech was longer and louder than any of the predecessors', but Gillian wasn't certain whether they were applauding what Mike had said and his restraint from personal aggrandizement or simply that the speeches had ended and they could return to town for the barbecue.

Held in the town's largest park, the barbecue was both a fundraiser for the local veterans' group and an opportunity for residents to share stories of their families' bravery. As Gillian had expected, a reporter from the Blytheville paper was present, interviewing both mayoral candidates as well as a cross section of ordinary citizens.

"Nice hat, Mike," the reporter, who wore a red and white polka dot blouse with one of the shortest navy skirts Gillian had seen, said with a grin. "And who's your companion?"

Mike raised an eyebrow. "As if you didn't know, Rita. If you didn't see all those pictures of us on the internet after the concert, you're slipping up." The words were accompanied by a smile that confirmed Mike and Rita's friendship.

"Nice to meet you, Gillian. Are you hanging around for the basketball game?" When Mike shook his head, Rita informed Gillian that Mike had been the star of Blytheville High's basketball team. "But you probably already knew that."

"Actually, I didn't. Mike's one of the most modest men I've met."

"And modest men finish last."

No matter what Rita said, Gillian didn't want to believe that. She was hardly an expert on Blytheville politics, but she knew enough about politics in general to know Mike would be a good mayor. Honor and integrity combined with modesty was what every town in America needed.

"I hope not."

Mike slid his arm around Gillian's waist. "I hate to break up this fascinating conversation, but you're making me uncomfortable, talking about me as if I'm not here. Besides," he said after a glance at his watch, "I promised my parents we'd be back at the ranch by four."

A couple hours of lazy conversation alongside the pool were followed by a fried chicken supper. The Tarkett family obviously enjoyed being together, and Gillian was happy to be included.

As the sun began to set, everyone piled into their trucks, leaving Mike and Gillian to follow in his car. It was time for the fireworks, the culmination of Blytheville's Memorial Day, and the Tarketts would be there. To Gillian's surprise, when they reached town, the trucks turned left, but Mike did not.

"I thought your mother said the fireworks were at the park."

"They are," he agreed, "but that's not the only place to see them." He turned right and headed up the hill to a residential area. Single family homes lined one side of the street, while a row of two-story town houses occupied the other. Mike pushed the remote, opening the garage of one of the town houses and pulled inside.

"I thought you might like to see where I live."

When he'd switched off the engine, Mike helped Gillian out of the car and up the steps into his home. They entered through a modest kitchen, then climbed the stairs to the second-story den, which boasted a balcony overlooking the city. To Gillian's surprise, though she knew there were neighbors on both sides and suspected they also had balconies, they were out of sight.

"One of the things I like about this complex is that the architect managed to preserve privacy without using a lot of land," Mike said as he ushered her onto the balcony and closed the sliding glass doors behind them. "If I want open spaces, I can go to the ranch. This place is close to town and low maintenance."

"Plus it has a fabulous view." Gillian gasped as the first fireworks burst into the sky, huge red, white, and blue balls that hung in the air for an improbably long time before fading into darkness. They were followed by rockets, pyrotechnic waterfalls, and a not particularly successful attempt at an American flag. Gillian didn't care about the imperfection. What was important was the sentiment behind the fireworks. This was a town honoring its heroes.

For half an hour she and Mike stood next to the balcony railing, his arm around her waist, as they watched the magnificent display. When the show ended and the last shooting star disappeared, he turned to face her.

"That was wonderful," Gillian said, still marveling at the beauty. She'd attended fireworks displays before, but always as part of a crowd. Being here with Mike had made tonight extra special.

"Not as wonderful as you." Mike swallowed deeply, then cupped her cheek, his fingers moving slowly toward her chin. "There's a reason I brought you here away from everyone else. I love my family, but at times they can be overwhelming. I wanted tonight to be just the two of us."

Mike's hand touched her lips before dropping to his side. "When Mom insisted I go to Rainbow's End, I never expected this. I figured I was in for a week of boredom. Instead, these past two months have been the best of my life, and it's all because of you. I love you, Gillian. I want to spend the rest of my life showing you just how deep that love is."

Mike reached into his pocket and withdrew a square box that could hold only one thing. "Will you marry me?"

Gillian's heart began to pound. Was this the plan God had for her, the answer to her prayers for a family of her own? Stacy and Cal treated her like one of their children. That was what Gillian had always wanted, a family that loved her for who she was. It could be hers forever, if she said yes.

She looked at the man standing next to her, love shining from his eyes. There were so many reasons to say yes. She cared deeply for Mike. He would be a good husband. If she married him, she'd have both a mother and a father. She would even make her own father happy. Gillian felt as if she was ticking off the advantages on her fingers. Everything urged her to say yes, and yet . . .

"I don't know what to say."

Mike swallowed, and Gillian knew she'd disappointed him. "Say yes," he urged her.

"Marriage is a big step." In the second when she'd been ready to say yes, she'd felt as if she were on the edge of a precipice. A single step would take her into the unknown, and though she believed Mike would catch her, something held her back. Perhaps it was simply too soon. Perhaps it was the fear that she was like Brianna, in love with the idea of what a man could provide rather than the man himself. Perhaps it was the feelings for TJ that she couldn't dismiss, no matter how hard she tried. Gillian wasn't certain. All she knew was that she couldn't give Mike the answer he wanted.

"I guess I'm just not ready."

Mike was silent for a moment as he slipped the ring back into his pocket, his eyes troubled. "I'm sure you know that's not the answer I was hoping for. My family claims I'm a patient man, but they're wrong. I don't like waiting. But you, Gillian, are worth waiting for. I'll try to be patient until you're ready."

He managed a small smile. "I'm giving you fair warning, though. I'm persistent. I'm going to do everything I can to convince you. I'm also going to ask you the same question every two weeks until you say yes." Mike turned to face the house. "Now, let's get you back to Rainbow's End. It's been a long day."

42

TJ was not a happy man. He raced his bike up Ranger Hill, trying not to think about Gillian missing breakfast. Although no one was assigned a specific time, they'd resumed their habit of eating together. That was a fine way to start the day. At least TJ thought so. Why was today different?

Gillian's car had been in its normal spot, although that didn't prove much, since she didn't usually go into town for another hour. Perhaps she had overslept. There was no reason to imagine a sinister reason for her absence. It wasn't as if she and Mike Tarkett had eloped to Vegas after the fireworks display last night.

TJ's frown deepened. Why did that thought have to pop into his head? Why did he have to picture an Elvis impersonator performing the ceremony? Surely Gillian hadn't agreed to that. He was close—so close—to having one half of his future planned. Surely he wouldn't be too late for the second.

Trying to get his mind focused on teaching, he parked his bike in its usual spot and headed for the back entrance. As TJ entered the school, Jake Thomas emerged from his office.

"Just the man I wanted to see," the principal announced,

clapping TJ on the shoulder. "Will you stop in during your free period? There's something I want to talk to you about."

The day had just gotten worse. TJ had heard several of the teachers grousing about the upcoming end-of-school party. If Jake wanted him to chaperone the event, he'd be disappointed. That was one thing TJ had no intention of doing, but he nodded and muttered, "Sure." He had no choice other than to listen to whatever Jake had to say.

Two and a half hours later, TJ entered the principal's office and took the seat Jake indicated, prepared to offer a list of reasons he should not be a chaperone.

The principal leaned forward slightly, placing his elbows on the desk and steepling his fingers. "All the classes I've attended tell me to start with pleasantries," Jake said. "I never saw much point in that, so I'm going to cut to the chase. I've been impressed with what you've done here. I don't want to give you a swelled head, but I've heard nothing but good things from the students, their parents, and the other teachers."

TJ blinked at the unexpected praise, wondering where this was leading. This sounded like more was at stake than the party.

The principal nodded, then picked up a folder from the middle of his desk. "The bottom line is, I'd like to offer you a full-time position for next year. I've got the contract here."

TJ stared in amazement. "I'm honored, sir." Flabbergasted was more like it. The ever-active grapevine had told him Jake had been reviewing résumés and was leaning toward a woman who'd left a few years earlier to raise a family.

Jake frowned. "What's this 'sir' business? I thought we were on a first-name basis."

"You're right, Jake. I guess I'm more surprised than I realized." This could be the opportunity he needed, a chance to save the money for seminary, a chance to be certain that was what God intended for him. Though the call to ordination was strong, it had not been accompanied by a sense of urgency. Instead, TJ felt as if he were being cautioned to move slowly. Perhaps this was the reason why. Perhaps he still had more to do in Dupree.

"I hope the surprise was a pleasant one."

"It was. It is. I just need to think it over a bit. I want to pray about it." A month ago, TJ would not have said that, much less been comfortable mentioning his prayer life with the principal, but that was a month ago. TJ was no longer the same man.

Jake nodded. "I understand. Take your time, TJ. I want you to be certain this is the right decision for you." He paused and glanced at the calendar posted on the side wall. "Do you think you'll have your decision by the time school ends?"

Though it was less than two weeks, TJ had no difficulty nodding. "That'll be fine." That would give him time to think, to pray, and to talk to Gillian.

Though the last need nagged at him, TJ couldn't simply leave the school in the middle of the day. Instead, he found himself watching the clock, counting the minutes as eagerly as any of his students did. When the final bell rang, he practically sprinted to the parking lot. Three minutes later he arrived at Hill Country Pages. Though Gillian had normally left by this time, there was always the possibility she was working late. He didn't want to ride out to Rainbow's End only to discover she was still in town.

"I'm sorry, sir," the woman who was manning the cash register told him. "Gillian left on time today. I imagine she's back at Rainbow's End."

But she wasn't. Her car was missing, and when TJ knocked on the door to her cabin, there was no answer. He headed for the office, hoping whoever was on duty would know where Gillian had gone. There he found Brandi, one of the teenagers who served meals as well as worked the front desk, laughing as she read a newspaper.

"Want to share the joke?"

She looked up, her face flushing. "I'm not sure you'll find it funny." Reluctantly, she showed him a picture of Gillian and

Mike. Mike had his arm wrapped around her waist, and she was looking up at him as if he were the most wonderful man in the universe. "They sure look like lovebirds, don't they?" Brandi asked.

"Yeah." Unfortunately, they did.

If there were ever a time when retail therapy was needed, it was now. An afternoon of shopping might not bring about world peace, but it just might prevent an elopement.

"I hate her! She doesn't understand me!" Brianna clenched her fists and pounded the armrest, seemingly oblivious to the beautiful countryside outside the window.

Gillian bit the inside of her cheek, forcing herself to remain silent. There was no point in arguing when she knew Brianna would not listen. She considered it nothing less than a small miracle that she'd returned to Rainbow's End at the exact moment Brianna had stormed out of Firefly Valley, tears streaming down her cheeks, her face contorted in rage. The girl was almost incoherent, but between the screams and the obscenities, Gillian had pieced together the picture of a fight between Brianna and her mother culminating in Brianna's threat to run away with Pete.

"He's the only one who understands me," Brianna had declared. "He's the only one who sees I'm a woman. Mom thinks I'm still a little girl. Well, I'm not!"

Though Brianna's behavior more closely resembled that of a child in the midst of a tantrum than the grown woman she claimed to be, Gillian refused to become involved in the argument.

"I need some new clothes," she told Brianna. "Want to help me pick them out?" When the teen hesitated, she increased the stakes. "Who knows? You might find the right dress for the end-of-school party. If you do, I'll buy it for you."

As Gillian had hoped, Brianna's eyes had brightened, and she'd climbed into the car. Though Brianna had refused to speak to her mother, as soon as they were once again in cell range, Gillian had coaxed the number from her and had called Natalie, telling her her daughter was with her and would probably spend the night with her.

"Maybe you can talk some sense into her," Natalie had said just before she hung up. Though Gillian doubted that was possible, she could keep mother and daughter apart and ensure Brianna spent no time with Pete today.

As Brianna continued her diatribe, listing her mother's many flaws and Pete's many assets, Gillian said nothing. There were times when the best thing to do was let someone vent, and this was one of them. When Brianna paused to take a breath, Gillian said, "The decision's yours. There's a dress shop in Blytheville I've been wanting to visit, but I thought we'd go to the Angora farm first. Is that okay?" Stacy had told her that although it did not bear the Tarkett name, the farm and the shop Marisa had raved about were among the family's holdings.

Brianna relaxed her fists as she turned toward Gillian. "I heard they have cool clothes there." With the volatility so common to teens, all signs of Brianna's anger had disappeared, replaced by the anticipation of shopping.

Gillian tried not to smile at the abrupt change of mood. "Marisa said they carry mostly sweaters and scarves. I thought those were supposed to be warm, not cool."

Twisting her mouth into an expression that could have served as a Halloween ghoul's mask, Brianna said, "Yeah, right." She was silent for a second, then wrinkled her nose. "Oh, you were trying to be funny, weren't you? I hate to break this to you, but you'll never be invited to *Saturday Night Live*."

"And here I thought I had a career as a comedian." Gillian rejoiced in Brianna's grin and the visible relaxing of her shoulders. It seemed as if she'd put her anger behind her, at least temporarily.

"No chance." Brianna twisted in the seat so she faced Gillian. "What was it like being a famous pianist? It sounds so glamorous—all that travel, all those beautiful clothes."

Gillian had thought so once. "Believe it or not, it's a job, and like any job, it has its good and its bad. The hours of practice are exhausting, and after a while, all the hotels, restaurants, and airports start to look alike."

"But you kept doing it. Why?"

Gillian smiled, remembering. "The applause made it all worthwhile."

"That must have been cool, all those people standing up and clapping for you."

"I didn't get a standing ovation every time, but you're right; it was cool." Each time it had happened, Gillian's heart had pounded with the realization that the audience cared enough to give her more than polite applause. She'd quickly learned to distinguish between perfunctory clapping and genuine enthusiasm, and the real thing had made her rejoice.

"I wish someone would clap for me. All my mom does is criticize me. I can't do anything to make her happy." Brianna's voice held wistful longing, a far cry from the anger that had colored it only minutes earlier, leaving Gillian wishing there were something she could do or say to comfort her. TJ would have known what to say, but TJ wasn't here. Gillian was on her own.

"You probably don't believe it, but I envy you," she told the teen. "You have something I always wanted—a mother."

Brianna's face registered disbelief. "What happened to yours?"

"She died when I was born, and my dad never remarried."

Brianna's expression had changed, and for a second Gillian thought she saw pity in her brown eyes. "So what did he do?"

"He hired a nanny. A lot of them. They never seemed to last more than six months."

"But at least they were nice."

"If you say so." To be fair, the nannies had been kind, but

kindness wasn't what Gillian had sought. Love was. "The best thing that happened to me was when Kate moved in with her grandparents down the street. They became my second family."

"That's sad." Brianna's expression underwent another of the mercurial changes that seemed to be the order of the day, her lips curving into a mischievous smile. "I've got an offer you can't refuse. I'll give you my mom if you let me move into your cabin."

"Let's see how you like the sleepover tonight. You might discover I'm an old fuddy-duddy who snores so loudly you can't sleep."

As Gillian had hoped, Brianna giggled. "Just tell me you've got good food in your fridge."

Gillian shook her head. "Juice and milk's the limit, but I have a secret weapon: Carmen. We can raid her refrigerator if we're hungry."

"Good deal."

A few minutes later, they pulled into the driveway leading to the Angora goat farm. If the sign was any indication, the products would be unique, for the goats certainly were. They had the usual muzzle, beard, and floppy ears, but their fleece was long and curly. "Let's see if we can find something for Sally here."

Gillian parked in the lot, pausing while Brianna admired the dozen or so goats grazing in the pasture, clearly unaffected by the presence of customers.

From the outside, the store looked like an ordinary barn, but once they were indoors, Gillian realized why both Marisa and Stacy had raved about it. For anyone who enjoyed woven or knitted goods, this was a shopper's paradise. Tables piled with a seemingly endless variety of merchandise, racks bearing sweaters in every size and style imaginable, and bins filled with skeins of yarn all competed for the customer's attention.

"What do you think?" Gillian asked Brianna.

"I think I need one of everything."

Brianna helped Gillian select an open-weave sweater in light blue for Sally, seeming to enjoy being included in the decision. And, though she oohed and aahed over most of the merchandise, she bought only one item, an afghan she declared perfect for her bedroom in the new apartment. Gillian smiled, as much at the fact that Brianna had abandoned the idea of running away as at the intricately patterned afghan.

Though they explored not only the dress shop Kate had recommended but also three other stores, Brianna found nothing that appealed to her in Blytheville. "It doesn't matter," she told Gillian. "I don't need a new outfit for the party." But it did matter. Gillian knew that.

"Maybe you can find something of mine that suits you," she suggested. "I've got a closet full of clothes. Two, actually." When she'd decided to extend her stay at Rainbow's End, Gillian had had the housekeeper ship the majority of her summer wardrobe to Texas. There might be something that appealed to Brianna.

"Really? You'd let me borrow your clothes?"

"Why not?"

Brianna grinned. "That would be cool."

She also found the barbecue dinner and the movie followed by ice cream to be cool. By the time they arrived back at Rainbow's End, it was after ten.

"Thanks, Gillian," Brianna said as she grabbed a pair of borrowed pajamas and headed for Gillian's second bedroom. "I had a good time."

So did Gillian, although she was more exhausted than she'd been in months. This pseudo-parenthood business was harder than she'd imagined, but at least Brianna was still here.

43

Where was she? She'd missed supper, the evening in Firefly Valley, and now breakfast, all without a word of explanation. That wasn't like Gillian. She normally made a point of saying something if she was going to miss the time with the teenagers.

TJ had told himself he wasn't being nosy, that he was simply checking on a friend's welfare when he'd walked by her cabin last night. No lights. No car. Gillian was definitely not there. The question was, where was she? The only answer that made sense was that she was spending the evening with Mike, but if that was so, why was her car gone? Mike normally picked her up.

The last time Gillian had been gone so long had been the day she'd spent at the hospital waiting for Baby Vange to arrive. Kate and Greg's presence at supper told TJ nothing was wrong with either the baby or Kate's grandmother. That left Mike as the most likely reason for Gillian's absence. Perhaps there had been a late-night event and she was staying at the ranch with his parents. But if that was the case, it didn't explain why she hadn't told TJ she'd miss their time in Firefly Valley.

Trying to shake off his disgruntlement, TJ climbed onto his

motorcycle. It was time to get to school. But though he told himself he shouldn't, TJ couldn't stop himself from detouring toward Gillian's cabin.

The car was there. Elation flowed through his veins at the proof of Gillian's return. It might be a whole day later than he'd expected, but he would be able to get her spin on the teaching contract this afternoon.

As TJ started to turn the bike, the cabin door opened and Brianna Carter emerged, wearing an outfit TJ recognized as belonging to Gillian and carrying a large shopping bag.

"Thanks for everything." Brianna waved at Gillian, who stood behind her. "That was the best sleepover ever."

Even from this distance, TJ could see Gillian's smile. "You're welcome," she told the teen.

Relief that Gillian hadn't been with Mike flooded through TJ as he switched off the motorcycle and approached the cabin.

"Good morning, Gillian," he said when Brianna was out of earshot. He hoped it was a good morning for her, because the dark circles under her eyes told TJ sleep had not been a major component of the sleepover. "I missed you last night." And yesterday afternoon and this morning.

"I'm sorry. I should have left you a message, but things got a little crazy. I was trying to convince Brianna not to run away with Pete. She had a fight with her mom and decided the answer was to stow away in Pete's truck so he'd marry her."

"I don't think Pete's interested in marriage."

Gillian's expression left no doubt that she agreed. "I didn't tell her that. Instead I bribed her with a shopping trip and a girls' night out. It was the only thing I could think of to distract her."

"It looks like you succeeded."

Brushing a lock of hair from her face, she nodded. "Temporarily. I did learn one thing, though, and that's that this counseling business is tough."

"True, but it's also rewarding." TJ glanced at his watch and frowned. "I'd like to talk to you about a couple things, but I've got to get to school. If you're free this afternoon, we could take a picnic to Paintbrush Island and still be back in time to go to Firefly Valley."

Gillian was silent for a second or two, as if she was as surprised by the invitation as TJ was. He hadn't planned a picnic, though Greg had told him on several occasions that the small island on the other side of Bluebonnet Lake was an ideal spot for one. Somehow the words had popped out, seemingly on their own.

"Sure," Gillian said. "That sounds like fun."

Gillian was having a difficult time concentrating on work. Fortunately, there weren't too many customers, and the one she'd directed to cookbooks when she'd wanted a gardening guide was unlikely to tell the rest of Dupree that Gillian Hodge was having a bad day. She could blame her lack of concentration on being tired, but that was only a tiny part of the cause. The real reason was TJ's invitation.

It had been almost a month since they'd attended the rodeo. Since then, with the notable exception of that unforgettable kiss, they hadn't been on anything that resembled a date. Now he'd suggested a picnic for two. What had changed?

Gillian felt a frisson of excitement at the thought of Paintbrush Island. Kate had told her it was the most romantic spot in the whole area, and Marisa's eyes brightened whenever she spoke of the island, as if she too had found it a special place. Of course, Gillian reminded herself, nothing in TJ's expression had led her to believe he had anything romantic in mind. It was Mike who had proposed, Mike whom she'd refused.

Perhaps TJ was simply looking for some exercise or perhaps he wanted a change of pace from having supper with other guests. He was probably one of those who believed in the buddy system when water was involved. That was it. Gillian was the designated buddy. She shouldn't read anything into the invitation other than a simple picnic supper and a chance to talk about whatever was on TJ's mind, but she couldn't help wishing he viewed her as more than a buddy. Though there were times when he looked at her as if she were more than a friend, he'd said nothing that could be construed as lover-like.

"You look like summer personified," TJ said seven hours later when they met on the dock. By the time Gillian arrived, dressed in hunter green shorts, a floral print top, and a straw hat, he'd gotten the boat out of the boathouse and had already loaded a picnic basket into it.

"Thanks. You look pretty summery yourself." TJ wore khaki shorts and a polo the same shade of green as her shorts. "It almost looks like we decided to color coordinate."

"I wish I could claim mental telepathy, but the answer is a lot simpler. This was the only clean shirt in the drawer." He extended his hand, helping her climb into the boat, then untied it and hopped in himself.

TJ rowed as if he'd done it before, his strokes seemingly effortless, although Gillian knew they weren't.

"Were you on the crew in college?" she asked, wondering where he'd gained such expertise.

"It's more recent than that. There was a small lake near our apartment and a fellow who rented boats. Deb and I used to row there occasionally."

Though his sunglasses made it difficult to be certain, Gillian heard no pain in TJ's voice when he spoke of his wife. Perhaps his efforts to reestablish his relationship with God were healing his empty heart. If so, another of her prayers was being answered.

When they reached the island, although Gillian had expected TJ to dock the boat on the edge closest to Rainbow's End, he continued to the opposite side, declaring the best spot was out of sight of the resort.

"This is it," he said, slowing as they approached a part of the island where the trees came closer to the shore but still left enough room for beaching the boat.

Though the other side of the island had been lovely, this one surpassed it. The ground rose from the lake edge to a small hill covered with hickory and mesquite, and while the trees weren't as tall as the ones that surrounded the resort itself, they were large enough to provide shade. With no houses or other signs of civilization in sight, it was a scene of both beauty and peace.

"I can see why Kate raves about this place," Gillian said as TJ pulled the boat onto the shore. "It's gorgeous."

"We're too late for the namesake Indian paintbrush to be in bloom, but this still looks like a good spot for a picnic. Are you hungry?"

Gillian nodded. "You bet. I ate a light lunch, because I've heard about Carmen's picnics." The tales of enough food to feed a small crowd were only slight exaggerations. As if she'd been unsure of what TJ and Gillian might like, Carmen had provided a variety. The basket contained large quantities of roast beef and tuna sandwiches, both potato salad and coleslaw, and thermoses of lemonade and sweet tea, along with a selection of enormous sugar, peanut butter, and chocolate chip cookies for dessert.

"This tastes even better than it looks," Gillian said as she bit into a cookie. It had been a pleasant meal, filled with good food and casual conversation, but now that it was almost over, she felt TJ begin to tense, and that made her shoulders tighten.

"As I mentioned this morning, I had an ulterior motive for bringing you out here," he said. "I need your opinion."

There was nothing remotely romantic about either his words or the way he delivered them. Gillian knew she shouldn't be surprised or disappointed, and yet she was.

"Go ahead." She broke off another piece of cookie, hoping the simple act of chewing would help her swallow her disappointment. Though she was tempted to cup her ears as TJ had, she did not. "As Sally used to say, I'm all ears."

TJ snagged a chocolate chip cookie, then leaned against a tree trunk. "Jake Thomas offered me a full-time position."

Whatever she'd been expecting, it wasn't that. Gillian tried to imagine what TJ wanted her to say. "That's good news, isn't it?" She knew he'd been reassessing his future. Although she had thought he was considering the ministry, this could be the answer he sought. Despite his own misgivings, Gillian knew he was a talented teacher. "Did you accept?"

"Yes and no. I wanted to see what you thought."

Again, she searched his face, looking for a clue to the kind of response that would satisfy him. "I'd say that all depends on what you want to do. Dupree is a nice town. You could make a difference in the kids' lives here. In fact, you're already doing that. Staying would simply give you a chance to have more of an impact on them."

He nodded slowly as he chewed the cookie. "That's what I thought. That's why I'm considering accepting for a year."

"Why put a time limit on it?" When it came to jobs, most people sought permanence and the security it brought.

Though his posture remained relaxed, when TJ pushed his sunglasses on top of his head, Gillian could see the tension in his eyes. "That's the main thing I wanted to talk to you about. I know my limitations. I'm a good but not a great teacher. I never really felt the calling to teach."

The admission didn't surprise Gillian. He'd told her teaching had been Deb's dream and passion, not his. Now that Deb was gone, it was logical that TJ would question whether it was the right future for him.

"But you do feel called to do something else." She made it a statement, based on his inflection when he'd said he hadn't felt called to teach. It had sounded as if he were about to say, "But I . . ."

"Yeah." Brushing crumbs from his hands, he leaned forward. "I want to become an ordained minister, and another year of teaching would give me the money I need to attend seminary. What do you think? Am I crazy?"

TJ sounded almost as vulnerable as Brianna had a day earlier. Though on the surface the rebellious teenager and the still-grieving widower had little in common, they were both at a crossroads in their lives. A shopping trip wouldn't help TJ, but perhaps some words would.

"You're not crazy," Gillian assured him. "If you believe ordination is what God wants you to do, you should do it." For the man who'd been called the RV Reverend, it wouldn't be a change of direction but simply formalizing what he had already been doing.

TJ popped the last piece of cookie into his mouth, brushing the crumbs from his hands as he chewed.

"I do believe it's God's plan for me," he said a minute later. "When I was in church on Sunday, I felt as if that was where I belonged, and not just as a member of the congregation. I could picture myself in Pastor Bill's shoes."

Gillian was glad she could see TJ's eyes, because she saw more enthusiasm in them than ever before. "You should do it," she said, infusing her words with every bit of certainty she possessed. "I think you'll be a great minister."

"I hope so. Even though there were times when I felt called, I never really considered the possibility before. Deb and I had a comfortable life as teachers. We had the same interests, the same schedule. Everything would have changed if I'd become a full-time minister. I didn't want that to happen to us."

TJ stared into the distance for a moment before continuing. "It's ironic, isn't it? I was trying so hard to avoid change, and then everything changed, even though I didn't pursue my dream.

Suddenly there was no 'us' anymore. In my grief and anger, I turned my back on God and the thought of sharing his Word with others. I was sure that was nothing more than part of my past, but it feels right now."

"Then you should do it."

And Gillian should decide whether what she felt for Mike was love. Despite what Sally had said about Gillian marrying a minister, it was clear TJ was not the man for her. He might be planning to become a minister. He might be changing his life, but he wasn't ready to marry again. Not once had he hinted that his future might include another person. Instead, he'd asked about what *he* should do, not what *they* should do.

Here they were in what both Kate and Marisa claimed was the most romantic spot in the area, and they might as well have been in a conference room somewhere. Not once had TJ done or said anything even remotely romantic. Though her heart ached at the thought, Gillian knew it was time to face reality. She had been deluding herself by thinking TJ regarded her as someone special. Today had proven that. To TJ, she was a friend, someone he could ask for advice. Nothing more.

44

Love. It seemed that was all anyone could talk about. Three times this morning a woman had come into Hill Country Pages asking for a romance novel. "The sappier, the better," one had told Gillian. "I want to cry my eyes out when the hero and heroine finally find true love."

As if that weren't enough, the Matchers had come in, ostensibly looking for a cookbook, though their pointed glances at Gillian's ringless left hand and the less-than-subtle questions about why Mike's Ferrari hadn't been seen in Dupree for two days told a different story.

Gillian had seen no reason to inform them that Mike had been in Dallas on business but was scheduled to stop by the store on his way home. Though this was the first Friday they could have gone on a date without impacting Gillian's time in Firefly Valley, the combination of Mike's business trip and Gillian's agreement to help Brianna dress for the end-of-school party had caused them to cancel their plans for a movie night. Instead, they were scheduled to have dinner tomorrow at a private club outside San Antonio. When Marisa had heard about the club, she'd practically squealed with delight, telling Gillian it was reputed to be one of the most romantic spots in this part of Texas.

"He's going to propose," Marisa declared.

No one—not even Kate—knew he already had. It had been eleven days since Mike had asked Gillian to marry him, eleven days when she had thought of little other than love and marriage.

"Do you have a book about the language of flowers?"

Gillian looked up, surprised to see Sally. "I thought you were at the senior center."

Sally shrugged. "I was, and I'll go back, but in the meantime, I need that book." When Gillian lifted an eyebrow, as if to ask why that particular book was so important, Sally continued. "It's for Roy. The only flowers he gives me are roses. He thinks they're the only ones that speak of love. Now, don't get me wrong. I like roses. Who doesn't? But I also like variety, so I'm going to give him a few hints."

Gillian couldn't help smiling at the image of Roy poring over the book. "Do you think he'll read it?"

"Of course he will. Just like I've been watching those golf videos he gave me. We're both trying to learn more about each other." Sally winked. "Marriage is a lot of work, but it's also a lot of fun. You ought to try it."

Gillian would. Soon. She had thought about it. She'd prayed about it. And while she hadn't heard any voices from a cloud or even a talking donkey doling out advice, whenever she thought about marrying Mike, she felt comfortable.

There were so many things about Mike to like—so many things to love, she corrected herself. He was a good man, a man of deep principles. She found his company stimulating, and when he spoke of his future, she could picture herself sharing it. Most of all, when she was with him, Gillian was content. They had a firm foundation on which to build a life together.

When Mike arrived bearing a box of chocolates from what

he told her was an up-and-coming candy maker, Gillian gave him a warm smile. The next time he proposed, she would accept.

Where was the girl? Gillian glanced at her watch and frowned for what seemed like the dozenth time in as many minutes. School had been out for over an hour, and while they hadn't arranged an exact time, Brianna had said she'd come as soon as the van dropped her off at Firefly Valley. She'd insisted that she needed Gillian to help with her hair as well as lend her the dress she wanted to wear to tonight's end-of-school party.

Thinking Brianna might have gone home to drop off her backpack, Gillian called the RV, grateful that although there was no cell service in Firefly Valley, Greg had arranged for landlines to be extended to the RVs. No answer. Though it had been over a week since their shopping excursion and Brianna's sleepover, Gillian had seen her only a couple times, most recently last night when she'd chosen the dress for the party.

Gillian had to give Brianna credit for good taste. She'd picked one of Gillian's favorites, an apricot silk trimmed with a slightly deeper shade of satin. It was probably too fancy for Dupree High School's party, but Gillian refused to say that, nor did she mention that she'd considered wearing it for her date with Mike tomorrow night. There'd be more dates with Mike. If tomorrow went the way Gillian expected, there would be a whole lifetime with Mike, but Brianna had only one last day of school.

Where was she?

Gillian punched the redial button. Still no answer. Perhaps Brianna was outside talking to one of her friends and didn't hear the phone. Determined to find her, Gillian headed for the RVs. She'd crossed the road and entered the RV park when she saw Todd in earnest conversation with another of the boys.

"I was looking for Brianna," Gillian said as she approached them. "Have you seen her?"

The other boy punched Todd in the arm, then sprinted off as if to distance himself from any discussion of Brianna.

"You're asking me?" Todd's voice rose with sarcasm. "She hasn't said a word to me in weeks. All I hear her saying is 'Pete did this' and 'Pete did that.' Can't she see that he's all wrong for her?" Todd scuffed the ground, refusing to meet Gillian's gaze. "I guess love really is blind."

A sense of urgency she could not explain filled Gillian. "I need to find her. When was the last time you saw her?"

"In the van. She came back from school with the rest of us." He glanced at his watch. "Sixty-three minutes ago." Of course Todd was precise. That was part of who he was.

"And she didn't say anything?"

"I told you she doesn't talk to me."

Gillian nodded and headed toward the RV Brianna shared with her mother, not surprised when Todd accompanied her. The boy might be only fifteen, but his emotions were deeply engaged.

"Brianna," Gillian called out as she knocked on the door. There was no answer. She waited a few seconds, repeated the call and knock, then turned the knob. The door was unlocked. Weighing the propriety of entering the RV without an invitation against her growing concern over the teenager, Gillian pushed the door open and entered. When Todd moved to follow her, she shook her head. "One of us is enough."

The interior of the RV was in its normal state of disarray with everything from discarded fast food containers to magazines covering the flat surfaces. Gillian looked around, hoping for a clue. And then she saw the bright orange sheet of paper on the coffee table. Brianna had been carrying a pad of the same color paper the day they'd spent together.

Gillian took a step closer and picked up the paper.

Mom—

By the time you read this, Pete and I will be married. I love you, but I love him even more.

Brianna

The note was short, succinct, and sent a shiver down Gillian's spine. She'd been right to be concerned.

"What is it?" Todd demanded as Gillian left the RV.

"Brianna's gone." She wouldn't tell him that the girl of his dreams was eloping with Pete. That would only hurt him. "I've got to find her."

"I'll help."

Gillian could see nothing good coming from that. "The best thing you can do is stay here in case she comes back."

"What are you going to do?"

"Find TJ." As the words came out, Gillian was filled with certainty. Certainty that TJ was the only one who could help and certainty that she had been prevented from making a serious mistake. The Bible was filled with stories of people receiving messages in unexpected ways and places—Jonah in the whale's belly, Saul on the road to Damascus. For Gillian, the revelation had come as she headed toward Lone Star Trail.

She ran across the street, her heart pounding as fear for Brianna mingled with the realization that she'd received the answer she sought. Gillian had prayed for guidance, to know whether Mike was the man God intended for her. There'd been no answer, no clear sign, but with each day she'd come closer to accepting his proposal. Today she'd thought she'd seen her path clearly, not understanding that that had been the wrong path.

Mike would have been a wonderful husband and father, and Cal and Stacy would have been loving grandparents. It wouldn't have been a one-sided arrangement. Gillian admired Mike's principles and knew she could have been the helpmeet he needed if he was to run for office beyond mayor of Blytheville.

She cared for him. Yes, she loved him. But in the moment of crisis, she'd seen the truth. The love she felt for Mike was for a friend or a brother, not a husband. If she married him, both of them would be cheated of the opportunity for true love.

It was TJ who filled Gillian's heart and thoughts, TJ to whom she turned instinctively, TJ whom she trusted to help her. She loved him with every fiber of her being, with a love as deep as the ocean, as pure as a mountain stream. Whether or not he returned that love, Gillian knew she could not marry Mike. He was not the man for her, and painful though it would be, she needed to tell him that.

But that would have to wait. What she needed now was to find Brianna before she made her own mistake. As she raced up the drive toward Rainbow's End, Gillian felt relief wash over her at the sight of TJ's motorcycle. He was somewhere at Rainbow's End.

"Have you seen TJ?" she demanded as she flung open the door to the office. If TJ had borrowed a boat, he would have told whoever was on duty.

Kevin shook his head. "I haven't seen him, but I heard his bike come in around five minutes ago. He's probably in his cabin."

"Thanks." Gillian ran outside, trying to ignore the stitch in her side. Within seconds, she was pounding on TJ's door.

"Where's the fire?" he asked, sounding slightly amused as he opened the door. Instantly, his expression sobered. "What's wrong?"

As quickly as she could, Gillian explained. "We've got to stop her. We can't let her marry Pete." Gillian took a deep breath, trying to slow her pulse. She wasn't alone anymore. TJ would help her.

He nodded briskly. "We need a plan." As if he knew that her legs would barely support her, TJ led Gillian to one of the

Adirondack chairs on his deck, then settled in the other one. "We need to talk to her mom and see if she wants to get the police involved. From what you told me about her reaction to talking to the police, I suspect she'd rather not, but it's her choice."

Gillian nodded. If she were in Natalie's shoes, she would try to find her daughter by herself. Hadn't she heard there was a twenty-four-hour waiting period before a person was considered missing and that there was a lot of paperwork? "Do you have any idea where they could have gone?"

"I can't say for sure, but my guess is Pete's taken Brianna to the love nest."

Trying to tamp down the images the term raised, Gillian said, "I don't like the sound of that. Where is it, and how do you know about it?"

"It's a cabin in the woods about half an hour from here. I heard some of the other construction workers talking about it one day when I was at the site. Apparently a distant relative of one of them owns it and doesn't care who uses it." TJ reached over and clasped Gillian's hand, the warmth of his palm and the strength of his fingers reassuring her.

"Before you ask, I've been spending a fair amount of time at the site. Since warning Pete didn't seem to keep him away from Brianna, I wanted to see what I could learn about him."

Gillian had been right. Not only could she trust TJ to help her today, but he'd been helping her all along, doing more than she'd asked. "What did you learn?"

"Not much, other than that the place in the woods is the most likely spot. Unless you can think of anywhere else, that's where we'll go." TJ disengaged his hand from hers and went into his cabin, returning with a motorcycle helmet. "You'll need this."

As frissons of fear made their way down Gillian's spine, she shook her head. She wanted to find Brianna—she needed to find her—but there had to be another way. "No!" she cried as blood drained from her face. "Not your motorcycle. We'll take my car."

TJ shook his head. Keeping his voice as calm as if he were trying to coax a frightened animal out of a trap, he said, "Your car will never make it. I've heard about the roads out there. They're like those wagon train ruts I saw in Wyoming. We need a high-clearance vehicle or a motorcycle. Kate and Greg have gone out in their SUV and Eric's taken the truck, so that leaves my bike. I'm sorry, Gillian, but I don't see any alternatives. If you don't ride with me, your choice is to stay here."

And that was no choice at all. "I can't do that. I don't know what Brianna will do if she sees you. She trusts me. At least I think she does."

His eyes serious, TJ laid his hand on Gillian's and squeezed it. "I guess the question is whether you trust me. I can't make any promises other than to do my best to keep you safe."

There was no alternative. Gillian knew that. She stared at the helmet for a moment, then reached for it. "I trust you, TJ." With her heart as well as her safety. "Let's go."

45

After her helmet straps were secured, TJ led Gillian to his motorcycle. Once she climbed onto the passenger's seat, he said, "You can lean back, or if you prefer, you can wrap your arms around my waist. You might feel more secure that way."

She did. Feeling as if she'd somehow landed in the middle of a nightmare, Gillian hugged TJ's waist and leaned her face against his back, not wanting to see where they were going. But as TJ rode slowly out of Rainbow's End and up Ranger Hill, talking all the while, Gillian began to relax.

She'd told TJ she trusted him, and she did. He'd ridden thousands of miles without an accident before the day she'd met him, and that crash, he'd explained, had been the result of hydroplaning in the rain. There was no rain today, no reason to believe they'd have an accident. Instead, Brianna was in danger of making a serious mistake, and TJ was doing his best to help prevent that.

"Natalie'll be at the grocery store," Gillian said as they entered Dupree. Fortunately, there were no customers waiting for checkout when Gillian and TJ entered the small store. Though

Natalie gave them a broad welcoming smile, the smile faded as Gillian explained about the note.

"I don't want to call the police yet," she said, confirming Gillian's thoughts. "Let's see if we can find her and talk some sense into her. I'm going with you." Natalie's face was haggard as she realized her worst fears were coming true. Brianna was repeating her mother's mistake.

Though his eyes radiated sympathy, TJ shook his head. "I'm not sure that would be a good idea. I think Brianna might respond better to Gillian." When Natalie started to protest, TJ continued. "There are times when a neutral party is the best idea."

Gillian looked around the store. Though no one was waiting for checkout, there were half a dozen people shopping. Natalie couldn't simply leave them, nor could she close the store without the manager's approval.

"Can you get someone to take over here? We'll call you as soon as we find Brianna," Gillian promised. "Once we've gotten her away from Pete, you can pick her up. My guess is she'll need you then." And she wouldn't want TJ and Gillian to listen to what her mother had to say. Gillian refused to consider the possibility that Brianna would refuse to leave the man she thought she loved. If everything went well, Brianna and her mother would be reunited within hours.

"We may have to meet you at the main road," she told Natalie. "TJ doesn't think a sedan will make it all the way to the cabin."

Natalie bit her lip, then glanced at the back of the store. "My boss has an SUV. He's running an errand, due back in half an hour." Natalie gnawed her lip again. "When he hears what happened, he'll take over here and let me borrow the SUV."

"Perfect." TJ nodded his approval.

"What else can I do?"

TJ's answer was simple. "Pray."

When they were back on the bike, Gillian expected TJ to

continue straight down Lone Star Trail to the highway. Instead, he turned left on Cypress. The reason for the detour was clear a few seconds later when they reached the construction site.

"I want to be sure Pete isn't here," he explained as he dismounted. "It's unlikely, but he may have had a clearer head than Brianna and decided that eloping with a minor wasn't a good idea. He told me he had no intention of facing a felony charge."

But there was no sign of either Pete or his truck.

"It must be Pete's day," the foreman said when TJ asked to see him. "Everyone's looking for him. 'Fraid you missed him, though. He left early. Said his missus burned her hand real bad. He was gonna take her to the doctor."

"His missus?" Though Gillian hadn't intended to say anything, the words tumbled out. She had had concerns about Pete's relationship with Brianna, but not once had she considered that he might be married. Did Brianna know that? Gillian doubted it.

The foreman nodded. "Never met her, but some of the other fellas say she's real nice. Got a baby due in a month or so."

"Do you believe that?" Gillian asked as she and TJ headed back to the bike. She was still shocked by the thought of Brianna running away with a married man. A bad situation had just become worse.

"Do I believe that Pete's married and expecting a baby? I'm afraid I do." TJ touched the back of Gillian's waist, a gesture designed more to comfort her than to help her onto the bike. It helped, but only marginally. Gillian didn't want to think about Brianna's reaction when she learned the truth about Pete.

TJ climbed onto the bike and started the engine. "I don't have a lot of trouble believing Pete's got a wife, but I don't imagine his wife called or that he went home to be with her. That sounded like an excuse to leave early with Brianna."

Wrapping her arms around TJ's waist, Gillian leaned forward. "You don't think he married her, do you?"

"No. That was pretty farfetched from the beginning. Texas

has a three-day waiting period after you get a marriage license. From what you said, as of yesterday, Brianna was planning to attend the party tonight. That doesn't sound like she's got a marriage license in her pocket. Besides, she's underage. Natalie would have had to give her permission, and we know she didn't."

"That's what I thought." Though Gillian shuddered as they turned onto the highway, her shudder had nothing to do with being on a motorcycle. The fear she had of being so close to a reminder of her accident had dissipated, replaced by worries about Brianna. "Pete's planning to take advantage of Brianna's innocence."

Gillian saw TJ nod. "I don't understand what changed, but I'm afraid so. Hang on now. We're going to go as fast as we can."

Though she knew she'd have sore muscles tomorrow, Gillian found the ride wasn't as bad as she'd expected. It felt a lot like being on a bicycle, only much faster. The sound of the engine was somehow soothing, and the sensation of the wind on her face was pleasant. If their mission weren't so serious, Gillian realized she might have enjoyed the bike. As it was, she took comfort from being with TJ and working together to find Brianna.

The time went more quickly than she had anticipated, perhaps because TJ was paying little attention to speed limits. Once they turned off the main road, Gillian realized why he had insisted her car couldn't handle the route. Instead of smooth macadam, they were on a deeply rutted dirt road. While a high-clearance vehicle would have no trouble and a motorcycle could travel in one of the tracks, a sedan would have hung up.

The road, if it could be called that, led into a heavily wooded area, the cypresses so close together that they blocked the sun, making Gillian feel as if night had fallen. She tried not to shiver at the thought of what might be waiting for them at the end of the road. The love nest.

Gillian almost laughed at the sight of the cabin that had earned that name. Little more than a shack, it needed a good coat of paint and more than a few roof shingles. A black truck was parked outside, and a light was on inside.

"That's Pete's," Gillian confirmed as she saw the faded flag decal on the left rear bumper.

TJ parked the bike, then touched the truck's hood. "It's still warm," he told Gillian as she attempted to regain her balance. Her legs were vibrating so much that she could barely stand. TJ put his arm around her. "That's a good sign. It means they haven't been here too long."

"Thank God." Perhaps the prayers she'd been offering as she and TJ raced down the highway had been answered. They might have arrived in time to save Brianna from a huge mistake. Gillian looked at the front door. "Do we knock? I'm not sure of the etiquette in situations like this."

"Knocking never hurts." But the knock TJ delivered was more like a pounding. "C'mon out, Pete," he shouted as he gave the door another firm rap.

The door flew open, revealing a shirtless, barefoot Pete and Brianna dressed in a pale pink negligee that revealed more than it concealed. Gillian saw anger on Pete's face and shock on Brianna's.

The girl looked behind Gillian and TJ, as if expecting to see her mother. Gillian couldn't tell whether she was relieved or disappointed that there was no sign of Natalie. All she saw was Brianna gripping Pete's arm, clinging to him as if he were a lifeline.

"You got no business here," Pete snarled. He brushed off Brianna's hand, then reached to the other side of the doorway to pull out a shotgun. Pointing the weapon at TJ, he said, "Better leave. You'll be sorry if you don't."

"We're not leaving without Brianna." Gillian kept her eyes on the would-be bride as she made the announcement. Though Brianna had said nothing, Gillian had seen the apprehension in her eyes when Pete grabbed the shotgun.

"She's here because she wants to be here. Right, sweetie?" Though the question was directed at Brianna, Pete's eyes remained focused on TJ.

Brianna bit her lip, nodded, then shook her head. "I'm not sure."

That got his attention. "What do you mean you're not sure?" Pete swiveled his head to glare at Brianna. "You were mighty sure back in Dupree."

To Gillian's surprise, TJ said nothing, nor did his posture reveal any fear, even though Pete had a weapon trained on him. He stood next to Gillian, apparently relaxed, one hand on the back of her waist, as if he knew she still needed support. Her legs no longer vibrated from the motorcycle, but her stomach felt as if it were tied in knots. Though she hadn't expected this to be a pretty scene, the shotgun turned ugly into terrifying. Gillian had read far too many accounts of injuries or worse when guns and tempers were involved. She had to get Brianna away from Pete.

"It's not too late, Brianna. You can leave now and put all this behind you." Gillian infused her words with every bit of persuasion she possessed.

Brianna's eyes shifted from Gillian to Pete and then back to Gillian. "I don't know what I want. He promised we'd get married this afternoon, but we didn't."

TJ took a step forward. Though there was nothing threatening about his action, Pete's grip on the gun tightened.

"It seems like both of you have been keeping secrets." TJ's tone was conversational, as if it were normal for him to be facing a shotgun and a frightened teenager. Fixing his gaze on Pete, he said, "You probably thought this would be fun, but I don't imagine that a statutory rape charge is going to sit well with your pregnant wife."

There was a second of silence as the words registered. Brianna reacted first. "Wife?" she squeaked, and her face turned red. In that instant, she looked far younger than fifteen, and Gillian suspected that if Natalie were here, Brianna would have thrown herself into her mother's arms. Though Gillian longed to comfort her, Pete still blocked the doorway.

"Wait a minute." For the first time, Pete's confidence seemed to shrink. "She said she turned eighteen yesterday."

TJ snorted. "Then she lied. I don't know when her birthday is, but Brianna's fifteen."

Pete slid the shotgun back on the rack, his face suddenly ashen. Gillian wouldn't be surprised to see him running to his truck in an attempt to get as far away from here as possible.

"Did he say wife?" Brianna stared at Pete, willing him to deny the accusation. "Is it true? Are you married? You're gonna have a baby?"

When Pete nodded, Brianna burst into tears and ran back into the cabin. It was time to act. Pushing her way past the burly man, Gillian entered the love nest. It looked like a cheap motel room, with a bed dominating one side and what was probably advertised as a kitchenette on the other. Though there was no stove, the kitchenette boasted a table with four chairs, a small cupboard, and a microwave-refrigerator combination.

Brianna stood in the middle of the room, staring sightlessly at the door. Trauma. Recognizing the symptoms, Gillian took a few steps forward and wrapped her arms around Brianna.

"Where are your clothes?" she asked. The sooner she had Brianna properly dressed and out of here, the better. When Brianna nodded toward the bathroom but still seemed frozen in place, Gillian propelled her to the small room. "I'll be right here if you need me," she said as the girl's trembling increased.

While Gillian stood outside the bathroom, TJ entered the cabin, forcing Pete to move aside. Though the man had not fled as Gillian had expected, he looked distinctly uncomfortable.

TJ kept his voice even as he addressed Pete. "I'm not sure whether Brianna's mother will press charges, but my advice is to look for another job site. If you do, this may all blow over. If you don't, I'll talk to Drew Carroll and ensure that you're banned from his site and every other one within a hundred-mile radius."

Pete clenched first one fist, then another, and for a moment Gillian feared he would hit TJ. Instead, he grabbed his shirt and headed for his truck. Seconds later, the sound of a powerful diesel engine filled the cabin.

TJ waited until they could no longer hear Pete's truck, then turned to Gillian. "I'm going to find cell service and call Natalie."

Though she'd said nothing when Pete left without saying a word to her, Brianna burst from the bathroom, still buttoning her shirt as she shook her head violently. "No! You can't tell my mom."

Gillian put her arms around the girl, trying to soothe her. "She already knows," she said quietly. "You left her a note, remember?" As Gillian stroked Brianna's back, comforting her as she would have a child, she nodded to TJ. Brianna might not want to face Natalie, but whether she recognized it or not, she needed her mother.

Hanging her head in shame, Brianna nodded. "She wasn't supposed to find the note until later. After we were married." New tears joined the ones that had dried on her cheeks. "He promised me, Gillian. He promised we'd get married. He said it was too late to get a license today, so we'd have a weekend honeymoon, then get married first thing on Monday."

Knowing there was no point in mentioning the three-day waiting period or the need for Natalie's permission, Gillian simply nodded and continued stroking Brianna's back.

"I was such a fool." Brianna's tears had resumed in earnest. "I believed him. I thought he loved me, but he didn't."

There was nothing she could say to refute that. Instead, Gillian cupped Brianna's chin and forced her to look at her. "Your mom loves you. I know she does."

"Yeah." The thought seemed to comfort Brianna. "But what

am I gonna say to her? She was right. I shouldn't have trusted Pete."

"You've learned from your mistake. That's all anyone can ask."

Before Gillian could say anything more, the sound of a motorcycle announced TJ's return. He sprinted into the cabin. "Natalie's on her way, but it'll be half an hour or so."

Half an hour for Brianna to cry and worry. Desperate for something to take the girl's mind off the way she'd been deceived, Gillian rubbed her stomach. "Let's see what we can find to eat. Brianna, will you look in the cupboards?"

When TJ raised an eyebrow, Gillian simply nodded, mouthing, "Trust me."

"Not exactly a feast," Brianna said a minute later as she held up a jar of instant coffee, an unopened sleeve of crackers, and a fresh jar of peanut butter.

"It'll do." Boiling water and spreading peanut butter didn't require much effort, but it was the only distraction Gillian could find for Brianna.

"I might have something in my saddlebags," TJ offered. Returning a minute later, he held out some beef jerky and two energy bars as if they were shrimp and lobster.

"You call that food?" Brianna demanded. "When I get home, my mom will make me a big steak and a baked potato."

Gillian suspected Natalie would give Brianna anything she wanted, at least tonight. In the meantime, she laid three paper towels on the table and pulled three more to serve as napkins. "Let's eat." Turning to TJ, she asked him to give thanks. And he did, thanking the Lord not just for the food but also for Brianna's safety.

The simple act of sitting at a table, eating crackers and sipping coffee, seemed to restore enough normalcy to Brianna's life that her shoulders no longer shook, and her eyes lost their glazed look.

In less time than she'd expected, Gillian heard a vehicle. Natalie must have broken every speed limit to get here this quickly, and Gillian couldn't blame her. She'd have done the same had she been in Natalie's position.

Brianna started to rise, then sank back in her chair, as if her legs would not support her. Her eyebrows rose when she heard not one but two doors slam. Natalie was not alone. Perhaps the store manager had insisted on driving. But seconds later, Brianna's mother ran into the cabin, followed by Todd.

Gillian looked at the new arrivals, not sure who seemed more upset, but Brianna had eyes only for her mother. As Natalie opened her arms, she rose so quickly that the chair toppled over. "Oh, Mom, I'm sorry," Brianna cried as she wrapped her arms around her mother's waist and began to sob. "You were right. Pete didn't love me."

Natalie stroked her head, her eyes glistening with tears as she looked at Gillian for a second, telegraphing her gratitude. "It's okay, honey. I love you. Nothing you can do will change that. I just wish you hadn't had to learn about Pete this way. You had me mighty worried." Natalie's gaze turned to Todd. "You also caused this young man a lot of worry. He would have ridden his bicycle all the way out here if I hadn't agreed to let him come with me."

Brianna turned a tear-stained face toward Todd, hope mingling with disbelief. "You still want to see me, even after all I did?"

Todd shrugged. "We need to talk."

It might not have been the response Brianna wanted, but it was a beginning.

46

That was a close call," TJ said as he closed the cabin door behind him and Gillian. Relief and a sense of rightness filled him. The relief was understandable. He and Gillian had arrived in time to save Brianna from Pete and the love nest. Love nest! TJ shook his head at the term. Love had nothing to do with it. The men should have called it their lust nest.

The sense of the rightness surprised him, and yet he could not ignore how right it felt that he and Gillian had worked together in the rescue. They had been partners, and as was true in the best partnerships, they'd accomplished more than they would have alone. They'd protected Brianna and, unless TJ was mistaken, they'd helped mend the girl's relationship with her mother and Todd. Without a doubt, it had been a good couple hours' work.

Gillian nodded slowly. "I can't begin to thank you for all you did."

"It wasn't what *I* did," TJ said, wanting her to understand the depth of the feelings that had swept through him. "We did it together. You were pretty amazing back there, keeping Brianna as calm as you did."

"Me, amazing?" Though she'd been walking steadily toward

the motorcycle, Gillian stopped and looked up, her eyes filled with tears, her hands shaking almost as much as Brianna's had. "Look at me," she said, holding her hands in front of her. "I can't remember the last time I was so scared. All I could think about was getting there before Pete had a chance to . . ." Gillian's voice faded, her reluctance to pronounce the words obvious. She stared at her hands. "You'd think I'd be relaxed now that it's over."

"That's normal." TJ wrapped his arm around her waist and drew her close to him, hoping his warmth would soothe her. Whether or not she wanted to admit it, Gillian had been through a traumatic situation, and while TJ had emerged feeling victorious, she had not. "You did a great job, Gillian. No one could have done better." She looked dubious, and her hands continued to tremble. "There's nothing wrong with the way you're feeling," he assured her. "You had another adrenaline overload, and now you're crashing."

Gillian's eyes widened and she flinched. "Crashing, huh? Don't use that word when I still have to get back on your motorcycle." Her attempt to laugh failed.

"I'm sorry." He'd spoken without thinking, but though he wished he could retract the word, he could not. It was time for damage control. "Do you want to wait a bit?"

"No." Gillian's reply was more emphatic than he'd expected. "The sooner I leave here, the better."

"Then let's go. This place is a dump." TJ shared her opinion of the cabin. There was no reason to linger in such a tawdry spot. To TJ's relief, Gillian appeared to relax, and her voice had lost its tremors as she said, "I can't believe how calm you were when Pete pointed that shotgun at you. I know good guys are supposed to rescue damsels in distress, but I've never seen anyone actually do it. You were amazing, TJ."

"I'm glad you put me in the good guy category." That Gillian regarded him as amazing made TJ want to grin. The truth was, he wanted her to view him as more than a good guy. This afternoon had confirmed his belief that Gillian was the woman with whom he wanted to share the rest of his life. She was the perfect partner—a woman he could love and cherish, a woman whose strength would fortify him, a woman who would fill each day with joy.

TJ couldn't see himself as the perfect man for her—he was far from perfect, and he still didn't have his future all sewn up—but he couldn't go another day without telling Gillian how much he loved her. As much as he wanted to share his love with her, this was neither the time nor the place.

Though she had no way of reading his thoughts, Gillian laid her hand on the side of his cheek and smiled. "Of course you're a good guy. There was never any doubt about that."

TJ stayed well within the speed limit as they returned to Rainbow's End. There was no need to rush, and he wanted to savor every minute with Gillian. If he had his way, they'd never stop. They'd ride off into the sunset like in those mushy movies his mother used to watch. Perhaps he and Gillian would go to Big Bend. Perhaps to the Gulf Coast and Padre Island. They might even head north so she could show him Lake Erie and Niagara Falls. He didn't care where they went as long as Gillian was his companion.

Though they'd talked on the way to the cabin, exchanging terse comments about what they might find once they arrived, neither of them spoke on the return trip. TJ felt no need for conversation. It was enough to have Gillian's arms around his waist, her face so close to his back that he could feel the warmth of her breath each time she exhaled. Her breathing was slow and even now, proof that the adrenaline rush had subsided along with her fear. That was one more reason to give thanks.

When they arrived at Rainbow's End and he helped her off the bike, TJ glanced at his watch. "Looks like we missed dinner. Do you want to go to the Sit 'n' Sip? We don't have to rush."

Though she often had dates with Mike, Gillian had said nothing about this week, leading TJ to believe she had no plans for the evening. Perhaps he could convince her to go back to Paintbrush Island. It was a pretty spot, and they'd have no interruptions. Yes, the island would be an ideal place to tell Gillian all that was in his heart.

Anticipation rushed through TJ as she unstrapped her helmet and handed it to him. Though he'd hoped for a smile, Gillian's expression was solemn. "I wish I could, but there's something I need to do." She paused before adding, "Somewhere I have to go."

"Can I help?"

Gillian shook her head. "It's something only I can do."

Though she said nothing more, TJ knew exactly where Gillian was going.

Gillian gazed into the mirror one last time, hoping that all that had happened tonight wasn't visible. Fortunately, though she felt different, her face didn't betray her.

Mike had sounded surprised when she'd called, saying she needed to see him, but he'd assured her that he had time for her. "Always," he'd said. But there was no always. There was only tonight.

Gillian slipped into white capris, then buttoned the navy and white shirt. Though the red Stetson would be the perfect finishing touch, she would not wear that. Instead, she laid it carefully on the passenger seat. It was time to go.

Less than half an hour later, she pulled into Mike's driveway. Even before she'd switched off the ignition, he opened the front door and hurried to help her out of the car.

"You look great," he said, his eyes moving slowly from the top of her head to her toes. "You're even more beautiful than usual, if that's possible." Though he leaned forward, as if to kiss her, something in her expression must have stopped him, because he pulled back.

"Thanks." Gillian wasn't certain whether she was thanking him for the compliment or the lack of a kiss. The truth was, she was grateful for both. She saw Mike's puzzled look when she carried the Stetson into his condo and laid it on the console table just inside the door. Though she knew he would never ask her to return it, Gillian did not feel right keeping something so closely associated with the Tarkett family.

"Can I get you some iced tea or a soda?" he asked. That was Mike: the perfect host.

"No thanks. I hope I didn't interrupt something important." Even to her ears, the words sounded stilted. She'd known this would be difficult, but she hadn't expected it to be quite so hard. This was Mike, her friend, one of the nicest men she knew. Gillian hated knowing she was going to hurt a very good man.

"There's nothing more important than you." Mike touched the small of her back in what might have been designed as a comforting gesture, then let his hand fall away. "Now, tell me what I can do to make you less nervous." He led the way into the living room and gestured toward the sofa.

Gillian took a seat on one end, waiting until he'd settled next to her before she spoke. "I'm sorry. I didn't realize it would be so obvious. Something happened today." When she saw the curiosity in his eyes, she shook her head. "What it was doesn't matter. What's important is that it made everything clear to me. Oh, Mike." Though she wanted nothing more than to clench them, Gillian forced her hands to relax. "I wish there were an easy way to say this, but . . ."

"You've made your decision." He completed the sentence.

"I have." Gillian turned so she was facing him directly. "I love you, Mike, but I realized that I love you as a friend or a brother, not a husband."

She wouldn't tell him that this morning she had thought she was ready to accept his proposal. Saying that would be cruel, and the last thing she wanted was to cause this wonderful man any more pain.

"I wish it were otherwise, but I can't marry you. You deserve a wife who'll love you with her whole heart. I'm not that woman."

Mike's eyes clouded with pain, and she saw his lips tighten. "I wish I could say I was surprised, but when you called, I was afraid this was the reason." He reached for her left hand, stroking her ring finger as if he were placing a ring on it. "I love you, Gillian. I'm not sure there will ever be another woman for me."

"Yes, there will. You'll find her, and when you do, you'll realize that what you felt for me was only the prelude. She'll be the full symphony."

Mike wrinkled his nose at her musical analogy. "If you're trying to make me laugh, you almost succeeded. Almost." He clasped her hand between both of his. "While I waited for you, I tried to imagine what I could do to make you change your mind if you said you wouldn't marry me. I had all kinds of crazy schemes, but I know they would be wrong."

Though he'd been looking at her, Mike's gaze dropped to the floor, and Gillian saw him swallow deeply, as if he were trying to control his emotions. But though he gave no other outward sign, Gillian knew he was hurting inside. She wished—oh, how she wished—she hadn't been the one to inflict those wounds.

Mike tightened the grip on her hand. "I wish there were something I could do, but I know you wouldn't be happy with me when you love someone else."

"How did you guess?"

Mike shrugged. "I tried to tell myself I was mistaken, but it's written on your face when you talk about him. All I can say is that I hope TJ knows how lucky he is."

Mike rose and tugged Gillian to her feet. "It's time for you to go back to Rainbow's End and the man you love, but before you go, will you give me a good-bye kiss?"

Without hesitation, Gillian moved into his open arms and

raised her face. The kiss was short and sweet, a reminder of the good times they'd shared, of the future that might have been theirs. When it ended, Gillian knew she had done the right thing. Though she'd never forget Mike, he was not the man God had planned for her.

Half an hour later, she mustered every ounce of courage she possessed and knocked on the door to TJ's cabin.

He swung it open, his eyes widening in something that looked like surprise. "I didn't expect to see you tonight." His voice was rough, as if he was having trouble forming the words. "If you came for my congratulations, you've got them. Mike is a great guy."

There was no disguising the pain in either TJ's voice or his eyes, and that pain set Gillian's heart to pounding. If the thought of her marrying another man hurt that much, it must mean TJ cared. And if he cared, perhaps her dream had a chance of coming true.

She had thought he would invite her into the cabin or at least come out to be with her, but instead he stood inside the doorway, leaving her standing on the porch. Though this wasn't the way she had pictured the scene, Gillian wouldn't back away. Not now, not when she was so close to knowing whether she would find the happily-ever-after she'd dreamt of for so long.

"You're right," she said firmly. "Mike is a great guy, but he's not the man I love or the man I want to spend the rest of my life with."

As her words registered, TJ's expression began to change, the pain seeming to drain from him, replaced by something that looked like hope. And that glimmer of hope ignited a flame inside Gillian.

"Mike knew that," she told TJ. "I think he realized it before I did."

"What do you mean?"

Gillian paused. In the movies, the man was the one who declared his love, pursuing, then persuading the heroine to marry him. When she agreed, he swept her into his arms as the credits rolled.

This was not a movie. It was real life, and in real life sometimes a woman had to be the first to speak.

"I love you, TJ." Though it was the first time she'd said them, the words came out easily. When he opened his lips to speak, she shook her head. She wanted TJ to hear everything she had to say before he responded. She took a quick breath, then continued. "I know you're not ready to think about marriage, but I want you to know that I'd never try to take Deb's place."

"You can't."

Two words. Two simple words, but combined with the finality Gillian heard in TJ's voice, they doused the flame of hope, leaving her feeling as if she'd been bludgeoned. Though she had tried to tell herself this was possible, her heart had refused to believe it. Now she was faced with the reality that her dream of love and marriage would never come true.

"I—"

TJ raised his index finger to his lips in the universal signal for silence. "You need to let me finish my sentence. What I started to say was that you can't take Deb's place. She'll always be my first love. But you're my last love. You have your own place in my heart."

Though the smile he gave her made Gillian's heart begin to pound, it was his words that brought tears of joy to her eyes. TJ loved her. Dreams really did come true.

"I'm surprised you didn't give up on me. I was blind and I was stubborn," TJ said, his smile turning rueful. "I didn't want to admit what was clear to others. I was so caught up in my own misery that it took me far too long to realize God had given me something I never expected—a second chance at love and a woman who's more wonderful than I dreamt possible. He opened the window, but I wasn't brave enough to climb through it."

There was a second of silence when all Gillian heard was the pounding of her heart. Though she wanted to speak, to tell TJ how deeply she loved him, she could not force the words past the lump in her throat. Then TJ stretched out his hands, reaching for hers.

"I don't have much to offer you. I can't promise you a life of luxury. I can't even promise we'll be able to put down roots in one place. You know there are no guarantees like that with the ministry." TJ paused. "The truth is, I don't know what the future will bring, but I do know that I want you to be part of that future, and if you agree to share it with me, I'll do everything I can to make you happy."

TJ tightened his grip on her hands as he stepped through the doorway, closing the distance between them. When he was only inches away, he smiled again. "Gillian, you're the best thing that's ever happened to me. You challenge me to be better than I thought I could be. You fill my thoughts and dreams. I didn't think it was possible, but you've filled all the empty spaces in my heart. Now it's overflowing with love."

Gillian felt as if her own heart were about to explode from the sheer joy TJ's words brought. A moment ago, she had believed they had no chance at happiness together, but now the man she loved was saying everything she'd longed to hear. The words were wonderful, his expression even more so, for there was no question that what she saw shining from his eyes was love. Love for her.

"I love you, Gillian," TJ said, the firmness of his voice underscoring his sincerity. "Will you marry me?"

"Oh yes!"

As TJ opened his arms, Gillian moved into them and raised her lips for his kiss. It began as softly as a single note but swelled into a concert of love that filled each and every corner of her being. Against all odds, she had found her heart mate, the man God had brought into her life.

Gillian sighed with pleasure as TJ stroked her hair, then wrapped his arms around her again, drawing her closer. She'd traveled thousands of miles. She'd taken detours along the way, but at last she'd found what she sought: the road to her future.

Author's Letter

Dear Reader,

Each time I start to write a book, I picture you. I don't know what you look like, whether you're reading a paper or an ebook. I don't know whether you prefer to read in the solitude of a corner of your home or in a busy coffee shop. What I do know is that if you picked up one of my books, you're looking for a few hours' respite from the real world, and that while you want to escape reality, you also want a story of real people facing real challenges and overcoming them, even though it may not be easy. My prayer as I begin each book is that the story will touch your heart and deepen your faith. Did I succeed? I hope so.

On Lone Star Trail *is the final book in the Texas Crossroads series, and as always happens when I reach that milestone, my thoughts are bittersweet. There's satisfaction in finishing the book, but that's mingled with regret that I won't be spending my days at Rainbow's End. I hope you're like me and enjoyed seeing the changes in not only the resort but, more importantly, the people who called it home.*

If this is your first Texas Crossroads book, I encourage you to pick up a copy of the first two. The story of Rainbow's End begins with At Bluebonnet Lake, *where Kate and Greg meet and fall in love. You know how their story ends, but I assure you, it wasn't an easy path. Marisa meets her future husband in* In Firefly Valley, *and once again, the road to happiness has more twists than she expected.*

If you've read the other books, you know that I enjoy sharing Carmen's healthy recipes. Here's another of my favorites. Not only do these bar cookies travel well for bird-watching or anything else that's on your agenda, but they also freeze well . . . if there are any left.

One of the things I enjoy even more than sharing recipes is hearing from you. I hope you'll visit my website (www.amandacabot.com) to sign up for my online newsletter and, if you're so inclined, to send me a note. As I've said before, you're the reason I write.

Blessings,
Amanda Cabot

Raisin-Oatmeal Bars

Please note that because this is low fat, all mixing is done by hand. No high altitude adjustments are needed.

Grease and flour a 9x13 pan. (I use a floured spray like Baker's Joy.) Preheat the oven to 350 degrees.

Combine until well mixed:

2	egg whites
2 tbsp	unsweetened applesauce
1 cup	plain fat-free yogurt
2 tbsp	skim milk
2 tsp	vanilla
¾ cup	brown sugar, firmly packed
½ cup	sugar

Add and mix well:

3 cups	old-fashioned oats
1 cup	raisins

Combine and stir in:

1½ cups	all-purpose flour
1 tsp	baking soda
1 tsp	cinnamon

Spread in pan and bake for 25 minutes.

Cool completely before cutting.

Dreams have always been an important part of **Amanda Cabot**'s life. For almost as long as she can remember, she dreamt of being an author. Fortunately for the world, her grade-school attempts as a playwright were not successful, and she turned her attention to novels. Her dream of selling a book before her thirtieth birthday came true, and she's been spinning tales ever since. She now has more than thirty novels to her credit under a variety of pen names.

Her books have been finalists for the ACFW Carol Award as well as the Booksellers' Best and have appeared on the CBA and ECPA bestseller lists.

A popular speaker, Amanda is a member of ACFW and a charter member of Romance Writers of America. She married her high school sweetheart, who shares her love of travel and who's driven thousands of miles to help her research her books. After years as Easterners, they fulfilled a longtime dream and now live in the American West.

MEET
Amanda Cabot

VISIT

AmandaCabot.com

to learn more about Amanda,
sign up for her newsletter,
and stay connected.

"Cabot engages and entertains in equal measure."

—*Publishers Weekly*

"Crafting characters rich with emotion, Amanda Cabot pens a compelling story of devastation and loss, of healing and second chances. But most of all, of transcending faith."
—Tamera Alexander, bestselling author

Available wherever books and ebooks are sold. 

"One thing I know to expect when I open an Amanda Cabot novel is heart. She creates characters that tug at my heartstrings, storylines that make my heart smile, and a spiritual lesson that does my heart good."

—Kim Vogel Sawyer, bestselling author

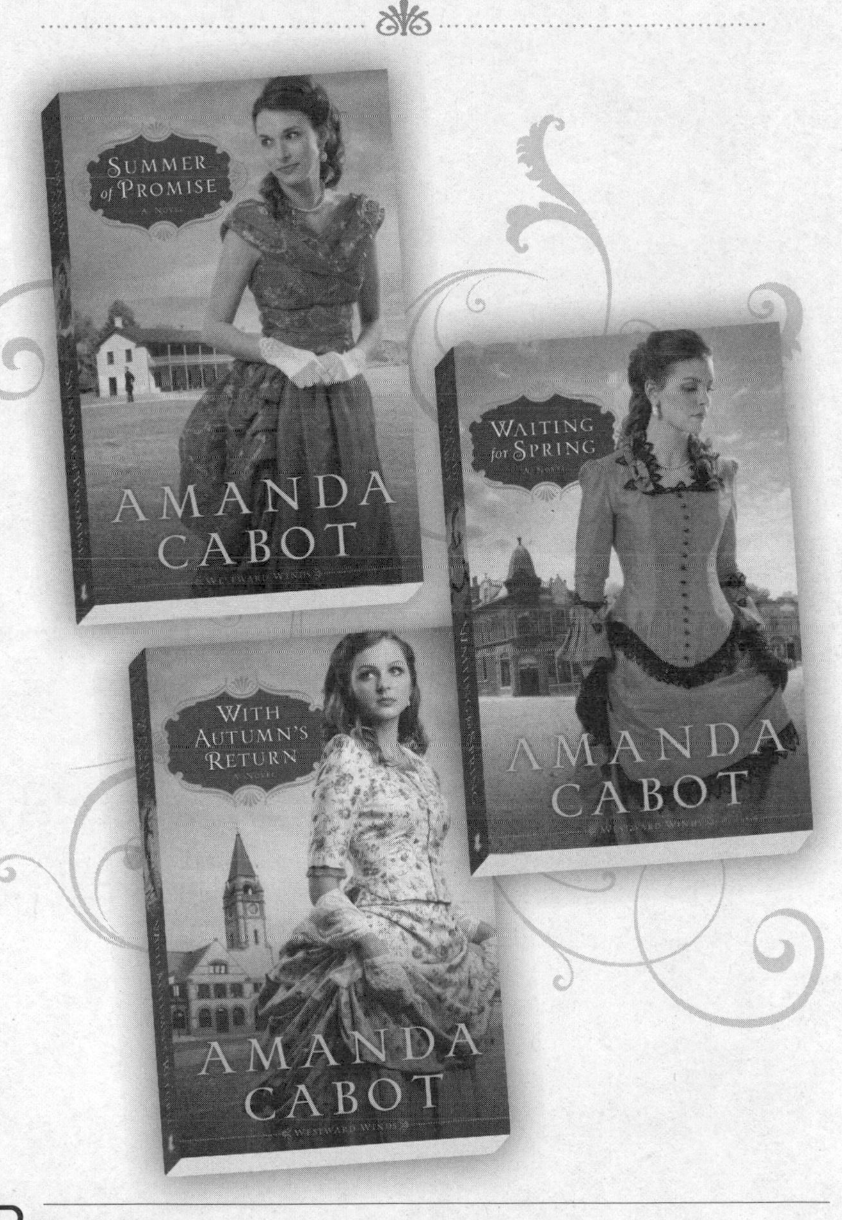